A History of the Future

JAMES
HOWARD
KUNSTLER

A History of the Future

A World Made by Hand Novel

Atlantic Monthly Press
New York

Published simultaneously in Canada
Printed in the United States of America

FIRST EDITION

ISBN 978-0-8021-2252-0
eISBN 978-0-8021-9247-9

Atlantic Monthly Press
an imprint of Grove/Atlantic, Inc.
154 West 14th Street
New York, NY 10011

Distributed by Publishers Group West

www.groveatlantic.com

14 15 16 17   10 9 8 7 6 5 4 3 2 1

This book is for Peter A. Golden,
comrade in the trenches of lit

You weary heavy-laden souls
Who are oppressed sore
You travelers through the wilderness
To Canaan's peaceful shore
Through beating winds and chilly rains,
And waters deep and cold
And enemies surrounding you
Have courage and be bold

"Florence" (hymn)
T. W. Carter, 1844

In the not-distant future . . .

The electricity has flickered out. The automobile age is over. The computers are all down for good. Two great cities have been destroyed. Epidemics have ravaged the population. The people of a little town named Union Grove, in upstate New York, know little about what is going on outside Washington County. A messenger is returning with the news . . .

ONE

Two days before Christmas in the year that concerns us—a year yet to come in an America much beset by change—Brother Jobe, pastor, patriarch, and head honcho of the New Faith Covenant Brotherhood Church of Jesus, supervised the finishing touches on his pet project of the season: a tavern and place of fellowship on Main Street in the village of Union Grove, Washington County, New York.

Despite the hardship of recent years that had followed the bombs that destroyed Los Angeles and Washington, DC, and the attendant travails of a collapsed economy, and other serial calamities, this was a happy week for most of Union Grove's people. The growing season, which extended three weeks longer than in the previous decade, brought a bounteous harvest (apart from the troubling appearance of a previously unknown corn smut in a few farmers' fields). The town had gotten through the year without suffering a major epidemic like the ones that had burned through the region in past years and decimated the population, though there was plenty of routine illness for the weak and unlucky. A community laundry was close to opening in the repurposed Union-Wayland paper mill building beside the Battenkill River. It was the first new enterprise of size that the town had seen since the modern age drove itself into a ditch, a joint effort between the regular town folk and Brother Jobe's New Faith brethren. They had arrived in late spring seeking refuge from the disorders elsewhere in America, bought the vacant high school, moved their seventy-eight members into it, and done much to stimulate a revival of community spirits in Union Grove, for all their odd ways.

Being Christmas week, the townspeople did their best to make festivity visible without electric lights. Fir swags festooned the porches and wreaths hung on doors. Lighted candles on windowsills flickered defiance against the year's longest nights. Men and their children dragged balsam trees out of the woods and pine scent filled the crisp air all over town. Women pinned bright red sprays of winterberry onto their knitted hats as they went around trading and visiting. Horses wore holly sprigs on their cruppers as they clip-clopped along the streets. A bright sense of the holiday affected even the gloomier personalities around town, those who struggled in adjusting to the new ways of the new times. All that was missing was snow. The bare ground made everyone impatient for a new look. It had rained a few times the previous week, but when colder air finally swept through it felt as dry as the distant Canadian prairie it came from.

The farm laborers who lived in the village had been given the whole week off, with most of the year's work completed. Many were out and about in town enjoying their rare hours of leisure, stopping to chat with friends, and visiting the other Main Street businesses that the New Faith people had set up, including now the barbershop, the smoke shop, and Brother Jobe's "haberdash," which sold new-made clothing to people who had all but run through the last ragged remains of their off-the-rack manufactured casuals from the old times. Russo's bakery had received a shipment of scarce wheat flour from Albany that Stephen Bullock's Hudson River trade boat brought back on its weekly run, and the bakery shop window was filled with Christmas cookies, confections, fruit jellies, panettones, gingerbread men, and a wondrous great *bûche de noël*, the buttercream frosted roll cake tricked out like a Yule log, baked just that afternoon, with meringue mushrooms and holly leaves of filbert paste—which was rumored to be destined for Bullock's own table. Einhorn's general merchandise store had laid in a stock of goods intended to please children: sleds, chess boards, lacrosse sticks, dolls (in costumes that looked suspiciously like the New Faith getups), puppets, a rocking horse, skittles and bowls, knock hockey, marble mazes, jigsaw puzzles, all things made by hand. There was nothing electronic on display and few of the town's children would have even remembered what computer games were like. Terry Einhorn kept a big pot of cider warming on the woodstove for customers. His chore boy Buddy Haseltine, who had the mind of a child, wore a floppy Santa Claus hat and a broad smile as he carried in an armload of stove billets from out back. He loved this time of year when the store was so busy.

Brother Jobe's new Union Tavern stood at the center of all this activity, in the generous corner storefront where Van Buren Street came to a T at Main. The space, in a fine three-story redbrick business block with marble steps, lintels, and string courses, had originally been built to house Alger's Drug Store in the year 1902. It was operated by Alger's grandson until 1981 when a Walgreens opened in the strip mall at the edge of town. The loss of the soda fountain alone was a blow to the life of the town. For decades after that, the shop front was given over to Luddie's Pizza, with a big internally lighted plastic sign that spanned the frontage and turquoise paneling above. It covered up the whole Main Street facade, including all the upper-story windows. The interior was a motley assemblage of vinyl, linoleum, stainless steel, and other clashing materials, which had all looked even worse under the harsh fluorescent lighting. In those days, Americans virtually lived on pizza and consumed it in settings that would make livestock feel queasy. As it happened, the entire Luddie family perished in the Mexican flu epidemic, and that was that. Meanwhile, the wheat flour scarcity, the lack of gas for the ovens, and changing work routines put an end to the century-long pizza craze. Like a score of other shop fronts along Main Street, Luddie's remained dark and vacant for years as the economy sank.

Brother Jobe's crew had taken off the turquoise paneling to reveal the old brick and the graceful arched upper windows. Then they set about gutting the first-floor interior, including the now useless stack of pizza ovens, and rearranged the kitchen in the back. The renovated middle room featured cherrywood wainscoting, a selection of castoff sofas and easy chairs arranged in sociable groups about a big woodstove, and a row of cozy booths along the other wall. Removing the greasy drop ceiling revealed magnificent old pressed tin twelve feet high. Up front, the New Faith crew had installed a twenty-foot-long cherrywood bar backed by an impressive array of mirrors above a row of kegs that contained the best ciders, beers, and ales produced around Washington County. The original transom that spelled out ALGER'S DRUGS in ethereal green, sapphire blue, and opalescent yellow stained glass had been rescued from the basement and was back above the door, while a new handpainted wooden sign over the breadth of the frontage spelled out UNION TAVERN in ocher letters that looked like old gold on a black background, with a welcoming pineapple stenciled at each end to denote hospitality. Both outside and in the place were decorated for the holiday with pine garlands and holly.

Brother Jobe paced fretfully in the front barroom, stopped, and pointed up at the chalkboard menu behind the bar.

"What do you mean 'hot soup'?" he asked Brother Micah, the bartender and nominally manager of the new establishment, which would open its doors to the public for the first time in just a little while.

"Hot soup?" Brother Micah said. "Everybody knows what that is."

"All soup is hot," Brother Jobe said. "Why not just say soup?"

"Well, you say 'hot' to give folks the idea that it'll warm them up on a cold day, make 'em feel good inside," said Brother Micah, who had once worked in a Golden Polenta franchise restaurant back in the old times.

Brother Jobe just stared wearily with a sour expression on his face. A wintry ache crept through his joints. Along with all his other duties and responsibilities, getting the tavern ready had worn him out. Back in the middle room, two New Faith sisters bustled about. One set out jars of the New Faith red hot chile sauce on the tables in the booths and another lighted candles in the tin wall sconces. Daylight was fading at four o'clock in the afternoon this time of year. A painted sign that hung beside the woodstove said NO CARD PLAYING, MARIJUANA, SPITTING ON THE PREMISES.

"Ain't it self-evident that soup is hot?" Brother Jobe said.

"It's the psychology of the thing," Brother Micah said. "You see?"

"Hmph, psychology," Brother Jobe muttered. "I'll take a dram of whiskey."

"The Battenville light rye, the Eagle Bridge corn, or the Shushan what-have-you?"

"What-have-you? Did they stick a possum in the barrel or something?"

"It's not half bad."

"I'll try half a dram then. Sounds indifferent."

"It's different enough."

Brother Jobe scanned the other menu items on offer from the kitchen as he sipped the whiskey. Ham plate. Cheese plate. Hard sausage plate. Pulled pork plate. Variety plate. Chicken liver fry-up. Meatballs and gravy sauce. Corn dodger with pepper jelly. Tater tots ("our own!"). Cheese toast. Pickled eggs. Pickled peppers. Mixed pickles. Popcorn.

"What all is the darn soup, anyway?" Brother Jobe asked.

"Split pea with lard cracklings, I believe," Brother Micah said as he pounded a bung valve into a keg of Holyrood's special Christmas brew, pear scrumpy, a carbonated cider with a greater than average kick. A knock on the front window prompted both brothers to turn their heads. Peering through the glass was Robert Earle, carpenter by trade and, since last June, mayor of Union Grove. Brother Jobe waddled over to the door and let him in. Three other townsmen who had gathered out on the sidewalk made to follow Robert inside but Brother Jobe stopped them.

"Hey, let us in, too!" said Dennis Fontana, chicken house manager at Ned Larmon's big farm on Pumpkin Hill.

"Four-thirty, boys, like it says on that there sign in the window," Brother Jobe said.

"Aw, come on—"

He locked the door briskly behind Robert, who carried his fiddle case.

"You gonna grace us with some tunes here on our opening night?" Brother Jobe said. He pronounced it *chunes*.

"I'm on my way to Christmas practice," Robert said. By this he meant the music circle at Union Grove's First Congregational Church. They'd been rehearsing for months.

"I hear you all gonna put on a musicale Christmas Eve."

"That's right. Your bunch is welcome."

"We was thinking of putting on some carol singing ourself, mebbe Christmas Day, proper. You think some of your town folks might want to come over to our sanctuary for it? We got a heat system all rigged up. I aim to see we all mix more, your people and ours."

"Hang up a sign for it in the window here," Robert said. "Folks will see it. This place is all the talk of the town."

"Is that so?" Brother Jobe said, perking up visibly. Now there were five men and two women waiting outside for the place to open, one pressed right up against the window peering in. "You suppose they'll come regular, like?"

"Look at them out there. You're not insecure, are you?"

"Hmph," Brother Jobe said. "What do you think of the joint?"

"I like it. Your boys did a nice job."

"It ain't exactly a come-to-Jesus spot, but we're all for fellowship whatever style it comes in."

"How'd a guy like you ever learn the bar business?" Robert said.

"It ain't brain surgery. My daddy had a half-interest in a road-house in Gate City, Virginia. Ugly little burg full of hillbillies. I worked there one summer as the fry cook and learned just how the partner was robbing us. Daddy burned the place down and collected on the insurance. The partner happened to electrocute himself in his own hot tub a month later. Vengeance is the Lord's, I guess. Won't you have a taste of something on the house?"

"I came by to give you my invoice."

Robert handed Brother Jobe a folded sheet of paper. Robert had been working for two months outfitting the interior of a special chamber over in the former high school. The work had involved very exacting marquetry and a coffered ceiling. It was designed to be the winter quarters of the New Faith's clairvoyant epileptic spiritual guide Mary Beth Ivanhoe, also known among them as Precious Mother or the Queen Bee.

"We appreciate the fine job you done," Brother Jobe said. "I was just sampling this here whiskey, the Shushan what-have-you. It's got bark and bite both. Try a glass."

"Sure, thanks," Robert said.

The crowd was yet growing outside on the sidewalk. A few were clean-shaven New Faith members in broad-brimmed hats. Carol singing could be heard among them.

Brother Jobe called for two more whiskeys, then glanced down at the invoice.

"Shoo-wee," he said. It was for $350, payable in silver. "You kept track of your hours, I suppose."

"Yes I did."

"Sure you won't take paper money? It'll work out to more than a half million bucks if you do."

"People don't like paper dollars anymore."

"You'd feel rich, though."

Robert shifted his weight on the stool. "I'd only be fooling myself," he said.

"I'm just funnin' with you, old son. Come by my office at headquarters and you'll be paid in full in hard silver coin. Say, what if our choir put on a free concert on Main Street on Christmas Day? Right on the town hall steps or something. Think your townies would turn out for that?"

"It's possible."

"Spread the word, then. We'll do it! Now lookit, I'm about to throw the doors open, first time ever. Won't you give us just one tune to kick her off?"

"Oh, all right."

By the time Brother Jobe let the public in there were twenty-three people waiting. Seven were women. Robert Earle played a medley of "Deck the Halls," "God Rest Ye Merry Gentlemen," and "Jingle Bells," and by the time he stopped there was such a groan of protest from the now thirty-five people standing three deep at the bar that it was all he could do to get out of the place.

Two

When dire events overtook American life and the economy collapsed and so many once normal arrangements dissolved with it, and everything changed in a matter of months, Andrew Pendergast's true romance with the world began. It manifested in a rebirth of his gratitude for being. The world tilted, but he had anticipated and prepared for it and the tilt affected him favorably, especially his internal demeanor, which was one of a cheerful engagement with reality. His work as a freelance editor of scientific books and journals evaporated, of course, as so many livelihoods did, but before long so did any need to make monthly mortgage and car payments to a bank that no longer functionally existed, nor to an electric company that no longer delivered service, or the phone company, or the Internet provider, or any other entity that had formerly claimed some obligation from him. With every far-flung corporate network down, from the state and federal governments with their tax collectors to the skein of rackets that had posed as health care, the vast parasitical armature of institutions and corporations lost its grip on those who had survived the difficult transition and the epidemics, and Andrew Pendergast, for one, blossomed.

Andrew had no family left. He had lost his only sibling, a sister he had idolized, in a waterskiing accident when she was sixteen and he was twelve. His parents never lived to see the global collapse. Andrew was a bachelor who lived alone. In the old times, he defined himself and the precinct of his daily life as *gay,* meaning homosexual. Now, with the old contexts dissolved, it was no longer possible to think that way. His personal map of the world had changed as much as the geography he was immersed in.

He had survived a decade of adventures in the New York City publishing world and its extracurricular social venues. He had felt himself an outsider even in that lively subculture. Then, seeing the disorders blossom in politics, banking, and oil, he very deliberately planned his escape from that life to a new one in the distant upper Hudson River valley, a region he had discovered on B & B weekends before everything fell apart. On one of those forays upstate, he had seen the house for sale on Cottage Street. The seller was "highly motivated" due to financial reverses, the realtor disclosed in a low whisper. This was the case for a lot of unfortunate people at the time. Andrew bought the house, moved up from the city, and worked his freelance editing jobs at a remove until the bomb in Washington, DC, tanked the nation's economy altogether and scattered the remnants of its government. By then, though, he had made a beachhead for himself in Union Grove.

A person of diverse skills and interests, Andrew found many roles to play in the post-collapse village of Union Grove, Washington County, New York. He took charge at the town library after Mrs. Downs, librarian since the 1990s, lost her life to the vicious encephalitis that winnowed the region's population by a good third. Nobody else stepped forward at a time when the townspeople were consumed with grieving for their dead and finding some way to salvage their lives by practicing useful occupations that they had never planned on and were not trained for. Andrew took charge of the library building, resurrected the mothballed card catalogs stored in the basement, and opened up the place three evenings a week plus Sunday afternoons. As well as reopening the library, he had helped form the public volunteer burial committee when the Mexican flu followed the encephalitis epidemic and the bodies piled up like stacked cordwood outside Dr. Copeland's infirmary. He established a model garden on his half-acre property and his methods were emulated by other householders for whom gardening was a lost art that necessity required them to relearn. He repaired old mechanical clocks, which were much in demand, with the electricity down for good. He painted portraits, now the only method for recording likenesses. He organized and directed the stage shows put on in the old theater on the third floor of the town hall, most recently Rodgers and Hammerstein's *Carousel* the previous fall. And he presided over the music circle of the Congregational Church, which was the heart of the one reliably enduring institution in Union Grove that the townspeople could organize their lives around.

This glowing winter evening, Andrew stepped lightly down the porch stairs of his house, leaving the front door unlocked, one of the pleasures of living in a tightly knit village in these new times. His house was the oldest surviving in town with its original details intact, an 1841 center-gable Gothic cottage with a trefoil window in the peak under the figured bargeboards. Before the Civil War it had been a station on the Underground Railroad, the network of safe houses that had sheltered escaped slaves on their journey to Canada. Robert Earle helped Andrew restore the sills, the porch, and the scrollwork ornaments. Andrew fixed the old windows himself, one by one, even rebuilding the sash-weight counterbalances. He made his own house paint from boiled linseed oil, turpentine, and an oxide yellow ocher pigment he discovered in a cliff face on one of his rambles along the Battenkill. His neighbors thought it strange that Andrew put so much effort into fixing up the old house, while they neglected theirs in melancholy discouragement. His mental state was not like theirs. The world was singing in all his cells.

This evening, with the scent of fir mixed with wood smoke on the crisp air, Andrew wore a fine wool overcoat over his customary worsted trousers and waistcoat. He had an impressive collection of vests from his days as a young dandy in book publishing. Andrew had devoted much of his meager income in those years to assembling a wardrobe of the highest quality, which he now cared for meticulously. His feet were shod in lace-up ankle boots, made to order for him in town by Walter McWhinnie, Union Grove's cobbler and harness maker. Andrew was thrilled when the New Faith people opened their haberdash, because they sold a pretty good bib-front cotton shirt that went well with his outfits after his old Ralph Lauren shirts grew threadbare with pilled collars. On his head this cool winter evening, Andrew wore a felted wool slouch hat, collected with other hats during his city years. Unlike most of the regular townsmen of Union Grove, he was clean-shaven.

Andrew did not have a close companion or a romantic partner. He was careful and guarded with his emotions, the opposite of impulsive. Even back in New York he had been prudent in his sexual adventures. In Union Grove, he had avoided the appearance of seeking liaisons. He did not want to tempt the fearful reactions of frightened people struggling among the remnants of their culture. More to the point, however, since the world and everything in it had changed he had come to reexamine the question of his sexual orientation, wondering whether it even was an orientation or something less fixed in his persona than a figment from a bygone cultural ideology. He wondered how much of the story he had told himself back then was just a story scripted for him by others, a convenient explanation for a sequence of acts undertaken to stick to the script. Despite the enormous pressures to conform to it, the script did not validate his deeper feelings of uncertainty and shame. He wondered how much of it had come from sheer avoidance of the tension he felt around women, and whether there was perhaps something marvelous in meeting that tension that he had avoided just because it was easier to do so. He wondered above all why, for years after he'd grown up, he could not quite conceive of himself as a genuine adult. He recognized the paradox of wanting to escape into femininity, as represented by his idolized dead sister, while associating sexually only with other males, many of whom made a fetish of mocking the femininity they affected to imitate. His episodes with other men had been furtive encounters of priapic ritual not so different from sex with himself, except they left him in a state of enervated anxiety. Of all the feelings they generated, pride was not one of them, whatever the script insisted. That was all over for him now. He hadn't heard the word "gay" in as long as he could remember and at one point he realized what a relief that was. The memories of his acts with other men resided in an emotional compartment that he rarely revisited. He was more than content, at age thirty-seven, to sublimate the terrors of sex in all the other activities that lately engaged his hours.

The thoughts that preoccupied him as he left the house this winter evening revolved around pieces he was about to rehearse with the other members of the music circle: "The Boar's Head Carol," "While Shepherds Watched Their Flocks by Night," "Es Ist Ein Ros Entsprungen," "The Wexford Carol," "In Dulci Jubilo," "The Gloucester Wassail," and about ten more. The regular music circle was composed of seven instrumentalists including himself on piano and harmonium, Robert Earle and Bruce Wheedon on violins (fiddles, they called them), Leslie Einhorn, cello, Dan Mullinex, flutes and clarinet, Eric Laudermilk on guitar, and Charles Pettie on bass fiddle and trombone. This group met once a week all year round and played at the many balls, fetes, and levees that composed the social life of Union Grove now that canned entertainment no longer existed. In addition to this lineup was the Congregational Church choir, which came on board with the music circle only at Christmas and Easter. Andrew's mind was crowded with orchestrations as he proceeded down Main Street toward the center of the old business district. He was distracted from his musical ruminations when he noticed the unusual number of people on the sidewalks, in particular the crowd that had formed outside the New Faith group's new tavern. It looked so wonderfully cheerful in the December twilight, like the best bars in downtown New York on a TGIF night back in the day. He was tempted to go have a look for himself, but he wanted to be on time for rehearsal so he stayed on the opposite side of the street.

As he rounded the corner onto Van Buren Street, he saw a figure in a battered and patched goosedown jacket pissing against a vacant storefront that had last been a Verizon wireless phone store and, before that, a farmers credit union, a liquor store, a psychedelic head shop (briefly), a jewelry and watch repair emporium, and for decades, starting when the building was erected in 1912, a greengrocer. As Andrew passed him, the ragged figure, named Jack Harron, age twenty-six, turned around and directed the stream of his piss toward Andrew so that a little bit of it actually splashed on the bottom of his wool overcoat. Andrew was so amazed that he stopped in his tracks.

"What are you looking at?" Harron said.

"You . . . wet my coat."

"So I did," Harron said, slurring his words. He wove and listed in his laceless boots, barely keeping upright.

Andrew searched Harron's haggard face for something that was not present behind the scraggly brown beard. Harron returned his gaze with a chilling look in his red-rimmed eyes that denoted more an utter vacancy of purpose than actual malice.

"I have to go now," Andrew said, thinking himself ridiculous for saying so.

"Too late for a pissing match anyway," Harron said. "I'm all out of piss. What makes you think you're better than other people?"

"I'm not better than other people," Andrew said.

"Sure you are."

Andrew spun on his heels and resumed his journey up Van Buren Street. He could see the white steeple of the Congregational Church two blocks ahead gleaming in the last moments of twilight while his brain spun out one fantasy after another about how he might have defended his honor. As he neared the church and heard the sound of instruments tuning in the community room, his fantasies of violent combat turned to a vague searching curiosity as to what this antagonist had been doing in life before the great hardships of the new times scuttled just about everybody's hopes, dreams, and expectations—everyone except himself, Andrew Pendergast, who was thriving. Perhaps the drunken young man was right. Andrew gave the appearance of being better than other people, certainly of doing better. Was that okay, he reflected, something to be ashamed of, or just a plain fact in the new order of things?

THREE

Mandy Stokes, thirty-two, left her brick cottage in the Mill Hollow section of town at the prompting of a voice she called the "spirit guide" that had taken up residence within her beginning the previous summer after a brief, violent illness during which something happened in her mind. As a result, the everyday world had become for her a shadowy backdrop to a more vivid beckoning interior realm of colorful event populated by dream figures who alternately tempted and persecuted her. Mandy carried her fourteen-month-old infant boy, Julian, in an ash-splint backpack made by her husband, Rick, chief foreman on Ned Larmon's farm. Rick was still out at the farm, baby-sitting a sick horse.

Rick was aware that his wife had come through her illness changed and distant, but she did not tell him about her new familiars—they had warned her not to—and he had waited patiently all these months for her to "come back to herself," as Dr. Copeland told him to expect she would, while Rick continued to take the doctor's hopeful words literally, against the evidence of his senses. If anything, Mandy became more unreachable as the weeks went by. She appeared at times to talk to herself, but when Rick asked if she had said something she denied it. In the days that beat a quickening path to the December solstice, Rick sometimes came back home from his duties at the Larmon farm to find Mandy sitting in the dark, with the baby crying on the floor and the ashes from the morning's fire cold in the woodstove. He was afraid to leave the child alone with her but ashamed to admit to anyone that she was unwell and so unable to manage.

Rick and Mandy were the sort of people for whom the economic collapse had harshly undone all of their own early programming. Rick was an Amherst grad, fortunate to find a job as an on-air reporter at the NBC affiliate TV station in Albany when the bomb went off in Washington. Mandy had just completed her master's thesis on gender relations in Roosevelt's Works Progress Administration. The SUNY Albany campus shut down a week after the bombing when supply chains for everything from cafeteria stocks to payroll funding broke down. Rick's TV station suspended paychecks the following week, though by then the banks were on a government-declared "holiday" and cash money was vanishing everywhere. The two of them stayed in the sizzling apartment in a not very good neighborhood of central Albany waiting for something like normal life to resume. Up until then, Mandy had entertained furtive thoughts of leaving Rick, who she saw as hopelessly conventional in habits and aspirations, but in the first weeks of the emergency his stolidity impressed her and she clung to him as if he were a lifeboat after a shipwreck.

Meanwhile the supermarket shelves grew bare as the jobbers quit their resupply deliveries and angry, unoccupied people milled in the streets at all hours, giving the city a vivid sense of constant menace. The state government affected to distribute food, but diesel fuel was in short supply, too, and the few trucks sent out were easily hijacked. As Mandy and Rick ate through the last of their dried lentils and the jar of years-old curry powder, their situation grew desperate.

Rick had a college roommate, Matt Larmon, whose father ran a farm, a big successful dairy operation, in the little town of Union Grove, some thirty-five miles northeast of Albany. Rick had spent one memorable July there, after his junior year, haying, fixing machinery, running cows, and hanging out on country roads drinking beers with Matt and some local girls on hot nights. Mr. Larmon had told him more than once that he was a good worker. It had been seven years since then, and he'd fallen out of touch with Matt, but Rick proposed that he and Mandy now try to get to the Larmon farm and ride out whatever craziness was going on in the world there, if possible. The phones were down and they could not contact Matt's father, Ned Larmon, but the city was quickly growing untenable with scavengers invading apartments, so Rick and Mandy decided to get going. They took only what they could carry in two small backpacks. Rick left his now useless Honda Civic behind. For three days they made their way north on foot in pleasant summer weather, eating early corn out of the fields and getting some hot meals here and there from kind people along the way. The people they met on the road were as baffled as they were frightened. How could something like this happen in the United States?

Rick and Mandy succeeded in finding their way to the Larmon farm. Matt was already there, too, it turned out, having left his apartment in Brooklyn and his job managing the web advertising revenue for a sports magazine group. Within an hour of the Washington bombing, with a full tank of gas, Matt had crossed the Willis Avenue Bridge out of Manhattan and then navigated his way north on back roads, avoiding the interstates. That first evening at the farm was pervaded by a strange combination of giddy excitement and dread, like a class reunion in wartime. In the background, behind the flowing liquor and the plentiful local viands, they were all painfully aware that the economy was failing, that many things had stopped working, and it had begun to look as if there would be no going back to anything that resembled the normality of life before the bombings.

By August of that year, as their predicament became clear, Ned and Matt Larmon worked to reorganize the farm to operate as though the modern age had permanently ended. They acquired draft horses, Belgians and Haflingers. Matt and Rick scoured the countryside buying up antique horse-drawn machinery, mowers, seed drills, and balers and learned step by step to rebuild them. They repaired several outbuildings on the property and constructed a new creamery, anticipating that all the old long-distance supply lines would unravel now that the tanker trucks no longer made their routine bulk collections of milk for the conglomerate food companies—meaning that value-added goods, such as butter and cheese, had to be produced on site. Mandy went to work in the creamery. It was not a life she could have anticipated the previous spring as she completed the work for her master's degree in Women's Studies.

It was obvious that much of the work done previously by machines and fossil fuels would now have to be realized by human labor. Rick's role was enlisting local men from Union Grove to sign on to work on the Larmon farm under terms that would have seemed crazy in the old times—shares of the food that was produced there, no cash because there wasn't any as the weeks went by. Few of the people in Union Grove were keen to do farm work. They were used to offices or, at least, to manual jobs aided by power equipment. Rick found twelve willing men and organized several crews rotating between the fields, the barns, and the pastures, and five women for milking and the creamery. Many other townspeople just waited fretfully for normality (and their accustomed jobs and paychecks) to return and wouldn't consider stooping to farm labor, and in the first winter these would be among the people who froze to death in unheated houses, or went hungry in ways unimaginable to a nation of former Walmart shoppers, or ran down their immune systems with liquor and drugs just as the first wave of the Mexican flu hit. The more nimble personalities understood that the great changes wracking the U.S. economy would probably be permanent. The Larmon farm's system of shares and bonuses was different from Stephen Bullock's more explicitly feudal operation, located seven miles east on the Hudson River, where the workers and their families lived on the premises and sold their allegiance to Bullock in exchange for security. But as the first planting season of the new times got under way, the Larmon system seemed to work, and the model was adopted by other landholders in the neighborhood of Union Grove, including Ben Deaver, Carl Weibel, and Bill Schmidt.

Rick and Mandy's lives moved from the grinding anxiety of those first weeks in Albany to the settled routines of farm life alien to everything their culture had prepared them for. They slept in a spare bedroom in the Larmons' big house and became a part of the family. In November, Matt was crushed to death by a falling king post while he and Rick were working on major structural repairs to the horse barn. Things were not the same afterward. Ned tried to suppress his devastation, but a raw, resentful gloom pervaded the household like the odor of a dead animal in the walls. One time, after the older man had more than a few whiskeys, and Rick was helping him up the stairs to bed, Ned muttered the phrase, "Why him and not you?" As the epidemics and attendant hardships winnowed the population that winter, and as houses were abandoned and the county courts and deed registries ceased operations, Rick and Mandy found a vacant house in the village that they could move into. They kept their positions on the Larmon farm but no longer lived there, and that was how their lives had wended in those years until Julian was born.

Now, this winter evening two days before Christmas, Mandy walked up Elbow Street out of Mill Hollow to Main Street, at the urging of her spirit guide, an entity who called himself Caim or Caym (she was not sure how it was spelled because he specifically forbade her to write it or speak his name to anyone else). He took the form in her mind of a big black bird and radiated an overpowering aura of wisdom and authority made visible in shimmering gold pulsations that Mandy saw in the third eye of her fervid imagination. She could not resist the instructions he uttered in a reverberating voice plangent with intimacy, like a lost ancestor speaking to his posterity with a fiery love. "Go to the town and find the people," the voice urged her.

As Mandy turned onto Main Street she saw lights glowing in the windows of the big storefront on the corner of Van Buren and people coming and going through the door. A light snowfall, the first of the season, was beginning to stick on the sidewalk and the smooth soles of her fleece-lined moccasins slipped against it, causing her to stumble. As the back of Julian's head bonked the back of Mandy's head, he started to cry.

"Be still," she said.

She came up to the new Union Tavern and stared through the window at the crowd within and the bright, merry scene, the burning candles, the holiday swags. Here were the people, she thought.

"Go inside," Caym said.

She entered into the front barroom where some thirty men and far fewer women stood and milled about with glasses in their hands. Though the thrum of conversation was loud, heads turned at the shrill sound of her crying baby. Some of the turned heads saluted her with a raised glass or a tipped hat. One of them was Dennis Fontana, a hand on the Larmon farm. She knew him from the years before Julian was born, when she worked in the Larmon creamery. He was a gangly, sharp-featured bachelor, twenty-six years old, with a thick sandy beard. He lived in the deconsecrated Methodist church on John Street with three other young single men who had barely known the old times and were still looking for wives from a population stock reduced by repeated visits of epidemic disease and other hardships. He spoke to her but in the commotion of voices she couldn't understand what he said. Caym told her to nod her head to whatever anyone said. Dennis corkscrewed around to hail Micah the barman and got two more pints of the Mount Tom Golden Cider. He handed one to Mandy, saying, "I bet you can hardly hear what I'm saying, it's so loud in here." Mandy nodded.

A gang of four hands from the Deaver farm were singing Christmas carols at the other end of the bar. Mandy tried the cider. It was very sparkly and sweetened with honey and tasted a little like the soda that had been ubiquitous in everyday life years before. She realized at that moment how much she missed soda, zero-calorie Fresca in particular, her favorite. The bubbly cider provoked an awareness of how thirsty she was and she drained the glass. Then she became aware of the warmth spreading inside her. Caym thanked her for it. Dennis pantomimed a look meant to inform her that he was impressed with her drinking prowess. Then he drew a circle with his finger in the air and reached for her glass. He got Micah's attention and had him refill it. A waitress brought a plate of the establishment's own tater tots to Dennis, with a little monkey dish of New Faith tomato ketchup to go with them. He extended the plate in Mandy's direction. Mandy nodded but did not take any. The baby was shrieking even more loudly than when they came in. Dennis held up a tater tot and pointed over Mandy's shoulder.

"Little feller must be hungry," Dennis said.

Mandy nodded.

Dennis stepped around Mandy and waved the tater tot in front of him. The child stopped shrieking and eyed the offering. Dennis held it in front of the child's face, allowed him to get a grip on it, and watched him first sniff it and then nibble it. A moment later, the child jammed the rest of the tater tot in his mouth, chewed and swallowed, and smiled broadly with delight. Then he commenced bobbing up and down in his backpack and waving his stubby arms. Mandy turned quickly to face Dennis.

"He likes 'em real well," Dennis said, and put a tater tot in his own mouth.

Mandy nodded. Julian shrieked again and bobbed violently in his pack.

Dennis circled around to him again and offered another morsel, which the child snatched out of his fingers. He ate it rapidly and made it clear he wanted more. As Dennis Fontana continued to feed tater tots to Julian, Mandy drained her second pint of cider. It was stronger than the manufactured beverages of yesteryear. Soon other people were giving the baby other tidbits: little pieces of cheese, sausage, a meatball, and even some pickle, which made him cough. Dennis held his glass up to Julian's lips and the baby managed to gulp some, though quite a bit of the cider flowed down his neck and into his clothing.

"That's enough for you now," Dennis said and circled back around to Mandy. She was easy on the eyes, he thought. She wore a long patchwork skirt with wild highlights in turquoise and scarlet satin. The backpack straps tugged against the fabric of her ancient wool mackinaw jacket, outlining her figure nicely. Her hair, unwashed for a week, was tucked under a knitted wool cloche, but wisps leaked out appealingly around her neck and forehead. Dennis knew that she was the wife of Rick Stokes, Ned Larmon's field foreman, and he wondered why she was downtown on her own—though he understood that the opening of the tavern was a special occasion as for years the people of Union Grove had not had any place to congregate in the evening besides the church. "Rick must still be up to the farm, huh?" he said.

Mandy nodded.

The effect of the cider was to make Caym's voice a bit lower, a bit harder to hear, as if he were speaking to her through a long drainpipe. The warmth of the scene in the tavern had replaced the bleak landscape of her mind with a more pleasing new topography and rich yellow light. Dennis's lips were moving. Mandy didn't understand a word he said but she enjoyed his attention. She just kept nodding her head.

Then, she heard Caym say, "Take this man outside." Mandy didn't quite understand what this meant but the spirit guide added, "Show him that you are love incarnate."

A moment later, she reached for Dennis's hand. It was warm and a little sticky from the cider. She gestured at him with her eyes to come. His uncertainty prompted a half-smile back at her. She jerked her head toward the door. He pointed at himself and raised his eyebrows. She nodded. He made yet another face that signified he was open to suggestions. Still holding his hand she turned and led him through the crowd out of the bar. Outside, snow coated the sidewalks and streets and flakes fell sparsely in the still air. A few dim lights burned upstairs in the buildings of Main Street, but there were no streetlights anymore, with the electricity down for good, and no automobile traffic, with Happy Motoring over forever. The townspeople who were not in the tavern or over at the church now had all gone home. A raucous silence filled the streets.

"Give this man what he wants," Caym said. "Find a place."

There was an alley between the tavern building and its neighbor, the Sohn Building (1905), where the storefront, once a bridal shop, was empty. Mandy led Dennis by the hand down the alley to a mid-block service courtyard filled with stacks of lumber, old plastic barrels and the new wooden ones that were coming to replace them, snow-covered tarpaulins in turn covering unused extra tables and chairs, and a four-wheeled horse cart empty except for a half inch of snow. Mandy spun Dennis around, reached up, and pulled his face down to hers, kissing him violently. His hands found their way inside her mackinaw jacket. She momentarily pulled herself away from his hungry mouth. His eyes opened stickily, as though he desperately wished to remain in the dreamy realm of unbidden romance. Her dark eyes drilled back at him with a gaze so fierce that it both frightened and excited him. She took off the backpack with baby Julian and leaned it against the tarpaulin-covered furniture. Julian had gone to sleep, his face smeared with ketchup. Mandy climbed into the cart's cargo bed and lay on her back throwing her colorful skirt up and lifting her knees. Dennis followed avidly and lowered his trousers. He loomed above Mandy. A pair of black wings seemed to spread from behind him and his sharp-nosed face appeared suddenly birdlike as he moved to his exertions. In a little while he subsided, breathless, against her.

"Disgusting whore," Caym said.

"What?" Mandy said.

"I didn't say anything. You're lovely."

"I'm a whore."

"I have some money."

"No!"

"Silver money."

At that moment, a back door to the tavern's kitchen opened and out stepped Brother Enos, sixteen, one of the helpers in the kitchen, a bucket swinging from his arm. He waddled down three steps, lifted a square of plywood off a plastic barrel, and deposited a load of kitchen scraps among what would be tomorrow's breakfast for the New Faith pigs. Returning to the kitchen door, Brother Enos with a sideward glance noticed Dennis and Mandy across the way in the cargo bed of the cart. Dennis was propped on one arm staring right at him. Mandy tried to turn her face away. Brother

Enos did not linger. He waddled back through the door with his bucket more rapidly than he emerged.

"Stupid, filthy girl!" Caym said. His voice was now like a loudspeaker inside her head. "Insect! Worthless piece of shit! Go home! Now!"

Mandy struggled to draw her legs out from under Dennis.

"Wait," he whispered.

"I can't."

"Go home now or I will kill this man," Caym said.

Dennis unpinned her. She swung herself awkwardly out of the cart bed, hoisted the baby onto her back again, and hurried out of the courtyard through the alley, tears streaking her face. Propped up on one arm in the cart's cargo bed, snowflakes alighting on his hair and woolly beard, Dennis watched her exit the alley. Every dozen steps Mandy broke into a run. Julian started crying again, too, as he bounced up and down on her back. Mandy just happened to be across Main Street from Einhorn's store when the baby threw up and the warm vomit flowed down the back of her mackinaw jacket. Mandy stopped in her tracks, groaned, and struggled to squirm the backpack around so she could seize Julian.

"Don't you just hate him?" Caym said.

Raging now, Mandy managed to hoist Julian up by his armpits and shook him violently several times, hissing, "Goddamn you!" through clenched teeth. The baby shrieked once sharply and then went silent. Across the street, Buddy Haseltine, the child-man who did chores in Einhorn's store and lived in the back room, watched Mandy from the wicker chair on the porch where he had been counting snowflakes. He'd gotten to one hundred and two.

"I just hate you!" Mandy said and shook Julian twice more on the words "just" and "hate," but he was silent now. Buddy Haseltine, swaddled in wool clothing, had been balancing on the rear legs of the wicker chair with his own stumpy legs up on the porch rail, but he now let the chair down as he leaned forward to watch and it clattered audibly on the porch floor. Mandy glanced over at Buddy as she stuffed Julian back into the ash-splint pack. Buddy's face was disposed in its usual way, mouth open and tongue protruding slightly like a small pink animal that lived in a cave, but his eyes appeared to register the scene.

"He's fine," Mandy said. "See?" She hoisted the pack as if to show, then slid the rig onto her back again, aimed a broad false smile at Buddy, and hurried away in the direction of Mill Hollow.

FOUR

Stephen Bullock, owner of the great five-thousand-acre farm (or "plantation," as some called it) four miles west of Union Grove, where the Battenkill River emptied into the mighty Hudson, was a personality of byzantine complexity, of hard edges and melting sentiment, comfortable with reality but eager to improve upon it, a visionary, a dreamer. More than anyone in Washington County, perhaps, he actually enjoyed these new times better than the old— back when the juice of modernity ran through everything like God's own adrenaline. He was much less nervous these days.

Being the only establishment in the district with a small working hydroelectric installation, Bullock even enjoyed some of the residual comforts of the bygone age. He could play recorded music on a stereo system and run a washing machine. He could enjoy electric lights in his house—though replacement bulbs had become almost impossible to find anymore and they were something he was just not equipped to manufacture on the premises, unlike saddlery, distilled spirits, smoked hams, or the linen sailcloth he used on his own trading sloop, which went to and fro to Albany weekly to buy whatever goods might still be had from the outside world.

Bullock's farm ran on a different model than the farms of Ned Larmon, Ben Deaver, Carl Weibel, Todd Zucker, and Bill Schmidt, the other successful big landholders. These men had refitted their formerly modern operations on a mid-nineteenth-century basis, employing hired labor who lived in the nearby town and who reported for work every day as for any job. Bullock's system was more like a seventeenth-century Hudson River Dutch patroonship, with feudal overtones. (His distant ancestor Joost van Druton, or Drooton, was granted just such a colossal holding of sixty-seven square miles, in the vicinity of Kinderhook, in 1648). Bullock's *people*, as he called his workers and their families, lived on Bullock's own property. Their relationship to Bullock and the land was more an entire way of life than a job. He'd allowed them to construct a village of their own and given them the materials to build with. Bullock didn't care for religion, so there was no church, but he'd provided a community center building for his people that looked like a church, to be used for common meals, festivals, dances, weddings, funerals, and services of their own devising. It also contained a commissary or small retail operation where his people could purchase the goods that his trade boat brought in from receding precincts of the troubled wider world. His people called the building the *grange*, because it resembled a grange hall of yore, with tall stately windows, a grand front door dignified with pilasters and a fanlight, and a graceful cupola with a small dome painted in yellow ocher. A graveyard occupied a half acre beside it where, over recent years, victims of the Mexican flu, the encephalitis, and the general decline of advanced medicine were deposited to begin their journeys to the infinite.

The living, who numbered sixty-three adults, had traded their allegiance to Bullock in exchange for food, security, purposeful work, and a sense of community on his property. Against the background of a society that had lost its bearings so completely, the future, for many of these people, seemed something worse than a broken promise—a dreadful, certain swindle. Bullock afforded his people not only shelter from a terrible storm of history but a practical faith in the continuation of an ordered existence, the prospect of remaining civilized. These were men and women who had had regular lives around the region and regular vocations: pharmacists, car dealers, bureaucrats, insurance reps, who had been left high and dry by the mighty changes sweeping the land.

This evening, two days before Christmas, Bullock would attend the annual holiday ball, or levee, for his people at the grange. It was not so different from the Saturday night dances held throughout the year, except that the outside public of Union Grove was not invited. This traditional Christmas levee—in its seventh season— would be limited strictly to the greater Bullock farm family, his people. As usual, he intended to supply plenty of the farm's own champagne-style "bright" cider, hams, fowls, and roasts with all the trimmings, a very large, grand cake constructed to resemble a Yule log, made by Union Grove's master baker Danny Russo, with ice cream churned on the premises, cookies, puddings, and other sweets for the twenty-two children of his people, and the distribution of gifts from the goods acquired over the preceding year in trade for the prodigious outputs of his farm, which derived, of course, from his people's labor.

But first there was a disagreeable matter to dispose of: the possible expulsion of one of his people, a very rare occurrence. He had asked Travis Berkey to report to the library in his house, the old manse, as they called it, at six o'clock in the evening. Bullock was already dressed for the levee in his customary riding trousers, shiny high black leather riding boots, a long green velvet frock coat, and a holly berry red satin vest within. He wore his long white hair in a tidy queue this evening. The large bookshelf-lined library contained an eight-foot-long map table covered with charts and drawings of Bullock's ongoing projects—the sorghum mill, an expansion of the cement works, a contraption for sifting large batches of compost—as well as Bullock's regular desk. A forty-watt bulb burned in the banker's lamp there leaving the rest of the room shrouded in dimness.

Two of Bullock's most trusted lieutenants, Dick Lee and Michael Delson, occupied comfortable leather club chairs in far corners of the room. Both wore their best clothing for this special evening and both were armed but did not display their weapons. An old mantel clock chimed six times above the blazing fireplace between where the two men sat. Bullock poured whiskey made on the property into three pony glasses and brought the drinks to his two men. He put a disc of carols by the Choir of King's College, Cambridge, on the CD player. The first carol, "In Dulci Jubilo," struck just the right tone of gravity for the occasion, he thought. "Chestnuts Roasting on an Open Fire" would have been all wrong, smacking of everything that had ruined the country in the way of late-twentieth-century complacency, narcissism, and hubris . . . yuletide in Las Vegas, chorus girls in Santa Claus getups, and cash registers ringing everywhere . . . It made him shudder.

A knock on the door brought Bullock out of his reverie. The clock said 6:10. He put down his whiskey glass. Sophie Bullock, resplendent in a close-bodied silver satin gown that made her look like a Christmas tree ornament come to life, and which contrasted radiantly with the dim ambience of the library, showed Travis Berkey into the room, then withdrew into the hallway and closed the door, leaving all concerned in a resonant silence.

"You're a little late," Bullock said eventually.

"I had my duties," Berkey said. He was sinewy and curved like a human scythe blade, as if well worn by physical labor, though he was not out of his thirties. He wore a greasy leather wool shearling-lined vest and wool trousers with holes in the knees. "Had to rebuild a singletree."

"How'd it break?"

"Things get used hard around here."

"Yes, well, I'll just come to the point then," Bullock said. "You have to leave."

"Leave?" Berkey said. "I just got here."

"I mean the farm."

Berkey recoiled as from a blow and then visibly shrank within himself.

"What for?" he said.

"You beat poor Perses nearly to death." Perses was a Belgian gelding used by the logging crew of which Travis Berkey was chief teamster. He seemed to search the air in front of him for an explanation.

"He stepped on my foot."

"I suppose he did that on purpose."

"It wasn't the first time."

"Perhaps you're not so good around horses."

"He's a bad-tempered horse."

"Horseflesh is dear. We can't breed them fast enough these days. And we can't be prima donnas about their temperament. We certainly can't abuse them with ax handles. He was pissing blood, you know. How would you like it if I took an ax handle to your kidneys?"

Berkey seemed to search the dim corners of the ceiling for something to say.

"I'm sorry," he finally said. "I won't never do it again."

"Of course you would. That's your temperament."

"Put me on some other crew, then. I'll work. I'll do whatever you say."

"I hear that you hit your wife now and then too," Bullock said.

Dick Lee coughed into his sleeve. Berkey stared into the carpet and seethed.

"Who told you I did that?" he said.

"Does it matter? More than a couple of people."

"How come I don't get to defend myself in front of my accusers?" Berkey said. In the old times, he'd been a deputy building inspector for the city of Glens Falls. He was not ignorant about official procedure. "Bring them in here and let's hear it out face-to-face."

"This isn't some civil service union grievance."

"I'm entitled to a hearing. It's still America, goddammit."

"That's debatable. But this *is* my farm. I decide what happens around here, and I'm inclined to kick your ass out."

Bullock sighed and puffed out his cheeks. He wanted to pour himself another whiskey, but Berkey was also reputed to be a problem drinker and he didn't want to further aggravate the man's state of mind.

"I've got a family here, a house," Berkey said. His tone had shifted from defiant to pleading.

"I wouldn't let your wife and child go with you, the way you act. They can stay here in that house. Sooner or later she'll find a better man than you to keep company with and in the meantime we'll see to their needs."

"You can't come between a man and his family!"

"You bet I can. And I will."

"It's Christmas, goddammit," Berkey said and began to weep great heaping sobs. "Show a little mercy? I'm sorry. I'm sorry for anything I done. Please. Have mercy. Please . . ." Berkey sank into his haunches on the carpet and blubbered.

Dick Lee got up to poke the logs on the hearth.

Delson put his hand over his eyes so he didn't have to look.

"Please don't cast me out," Berkey blubbered. "Have mercy. Oh, Jesus. Have mercy."

If the man sank any lower into the carpet, Bullock thought, he'd vanish and leave a mere stain. Then Bullock swung behind his desk with catlike grace, took a seat behind the desk where he didn't have to see Berkey on the floor, and poured himself another whiskey after all. He let Berkey carry on for a good five minutes. The clock ticked between carols and then the King's Choir segued into "The First Noel," and the music got to him as images of poor shepherds keeping their sheep softened his heart.

"Get up off the floor," he said.

Weeping quietly now, Berkey gathered his loose limbs together and arose from the floor.

"Quit blubbering and look at me."

Berkey hocked down a draft of phlegm and turned his rheumy eyes to meet Bullock's.

"I'm putting you in the lockup tonight and you're going to remain in there the next few days until Christmas is over," Bullock said. He'd established a brig in a room behind the smithy where it stayed reasonably warm on a winter night. "We'll send in rations and take out slops, and you're going to reflect on your behavior while you're there. When work resumes after the holiday you'll report to the sawmill. I don't want you around animals anymore."

"You mean you're not going to kick me off the premises?"

"I'm going to let you stay."

Berkey shuddered.

"If I hear of you harming an animal again, I'll hang you from a locust tree on the River Road. If you lay a hand on your wife or your child, I'll take an ax handle to you. And if it happens that Perses dies from the injuries you inflicted on him, I will run you off after all."

"Thank you, sir."

"You can thank whoever invented Christmas," Bullock said. He looked across the room at his two trusted men and jerked his head.

Michael Delson and Dick Lee steered Berkey out the door by his elbows.

FIVE

Rick Stokes came home to his cottage in Mill Hollow to find the wood-fired cookstove stone-cold. The past two winters with the baby, he and Mandy had closed off the upstairs rooms and lived on the first floor, with their bed set up in the former sitting room and the baby's crib near the stove in the kitchen. In recent weeks, his every homecoming from the long days at the Larmon farm filled him with dismay and not a little fear. Every week the house was in more and more disarray. There was something wrong with Mandy and really no place to take her now, no hospital, no facility, just Dr. Copeland, who could not explain her malady. How could she not be moved to light a fire on such a cold winter night, Rick wondered? They had plenty of stove billets and kindling and he regularly bought matches from Roger Hoad, who made them according to a formula that reputedly included his own dried urine.

Rick found a candle stub on the kitchen counter and lit a match.

"What the hell, Mandy?" he muttered, more to himself than to his wife. He set about starting the firebox on the cookstove, and when he got a few splints going he put in some oak billets and closed the iron door. He had been keeping watch at the farm on a colicky horse since two o'clock in the afternoon. The horse, a well-mannered Haflinger gelding named Duffy, had been in great pain, assuming tortured positions on its haunches in its stall, and sweating copiously. Around eight that evening, it shat out a bloody mass that looked like an afterbirth, but by nine o'clock it was back on its feet taking water and a few handfuls of grain. Ned Larmon and Rick concluded that Duffy was going to be all right. Rick was exhausted, having left the house before daylight that morning.

Rick was losing confidence that Mandy was ever going to be all right again. She seemed to be straying deeper and deeper into a distant hinterland of the mind from which return was increasingly unlikely. It had begun to occur to him that they couldn't go on like this. And now coming home to find the house like a cold storage locker, he realized the baby was no longer safe in her care. He would have to find a family with a competent adult female to look after Julian, at least during the days. However, Rick had no idea who might look after Mandy while he was off working on the farm. And what might she do then? Search desperately around town for her child? Throw herself in the river? These ruminations vexed and grieved Rick. He'd spent weeks thinking round and round about what to do. Now, he was ready to act. And all of this just as Christmas was coming, he thought, in what should have been the happiest time of year in these years of hardship and tribulation. It made him so heartsick he wobbled in his boots.

He took the candle stub and moved quietly to the sitting room. Mandy lay under a heap of blankets and quilts with her back toward the kitchen. Her body was motionless. He padded back into the kitchen and held the candle high above the crib where Julian slept. The baby, too, lay motionless beneath a heap of quilts. Rick watched Julian a full minute. He had the impression in the flickering candlelight that the baby's little body seemed unusually inert.

"Hey little pup," he said softly and reached under the quilts to get a grip on the boy. His discovery that the boy's body felt very cold sent a bolt of fear through him that seemed to explode in his head like a bomb. He put the candle down on a nearby sideboard, lifted Julian out of the crib, and held him to his chest. The boy's head lolled lifelessly, and his face, bundled in his colorful knitted wool hat, looked ashen gray.

"Mandy!" Rick called across the room. Then again, with more urgency, "Mandy!"

As he wheeled around, he heard her stir. The bedsprings groaned. The floorboards creaked. A dark shape arose in the dim light. Then, Mandy hurtled across the room, shrieking like a raptor, and plunged a nine-inch cook's knife into a soft space between her husband's sternum and rib so that the blade neatly sectioned the right atrium of his heart and severed the pulmonary artery. Rick dropped Julian and fell backward onto the crib that he had made himself out of cherrywood in the months preceding the baby's birth. He had no clear sense of what happened to him in the elongated moment when the crib splintered beneath him and he came to rest on the floor at the sudden end of his life. He certainly did not hear the keening wail that Mandy emitted as the blood ran out of him, which soon drew several neighbors to the house.

Six

Christmas music practice at the Congregational Church was reaching its triumphal climax with the concluding song of this year's program: "Angels from the Realms of Glory," with Andrew Pendergast directing the choir in its soaring invocations of *Come and worship, worship Christ the newborn king* in place of the latin *Gloria in excelsis deo* and all the musicians variously pounding, blowing, and bowing away on their instruments in a transport of yuletide jubilation. It is true that a certain amount of cider had been consumed during the two hours of rehearsal, courtesy of Dan Mullinex, flutes and clarinet, who happened to be the ramrod at Holyrood's cider works and who brought a keg of 12 percent alcohol "farmhouse draught" to the proceedings. Platters of cakes, sweetmeats, meringues, and cookies also had been brought and devoured in the course of things so that the twelve musicians and twenty-two chorale members were well sugared too. Spirits ran high. An old Harmon top-loader stove warmed the big community room aided by the body heat of thirty-four people. And the room was well lighted by the standards of the new times with a central eighteen-taper chandelier and candles deployed wherever a musician or chorale member needed to read sheet music.

Charles Pettie, bass fiddle, proprietor of the Battenkill creamery, a modest man of forty-eight years renowned for his way with fresh cheese and a knowledge of music theory second only to Andrew Pendergast, could not contain his agitation.

"That's too damned bombastic for a finale," he said to Robert Earle, first fiddle, who had risen from his seat.

"What would you prefer?"

"'I Will Bow and Be Simple,' a cappella," Pettie said.

"We do that early in the set."

"I'm saying move it to last."

"It's kind of austere for a Christmas finale."

"It's sobering. And the tone's right," Charles said. "Times being how they are."

Robert was about to argue when a commotion erupted at the far end of the big room. There were screams and shouts of "murder" and "come quickly," and it turned out that Don Burkhardt, a farm worker on Deaver's place and a Mill Hollow denizen, had responded to Mandy Stokes's wailing. He and several neighbors had discovered a scene of bloody mayhem upon entering the house and, being twenty-four years old and a swift runner, Don was sent by the others to fetch help. The musicians now put their instruments down, grabbed their coats and hats stashed in every corner, and moved as a mob out the door. The Reverend Loren Holder prevailed on several of the older women to stay behind and mind the lighted candles and the woodstove so the Congregational Church would not burn down.

Robert and Loren followed the mob out to Van Buren Street, then downtown, on Main Street. The new Union Tavern had already emptied out and that crowd had also moved down to the scene of the tragedy. The music circle crowd finally passed under the ancient railroad overpass that led into Mill Hollow, the site of Union Grove's first industrial establishment, a flax braking works, built in the 1820s. Several dozen men and not a few women stood grimly outside the Stokes cottage. Candles flickered within and dark shapes moved around. Robert Earle had to fight his way up front through the combined mobs before he climbed four steps to the front door. Loren Holder, who held the so far largely ceremonial office of village constable and was the sole police presence in Union Grove, joined Robert on the deck to the entrance portico. The crowd appeared to them as more than the sum of the individuals in it—a threatening organism of uncertain appetites.

"What do I say," Robert asked Loren who, as a minister, had much more experience speaking before groups of people. Robert had been elected the village mayor by happenstance in June and was not a natural politician.

"Thank them for showing concern," Loren said leaning close to Robert's ear.

About a hundred faces looked up at Robert and Loren, dim in the meager light that came only through the windows from the rooms within.

"Thank you for showing concern," Robert said. "I don't know as it's necessary for all of you to stay around here."

"We want to know what happened," said Eric Laudermilk.

"What if there's a killer on the loose?" said Petey Widgeon.

The whole mixed crowd of musicians and tavern patrons rumbled anxiously.

"If you show a little patience, we'll try to find out what went on here and fill you in as soon as we have some information," Loren said.

"We may need some help carrying messages around town," Robert added.

"We already sent for the doc," said Ian Hindley, a Schmidt farmhand who had been enjoying himself at the new bar some minutes earlier and was now shivering under a crude blanket poncho with no hat.

"When he gets here, tell him to come right in," Robert said. "The rest of you, please stay outside. We'll let you know what's up as soon as possible."

Robert and Loren entered the cottage. Three candles guttered around the first-floor rooms. Deeper inside, in the sitting room turned bedroom, Mandy Stokes sat on the bed staring into the rug, being quietly comforted by a neighbor woman on each side. Loren and Robert turned their attention to the figure of Rick Stokes splayed atop a heap of splintered cherrywood. The handle of a cook's knife protruded conspicuously from the vivid dark splotch in the center of his wool coat. His eyes were fixed wide open and his mouth frozen in a morbid rictus of stupefaction. A dark viscous pool of liquid spread out on the floor beyond the splintered wood he lay upon. A much smaller bundle lay near him on the floor. Loren fetched a candle stub closer. He and Robert got down on their hands and knees to look.

"Aw, jeezus," Loren muttered, discerning that the bundle contained a baby and that the baby was motionless, its face gray.

"What do you think?" Robert said.

"Both dead," Loren said.

They lingered near the floor watching closely a good minute.

"Do you suppose she killed him?" Robert whispered.

"That might be one theory," Loren said. He got up off his hands and knees and Robert did likewise.

Of the several Mill Hollow men inside the house, Loren was slightly acquainted with Brad Kimmel, who ran one of the town's few going cash businesses: a "fix-it" shop. In the old times he'd sold power tools at the Lowe's big box store in Glens Falls.

"Is that the husband and their child there on the floor?" Loren asked.

"Yes it is," Kimmel said. "Name of Rick. A decent fellow."

"You live down here, right?" Loren asked.

"Yes I do."

"Did you hear any quarreling tonight?"

"Not a thing, until . . . this. There was yelling. I figure he killed the baby and she killed him?" Kimmel said in a low whisper.

"That may or may not be," Loren said. "I wouldn't go spreading that story."

"I'm just saying," Kimmel said.

"Was there some other party around here tonight?" Robert said.

"Party?" Kimmel said. "I don't know. That tavern opened up today—"

"No, some other person," Robert said. "Someone who doesn't belong down here that you might have noticed."

"Oh," Kimmel said. "No. I didn't see anyone."

"How about you others," Loren asked the men with Kimmel: Ralph Horsley, a laborer on the Deaver farm, and Bob Bouchard, a woodcutter.

"No, sir," Bouchard said while Horsley shook his head.

"I hope nobody touched anything," Loren said. He knew next to nothing about the correct procedure. It occurred to him that forensics were now a thing of the past. There were no labs to send things to. The legal system of the old times was defunct: the courts, professional police, all of it. The truth of this tragedy would have to be determined by other means, and Loren was not sure it would be the truth.

"We didn't touch nothing," Kimmel said. The other neighbor men nodded.

"Thanks," Robert said. "We'll take it from here."

They didn't seem to understand.

"You guys can go now," Loren said. Irritation was creeping into his voice.

When they had left, footsteps resounded overhead, and soon a familiar boxy figure resolved out of the shadows where the stairway opened into the dim hall. Brother Jobe wore a knee-length gray blanket greatcoat with a wool muffler draped about his neck. He carried his broad-brimmed hat in his hands.

"You fellows figure it out yet?" he asked Loren and Robert.

"No," Loren said. "How about you?"

"Working on it."

"Did you find anything upstairs?"

"Appears to me they don't use it in the winter."

Loren held his candle stub aloft and poked around the kitchen. Part of a round skillet–made corn bread sat on a cutting board with crumbs all around. It struck Loren as odd in a time when food was dear and manufactured mousetraps and chemical poisons were hard to come by. Mice were everywhere. Most people were careful about food. They put leftover food away in tins, old plastic storage tubs, and cabinets. There was some odd dark thing next to the corn bread. Loren looked closer with the candle. It was a fish head, from a smoked trout, he surmised, all desiccated, with a fragment of spine still attached. It was very cold in the cottage. Loren carefully touched the cookstove surface. It was barely warm. He opened the firebox and looked in. A few embers glowed.

"You better might have to take the girl into custody," Brother Jobe said.

Loren digested the idea. "She's not a suspect yet."

"No?" Brother Jobe said. He stepped around Loren and gazed down at Rick's body. "Got any other idears?"

"An intruder, maybe," Robert said. "Someone who did this and fled the scene. A secret boyfriend maybe. I dunno . . ."

"You try to talk to her yet?" Brother Jobe said.

Loren stepped carefully around the body and the splintered crib and went into the room where the women sat on the bed. The woman and her dead husband were among the few people in town who did not attend the Congregational Church or belong to any of its social organizations. Loren had never spoken to Mandy though he had seen her occasionally around town. He stood before her for a full minute. The neighbor woman on her right stroked Mandy's arm. Everyone's breath was visible in the dim light. Mandy did not look up at him so Loren squatted down on the rug before her.

"Tell me your name?" he said.

Mandy did not respond.

"It's Mandy," said the neighbor woman on her right side, Anna Klum.

"Mandy, I'm Loren Holder. I'm minister of the Congregational Church and I'm the town constable as well. It's up to me to find out what happened here."

Mandy didn't respond. She just stared through Loren.

"Can you tell me what happened?"

She would not. Mandy's mind was a vast cavern of roaring reverberating voices, none of them making any sense. It left her numb and mute.

"Has she been like this all along?" Loren asked the other women.

"Yes," said Tracy Tolleson on Mandy's left. "Since we got here."

Just then, Dr. Jerry Copeland entered the cottage. He nodded a greeting to the others. He saw the bodies on the floor and stooped down to take Rick's pulse at the carotid artery. He lifted the baby off the floor, undid the baby's swaddling on the kitchen table, and searched for a pulse. He palpated Julian's little arms and jaw. The muscles were still flaccid; rigor mortis had not set in. The baby's exposed pale skin and lifeless face made Robert shudder.

Loren quit his spot in the back bedroom and strode back to the kitchen. He, too, took a long hard look at the baby on the kitchen counter. All the men spoke lowly, in whispers.

"Not a mark on him," Loren said.

"He's sufficiently dead," the doctor said.

"What do you think?"

"I'll have to perform an autopsy."

"How about Mandy," Loren whispered.

"You need to find a place for her," the doctor said. "Some place secure, where she'll stay put." The doctor paused a moment. "Some place she won't hurt anybody."

"My sentiment too," Brother Jobe weighed in.

"Is there something wrong with her?" Robert said.

"She was a patient of mine last summer," the doctor said. "She had some kind of meningitis. Of course, I didn't have any antibiotics or antiviral drugs. People can get over it. I thought she mostly had. Her physical symptoms resolved. But she showed some apparent thinking problems afterward."

"Is she psychotic?"

The doctor looked abashed. "Actually, I haven't seen her since maybe back in October," he said. "But she appeared capable of functioning. I certainly didn't think she was a danger to herself or others." He turned his glance down to Rick's body on the floor with the handle of a cook's knife protruding from his chest. "Now I'd have to assume she could be," the doctor said.

"We don't have any place to put her," Robert said. "The town jail is unheated. She should be in a mental health facility."

"Well, that's not an option," the doctor said. Along with the legal system, the hospitals in Bennington and Glens Falls had ceased operating.

"Yeah," Robert said, puffing out his cheeks. "Not an option."

"What about your infirmary?" Loren said.

The doctor ruminated awhile. "The windows don't lock," he said.

"We have a place for her," Brother Jobe said.

The others turned to him.

"Warm, secure, and plenty of men to keep watch out in the hall. It's heated and she could get meals and all. We'll even pray for her."

The four men swapped glances. They understood their mutual assent without having to express it out loud.

"I'll send for a cart," Brother Jobe said. "You'll also have to get a message over to Bullock. It's high time that sumbitch took his magistrate duties seriously."

While they waited for the cart, Loren found some paper and an old ballpoint pen and drew a diagram of the first floor of the house and where the bodies had been found. When the cart came, the women attempted to help Mandy off the bed and out of the house. They got her to her feet but, as they attempted to steer her out of the back room, Mandy became hysterical, shrieked, scratched at and struck the women with her fists, even tried to bite them. Loren, the doctor, and Robert had to step in. They seized her and brought her back over to the bed where she continued to carry on wildly, even while Loren and the doctor held her down. She screamed at them in words that were not from a language any of them recognized. Meanwhile, Robert went outside. The crowd had dwindled now to about twenty persons, mostly men, stamping their feet in the cold and dark. He asked for someone to fetch a length of rope.

"Are you going to hang somebody?" said Troy Cotterill, a cooper, who was still quite drunk from his evening in the Union Tavern.

"I suppose you already heard that we have two bodies in there," Robert said, ignoring Cotterill.

There was agreement that this was so among the crowd.

"Don't she get a trial?" said Kyle Tripp, another farmhand.

"Nobody's been charged yet and there won't be any lynchings," Robert said. Just then, a two-wheeled cart raced under the old railroad bridge into Mill Hollow pulled by a fine bay gelding. Somebody came up with a length of old nylon rope, the really strong kind that was not manufactured anymore. Robert gave it to the doctor and Loren, who bound Mandy's wrists behind her, and hobbled her ankles, and wrapped her in a blanket, and conveyed her out the door to the cart driven by Brother Boaz from the New Faith Brotherhood Covenant Church of Jesus.

There was plenty of time to take the bodies where they needed to go.

SEVEN

Hours later, Loren Holder returned to the rectory of the Congregational Church where he lived with his wife, Jane Ann, and his four little orphaned boys. The presence of the boys in their household—since their rescue from the criminal child trafficker Miles English in the nearby village of Argyle—had lit up their lives, even while Loren and Jane Ann grieved for their own missing twenty-year-old son, Evan, who had gone off two years earlier with Robert Earle's son, Daniel, to see what had happened to America beyond the boundaries of Washington County. Nothing had been heard of them since. The big white clapboard rectory house with its figured gables and arched windows had once again become, for Loren and Jane Ann, the beating heart of their spirits, instead of a bleak outpost in the realm between the living and the dead. Striding up Van Buren Street in two inches of fluffy snow, Loren fixed his gaze on the candlelight that glowed through the curtain in their second-floor bedroom. A three-quarter moon spread enough soft radiance through the clouds that the street looked as vivid as a miniature scene in a glass snowglobe.

Loren entered the house carefully so as not to wake the children sleeping upstairs. A big Christmas tree stood in the front parlor. With the electricity out for good, there was no need to worry about a short circuit in a string of lights burning the house down. By standards of the old times, the number of presents under the tree would have seemed paltry. Christmas was no longer the frantic commercial potlatch it had been in the late days of the so-called consumer society. It was the custom in the new times to give children only one special present each year. Instead of manufactured wrapping paper, the gifts were concealed in scraps of fabric and garments that would be used when the holiday was over.

Loren lit a candle and checked the woodstoves in the front parlor and in the kitchen. They were well stoked. It put him in mind of the chill dreariness of the murder scene and how delicate the devices were that kept anyone from a life of tragic futility in these harsh new times. In the kitchen he poured himself three fingers of rough plum brandy in a pony glass. Upstairs, he found Jane Ann in bed, in a flannel nightshirt, reading the biography of a long-gone movie star renowned for her feisty independence and battles with the studio moguls. Jane Ann could tell by the way Loren was standing beside the bed, sipping the plum brandy, that something was up. She put down her book.

"I think you have something to tell me," she said.

EIGHT

By the time Robert Earle returned to his 1904 arts and crafts–style bungalow on Linden Street, his housemate and girlfriend, Britney Blieveldt, was cleaning up the debris from her candle-making operation. It had taken her four hours to dip sixty beeswax and tallow tapers and fill two dozen old glass jars with triple wicks that she liked to use as lighting for other handwork—from basketry to sewing to making the candles themselves. She had hung the tapers to harden on a rack attached to a varnished wooden pallet that Robert had made for her to collect any wax drippings that could be scraped off and saved. Beeswax was dear. She was industrious because she believed she had to be, and at twenty-nine she still had the energy. In the old times, when she was a teenager, she spent countless hours supine in front of the flat-screen television following the so-called reality antics of strangers. The new times had transformed her as had the murder of her husband, Shawn Watling, half a year earlier by the thugs who managed the old landfill as a salvage operation. She had been left dangerously adrift with a seven-year-old daughter. In the new times, in a community demoralized by the failed religion of scientific progress, in what had become a hard subsistence economy, being without a man was an unpromising situation. Robert Earle had rescued her, quite literally, from her burning house. And so she and her daughter, Sarah, fell in with Robert, a widower who was a generation older than Britney, and she had joined his household.

Robert took his boots off and removed the heavyweight Polartec fleece jersey that had held up so remarkably since he first bought it for telemark skiing more than twenty years ago, when the world was full of miracle fabrics and miracles in general, and all that was necessary to beat back the dark of night was the flick of a switch when you walked into a room. Now everything that used to be automatic was a chore in a daily cavalcade of chores that some days added up to an ordeal of chores. He carefully placed his fiddle case on top of the upright piano and moved to the woodstove to warm his hands and face. The aroma of balsam pine filled the house from the tree in the corner farthest from the woodstove. It was covered with a mix of old manufactured glass ornaments and whimsical figures Robert had carved, festooned with swags of popcorn strung on sewing thread.

Usually, when he entered the house he had some news, especially if he had just come from a meeting where a lot of other townspeople were present, as he had this evening with the assembly of musicians and choristers for Christmas practice. News had no other way of traveling now that the immersive media of TV, radio, and Internet were not a presence in their lives. Britney observed him closely trying to guess what he was holding back from telling her. She concluded that Robert was making an effort to avoid eye contact.

"Would you like something hot to drink?" she asked.

"Yes," he said, not looking her way. "Milk with honey and whiskey, please."

She disappeared into the rear keeping room, which was far enough from the various stoves to serve as a place of refrigeration this time of year. She returned shortly with a saucepan of milk and placed it on the parlor stove because the kitchen cookstove had been banked for the night and she didn't want to stoke it again as their bedroom was upstairs from the kitchen and Robert hated to sleep in a hot room. Then she set about assembling a supper plate for him.

The cuisine of the new times was rich but monotonous, being limited mostly to what grew in the vicinity and what could be made from it. They had plenty of butter, cream, cheeses, meats, and sausage. Wheat would not grow in the northeast because of pervasive stem-rust disease in the soil, and deliveries of it from elsewhere were erratic at best. They got by on corn, rye, barley, oats. Stephen Bullock was experimenting with the ancient grain called spelt. He'd gotten one small crop in that year. In trials so far it made a dense, nutty loaf like rye and rough crumbly noodles, which his wife, Sophie, pronounced "inedible." The staple in the new times was corn bread and many dishes were made around it, for instance the so-called pudding that Britney cut a big oblong of and put on a plate for Robert, with pickled garden vegetables and a side of fermented cabbage spiced with hot peppers, garlic, and green onions, not unlike the Korean kimchi that had been catching on in America just when things fell apart. Britney's pudding this evening was a savory baked dish of day-old corn bread, eggs, cream, kale, onions, and leftover duck, of which she had used everything but the quack.

Robert seated himself next to the stove in a hoop-back rocking chair built with his own hands out of maple, oak, and poplar the month after his daughter Genna died of encephalitis at age eleven. It had required all his attention to build it correctly.

"You know, we could get a horse now," Robert said.

"Why would you want to get a horse?"

This brought him up short. He wondered for a moment if Britney was being snarky with him, but this was not her way.

"I have quite a bit of hard money due. Enough for a horse."

"You could always rent a horse from Mr. Allison," she said. Tom Allison had been a vice president for administration at the county community college in the old times. Now he ran the town livery, a business he had to improvise because the model for running it hadn't existed in a century. He rented out carts and wagons as well as saddle horses. In the new times most people not involved with the transport of goods did not have to go anywhere.

"I've wanted a horse for a long time," Robert said.

"It's not like having a car where you can just leave it sit until you need it," Britney said. "You have to care for them constantly. And they get sick fairly often."

"What do you know about horses?"

"I half-leased a palomino named Josie when I was twelve and thirteen. That is, my mom did for me. Josie got Lyme disease and we had to pay the vet bills. On top of everything else. All the routine stuff."

"I didn't know you rode horses."

"There's probably a lot we don't know about each other," Britney said.

"I guess so."

Britney poured Robert's hot milk into a mug, stirred in a golden glob of honey, and finished it with a liberal shot of rye whiskey. As she brought it over to him, she tried again to get him to look at her. He actually closed his eyes as he took the mug and savored the first gulp of the warm, sweet beverage and felt it go to work in his belly.

"Oh, that's good," he said, still avoiding her gaze. "At least there's no more Lyme disease since people jacked all the deer."

"There's always something going on with a horse," Britney said. "And the vet doesn't have what he used to have to deal with it."

When she brought his supper plate over to him, Robert finally looked right back at her. "I'm disappointed," he said. "I thought you would be thrilled at the idea of getting a horse."

"Sorry," she said.

"I thought Sara would like to have a horse to ride."

"I wasn't so crazy about it. Mom pushed me into it because the real well-off girls in town rode horses."

Robert savored his first bite of the duck and kale pudding. Nobody in town had a horse except for the farmers and Tom Allison, Dr. Copeland, and Terry Einhorn the storekeeper. These were the well-off in the society of the new times. Robert wondered whether he was considered well-off. He was getting by. He was paid in hard silver for his work. He had plenty of firewood and food. So many others were not doing so well and had little prospect of it. But the plain fact was, he liked riding a horse and he still wanted to have one. You could go places.

"What kind of riding did you do?" he asked Britney.

"Dressage, it's called. Fancy steps. Like dancing for horses. I didn't like it. I just wanted to gallop around and we weren't allowed to."

"Sara could just gallop around."

"Horses are very dangerous. What do you know about horses?"

"I rode one to Albany and back last summer. And then up to Hebron and back in October on one of Tom's saddle horses. They were both well behaved."

"How did you like it?"

"I guess I liked it pretty well. I like the smell and the feel of them. I like that they're alive like us, with personalities."

"I liked that about them too."

"Down in Albany we got shot at, you know. We rode through that."

"It must have been a very good horse," Britney said.

"I thought I would get a cart for carrying my tools."

"Don't you usually leave your tools on the job?"

"Maybe it's childish but I just want a horse."

"It's not like a car," Britney said again.

He finished his supper plate in ruminative silence, his thoughts once more turned on the murder scene. Britney cut the wicks on the finished candles she had dipped and began putting them away in a chestnut drink cabinet that had belonged to Robert's grandfather, an attorney in Hartford, Connecticut. In the old times, Robert had housed his stereo amplifier and CD player in it.

"I'm going to wash up," Robert said. Britney had put a pail of water on the woodstove as she did every night for their ablutions. The town water system still worked, miraculously, because it was gravity-fed from an old town reservoir at an elevation on a low shoulder of Pumpkin Hill. Robert carried the steaming pail upstairs with a rag around the handle.

Not long after Robert retired to the bedroom, Britney came in from her own turn in the washroom and looking in on her sleeping daughter. Robert was reading by candlelight, his usual habit. It was a biography of Stalin. Britney wore a flannel nightshirt with her hair down. She smelled of lilac. Her compact, muscular physical presence excited him. He put down his book and watched her maneuver around the bed to her side. They had evolved a comfortable protocol for sexual activity in the months since Britney moved into the household. On the nights when she was interested in lovemaking, she always made a little show of removing her nightclothes before turning up the covers. This night, she just climbed quickly into bed.

"I realized something tonight," Robert said. Britney turned to look at him through her eyelashes with her chin down, thinking she was going to be criticized about her opposition to getting a horse. "It was at music practice. Bonnie Sweetland sang a solo verse on 'Away in a Manger.' Not having microphones has changed everything about music. People sing differently now."

"Why do I get the feeling that there's something else on your mind tonight?" she said.

After an awkward moment of hesitation he told her what had happened in Mill Hollow that evening.

NINE

When Andrew Pendergast returned from the exhilarating and exhausting Christmas practice, and the subsequent march to the murder scene in Mill Hollow, he noticed that his front door was not quite closed. It gave way inward, creaking on its hinges, as he made to turn the knob. The spice of his balsam Christmas tree carried another note on its broad raft of fragrance, a sweet-rotten odor like a dead squirrel in the ancient walls. He had been careful every summer to patch all the spots under the eaves where they had invaded in decades past. The heavy front door closed behind him with the solid, definitive thunk of well-fitted latches. The darkness and silence of an unelectrified house closed in on him. He reached with assurance toward a mahogany stand beside the door for the candle holder that lived there and one of the matches that lived beside it in an antique glass tumbler, which, in daylight, was a very subtle shade of violet. He struck the match on a piece of slate placed there for that purpose and lighted the candle. The nimbus of light blinded him for a moment, and in that moment someone across his living room began to sing in a reedy voice "We Wish You a Merry Christmas." Andrew pressed backward against the front door, felt for the handle, and considered running out into the street. His heart fluttered. The songster knew only one verse of the song and repeated it. Andrew calculated where various defensive utensils lay close at hand about the house. There was an antique Berber sword in the umbrella stand about ten feet away. The crudely made weapon, which had belonged to his favorite uncle, a CIA spook in the previous century, was encased in a leather and ivory sheath and it would take some doing to draw it. There was a cast-iron poker with a brass spear point next to the woodstove roughly halfway between where he stood and where the voice seemed to be coming from across the room. Andrew advanced into the living room with the candle held aloft. He seized the fireplace poker and squinted the remaining fifteen feet to the far wall, where the man who earlier had accosted him on the street and pissed on his overcoat now sat in a reproduction Louis XV armchair upholstered in red silk damask. Even in the dim light the grime showed on his patched goose-down jacket.

"Do you need a friend?" Jack Harron said.

"I have plenty of friends."

"You can't have too many."

"First you piss on my coat and then you invade my home," Andrew said. "How is that friendly?"

"I'm a ghost," Harron said.

"No you're not."

"I might as well be. I pass invisible among you."

"You're making yourself very visible to me."

"I watch the life going on all around. Meanwhile this world is killing me. It wants me gone just like you want me gone. Is that fair?"

Andrew shifted his weight. A wide pine plank floorboard squeaked.

"What's fair about life?" he said.

"Exactly. Want to hear my sob story?" Harron said.

"If it'll inspire you to leave."

"I don't want to leave. I like it here."

"Sooner or later you'll have to leave and I'd prefer that it's sooner."

"Wait."

An antique clock ticked loudly on the mantelpiece behind the woodstove that occupied the old hearth before the fireplace. The beehive clock was one of the last made by the great Seth Thomas of Connecticut in 1858.

"I'm waiting," Andrew said.

"Be patient. This is not what you think."

"Did you have anything to do with that business in Mill Hollow?" Andrew said.

"What happened in Mill Hollow?"

"There's two people dead down there."

"That's sad."

"It's more than sad. It's horrifying. There could be a killer on the loose. You could be the killer."

"Well, I'm not. Who were they that got killed?"

"A man and his baby son."

"What's this world coming to?"

"That's what everybody wants to know. Why did you piss on my coat?"

"I was trying to get your attention."

"That's a pretty crude way to go about it."

"I was a little drunk."

"Are you still?"

"No. That was hours ago. I apologize."

"Okay, now you've got my attention. What's your story?"

"I have nothing."

Andrew waited for him to elaborate. He didn't. Andrew put the candleholder on the woodstove. He was tired of holding it up. "Is there more to it?"

"It's a short story. I have nothing. I'm a broken man."

"I'm sorry to hear that. How did you get that way?"

"Like so many others. These times," Harron said. "All I have left is my will."

"I've noticed."

"You fix things," Harron said.

"Yes, I do."

"Fix me."

"I can't fix humans."

"Did you ever try?"

Andrew paused to consider this. Indeed, he had tried to get people in his life to behave differently, to change, to be other than what they were, to be what he wanted them to be. It never worked.

"Maybe you should talk to the doctor," Andrew said.

"I'm not broken that way," Harron said.

"Don't you have some place to live? There are empty houses everywhere."

"That's it. They're empty."

"There's free furniture everywhere."

"That's not the kind of empty I mean."

"Look," Andrew said. "It's cold in here. I'd like to make a fire. If I put this poker down, do you promise to behave yourself?"

"Yes. What were you going to do with it anyway?"

"Defend myself. Thrash you, if necessary."

"Hasn't there been enough killing around here for one day?" Harron said.

Andrew put the poker back in its stand beside the woodstove.

Harron said, "I'll make the fire. If you let me."

TEN

The doctor told Brother Jobe's men to bring the bodies into the springhouse next to the old carriage barn that served as his office and infirmary. It was a little warmer in there than it was outside, as it was bermed deep into the hillside. When the men left and the doctor was alone with the corpses in the flickering light of a single candle, an overwhelming surge of sadness ran through him at the cruel destiny that had brought these two to the completion of their business on earth, a father and son, arrayed side by side on an old wooden table awaiting the grave. The doctor suppressed the urge to resort to his own medicinal pear brandy, whereupon his eleven-year-old son, Jasper, and wife, Jeanette, entered the springhouse, bringing the doctor back out of himself.

"What happened?" Jeanette asked, surveying the bodies.

"I think the man shook the baby and killed it, and his wife killed him for it. You remember her. She had the meningitis last summer. We treated her. It affected her mind afterward."

"Yes. I remember. Such a sweet girl. Smart too. She did this?"

"It seems that she did."

"What will happen to her?"

The doctor shook his head, then turned to his son, who had lately been assisting him in his practice, training to eventually practice medicine in his own right.

"Fetch some more candlesticks, and the instruments, and my rubber apron," the father said to his son.

ELEVEN

The brothers and sisters of the New Faith Brotherhood Covenant Church of Jesus had done considerable remodeling of the Union Grove High School, which they'd bought the previous spring. One of the many chambers in it was formerly a teachers' lounge shoehorned by the architect between the men's gym locker room and the cafeteria pantry. It had been converted into a small informal chapel. The room was lighted in daytime by a narrow band of clerestory windows along the top of a wall that even a desperate adult could not have squeezed out of. When Brother Jobe and his men returned to the compound that night with Mandy Stokes in custody, they installed her in the chapel, removing the pews and bringing in a bed, a small table, a chair, and a rug. One Brother Shiloh, handy with tools and fittings, installed a deadbolt and a sturdy black locustwood bar on the door to keep the room's occupant secure.

The first of a rotating set of brothers was posted on a chair outside this detention cell. A team of four sisters attended Mandy inside, helping her out of her rank clothing and into a simple linen frock to sleep in. The process required a lot of forcible assistance as Mandy snarled and scratched and resisted, all the while screaming in strings of unintelligible words. She was sitting on the edge of her bed, seemingly calm, with a wool blanket over her shoulders when Brother Jobe entered the room. He thanked the sisters and dismissed them. Mandy did not acknowledge him. Placing his candle on the table, he dragged the chair to a place about six feet squarely in front of her and sat down. He sat quietly with her for a time until his breathing synchronized with hers.

"I'm going to count to fifty," he said. "And then you're going to look right at me."

He pulled his chair much closer to her and commenced counting slowly in a low, steady voice, calibrated to her intake of breath and exhalations, precisely five numbers for each set of breaths. The building was otherwise dead silent at this hour, with most of the New Faith members asleep in their rooms. When that soothing, expansive recital of the numbers was complete, Mandy lifted her head so that they sat face-to-face in the flickering light, whereupon Brother Jobe raised his right index finger to the zygomatic ridge under his right eye, took possession of her will, and entered her mind.

He was aware right away of what a tumultuous, alien environment it presented, a flashing chiaroscuro of lurid colors and many competing voices at all pitches and tones, variously mocking, accusatory, pleading, giddy, and furious, along with a cacophony of nonvocal noises—clanking machinery, raging wind, and a racket of jungley animal cries. He struggled to survey the dark interior landscape, to see past jagged shapes and crackling dendritic bursts of light to discover the tiny distant kernel of Mandy's true persona hunched in the boggy, flashing dimness, sobbing. As he searched inside her mind, staring straight into her face, which remained otherwise motionless as if in thrall, tears formed in the corners of both her eyes, grew into droplets, and rolled down her cheeks.

"What happened tonight over there?" he said. "In your home."

I killed them, the tiny figure communicated in a message barely discernible above the vivid din. *Please help me.* Then, this hidden Mandy was subsumed in the discord of sound and image that was inside her. As that occurred, Mandy sitting on the bed a few feet from Brother Jobe took in progressively deeper inhalations as her damp eyes widened in terror and finally rolled up into her head. Her body slumped off the edge of the bed to the rug on the floor with a thud.

Brother Jobe was left a bit breathless himself by the experience, a strange and troubling novelty even for one as studied in the advanced practice of hypnosis as he was, and as used to entering the unknown reaches of other people's minds as an experienced spelunker was familiar with the strangeness of new caverns.

TWELVE

Brother Boaz, a trim, compact, capable fellow who had managed a La Quinta Motor Inn outside Kingsport, Tennessee, in the old times, and now served as Brother Jobe's messenger, valet, and all-around factotum, found himself in the novel situation of riding hard through the darkened countryside at a full gallop in lightly falling snow to Stephen Bullock's plantation, some four miles west of Union Grove. Boaz was well bundled against the cold in a long wool greatcoat and a sheepskin trapper's hat, with a thick muffler wrapped around his neck and lower face and heavy wool-lined gauntlet gloves.

He had become acquainted with horses only the past several years prior to which, in times that now seemed like ancient history, his personal vehicle of choice, like so many others of his region and class, was the Ford F-110 pickup truck. He reflected, as his rear end slapped against the saddle, that he never would have imagined himself doing this back in the day when he sat in the grandstand at Martinsville in Virginia, watching the NASCAR Kroger 200. But the journey in dim, ambient light that barely revealed the course of State Route 29 excited his senses in a way that driving a motor vehicle never had. He made it to the River Road in twenty minutes. The bodies of the nine men Bullock had hanged Halloween week for invading his property and threatening his life had been taken down after they had attained a state of ripeness that carried clear to town when the wind was right and everyone was sufficiently horrified. But the memory of that odious spectacle of revenge lingered along the River Road.

Boaz slowed to a canter up the drive to Bullock's Old Manse, as his family's house was called, and which Bullock himself called it in self-mocking acknowledgment of his strange fate in becoming something like a feudal lord in these new times. It was just after nine o'clock. Some windows were lighted in the big clapboard house. Boaz hitched his horse, a sorrel gelding named Brownie, beside the soapstone water trough and punched his gloved fist through the pane of ice there to free the water below. As Brownie drank, one of Bullock's security men came out the kitchen door. Boaz explained his business and was directed a mile up the hill to the agglomeration of cottages and other buildings that Bullock had allowed his people to build for their own habitation over recent years, as he attracted and absorbed those displaced from the shattered economy. Boaz mounted Brownie again and set off uphill. The New Village, which had no name other than that (Bullock recoiled from having it called after himself), looked like something out of an old-time Christmas card. Gentle snow fell in the breezeless air under thin clouds that allowed light from the three-quarter moon to penetrate.

The Christmas ball for Bullock's people was still under way inside the large community hall at the center of the village. Boaz could hear the music all the way over on such a cold, still night and as he approached the village he marveled to see electric lights burning in the village hall. He was aware that Bullock ran a small hydroelectric installation—Brother Jobe talked about it incessantly and was determined to get a system like it going over in town— but the sight of the dazzling strings of tiny colored electric lamps twinkling through the high windows, and the magnificence of the amplified recorded Christmas music playing over loudspeakers, startled one who had gotten used to the lower amplitude of things in the new times.

Though Boaz took care to enter the building unobtrusively, some kind of formal ceremony was going on and many heads turned to him as he shut the big door and leaned against it. Bullock himself was preoccupied rummaging over a wide plank table piled high with bolts of cloth, tools, cooking implements, and boxes of hard to get trade goods he had accumulated over the year and was passing items out to his villagers in a kind of Christmas potlatch he had devised over the years in the belief that it represented a sharing of his wealth. Boaz could not help but wonder at the starkly different sets of social relations between Bullock's establishment, his own community of the New Faith, and the sorry populace of Union Grove, who apparently had lost faith in God and progress and seemed to lack some crucial glue of belief that might support the town's collective spirit. Boaz wondered which mode of living would prevail in the uncertain future.

Shortly, a barrel-shaped man of medium height with a nonetheless imposing air approached him. This was Dick Lee, Bullock's own chief factotum, who asked the stranger what he wanted. In a short while, when the dispensing of gifts seemed to conclude and some of the villagers began bundling up to leave, and others repaired one last time to long buffet tables where quite a bit of holiday viands, cakes, sweetmeats, and puddings remained to be picked over as well as the pitchers of beer and cider and bottles of Bullock's own fine whiskey, Dick Lee brought Boaz to the front of the large room where Bullock stood speaking to a brawny younger man and a tall slender woman, his wife or companion, Boaz supposed. All were dressed in a manner that evoked older times than the old times, like characters in the storybooks of the War of Independence. Bullock himself was striking in his buff breeches, riding boots, red satin vest, and cutaway coat.

"A messenger, sir," Dick Lee said.

"Is that right?" Bullock said. He seemed to have a deranged smile on his face as he torqued around to take in the shorter Boaz, who discerned fairly quickly that Bullock had had a lot to drink. "You're one of *them!*" Bullock added with a rough, taunting humor he might not have employed if he were sober.

"One of who?" Boaz said.

"The uh . . . the cult!" Bullock said, the gleam in his eyes sharpening. "I hate to put it so bluntly but what else would you call it? Really?"

"We're who we are," Boaz said.

"That chief of yours, the Reverend Jobe. He's a strange breed of porpoise now, isn't he?" Bullock said.

"He has many burdens and responsibilities and he's as upright as they come."

"Maybe so," Bullock said. "Want to sign on here with us?"

"Uh, no, sir. I've come to—"

"Well, of course. We're always looking for new blood here. But then, so is your bunch. Aw, goddammit, Dick, where's my glass. Care for a beverage, son?" he asked Boaz. "You must be cold from your journey. Have a damn drink."

By this time the handsome young couple had excused themselves and Dick Lee had fetched two glasses of Bullard's special Christmas cider, one of which he held out for Boaz, the other he gave to his boss. The cider was fortified with jack brandy. The sound system played Judy Garland singing "Have Yourself a Merry Little Christmas," recorded before anyone in the room had been born.

"Thank you—"

"Now, what's up over in that sad-sack town of yours?"

"A serious and sensitive matter, sir. Two people killed over there tonight."

"What? A fire?"

"A double murder, sir."

Bullock bent a little closer and squinted at Boaz, who could sense the alcohol on the great man's breath. "What the hell! Why can't people behave?"

Bullock stared down at Boaz as though expecting an answer.

"I don't know, sir. Wickedness abides."

"This have anything to do with that new barroom your chief has got going?"

"Not as far as I know, sir."

"Not that I'm against it. That goddamn town needs some kind of spark to light its dim little fire. Pitiful what it's come to since I was a boy and it had its own newspaper, its own police force, two or three decent places to eat, and even a movie theater in the White

Swan Hotel. I tell you, it breaks my heart to think about it. Now who the hell got killed and under what circumstances?"

"It looks like the husband killed the child and then the wife killed the husband."

"Oh Christ. What's the world coming to?"

"It's already come a far piece to where it's going to," Boaz said.

"I'll drink to that," Bullock said. "I suppose they want me to do something about it."

"They do, sir. You're the magistrate."

"Why the hell does everybody keep reminding me of that?"

"I don't know, sir."

Bullock quaffed the remaining half glass of his drink.

"Where's this woman now?" he said.

"She's with us."

"What! Are you recruiting murderers now?"

"No, we're holding her in a secure room in our compound. There was nowheres else. She's under arrest, I guess you might say."

"Did she confess?"

"She appears to be out of her mind, sir."

"It would be easy to pretend you were crazy after killing your husband. Lots of times they do."

"I can't say, sir. I never kilt a loved one. Anyway, they say they have to start legal proceedings and you're the one to see to it. They would like you to come over to town tomorrow afternoon, if that would be all right."

"Who's 'they'?

"Mr. Earle, who's mayor, my boss Brother Jobe, the Reverend Holder. He's the acting town constable these days—"

"Tomorrow's Christmas Eve for chrissake."

"Not until sundown."

"What's the goddamn rush on this anyway?"

"The town's nervous, sir. They feel like there's no real law anymore."

"Well, there isn't," Bullock said. "We're just making it up as we go along now."

In the end, Bullock agreed to journey to town at a time and place specified in the written instructions Boaz carried on his person. Boaz felt the effects of the cider as he mounted up for the return trip. On his way down the hill he couldn't help turning around to behold the wondrous colored electric lamps glowing so magically in the big wooden building, while the upholstered voice of Nat King Cole singing "O Little Town of Bethlehem" carried on the still air of the hillside suddenly lambent with moonlight.

THIRTEEN

Andrew Pendergast took Jack Harron at his word. Having an enemy with an implacable animus toward himself was something Andrew could neither understand nor do anything about. Helping somebody was another matter, if the person in need of help was sincere about it. If Jack had wanted to harm him, Andrew reasoned, he could have coldcocked him when he entered his own house in the dark.

"I can use some help around here," Andrew told him. "Here's what I propose. I'll regard you as a project. You can sleep in the room behind the kitchen for now. There's a bathroom across the hall. We'll carry a bed down there. I'm going to give you lists of things to do and some instructions. Some of them you'll do every day and some of them will be occasional or special. If it's something you don't know how to do, I'll teach you how. From time to time we'll talk."

"What about?"

"Apart from just daily matters, we'll talk about you and how you came to where you are and what you're going to do from now on."

"I'm not interesting."

"I'll be the judge of that."

"What do I call you?"

"Andrew, like everybody else. And yourself?"

"Jack."

"Okay, Jack. Here's how we'll start. I'll show you around the kitchen. There's a wood cookstove in there. In general I'll expect you to fire it up in the morning, every morning. We'll stoke it tonight to show you how it all works. There's a hot-water reservoir on it. When the water is hot enough, you're going to take a bath. And I want you to burn those clothes you're wearing."

"What will I do for clothes?"

"I'll give you some clothes. These ones you're wearing stink horribly."

"They do?"

"Take my word for it. Are you hungry?"

"Yes. Very hungry."

"Do you want to eat something first?"

Jack hesitated as if he was not used to deciding anything.

"No. I want to wash up and burn these clothes," he said. "I can't stand myself how I am a minute longer."

"That would be a good start."

Fourteen

Ten minutes after one o'clock on the afternoon of Christmas Eve, the sky had darkened unnaturally to a metallic gray that seemed to mock the festive wreaths and catenaries of holiday fir that the people of Union Grove put up all over town. The clotting clouds above the modest parapets of Main Street withheld the snow they seemed to contain in their dark, fat bellies. The temperature crossed and recrossed the thirty-two-degree mark and the townspeople began to worry if the great night would be marred by rain. Meanwhile, Robert Earle, Brother Jobe, the Reverend Loren Holder, Dr. Jerry Copeland, senior village trustee Ben Deaver (a former United Airlines vice president in the old times, now a prosperous farmer who employed many townspeople), and Sam Hutto (a lawyer who ran a turpentine still on the back side of Pumpkin Hill in the absence of a functioning court system) all waited in a first-floor chamber of Union Grove's old town hall.

The new town hall (erected 1986), way out on State Route 29, a poorly constructed cartoon of the Federalist civic style, all executed in strand board and vinyl, now delaminating, was useless in the new times and had been abandoned some years ago. Whereas the old town hall, a sturdy Romanesque brick heap built in 1879, still contained all the original masonry flues for the parlor stoves it was designed to begin its useful life with—a life it had recently resumed. It stood on an honored site in the very center of Main Street, where it embodied in masonry and mortar the continuity of civic endeavor. In recent years, musical theater directed by Andrew Pendergast was performed seasonally up on the third floor, originally a temperance hall, with a proscenium arch beautifully decorated with motifs inspired by the great William Morris.

The men gathered in the first-floor room, which was used for winter meetings of the town trustees. The sheet metal woodstove heating the room was a more primitive device than the original cast-iron Windsor-Latrobe coal burners that the building had been outfitted with in 1879. Coal was no longer available in this corner of the country. Waiting for Bullock, the men made small talk about crops, weather, illnesses, and other matters to avert the difficult agenda they were called together to discuss. At twenty minutes past one, Bullock arrived in a cloak and a massive shearling hat that gave him the appearance of a Napoleonic hussar. Not everyone present was forbearing.

"You're late," Ben Deaver observed.

"Sorry," Bullock said, shedding his top clothes. "Some days you just have no sense of time."

"Ever notice," Deaver said to all present, "how people who say they have no sense of time never show up early." Awkward laughter ensued. Some coughing. Having worked high up in running an airline and then becoming one of the largest landholders in the county and a successful farmer enabled Deaver to speak this way to Bullock where others might not have dared.

Bullock ignored the remark.

"You've got two dead people and a woman in custody, I'm told," he said, and sat down with his leather folio of papers at the head of the big chestnut table that was one of the building's original furnishings. "We all know the law is not functioning the way it used to and we'll have to start from scratch here to create something like a fair procedure. Has she confessed, by the way?" Bullock searched the faces around the table.

Brother Jobe looked down at his hands, knowing that what he knew was both inadmissible and so far out of the normal sway of other people's expectations about reality that he dare not introduce it.

"What have you got, Loren?" Bullock said.

"Not much. A diagram of the scene. Notes on interviews, I guess you'd call them, with those who came to the house in response to the screaming."

"Well, what the hell, Loren?"

"What the hell do you mean 'what the hell,' Stephen?"

"I mean . . . is that it?"

"It's what we're able to do," Loren said, his voice rising. "We don't have a professional police force here, in case you haven't noticed."

"Believe me, I've noticed."

"Is there some crime lab I haven't been informed about where I'm supposed to send materials?"

"Okay, okay. Calm down. What about the murder weapon?"

"I left it in place," Loren said.

"Where?" Bullock said. "What place?"

"In the chest of the victim," Loren said.

Bullock made a face.

The others around the table swapped glances.

"I told him to leave it in there," the doctor said. "The bodies were brought over to my place. I conducted a postmortem examination to determine the exact cause of death. It was self-evident in the case of the man, of course."

"And . . ."

"I've written a report," the doctor said, retrieving a tri-folded, handwritten clutch of papers from his inner coat pocket and handing them over.

"Don't you miss the old Xerox machine?" Bullock said, taking the papers. No comments were offered. "Can you give me the verbal bottom line on this? Who killed who and how?"

"No, I can't do that," the doctor said.

"He can't do that," Sam Hutto, who had spent years in courtrooms, agreed. "Didn't you go to law school, Stephen?"

"Yeah, I went to Duke," Bullock said with visible pride. "Never actually practiced, though. The law just wasn't in my blood."

"Maybe you should eat a little more red meat," Ben Deaver said.

Bullock scowled at Deaver but did not retort.

"You understand that the coroner doesn't pronounce verdicts," Sam Hutto said. "That's what the regular procedure is for—hearing, grand jury, trial, and all that."

"Oh, all right. Sorry I asked. What about the baby? You can summarize your medical findings about the baby without pronouncing a verdict, can't you?" Bullock said, and then turned to Sam. "Can't he?"

Sam didn't object.

The doctor cleared his throat. "You have the spectrum of injury that's consistent with what's called shaken baby syndrome," he said. "Retinal hemorrhage, that is, bleeding, subdural hemorrhage, bleeding in the outer layers of the brain, but chiefly this child died of a broken neck, a severe insult to the brain stem. The other injuries suggest that he'd been shaken before, probably more than a couple of times."

"So, father shakes baby, kills him, and mother stabs father to death," Bullock said.

"We don't know that for sure," Robert said. "It's just conjecture."

Bullock visibly struggled to contain his irritation.

"Let's get the old ball rolling then, shall we," he said. "You want to prosecute or defend, Sam?"

"Gawd, I was afraid it would come to this."

"Well, how many lawyers have we got left around here? Not too goddamn many. There's you and Dale Murray." Dale Murray, Robert Earle's predecessor as mayor of Union Grove, was rumored to be spending his late innings on planet earth drinking Battenkill light rye whiskey from dawn to dark.

"Oh, please, let's not drag him into this," Loren objected.

"I have the degree in jurisprudence," Brother Jobe said, startling the others around the table, who now all turned at him.

"You're kidding me," Bullock said. "How is that possible?"

Brother Jobe now glared darkly at Bullock, and the latter seemed to shrink visibly from his hard gaze.

"I ain't kidding one ding-dang bit, your honor. And it's possible 'cause I applied and got in and grinded my goldurned way through the goshdarned program, is how."

"And where'd you obtain this alleged law degree?"

"Duke University, Durham, North Carolina. We're ole homeys, looks like."

Bullock cackled unconvincingly.

"Right there on Towerview Road, West Campus," Brother Jobe continued. "Sound familiar? I remember it like it was yesterday. Across the street on one corner was the science lab building and the Panda Express on t'other. I guess that outfit ain't there no longer. Well, far as I know the whole shootin' match is done for, things being how they are these days. Yessir, I been through that mill. Of course, I done it some years after you was there, I suppose. Didn't see you around, anyways."

Bullock's jaw had dropped sequentially lower as Brother Jobe spoke since the landmarks he described were indeed as things were at Duke Law.

"How in the hell did they let you in there?" Bullock said. "I mean . . . no offense."

"I think it was the interview that clinched it," Brother Jobe said.

The others around the table tried to conceal their enjoyment of Bullock's discomfort.

"But you . . . you don't talk like a lawyer."

"I guess you never met too many Virginia country lawyers."

"No I haven't."

"Well, I can serve up a *casus belli* from *a priori* to *a posteriori* all the livelong day when I want to."

"And I suppose you practiced," Bullock said.

"About eight months," Brother Jobe said. "Scott County, V-A. It was mostly hillbilly law. Folks burning each other's trailers, drug cookers, wife beaters, child rapers, and all like that. I didn't take to it so well. Anyway the Lord Jesus saved me from a life of *animus nocendi et alii*. He saved me in more ways than one."

"Can you act as prosecutor in this case?" Ben Deaver said.

Brother Jobe paused ruminatively before answering.

"I suppose," he said.

Bullock shook his head and smiled, yet awash in incredulity.

"All right, then," he said. "And you'll defend, will you, Sam?"

"I will," Sam said.

Bullock opened his leather folio with a flourish.

"Very well," he said. "I've prepared all the necessary writs. We'll arraign this poor girl this afternoon and proceed from there." He looked over his reading glasses at Brother Jobe. "She's held over at your compound, I understand."

"That is correct."

"Is it the appropriate place?"

"There's no other secure place to confine her," Robert said. "To use the old jail upstairs, we'd have to heat this whole building, and that would require cords of firewood and somebody standing by around the clock to keep it all going."

"I'm told she's not in her right mind," Bullock said.

"That would be my observation," the doctor said. "It's in my notes."

"Mine, too, at the scene of the crime," Loren said.

"Obviously there's no psychiatric facility with a locked ward," Robert said.

"She's safe and comfortable where we got her," Brother Jobe said.

The doctor explained to Bullock the particulars of Mandy Stokes's recent illness, and how it had affected her.

"Then it might seem this whole business will conclude in a verdict of not guilty by reason of insanity," Bullock said, looking from one man to another around the table. None of them offered a comment or opinion. "Hasn't that occurred to any of you? Okay, in that event what would we do with her then? Keep her locked up in a room at the old high school for the next fifty years like some crazy old aunt in the attic?"

"You're putting the cart before the horse again, Stephen," Deaver said.

"Why don't we get on with the proceedings and take these things as they come," Loren said.

"All I'm saying is that this case raises some very troubling issues," Bullock said. "And I hope you're all prepared for certain consequences." He slapped his folio of writs shut. "Shall we get on with this arraignment then?"

Robert Earle, as nominal chair of the meeting, called to adjourn. Back outside on the street, before Bullock, Loren, and the two lawyers proceeded to the old high school, Bullock took Robert aside. A fine drizzle fell, glazing the sidewalk and making it slippery, and fewer people were out on Main Street than the day before.

"You know, sooner or later I'm going to have to adjudicate your role in the death of that other young man," Bullock said. He referred to Shawn Watling, murdered in June at the town landfill, which operated as a salvage yard for building materials and other recycled manufactured goods no longer available. Robert had been in Shawn's company at the time of the murder, and subsequently came to cohabit with Shawn's widow, Britney Blieveldt. Aspersions were cast but no charges made against Robert. The matter had never been legally resolved.

"You do what you must," Robert said.

"Of course, I could order a hearing and dismiss a complaint at any time."

"Then why the hell don't you, Stephen?" Robert said. "I thought we were friends. This is starting to get under my skin."

"I understand. But all you people here in town, you wanted me to represent the law, to *be* the law, and the law doesn't have friends. The way things look right now, I might have to hang this girl in the final end of all this. How is the town going to like that?" Then, loudly to the others, who stood at a remove, Bullock said, "Gentlemen, let's go do our duty."

Fifteen

The arraignment was conducted in the room where Mandy Stokes was confined. She sat on the edge of her bed, still in her nightclothes, staring blankly ahead into some indeterminate space between herself and her interlocutors, and barely responded to the recitation of charges against her except to glance up at Bullock when he spoke the name "Julian." Sam Hutto, with his long flat face and sympathetic manner, was introduced as her court-appointed defense attorney. She said nothing to him. Bullock set bail at five gold ounces—a sum so high as to preclude any possibility of release—and a date was set for a preliminary hearing. When the ritual was complete Brother Jobe walked the others back to the old lobby of the former high school, where Brother Boaz waited with something in a picture frame.

"Thank you, son," Brother Jobe said.

Bullock acknowledged Boaz with a nod, but he wore a skeptical grin as if he suspected something was up.

"There she is, your honor," Brother Jobe said as he handed over his framed diploma from the Duke University School of Law made out to one Lyle Beecham Wilsey, complete with stamped seals and signatures.

"Who's this Wilsey?" Bullock said.

"That was my old times name. Our New Faith names are hand-picked biblical. Ain't that obvious?"

Bullock looked at the diploma and back at Brother Jobe several times.

"Don't worry," Brother Jobe said. "I got an old driver's license and all kind of ID back in my quarters." Bullock continued to stare at the document. "You think one of my people whipped this thing together on a computer the past hour since it first come up? Lookit here, this wax seal is the genuine article."

Bullock handed it back.

"All I can say is, this world is just one astonishing goddamn thing after another."

Brother Jobe appeared to take it as a compliment, but then the unusually small features of his large round face all bunched together fretfully.

"Uh, your honor, I'll have to ask you to mind your language. This here is a sacred outfit."

"Excuse me."

SIXTEEN

Despite the tragedy in Mill Hollow of the night before, the Christmas Eve service, called *Lessons and Carols,* went on as scheduled at the First Congregational Church of Union Grove with the Reverend Loren Holder presiding and narrating the vignettes from the Nativity, and all the musical instruments and voices soaring between lessons, and the children of town acting out in costume the doings long ago in the Holy Land. The spacious nave of the austere white wooden church was warmed by more than three hundred bodies, including farmers, tradesmen, and their families who had come from miles around, as well as a score of visitors from the New Faith compound with their own shepherd, Brother Jobe. The formal program was followed in the large, adjacent community room by a potluck feast of roasts, hams, sausages, smoked trouts, braised pikes, puddings, fritters, creamed this and that, pickles, cheeses, corn breads and pones, brandied fruits, glacéed pears, prune whips, custards, honey cakes, and hickory nut macaroons, with eggnog, beer, and cider to wash it down.

When the convocation broke up, and wagons and carts were mounted for journeys home, and the people of town walked to their homes, the rain that started earlier turned again to snow, an exuberant snow of large fluffy flakes whose wondrous hexagonal patterns could be discerned when they landed on wool mittens. Robert walked home arm in arm with Britney and eight-year-old Sarah, marveling at how much in love he was with them, and how unlikely it was that he had come to have another family after losing his first family—wife, Sandy, daughter Genna, both killed by epidemic illnesses, and son Daniel, who had left home at nineteen with Loren and Jane Ann's boy Evan, to see what had happened out in America. It disturbed Robert when he realized that he loved his new family as much as the one that he had lost, and he wondered whether his feeling for one was a betrayal of the other.

But his regret did not persist very long this holiday eve as they called good night to neighbors and entered the house with all the urgent need to stoke the stove and light some candles and heat some water for washing and get Sarah ready for bed so she would ride unicorns through dream forests and be rested for the morning, when Robert would present her with the violin he had found to buy in nearby Center Falls, a very nice one-hundred-year-old German violin that would be a pleasure to play, and would become a familiar extension of the girl's hands and, if she was fortunate, of her heart as well in the years to come. And after she was tucked in, Robert read to her from Anna Sewell's *Black Beauty, the Autobiography of a Horse,* which had been one of his favorites as a child, and Daniel's and Genna's too. It was about a way of life that more resembled the new times of the present than Robert's own boyhood in the days of *Star Wars,* computer gaming magic, and other techno-grandiosities that had come to such a shockingly abrupt end.

When Sarah slipped into sleep, Robert took the candle into the bathroom, where half a pail of warm water stood on the chest beside the sink waiting for him, and from there into his own bedroom where Britney waited for him naked beneath the quilt. He climbed in and gathered her in his arms, amazed at the generosity of the universe to have arranged things this way.

"When I was a little girl," she said, "I had sneakers with little red lights on the edge of the soles. They twinkled whenever I took a step. I couldn't get over how magical they were. I wore them one year to the big public Christmas breakfast when they used to hold it in the old theater on the top floor of the old town hall. Everybody followed my footsteps around the room while the high school kids sang carols on stage. It broke my heart when they wore out and the batteries stopped working."

"Couldn't you get another pair?"

"By then Daddy was gone and we were very poor. Everybody was poor. I used to be sorry that Sarah would never have a pair of magic sneakers like that, but I don't think so anymore. There are other ways to feel special and other kinds of magic in the world. Merry Christmas, Robert."

Britney slid on top of him and sat up with the quilt over her shoulders, a vision in the candlelight: compact, soft, fragrant, amorously ripe, and intent. Robert reached up and drew her face down to his.

Seventeen

When Andrew Pendergast came back to his house after directing the musicians (and playing piano) for the Christmas Eve program of lessons and carols, there were candles burning in two of the front windows and the woodstove had been tended to keep the house warm for his return, as he had instructed Jack Harron to do. More than one clock ticked around the big old house and the split logs hissed as they burned in the stove. He put his hat and overcoat carefully in the hall closet and proceeded to the kitchen, placing a splint basket down on the big farmhouse table there.

"Jack," he called into the darkness where the back room was.

Shortly, Jack Harron emerged from his room into the hallway squinting in the candlelight. He was physically transformed from the filthy furtive creature of the previous evening to at least the outward representation of a housebroken human being. He wore a pair of Andrew's old wool pants, tattered from years of outdoor excursions in pursuit of minerals for his paints, botanicals for his health, and spring trout for his frying pan, and an old, frayed, lavender-colored Calvin Klein button-down shirt from days when Andrew reported to an office in New York City. Because Jack was so emaciated, the pants were cinched and scrunched at the waist with an old belt that he had punched some new holes in. And because he was shorter than Andrew he had rolled up each trouser leg. He had trimmed his beard, as Andrew told him to do, and bathed more than once in the past twenty-four hours until he'd scrubbed all the layers of grime and grease off himself.

"Were you asleep?"

"I guess so."

"Not sure?"

"I was asleep. I haven't slept hardly at all lately in the cold."

"Thank you for tending the stove and lighting the candles."

"It's what you told me."

"Thanks for doing what I told you."

"It's comfortable here. I forgot what that's like."

"Sit down," Andrew said and Jack took a seat at the table. Andrew fetched a plate from a cupboard and some cutlery from a drawer. He removed various articles from the splint basket: slices of ham, corn bread, a deviled egg, dried fruit, and nut cookies. "Are you hungry?"

Jack shrugged his shoulders.

"Anyway, help yourself. I brought this back for you."

Jack nodded. Andrew sat down across from him.

"Do you have any idea why I did that?" he said.

Jack appeared puzzled. "No," he said.

"It's called an act of kindness, the important part of being human. Has no one been kind to you?"

Jack began to weep quietly with his head hanging, eyes on the table.

"When I came here last night, I think I wanted to do you harm," he said.

"I thought so too," Andrew said.

"But I don't know why. I'm so confused . . . about everything."

"Do you still want to harm me?"

"No."

"All right. Eat something."

Jack hesitated as if struggling to work through a conundrum, before he picked up the slab of ham and began nibbling on it.

"I don't understand what's happened," he said.

"Tell me who you are."

"I don't know where to start."

"Start at whatever part makes sense."

"Sometime this fall," he said, "I stopped showing up for work at Mr. Schmidt's farm. I was just a common laborer. If there was a hard or a filthy job to do, Mr. Schmidt put me to it. I don't know why."

"He's not a bad man."

"I was a bad worker. I know it. I showed up late. I didn't care how I did anything. I had no gloves. My hands froze. I couldn't stand another day of it. I walked away. I never expected it would go this way."

"What would go what way?"

"My life. Working in mud, in frozen pig shit. I can't believe what's happened in the world. Now I can't even take care of myself."

Andrew reflected that, given the tribulations of the society he was born into, he had been fortunate never to have felt so lost.

"When the world wants to destroy you, what do you do?" Jack said.

"I don't believe the world wants to destroy you. At the worst it's indifferent to us."

"That's an evil thing. It brings us here. I didn't ask to be born. Nobody does. You'd think the world would have some pity on its creations."

"It's up to people to care for other people," Andrew said.

Their eyes met. Jack's were moist with emotion.

"Why would you let me stay here?"

"I'm by myself and there's a lot to do just to run this household. I could use help."

"Why are you by yourself?"

"It's how I am," Andrew said.

"Then why let me stay here?"

"You asked to be fixed. In the meantime, I'll ask you to do things. And you'll get fixed."

"I'll do things," Jack said. "I won't do any . . . personal things."

"I won't ask you to do any personal things."

"All right then."

Jack ate the rest of the ham more earnestly and popped the deviled egg in his mouth.

"Do you mind if I ask," Andrew said, "what you were before?"

"Before everything went to shit?"

"Yes."

"A student at Adirondack. The community college up to Glens Falls."

"Studying what?"

Jack laughed ruefully. "Communications," he said. "After a certain point, I couldn't drive up there anymore because of the gas shortage. Anyway, the school shut down, like everything else after a while. My mom lived here, over on Southside behind the Cumberland Farms store. She died. My older sister, she died too. You should have seen her in high school. Sizzling hot. She had a kid. The baby daddy was a useless piece of shit. Blew himself up in a trailer over to Battenville cooking drugs. In the last years of the old times, my sister got hugely fat. Like a cartoon. Then the world turned upside down. Her baby died the same year as Mom from the same disease. There was no food coming into the supermarket anymore. Not the stuff she ate, which was only stuff you could put into a microwave. Then she got to be skinny as a scarecrow. Her teeth fell out. Killed herself. Drank some old cleaner from under the sink. That's my family."

"What about your father?"

"Out of the picture since I was three. I couldn't tell you what he was like, except loud."

"Where have you been living?"

"The old place on Southside. There's no fireplace or stove in it. It was colder inside than out."

"There are plenty of empty houses around town."

"I didn't have the means to get cordwood anyhow."

A clock in a distant room chimed twelve times. It had a muted velvety tone.

"Merry Christmas, Jack."

"Merry Christmas to you, sir."

Eighteen

He was a shadow of a man, a ghost, clothed in shroudlike shreds with a ragged blanket roll slung over one shoulder, stealing across a haunted landscape. He had lost count of the days as he trekked from the deep interior of the continent toward home, passing through an autumn season of glorious color and bright days to the frozen, dim sepia vistas and endless nights of the northeastern early winter. Comfort was a distant memory. For weeks, he had known nothing but pain, cold, hunger, exhaustion, and loneliness. He subsisted on things stolen: the gleanings of harvested cornfields, turnips and potatoes purloined from root cellars, chickens, not always cooked, small wild animals, whatever the roadsides and forests grudged up. Though he had once eagerly met and consorted with strangers in his two years of adventuring, he now avoided them because in his current condition he looked like trouble coming, and others looked like trouble to him. The wool balaclava he pulled down over his face in the cold gave him an outward demeanor of alien menace, but he was too sick and weak to defend himself against people who might rush to judgment about who or what he was.

What kept Daniel Earle alive was a repository of sense memories that he played and replayed in his mind as he staggered across the landscape: fragments of places, vignettes, sights, smells, and sounds that connected to his deepest emotional center. One particular sense scene he returned to constantly was the image of a small barn, like a carriage house, with a loading door up in the hayloft. It was always spring there, with a welcoming pool of sunlight in the forecourt. That's all. It was not any place he remembered out of his own history, and he didn't connect it with any particular beloved person, but it spoke to him in deeply resonant tones suggesting that someday he would come home to it. Another fragmentary scene was of a shopfront window of many small panes, from the inside, a warm and well-lighted refuge, looking out on a street gathered in winter twilight. He didn't know why it meant so much to him, but when he called it forth from the vaults of his imagination it stirred things deep within him and produced a sense of profound contentment that allowed him to keep swinging one foot in front of the other.

Throughout his day and its gathering night, which he did not know to be that of Christmas Eve, he passed through increasingly familiar landscapes. He had skirted New York's capital city, Albany, to the north, thinking all big cities to be dangerous traps now, and wended through the broken, desolate suburbs across the Mohawk River, an unresolved countryside of abandoned tract housing, scraps of woodland, scavenged malls and strip malls, highways without cars, and scarecrow people scuttling around the ruins of it all in the cold with arms full of sticks for their fires. In and about this terrain of failed modernity lay country roads that had never been *developed*, as the old term went for farmland waiting to be paved over, and the visible traces of the farms that preceded the suburbs still stood represented by barns with sagging roofs and see-through walls and silos shrouded in Virginia creeper. He had slept in such a barn for a few hours the previous night in a place called Rexford, a former dormitory town for General Electric executives from Schenectady back in the mid-twentieth century, now a liminal zone where the suburban expansion of the old times came to a dead stop with the shattered economy. The population there had been reduced so severely that even good farmland in the vicinity lay fallow and unused, with sumacs sprouting equally in the former cornfields as they did in the parking lots.

In the gray twilight of Christmas Eve, Daniel trudged east and made it to the town of Mechanicville for his first sight of the Hudson River in two years. Coming upon the beautiful familiar river in light so dim he could barely make out the far shore eight hundred feet away, charged his flagging spirit like a glimpse of redemption. As he stood there on the river road looking north at the rusty steel-truss railroad bridge, the fine drizzle that had started in the afternoon turned to snow. Mechanicville itself was a decrepit spectacle of forsaken overbuilt highway junctions, skeletal hamburger shacks, ugly and mostly empty houses clad in tattered, disintegrating vinyl, and factories inactive since the 1970s now overgrown with mature trees. Daniel knew from his travels through post-collapse America that many towns proved themselves unable to recover from the economic trauma and everything that followed, while a few others did better. In the decades previous, Mechanicville had become a county welfare sink where the unfortunate great-grandchildren of earnest factory workers lived on government handouts in purposeless anomie. These people were among the first to go in hard times, and the towns went with them.

On this cold, damp Christmas Eve, the straggling inhabitants of Mechanicville stayed shuttered inside their mean dwellings with few signs of the holiday on display, and none of the old electric kind. A putrid pall hung over the place as of burning garbage and rotting meat. Daniel did not happen to pass by the block between Spring and South Streets where twelve houses had burned to ground two nights earlier, killing five people, whose bodies remained among the smoldering ruins—the sort of event, so emblematic of the times, unnoticed by outsiders, like the proverbial tree falling in the forest that nobody hears. He was relieved when he left the town behind and followed Route 4, the river road north through countryside little scarred by the suburban fiasco because it was so far from anything that mattered.

He retreated inside his imagination as he trudged up the empty road in the falling snow, with the river always on his right, though not always visible through the intervening woods cloaked in darkness. He did not know the time, but in fact it was 8:30 p.m. when he walked out of Mechanicville. Just then the music circle and the choir and the members of the Union Grove Congregational Church—his father, Robert Earle, among them—had concluded their Christmas Eve lessons and carols and retired to the communal banquet that followed, unaware of the lone figure miles away struggling toward them in the darkness. Daniel had consumed countless feasts in his mind in recent weeks as he traversed the landscape, sick and wretched. Sometimes they included manufactured things he remembered from early childhood but which no longer existed: the cheesy corn fantasy puffs of yore, factory-made cakes with creamy white centers, soda pops in every color from orange to brown to an unearthly phosphorescent chemical green, Mars bars, hamburgers on sesame seed buns, ramen noodles, corn dogs, egg rolls, pizza, marshmallow and chocolate Easter eggs, jelly donuts, ice cream studded with fragments of cookies or toffee or sugared nuts or an ingenious elastic confection called gummy bears. At other moments he conjured up massive roasts and haunches of red meat, corn slathered in butter, sauerkraut and sausages, potatoes in bubbling cheese, buckwheat pancakes saturated in butter and syrup, Indian pudding, the simpler foods of the new time, his time.

By and by he came on the town called Starkville, where he would finally cross to the east side of the Hudson River over a disintegrating steel and concrete highway bridge and enter Washington County. Coming upon it, his heart wanted to soar but all it could manage was a dull sense of warmth rising out of a cold hollow vacancy at the center of himself that had been there for some time. Starkville, once a factory village of five mills that manufactured things such as wallpaper and cardboard boxes and had a population of two thousand in the 1970s, when the mills last operated, was now a ghost settlement of fewer than a hundred souls, many of them engaged in fishing on the river and then smoking and pickling the pike and sturgeon that had come back in such spectacular numbers when the industrial age ebbed. Daniel had kept company in the months before he left home to see what was left of America with a prankish and pretty sixteen-year-old red-haired girl there named Kerry McKinney, walking the five miles from Union Grove in all weathers to see her. He had met her at the harvest ball in nearby Easton the previous fall where she step-danced on the plank stage in a flouncy turquoise dress and orange tights that matched her flaming hair. Her father owned the only going retail concern in what remained of Starkville, a general merchandise and grocery that got all its dry goods from Bullock, who got them from Albany on his boat. Then one Saturday around Easter, Daniel made the journey to Starkville only to learn that Kerry had died of cholera two days earlier, along with one of her three brothers. Daniel had seen plenty of death in that time of plagues, epidemics, and afflictions, including the deaths of his mother and sister. But this one provoked him to leave home to see if there was any place left in America where death and failure didn't rule. He never found that place, though he saw a lot of things that opened his young eyes in places that were not like home.

By midnight, when Christmas Eve was turning into the holy day itself, Daniel slogged through three inches of accumulating snow up State Route 29, past the abandoned house with the word "GIFTS" painted in capital letters on its roof. In the old times, a woman had sold poorly made items of decor to tourists called "leaf peepers" who flocked north to behold the fall colors. The building stood among an ambiguous assortment of car dealerships and food dispensaries that had once marked the ragged edge of town. Now only pieces of the buildings stood since the windows were blown out, the flat roofs had collapsed, and the trusses and sashes had all been removed in the Great Collection of salvaged metal that had preceded the disastrous war in the Holy Land. The snow-filled parking lots were devoid of cars.

As Daniel drew closer to the old center of Union Grove, he felt as helpless as a swimmer caught in a powerful current, the pawn of tremendous natural forces that seemed determined to defeat him, and to do it with malicious humor just as he neared his long-sought goal. He had not eaten anything since that morning, pieces of a mushy, deliquescing, half-rotten pumpkin he found in the dooryard garden of a house in Rexford with the front door banging in the winter breeze, suggesting the people who lived there were dead or gone. He had been staggering forward on bodily reserves for so long he took for granted that they would keep him going forever, and now he was astounded to find himself utterly depleted. As he paused in his frozen footsteps, panting slightly and dizzy, he thought he could make out the white steeple of the Congregational Church above the rooftops of the town's darkened houses, like an arrow in the night pointing at the cold distant spaces of a baffling universe. He could barely lift his legs high enough above the accumulating snow to swing them forward toward the heart of Main Street and its familiar buildings. Instead of jubilation, a strange and exorbitant pain lodged in his chest like a big reamer hollowing him out, as though he were an apple being cored. His last coherent thought was how funny it would be if he dropped dead a hundred feet shy of his destination and the falling snow buried him so that his body would not be discovered until spring.

Nineteen

Robert rose up through the depths of sleep thinking that something was banging on the house in the wind, a loose shutter, a section of fallen roof gutter. Soon, he apprehended that it might be someone at the door downstairs. Oddly his next thought was that it was Christmas and he couldn't help imagining an old fat man in a red suit trimmed with white fur attempting to enter the house by the front door because the old chimney was blocked up with stovepipe. Robert's sudden motion sitting up in bed woke Britney. The only working clock in the house was downstairs.

"What?" she said.

"Stay here," Robert whispered. He swung out of bed in an economic arc of motion and groped for his trousers in the dark.

"Be careful," Britney whispered back.

The knocking from the front door was weak but persistent, more like a small animal working away at something than a human being signaling its presence. He approached the front door warily and tried to steal a glimpse out each sidelight but couldn't see much beside a humped shape in the darkness. The knocking came in no particular pattern except a cluster of several raps, then a pause, then more. If anything, it communicated defeat.

"Who's there?" he said, speaking to the door.

The reply from outside was a low muffled sound like the groan of a bear, incomprehensible and sinister. Bears were not infrequent visitors in town. The winter thaws of recent years had interrupted their hibernation pattern. But there was little trash to attract them. The people of Union Grove did not generate anything near the volumes of garbage as in the old days; little food was wasted, and scraps were collected for pigs and chickens. The rest was burned or reused in some way. The bears would molest chicken houses, sheep, and goats, though. The absence of cars for many years made the bears bolder and to get places they commonly used roads and village streets that they had avoided in the old times. Anyway, Robert thought, nobody ever heard of bears rapping on the front door to a house out of politeness. It occurred to him that it was a drunken human being, someone who had gotten hammered on Christmas Eve and could not figure out which house was his. It happened before, the preceding New Year's Eve when Donny Willits, the "hard cheese boss" at Schroeder's creamery, made a commotion at his doorstep insisting that it was his home, so Robert let him sleep on the sofa even though Donny's house was a hundred and fifty feet down Linden Street.

An umbrella stand beside the door held several walking sticks that his father had used in the last year of his life when he'd come to stay with Robert after the war in the Holy Land was lost and things began unraveling badly in the country. Robert seized a stout ash cane with a brass handle in the shape of a serpent's head. He saw a blur out of the corner of his eye in weak light: Britney on the stairway wearing a cotton nightdress. He gestured to her to go back but she only retreated up one stair. Meanwhile, the rapping at the door had stopped.

Robert crouched down and cocked back the walking stick, feeling the weight of the business end and tensing to strike. He pressed his ear to the door for a moment but could hear nothing. Thinking not to alert whoever or whatever might be on the other side of what he was about to do, Robert reached for the doorknob, silently turned the lock button, then the knob itself, and jerked the door open. Pressure against it from the outside accelerated the door's inward arc and the knob smacked Robert on his forehead, knocking him backward. A large blob-shaped thing fell inside over the threshold and pitched sprawling onto the rug, where it came to rest, inert. Britney gave out a choked little shriek. Cold air rushed into the room.

Robert righted himself and shook the pain out of his head. Britney hurried the rest of the way downstairs to the kitchen and lit a candle there, returning quickly to the front parlor. The heap on the floor was a man clad in odious shreds of clothing, sprawled on his face, with snow still humped on his shoulders. His hands looked like stumps under windings of filthy rags. The soles of his lace-up boots had partially separated from the uppers. Robert and Britney could see his torso rise and fall slightly in the candlelight. He was still breathing. Robert prodded the man's side with his cane. It produced no response.

"He's out of it," Robert said.

"What do you want to do?" Britney said.

"I'll pull his feet out of the way. Go shut the door." Robert pulled the body forward. It remained inert. "Come, help me roll him over."

"I'll do it," Britney said. "You stay back so you can whack him if he wakes up and gets violent."

Britney, petite but compact and strong, found a point of leverage and tipped the body over in a deft motion.

"God, he stinks," she said before recoiling at the sight of the wool balaclava the intruder wore, like the homicidal murderer in so many movie melodramas of the old times.

As frightful as the wool mask was, a different unbid thought formed in Robert's mind, the thought that he'd dared not think until this moment. With trembling hand and with his heart fluttering in his chest, he grabbed the top of the balaclava and yanked it off. Britney stepped closer with the candle. Robert gaped at the face below with hollow cheeks under its months-long growth of yellow beard, pores blackened with grease and soot, and swollen, bloody chapped lips. He looked up at Britney.

"It's my boy," Robert said, his eyes brimming with emotion. "It's Daniel."

TWENTY

Robert pulled on his boots and coat and ran five blocks to Dr. Copeland's house. The doctor appeared at the door tucking his shirt into his trousers and carrying his boots. He was accustomed to waking up in the middle of the night, knowing that it meant some kind of medical emergency. He let Robert into the kitchen, lit a candle, and pulled on his boots after asking what the matter was. Robert explained. The doctor grabbed a leather bag off the pew bench beside the kitchen door and the two of them hurried back over in snow that was now six inches deep.

When they entered the house, Britney had arrayed a battery of candles around the front parlor and was finishing the job of cutting Daniel's fetid clothing off him. She had removed his boots as well. Meanwhile, her daughter Sarah had come downstairs and Britney had put her to work lighting fires in the main woodstove and the kitchen cookstove, setting a large pot of water on it to warm up.

The doctor knelt down to examine Daniel, checking his pulse against a pocket watch.

"What is it?" Robert said, squatting beside the doctor.

"Thirty-eight," the doctor said.

"That's low, isn't it?"

"Yes."

"What does it mean?"

"Exhaustion, dehydration, starvation, hypothermia, sickness."

The doctor grabbed a candlestick off a nearby side table and handed it to Robert.

"Hold the light so it shines in his eyes," the doctor said.

Daniel remained unconscious. The doctor retracted both of Daniel's eyelids. The pupils constricted bilaterally even in the meager light.

"Take the light away," the doctor said, leaning in close to see. Both pupils dilated with the light at a remove, suggesting Daniel's neurological function was normal. His skin was covered with sores. His feet were so blistered and red that they looked like raw meat. A flakey red rash began at the edge of his hairline.

"Ringworm," the doctor said, then looked up at Britney still holding the scissors. "Start cutting his hair and his beard as close as you can."

The doctor listened to Daniel's breathing and heartbeat through his stethoscope, then listened to his abdomen. He took his blood pressure with an old-fashioned aneroid cuff.

"His heart and lungs sound all right," the doctor said. "He sure wore himself out getting here. His blood pressure's low. He's malnourished. We'll get some fluid in him right away. Uh, I've forgotten your name," he said to Britney. She told him. "I delivered your little girl," I believe.

"Yes you did."

"What's her name?"

"Sarah."

"Sarah," the doctor said, "can you stuff more billets in the parlor stove? We have to get the heat up in here for this man."

"Yes, sir," Sarah said and proceeded to follow his instructions. Back in the old times, Robert thought, an eight-year-old would never be trusted with such a chore involving a hot stove. Sarah was quite capable at her age. Britney had finished cutting Daniel's hair.

"Get those filthy clothes and shoes out of here," the doctor told Robert, "and when you're done come back and hold this IV bottle." Robert gathered up the rags and the boots in a splint basket and put them outside on the front porch, then he returned to the doctor's side.

The doctor took two clear glass pint bottles out of his bag, rigged one, and handed it to Robert. The doctor prepared many things himself that he'd formerly had for the asking in a hospital setting. He cooked his own solution of glucose and saline and filled sterile glass bottles with them and he had hoarded plastic tubing in the months when the economy whirled around the drain. He reused everything he could and sterilized articles in a nonelectric copper and brass autoclave of his own design. He swabbed Daniel's forearm with pure grain alcohol and inserted an IV line.

"You can start washing him," the doctor said to Britney.

These procedures took an hour. Daniel remained unconscious but his pulse rose as the fluids and sugar flowed into his veins. The doctor attended to Daniel's raw, blistered feet. Sarah kept feeding billets into the stove until the room was so warm everybody perspired, including the patient on the floor.

Robert fetched all the parts of a bed from Daniel's boyhood room upstairs—the mattress, box spring, and frame—and brought them down to the first floor. By this time gray light had seeped through the windows as Christmas Day dawned. The three adults hoisted Daniel onto the bed. Daniel groaned in the process but remained unconscious. The doctor ran a urinary catheter into an old half gallon juice bottle beside the bed. Then he departed, saying he would return before noon with more IV fluid. Robert arranged a wing chair beside the head of Daniel's bed and sat there watching his son's rhythmic breathing while he wondered at all the things his son had seen in two years wandering away from home. How far had he ranged? What was the country like? What had happened to its people? And what had happened to Daniel's companion on the road, Evan Holder, son of Loren and Jane Ann?

TWENTY-ONE

Brother Jobe entered the special chamber in the New Faith compound that had been built for Mary Beth Ivanhoe, also known as Precious Mother and the Queen Bee, the epileptic clairvoyant who was the spiritual guide of the New Faith Brotherhood Covenant Church of Jesus, the one who showed them the way out of the bloody wilderness of Old Dixie, first to Pennsylvania, which turned violent on them, and finally farther north to Union Grove in Washington County, New York, where they purchased the abandoned high school and made their stand, hoping to found here a "new Jerusalem."

The large room was at the center of a grid of rooms framed into the school's old gymnasium the past autumn, with Mary Beth's chamber at top center and the women who waited on her sleeping in rooms around her. A cupola at the top of the chamber gathered just enough daylight to make things visible, while the massively insulating effects of all the rooms around it kept the temperature quite warm, as its revered occupant required. The ceiling around the well of the cupola was coffered in cherrywood. The walls of the room were intricately figured with marquetry in geometric and botanical motifs executed by Robert Earle, who was hired as well to teach several of the New Faith men the finer points of finish carpentry.

Two handmaidens had just finished applying soothing herbal unguents of comfrey, chamomile, rose hip, elder flower, and lanolin to Mary Beth in her bed, from which she rarely ventured. She had grown to over four hundred pounds since giving birth months earlier. The automobile accident in a Virginia shopping mall parking lot years ago that had injured her so grievously left her subject to frequent epileptic seizures as well as strange new mental abilities to "see" things distantly in both time and at geographic remove, and to sense many unseen currents of emotion and circumstance in the people around her, whether they were present or not. However, the damage to her spine from that long-ago trauma also left her in chronic pain that distracted her, roiled her temper, and appeared to provoke yet more frequent seizures when she was in turbulent spirits. She suffered as well from asthma, edema, acid reflux, alopecia, migraines, constipation, and irritations of the skin from being bedbound and encased in overlapping folds of fatty flesh.

Brother Jobe let himself in to the chamber, admiring the balance of the heavy door and the way it was figured with hexagonal inlays representing honeycomb. The heat, too, impressed him instantly and he removed his heavy wool frock coat.

"You awake there, Precious Mother?" he asked.

"If I wasn't before, I am now," she replied in a voice full of broken reeds and phlegm.

One of the handmaidens, Sister Tirzah, winked at Brother Jobe as she made for the door with a washbasin, signaling that her mistress was in one of her moods.

"Git that outa my face," Mary Beth croaked at the other attendant, Sister Jewel, who had been trying to apply powder to her, and even raised a hamlike arm to bat her away. "Can't you all leave me be for a dang moment." Seconds later, the door clicked shut with mechanical precision and she was alone with Brother Jobe, who pulled a chair up close to the bed and sat down rather primly with a small box balanced on his lap.

"Merry Christmas, Mary Beth."

"It's got me all a-flutter, listening out for reindeers and whatnot."

"Lookit here. Santa brung you something." Brother Jobe held out the small box. She made a face and snatched it out of his hands.

"I prayed to Jesus for health. I don't suppose he give you a portion of that for me in this itty-bitty box."

"I wisht it was so."

"'Cept it would take more like a truckload to git me right." She lifted off the lid and peered inside. "Aw, ain't that cute!" She held up a small enameled and gold-plated brooch in the shape of a bumble bee.

"Brother Axel says them stones in the eyes is real rubies," Brother Jobe said. "He worked the jewelry counter at the Target store back when."

"Is that a fact. I'm sure they had some fine baubles in that place. All cut glass and rhinestones."

"Anyways he vouched for it."

"Did you see here on the backside where it says 'Made in China'?"

"Lemme see that!"

Mary Beth clutched the bauble tightly in her dimpled fist.

"That's all right. I'll keep it anyway," she said.

"China's up and coming," Brother Jobe said. "Folks say they put men up on the moon not long ago."

"Where'd you hear that?"

"Mr. Bullock the squire. He sends a trade boat to Albany once a week when the river ain't froze. His boatmen heard it. That was all the news down there recently."

"Well, somebody should tell them chinks America already done it many a year back, 'fore you and me was even born. We should charge them a parking fee for landing on it and rent by the hour. It's our dang moon. We was there first."

"I suppose you're right."

"You're well-told I'm right about it. Matter of fact, I wouldn't let 'em stay more'n an hour. Take some snaps and clear the heck off. Why, it burns my fanny just to think of them capering on it. You let them mess around up there, they could fix things so the moon only shines down on China. Wouldn't that be a pretty pass?"

"I'm sorry I brung it up. Obviously it rankles. How do you like your new digs?" he said.

"It's all right."

"All right! We spent over five hundred dollars, silver, on it. Look at all these inlays, woodwork, fine fabrics. Doesn't it give you any pleasure to watch them?"

"I'd druther watch TV."

"Well, there is no more ding-dang TV. We got to make do with beauty and art and such now."

"If you felt like I do, you wouldn't give a steamin' hee-haw for beauty and art. I'm cursed and afflicted. This here place you put me in is just like a big wooden tomb. This is where I'm going to die. I seen it already in visions."

"Don't be morbid, now, Mary Beth—"

"Don't you call me names, sumbitch. I got enough heartache with my lot in life. Anyways, that's not what you come in here for."

Brother Jobe rose out of the chair, cleared his throat, and went around to the rear of it, holding on to the backrest as if for support.

"You know we got that young woman here in custody," he said. "The one that killed her husband and baby night before last."

"Yes I do. And I know that Bullock aims to hang her. He might not know it yet, but he won't see no other way."

"I looked in on her," Brother Jobe said. "I got inside amongst her mind the way I can. She been locked deep in there by a sickness. She ain't a wicked person. She was just following the commands of illness."

"I know she was. But she done the deeds."

"Yes she did," Brother Jobe said. "But the wickedness was all in the sickness. Anyways, we got to plead her now."

"They got to plead her insane. There ain't no other way. And he'll try to hang her no matter what."

"How's that exactly?"

"Cuz there ain't nowheres to keep a madwoman in the world that we become."

"Yeah. They already saying that. Is there any way that this comes out good?"

"I don't know yet," Mary Beth said with a racking sigh. "I ain't been able to see ahead that far. It gives me headaches to try. Pin this here bee onto my wig hat, would you," she said referring to the turban she wore to conceal her hairlessness.

"Huh? I gathered you didn't care for it."

"Well, it's the thought that counts, ain't it."

"That is exactly so, Mary Beth. It gladdens my heart that you come 'round to that view."

"You still a sumbitch," she said. "Want to give me a real durn Christmas gift?"

"Name it and we'll see what we can do."

"Send up some chicken and waffles with the sorghum syrup. And watermelon pickles. I know you can manage that."

"I'll bite the head off the chicken myself," Brother Jobe said on his way out the door, enjoying her choked laughter.

TWENTY-TWO

The doctor returned to Robert Earle's house at ten o'clock Christmas morning pulling a small handcart through the snow with a crate of twelve additional IV bottles, attended by his son Jasper, eleven, who carried a metal IV stand in one hand and his father's black bag in the other. They found Robert at Daniel's bedside with Loren Holder, the Congregational minister and father of the other boy who had lit out with Daniel two years before. The patient appeared stable but remained unconscious. The receiving jug from the catheter had accumulated a few ounces of dark urine. Beads of sweat stood out on Daniel's forehead. It was quite warm in the room with both downstairs stoves going. The doctor got more fluids running into the IV and checked Daniel's vital signs again.

"Is he in a coma?" Robert asked after the doctor went about his business silently without explaining everything he was doing.

"I wouldn't say so. His pulse and blood pressure are still low. Temperature's a hundred and two. He's still dehydrated, his electrolytes are all screwed up, he's extremely exhausted, malnourished, probably full of parasites, his body's been cannibalizing itself for a while to keep going. He's young, though. They have amazing healing powers. I suggest we just let him sleep as long as he needs to."

The doctor had to leave. He'd received a patient in his infirmary very early that morning, one Hollis Ingram, an apprentice cooper from up in Battenville, with third-degree burns on his hands and thighs from a Christmas Eve accident involving an upset pot of hot lard he was trying to deep-fry a turkey in. The doctor had to go back and administer more of the raw morphine he made himself from the opium that farmers in the vicinity grew for him, and he had to change Hollis's dressings. He left Jasper behind in Robert's house with the task of changing the IV bottles as required. Britney had taken Sarah first to feed their cow, Cinnamon, kept in a small paddock with a barn around the block. Then they went, at Robert's urging, to put in an appearance when the New Faith choir staged its program of Christmas carols from the steps of the town hall, and to tell Brother Jobe why Robert, as mayor, could not be there.

When the doctor was gone, Robert put his hand on Loren's shoulder, in the chair beside his. There was a ghost in the room: Loren's son Evan.

"I know you're anxious to find out," Robert said.

"I can't stand it," Loren said.

"If you have things to do, I'll send for you when Daniel wakes up."

Loren nodded in resignation and got up to put on his blanket coat, shearling hat, and enormous shearling mittens. He was a large man and the thick clothing made him seem solidly mountain-like and intimidating. His reddened, damp eyes told more about his state of mind.

"I'll send for you," Robert repeated. Loren nodded his head, with his lips in a tight resolute line, and made for the door.

Then Robert was alone in the room with his unconscious son and the doctor's boy. A nineteenth-century console clock reconditioned by Andrew Pendergast ticked away the minutes from the mantelpiece. Daniel's face twitched now and again, a welcome sign, the doctor's boy said. In repose, Daniel's face was now so strikingly that of a grown man compared to the nineteen-year-old boy who had walked out of town on a May morning two years before. His ordeal had carved furrows of maturity above the bridge of his nose and on his forehead. When he left home his facial hair had been downy and sparse. Robert could see the vivid reminders of Daniel's deceased mother, Sandy, in his long nose with its slight bump, deep-set eyes, and full lower lip. It disturbed Robert to realize that he had not thought so much about Sandy in recent months. She had been dead for longer than Daniel had been away.

"You must have had quite an adventure back in October," he said to Jasper, while the boy switched out an empty IV bottle. In the fall, Jasper had run away from home. Robert had joined the doctor in a search for him, unsuccessfully, it turned out. The boy was later brought back to town by two of Brother Jobe's rangers. It made Robert nervous to watch Jasper perform these doctoring chores, though the boy seemed to know how and Robert was keenly aware that he himself did not.

"I don't remember it so well," Jasper said.

"You went places, met up with people."

"I think so."

"Who?"

"Nobody," Jasper said. Peculiar as it was, the boy had a way of shutting down that seemed perfectly natural, like someone drawing a curtain against a storm. Robert thought the boy much stranger than he had previously imagined. After Jasper was brought back home that Halloween night there were whispers of trauma and intimations that he had been involved in strange, violent doings out in the county. A rumor floated that he had killed Brother Jobe's stallion Jupiter for stomping his dog Willie to death, but the head of the New Faith never made any formal accusation. No one ever learned all the details of the boy's exploits, including, as far as Robert knew, the doctor and the boy's mother. It remained an incident shrouded in mystery. Choral music sounded dimly in the distance, the nasal, modal shape-note singing of the New Faithers. Their harsh songs gave a dark edge to the very idea of Christmas and, combined with the diffident presence of the doctor's boy, made Robert want to reach for the applejack in the kitchen. But he didn't want the boy to see him drinking at this hour.

"Do you have any books I can read?" Jasper said.

"Sure," Robert said. "I'll go get something."

He went upstairs to Daniel's boyhood room and brought down several books he thought a boy of Jasper's age would be interested in: the old Landmark Books history series for children, *Pirates of the New World, The California Gold Rush,* and *Guadalcanal Diary.* Jasper took the one about pirates saying he'd already read the other two and retreated into it at once, foreclosing any further conversation. Robert had fetched his own bedside reading of the moment,

Stalin in Power: The Revolution from Above, 1928–1941 by Robert C. Tucker, from the Union Grove library. Together, the two of them sat reading silently for another hour until Britney and Sarah returned to the house just after noon. Though they did not make a commotion coming in, something happened. Daniel's eyes opened wide very suddenly, glistening with panic as though a klaxon had just gone off in the room. Robert looked up from his reading to see Britney with her mouth agape and followed her eyes back to Daniel, who had managed to raise himself up and twist around to see Britney and the girl.

"I know you," Daniel croaked, panting slightly.

Britney glanced over at Robert and then back at Daniel.

"I was your babysitter years ago," she said.

Daniel, still panting, turned to his father, who had dropped his book on the floor.

"Am I dreaming?" he said.

"No, you're really home," Robert said, getting out of his seat and coming over to squat down at Daniel's bedside.

"Hope I don't die."

"We won't let you."

Daniel slumped back down again.

TWENTY-THREE

Andrew Pendergast had a long-standing commitment to host a Christmas Day dinner party for his closest friends, twelve in all, most of them from the music circle plus Carolyn Smallwood, his assistant at the library, farmer Ben Deaver, and his wife, Nancy, and Larry Praeger, Union Grove's sole practicing dentist, and his wife, Sharon. Andrew rose early on Christmas morning, went downstairs to the large, well-equipped kitchen, and called down the back hall to rouse Jack Harron out of his room. Jack emerged blinking, hair askew like shocks of oat straw, pulling a suspender up over his shoulder.

"A Merry Christmas morning to you, Jack."

Jack nodded his head gravely, looking somewhat baffled as to his exact whereabouts and his place in them.

"You're late getting up."

"I just woke up."

"Exactly. Well, it's Christmas after all. I'll get you an alarm clock. There's one kicking around here somewhere. Now, I'd like you to make a fire out in the parlor stove. I'll get this cookstove going. In the future I'd like you to fire this one up first thing after you get up and put the kettle on for tea."

"Uh, yessir."

Andrew bent to the task himself, breaking up some old cedar shakes into kindling splints and shoving them into the firebox.

"We've got a lot to do around here today. Bring in some more stove billets for me from the woodshed. When you're done firing the parlor stove, bring in extra cordwood and go shovel the snow off the front walk and the sidewalk. The shovel's out on the back porch. Then, feed and water the chickens and collect whatever eggs there are. After that—"

"If you pile too many chores on me at once I'll forget what I'm supposed to do."

"Yes, of course. I'll put some oats on and we'll have a good hot breakfast when you're done with the chickens."

Twenty minutes later they both sat down to breakfast at the big farmhouse table in the kitchen. There was honey from Andrew's own beehives and heavy cream from Schroeder's dairy to go over the oats.

"I've got twelve friends coming over at four o'clock for Christmas dinner," Andrew said. "You're going to help me here in the kitchen and then you're going to help serve the meal."

"You mean, like a waiter?"

"Yes, that's the idea."

Jack appeared horrified.

"I don't know how."

"You don't have to know anything. Just carry some platters and bowls from here to the dining room. Take away some dirty dishes. Bring in some new ones."

"But I'll be seen."

"We can't help that, can we?"

Jack didn't reply. His eyebrows scrunched together and his features clouded.

"Don't tell me you're afraid of what people will think," Andrew said.

Jack poked at his oatmeal in silence.

"Did you break into other houses around town?"

"No."

"Did you do anything else to annoy people?"

"No!"

"What's the matter then?"

"I get nervous."

"What's the worst thing that can happen?"

"I could drop something."

"Yes, I suppose you could. But it wouldn't be the end of the world."

"I could spill something hot on somebody."

"They'd survive."

"I'm always so nervous. I never feel relaxed. I hate being me."

"I've got news for you, you're all you've got."

Jack went pale. "What do you mean by that?"

"You're your whole world. Without you, there's nothing. Surely you see some good things in the world around you."

"Like what?"

"Beauty."

"What about it?"

"It's important. And it's there for us."

"Yeah, there's some beauty in the world, I guess."

"It's there for you, Jack, in your world. Try paying attention to it. And know wherever you see a little beauty, there's more there, beyond your vision and hearing, waiting for you to discover it."

Jack appeared intensely interested in the idea for a moment, but then his eyebrows crowded together again and he tilted his head slightly.

"No offense, but what if that's just some bullshit?" he said.

"Then it's harmless bullshit. You can take it or leave it."

The slightest smile for the first time crept up the corners of Jack's mouth.

"You're strange," he said, "you know that?"

"Oh yes. I've been told that many times," Andrew said. "You'll be fine today. Just follow some simple instructions."

Andrew had hung a sixteen-pound turkey in his keeping room two days earlier. The room lay off the back end of the house. Here, beneath the hanging turkey, he kept his stores of preserved foods in neat stacks of glass bottles and things in bulk supply that did well at a cold temperature above freezing. Garlands and sprays of drying herbs hung around the turkey from bare rafters, along with ropes of onions and garlic. Andrew had laboriously constructed his own grain bins out of recycled sheet metal. Potatoes had their own wooden bins. Andrew grew much of his food in his own gardens, but like most everyone else in town he bought some commodities at Einhorn's store.

He asked Jack to pluck the turkey while he began making pastry for two pies, pumpkin and mincemeat. He found that the ancient spelt grain grown by Stephen Bullock made exceptionally good pie crusts. It had a nuttier flavor than wheat and a lower gluten content. For shortening, Andrew cut in half lard and half butter. Instead of a few tablespoons of water, he used applejack to moisten the dough because the alcohol would evaporate a greater volume of liquid during the baking process, making the crust extra flaky and fine. His mincemeat differed from the old standard preparations in that he used dried apples, dried high-bush cranberries, black currants, and candied rose hips instead of citrus peels, because oranges and lemons came to Union Grove so seldom these days. Lacking cinnamon, ginger, nutmeg, and other tropical spices, Andrew flavored his pumpkin filling and the mincemeat with caramelized honey, that is, cooked until it polymerized to a deep golden brown piquant elixir. Some pear brandy found its way in as well. By the time he had constructed his pies, the oven temperature was up to speed and ready to receive them.

Then Jack came in with the plucked turkey, looking exhausted but triumphant, as though he had overcome an adversary by main force.

"Good job," Andrew said. "Did you save the big tail feathers like I asked?"

"Yeah. What do you do with them?"

"We use them over at the theater for costumes, and I tie trout flies and fletch arrows with them. You can make a pen out of the quill, though I still have plenty of steel nibs. Sometimes I just put them in a bottle like a bouquet of flowers."

Jack looked perplexed. His mouth had been incrementally falling open.

"What?" Andrew said.

"Nothing," Jack said.

"Go wash the turkey inside and out and drain it well."

"Yessir."

"Do you have cooking skills?"

"Not really."

"Why not?"

"Our family didn't cook. They just heated stuff up."

He handed Jack a four-quart saucepan. "Go into the back room and get me as many onions as will fit in this."

Andrew stuffed the turkey with stale corn bread, his own pork sausage, chunks of apple, and chestnuts acquired from Temple Merton's farm and orchard on Coot Hill, five miles north of Union Grove. He carefully worked a half pound of butter under the skin of the upturned turkey's breast. They shoved the turkey into the oven at eleven o'clock. An old railroad station master's clock with big Roman numerals hung on the kitchen wall above a nineteenth-century portrait of a Jersey cow.

"Who taught you all this?" Jack asked, thinking himself as blank of mind as the cow in the picture.

"Nobody," Andrew said. "I'm my own creation."

"Are you favored by God?"

"I never thought so."

"I felt cursed my whole life."

"You're not," Andrew said. "It's just something you tell yourself. The truth is we're blessed just to be here. In that college you went to, did you ever hear of a philosopher named Wittgenstein?"

"No."

"Oh, well, of course. He said, *It's astonishing that anything exists.*"

Jack flinched and his eyes widened.

"What if it's just an illusion?"

"I dunno," Andrew said. "If reality is faking it, it's doing a great job."

Twenty-four

The Reverend Loren Holder plodded out of town up old Route 29 on a dreary task in his capacity as town constable. At two o'clock in the afternoon, the temperature reached 46 degrees, with the low sun breaking through patchy clots of cloud. The six inches of snow on the road had turned into viscid slush. In the old times, the road would've been plowed by midmorning. Now, besides the melting tracks of one sleigh that had passed earlier in the day, and some deposits of horse droppings among the melting hoofprints, it was hard even to make out where exactly the road lay in the landscape. Loren's calf-high leather boots were well oiled with lanolin cooked with beeswax. His feet stayed dry but his blanket coat and shearling hat made him sweat as he slogged his way east toward the homestead of one Donald Acker, who was alleged by his next-door neighbor farmer Ben Deaver to be keeping a starved horse in his barn—so Loren had been casually informed by Deaver at the levee that had followed the Christmas Eve music performance, just in case, Deaver had said, Loren might want to do something about it.

Loren cursed his way out of town because there was no question that he had to do something about it and conditions were unfavorable for a long walk, not to mention a confrontation. He tried not to think about the end of his hopes for the return of his son Evan in the happy circumstance of Daniel Earle's return. He almost didn't want to hear what had happened from Daniel, and in the meantime he preferred to see about the starved horse, which might have a better chance of survival in this world of woe than his boy. Everything about the afternoon, from the low angle of the sun just days after the solstice, to the bleak appearance of the fields and pastures in their stark winter raiment, to the crashing silence of the landscape broken only now and again by the shrill debate of crows, oppressed Loren like the weight of a lifetime's last days.

It took him an hour to trudge the mile and three-quarters up Route 29 to Acker's place on Huddle Road on the shadowed east side of Pumpkin Hill, where the blue snow was icing back up again as the temperature dropped. Acker's house was an 1870s vernacular cottage that had received several ghastly additions and makeovers in the late twentieth century. These putative improvements were now decrepitating at a faster rate than the original sections of the structure, including a sagging bay window that, in the process of detaching itself from the exterior, pulled puffs of pink fiberglass insulation out from behind the broken vinyl clapboards like the frothy guts leaking out of a mortally injured animal.

He went directly into the barn on the property, an old wreck of a thing with blue daylight glinting through the ancient siding. When his eyes adjusted to the dimness within, he saw a brindle horse standing still in a box stall in such stolid suffering that tears came to Loren's eyes as he imagined the animal's many days of anguished perseverance. The horse's ribs were visible through a blotchy coat of thick winter fur and his pelvis jutted out as though he had swallowed a piece of furniture. As he made his way closer he could see that the horse's stall was piled deep with the animal's own excrement and, though the horse had obviously tried at first to shit in one corner, where it was piled higher, the entire floor had come to be filled. The horse appeared to be dead on its feet. Only the blink of its eye informed Loren that it was not frozen in place. Its water bucket held an inch of muddy slush and both its haylage rack and its manger were empty. The horse didn't flinch or, for that matter, move in any way when Loren ran his hand down its bony withers. It was still warm.

He left the barn and trudged up to the house, made his way through a careless strewage of cordwood on the front porch, and pounded on the door. A gruff voice within cried "all right, all right," and then Donald Acker threw the door open. Acker, once a State Farm Insurance adjuster, was one of those who had moved into an

abandoned property in title limbo, with the county courts closed
and its records in disarray and claimants either dead or too distant
to pursue any claims. Acker was hardy enough to have escaped
the epidemics of recent years, and determined enough, with no
background in farming, to subsist on ten acres, of which he barely
cropped about three, leaving the rest in scrubby pasture. When the
economy first came apart, he'd left a wife named Chrissie behind
in Ho-Ho-Kus, New Jersey—she'd refused to move to "the boon-
docks" even after the bombing of DC—and he hadn't heard from
her since he used his last two five-gallon plastic storage tanks of
hoarded gasoline to go north without her. That was years ago, and
the car he'd arrived in was long gone, too, picked up for steel scrap
during the Great Collection.

Standing in the slightly lopsided doorway of the house, Acker
was an inch taller than Loren, who stood six-foot-three. He had
a sallow moon face that disclosed no emotion, a gray-blond beard
cut to the nub in a patchy way that resembled his starving horse's
blotchy coat. He wore several layers of flannel and more than one
sweater, making him appear more physically robust than he was.
He appeared not altogether steady on his feet. Loren recognized
Acker dimly from seeing him around town, but he'd never spoken
with him before.

"Sorry to disturb you on Christmas," he said.

Acker flinched.

"Is it really Christmas?" he said.

"Yes."

"Wow. You lose track living out here." Acker scratched himself.

Loren scanned the dim interior of the place behind him. It
was sparely furnished to an extreme and yet also disorderly. A
broken-down plush chair and a small table were deployed close
to a woodstove. There was no candle on the table and no other
furniture was visible. Loren wondered if Acker had burned it for
kindling and if he spent the long winter evenings sitting in the
dark. The big front room was strewn with old magazines, some in
piles. Venetian blinds hung askew in several windows. Blankets lay

heaped onto the lone chair as if Acker had been sleeping there. The place gave off a vibrant stink, as of an old gym sock stuffed with Roquefort cheese, and maybe a decomposing creek chub thrown in, Loren thought.

"I've had a complaint about you," he said.

Acker gazed back blankly for an awkward interval.

"You're the priest in town, aren't you?" he finally said, scratching again.

"Congregational minister, actually."

"Somebody complain that I skipped services? It's a free country last time I checked."

"I'm the town constable, too, as it happens."

"Is that like the police?"

"It's sort of what's left of the police."

"So much for the Constitution, then. Separation of church and state."

"I'm not too mixed up about it," Loren said.

Acker stared into Loren's face as though attempting to impress upon him his slight height advantage, but a tremor in Acker's left eye made the lid flutter in a way that revealed infirmity and weakness. Loren could not help but think that Acker was only marginally more healthy than his horse. The stare down concluded when Acker reached for the doorjamb to steady himself. Then he scratched again.

"Do you want to come in out of the cold?" he said. "I've got a little whiskey."

"That's kind of you," Loren said, "but the way you're scratching I suspect you've got a nice hatch of fleas going in there, so I'll just come to the point. There's a mistreated horse on the premises and I'm afraid I have to take it away from you."

Acker flinched again.

"Did Deaver tell you that?"

"Yes, he did."

"How does he know about it? That horse lives in the barn."

"Maybe he had a look inside."

"Maybe you should go arrest him for trespass."

Loren hitched up his coat and closed the top flap on the high collar. He was getting cold again standing on the porch in the evening shadows.

"You're a squatter here," Loren said. "You don't have standing to be trespassed on."

"How do you know I don't own the place?"

"Because at least a year before you moved in I presided over the burial of George Lund, who last owned it."

"Half the people around here live in houses they don't own and don't pay rent on," Acker said. "We still have rights. Deaver's trying to get a hold of this place. He wants to put me off it and take it over."

"This isn't a land dispute," Loren said. "It's about the horse. Anyway, I've looked in on the horse myself. It's suffering. I'm taking him with me."

"Do you have a warrant?"

"This doesn't require a warrant," Loren said.

Acker searched the porch ceiling as though seeking a useful argument that might be inscribed up there.

"Look," Acker said, "I have no money left to buy hay or grain. What am I supposed to do?"

"You have money for whiskey," Loren said. "You could have at least let the horse out of the barn. We didn't have any snow cover until yesterday. It could have been grazing in the weeds up until then. Why did you shut it in a stall filled with shit?"

Acker's thin-lipped mouth quivered at the corners.

"I was ashamed," he said, and looked down at his shoes.

"Well, you should be. We all have feelings, but this comes down to plain cruelty."

"Do you have any idea how hard it is to scratch a living out of the ground in these times?"

"I think so," Loren said. "I feel for you and for the people like you who never imagined they'd end up living this way."

"I'll need that horse to put in my potatoes next year."

"If I left him here with you, he wouldn't be alive at planting time," Loren said. "It'll be dark in an hour. I'd better be getting along now."

"You taking the horse?"

"Haven't I made that clear?"

Acker started shivering and seemed to retreat inside himself. Loren felt sorry for him but he felt sorrier for the horse. He left Acker on the porch and started for the barn. He had trudged through the crusty snow about three-quarters of the way to the barn when he heard a commotion of footfalls behind him and then felt a blow across his back that pitched him forward clean off his feet. The muscle memory from his days as a midfielder on the Middlebury College varsity lacrosse team propelled him into a shoulder roll that brought him back up into a crouch facing Donald Acker, who stood a few yards away with the stub of a broken tree limb in both hands and the same blank expression on his moon face. Acker wobbled in his tracks and tossed aside the tree limb as if that would make him appear to be an innocent bystander. Loren lunged for it. As he did, Acker attempted to turn around and flee, but his shoe caught in the crusty snow and he toppled over sideways. A moment later Loren was on top of him with the tree limb pressed against Acker's throat.

"Are you crazy?" Loren said.

"That horse is all I've got," Acker said. His eyes had gone watery. Loren began to register the pain he felt from the top of his right shoulder clear down to his kidney.

"You hurt me, you asshole," Loren hollered into Acker's reddening face. He took one hand off the tree limb in order to smack Acker upside his head.

"Ow!" Acker yelled and commenced bawling, his features bunching in pain.

"Don't give me any more trouble," Loren said, smacking Acker again, harder.

"Are you gonna arrest me?"

Loren expelled a guttural bellow of exasperation.

"Get up and go inside your house," he said, climbing off. "And don't even think about showing your face while I'm still on the premises. Go on!"

Acker struggled to his feet and limped back to the house.

Loren found a lead rope and a halter hanging in the barn and brought the horse outside into the purple twilight where it seemed to blink in amazement. With the strength it had left, the animal followed Loren down Huddle Road and then onto Route 29 another mile back to town. Loren had determined to bring it over to Brother Jobe's well-run stable adjacent to the old high school. He and the horse found a slow steady rhythm of progress that got them back into town in an hour. His shoulder and back ached and began to stiffen in the cold and he wondered what might have happened if Acker had had a firearm at hand. Loren did not have a pistol of his own and it occurred to him that he might think about acquiring one.

Main Street was dark and quiet on Christmas night and the new tavern was closed, but candles burned cheerfully in the windows of the houses around the corner on Van Buren Street. Here and there a parlor piano and singing could be heard and the horse's step seemed to quicken a little at the sights and sounds of town life. Shortly, Loren and the horse arrived at the former high school. Several of the New Faith men were in the stable at that hour, having just brought in the dozen horses and several mules from their paddocks for the night. The scene inside was a welcome contrast to the squalor of Acker's farm. Candle lanterns hung on the six-by-six posts along the center aisle, revealing a place of order, discipline, and human attention in soft golden light. The place smelled clean, more the aroma of hay than the odor of horse manure. The animals were busy eating from their mangers and glanced at the newcomer with interest as Loren led it down the aisle. The brothers helped settle the brindle into a stall and then led in a jennet donkey about half its size to keep it company. The donkey nuzzled the new arrival's drooping head.

"Everyone needs a little friend," said Brother Eben, the stable's evening manager. "She'll speed his recovery." He then went to fetch water, hay, and grain while Brother Zuriel, the New Faith farrier, examined the horse's neglected hooves and Brother Jonah began brushing the dirt out of its coat. Loren watched them with deep satisfaction that something had gone right in the world this day. The horse drank greedily when Brother Eben brought in a bucket of clean water. Then he hand-fed flakes of hay to it. Presently, Brother Jobe, who had been alerted to the situation, stopped in.

"I hear you brung me a Christmas present."

"Another mouth to feed," Loren said and explained.

"Oh, hey now, isn't that a sad sack of a feller, poor old boy," Brother Jobe said, coming into the stall. "Throw a stable sheet on him tonight, will you, Eben?"

"Yessir."

"You done the right thing," Brother Jobe said to Loren. "We're glad to take it in. He'll come back from his tribulation, just watch. Horses are wealth nowadays. Folks are beginning to realize it. There wasn't enough of them when the old times up and quit on us. We're breeding 'em as fast as we can. I aim to build another barn and go all out for mules this year. The mule is misunderstood and undervalued." Brother Jobe paused a moment. His demeanor grew quiet and he steered Loren out of the stall into the center aisle. "I've heard that Robert Earle's son turned up last night. And that your boy who lit out with him did not."

Loren sighed and nodded his head.

"I've lost a son too," Brother Jobe said, referring to Brother Minor, killed in a shoot-out the previous summer with the gang that ran the town landfill as a cash salvage business. "It's very hard, I know."

"We don't know what happened yet," Loren said. "Daniel's still out of it."

"Anytime you want someone to talk to, my door is open."

"Thank you."

"And you need a horse for any reason, you just take one of ours, hear? I'll tell my boys."

"Thank you for that too. How is Missus Stokes doing?"

"Under the circumstances not exactly thriving, but she's safe and warm and taking her food," Brother Jobe said.

Loren sighed and nodded. His shoulder and back muscles throbbed.

"I aim to persuade the squire to hasten proceedings, get the grand jury convened ASAP and the trial set," Brother Jobe continued. "That poor girl might have done a terrible dark deed but I feel for her nonetheless. I wonder if in the meantime she could stand a little company from one of her own townspeople. I have in mind a mature and sensitive woman such as your wife. I know she makes ministerial calls among your sick and bereft. I think our folks frighten Miz Stokes."

"I'll speak to Jane Ann," Loren said. "I'm sure she'll come over."

"Thank you. This gal ain't right in the head, poor thing. I'd go along with Mr. Hutto if he pleaded her insane, but I think the squire will try to hang her anyways."

"Bullock can't just do whatever he feels like."

"I'm not so sure about that," Brother Jobe said. "The law is a tattered and flimsy thing nowadays. Not so long ago in history, right here before this was its own nation, a woman who done such terrible deeds could be burned for a witch, legal proceedings and all, and sentenced to it with the full authority of a sage and solemn magistrate like our squire Bullock. Real justice is a fugitive thing in the long run. I look back on the times of my youth and marvel that the mills of the law worked as fair as it did. We weren't such a bad country then, after all. *He has showed you, O men, what is good. And what does the Lord require of you? To act justly and to love mercy and to walk humbly with your God.*"

"Micah 6:8," Loren said. "*All the works of Ahab's house are done. And you walk in their counsels, that I may make you a desolation, and your inhabitants a hissing.* Micah 6:16."

"I'll be ding-danged," Brother Jobe said. "You know your Bible after all."

"We're in the same line of work," Loren said.

TWENTY-FIVE

The big table in Andrew Pendergast's dining room was set for twelve with his Villeroy & Boch china in the red basketweave pattern and his antique steel flatware with cream-colored Bakelite handles on a pink damask tablecloth figured with cabbage roses. In the years of crash and collapse it was easy to buy fine things for next to nothing as households desperately liquidated their chattels for cash. Andrew lighted the eight beeswax candles arrayed in pewter holders molded into whimsical figures of forest animals: bear, bobcat, fox, and so on. They were low so his guests could see over them around the table. The centerpiece was an art nouveau silver bowl figured with leaves, blossoms, and nymphs. It was occupied by a small potted rosemary plant on which Andrew had hung a few tiny red and gold glass Christmas balls. On one side of the dining room, an oval mirror six feet in diameter hung over a 1920s reproduction serpentine Hepplewhite sideboard between two windows that looked out to his snow-blanketed garden. On the other side of the room a fire burned in a hearth behind a fitted glass fireplace door.

It was not so easy for Andrew to get his guests away from the woodstove in the adjoining parlor where they had been enjoying cocktails. All the talk initially was of the return of Daniel Earle and the sad absence of the companion he set out with two years before, Loren Holder's boy. Dr. Copeland told the gathering about Daniel's condition, and said that nothing yet was known of his adventures or tribulations, for he remained in a febrile sleep. He had no more to say about it for the moment, and the effects of the drinks was putting the company in a lighter mood.

"You know what I like about coming to your house?" Sharon Praeger said as Andrew poured her a second glass of extra-dry

German-style sparkling *apfelwein* cider, which tasted almost like champagne. "It's like the way everything was before."

"It's nice to pretend, anyway," said her husband, Larry, the town's only dentist, who, like the doctor, had to improvise constantly in his practice to make up for lost technologies and materials of the no-longer-modern age.

"Back in the day, we'd watch *It's a Wonderful Life* on Christmas night," said Dan Mullinex, whose wife was among those taken in the Mexican flu epidemic. He had been a young economics prof just starting out at Williams College in the old times and now worked for Holyrood, the cidermaker. He had brought several bottles with him.

"I loved that movie," said Linda Allison. "It breaks my heart that I may never see it ever again."

"We could put it on as a play, next Christmas," said Andrew. "If we could find a way to heat the theater."

"Did you ever notice in the movie that George Bailey's bank's main business was loaning money for the first suburban houses built after the war?" said Linda's husband, Tom Allison, another former academic left high and dry by the crash, who now ran the only livery in town.

"Which war?" said Larry Praeger.

"The Second World War," Dan said. "The movie came out in 1946. It was a box office flop, by the way."

"Maybe it would have been better if his bank had failed," said Maggie Furnival, with a glance toward her husband, Robbie, who had been in on the final burst of McMansion development as a building contractor before the collapse. He had lost everything for a while and his hatred for banks was assuaged when they all collapsed in a single week after the DC bombing. Now he was Union Grove's chief purveyor of cordwood, who employed eight roughneck woodcutters and had a stable of four Percheron horses for his logging operations.

"Well, finally, they all did." Robbie said. "In real life."

"It's hard to tell what's real life anymore," Larry said.

"The suburbs that George Bailey lent money to build eventually destroyed his little town, Bedford Falls, and everything else like it in America," Tom said. "You know that part in the movie where George wants to commit suicide on the bridge and the angel, what's his name—?"

"Clarence!" Dan said, like a good student.

"—and Clarence shows him what his town would be like if he had never been born. It would have been an evil little burg named Pottersville, named after the town villain played by, uh—"

"Lionel Barrymore!" Dan said.

"How do you remember these things?" Tom said. Dan just made a face and emptied his glass. "Anyway, in the dream sequence we see the Main Street of Pottersville. It's all gin mills and people getting in and out of taxicabs. Lights are blazing. The sidewalks are bustling. The town may be wicked but it's alive! Main Street business is booming. The shop fronts are all occupied. If the supposed nightmare of Pottersville had come true, this would have ended up a way better country. So, you see, George Bailey was the real villain of *It's a Wonderful Life*."

"Funny, how things work out," said the doctor, who always seemed preoccupied and indeed almost always was, given the many cares for the many he cared for in town.

"And now look at us," said Ben Deaver.

"Go ahead and look. There's a lot to like now, actually," said Tom.

"You don't miss electricity?"

"Not as much as I might have thought before. Look at us here. This is a happy gathering. We're all occupied doing worthwhile things. We probably eat better than before—I'm sure we will tonight, knowing Andrew. We're healthier than we would've been if we were still driving around in cars all day long, scarfing pizza, and watching Larry Kudlow on CNBC."

"You watched him?" Dan said.

"For laughs."

"Not much to laugh at there, in my opinion," Ben said.

"We're the lucky ones," Robbie said, thinking of the people he knew who could buy only a half cord of firewood at a time and lived in cold houses and didn't have enough to eat.

"I'm glad the whole rotten thing went down," said Nancy Deaver, who was working on her third glass of cider.

"She was a doomer," her husband, Ben, said.

"I was not," Nancy said. "I was just paying attention. It was obviously all a Ponzi scheme. You all were just too busy watching CNBC."

"Not me," Dan Mullinex said.

Andrew held up his glass. "A toast. To Mr. Charles Ponzi. For making it all possible."

The others smiled, not all of them comfortably, and drained their glasses, which Andrew refilled again.

"Well, I sure miss good crusty bread," Ben Deaver said. "How can this country be so screwed up that we can't even get regular shipments of wheat up the Hudson River. I tried growing a few acres five years ago but the stem rust got it right away."

"Have you tried Bullock's spelt?" Andrew said.

"I asked him for some seed and he wouldn't give me any," Ben said. "He wants the market all to himself, which is ridiculous because he can't supply it all."

"That's Bullock for you," Dan said.

"I don't mind corn bread," said Carolyn Smallwood, Andrew's assistant at the library, who had worked there through the entire transformation of life in recent times and had lived in the same house built by her great-grandfather on Van Buren Street all her life. "I'm quite fond of it, actually."

"People, people," Andrew said. "Can I ask you to move to the table?"

Early twilight had begun to gather under the eaves and Andrew lit the candles in the dining room. The aroma of good things roasting filled the first-floor rooms. When everybody was seated, Andrew picked up the lid of a silver chutney dish and banged it with a spoon. It produced a ringing musical tone that was Jack's cue to enter the dining room with serving bowls of mashed potatoes and Brussels sprouts braised with bacon and cider. The women in particular watched him come and go and return with a platter of carved turkey and stuffing. As instructed, Jack held the platter so each guest could help him- or herself and moved briskly along. Jack's hair was plastered down and he wore another of Andrew's old striped shirts so that he looked a little like a character out of a 1920s magazine advertisement for men's clothing. Dr. Copeland's wife, Jeanette, who was born in Normandy, said, "*merci*," and giggled when Jack moved on to her husband, who struggled against pouring himself a fifth glass of the sparkling cider. When they were all served, Jack put the platter on the sideboard, went to the kitchen, and came back out with a large gravy boat, which he deposited next to Nancy Deaver.

"Who are you?" she said to him softly.

"Nobody," Jack said, and hurried back toward the kitchen again.

Nancy, seated in the middle of the long table, leaned toward the host's end and said in stage whisper, as though eager for all the others to hear, "Tell us, Andrew, who's your new companion?"

Andrew flinched. "You mean him?" he said, pointing toward the kitchen.

"You found someone at last," Nancy said, very satisfied with her perspicacity and rather drunk.

"He's not my companion," Andrew said, his sense of comedy aroused. "He's my servant."

TWENTY-SIX

Around the same time that Andrew Pendergast and his friends addressed their plates of Christmas victuals, Jane Ann Holder, the minister's wife, turned up at the front door of the New Faith headquarters, formerly the town high school. She huddled inside her hooded wool cape, fashioned from a blanket, with a basket clutched to her body, and waited in the evening murk for the watchman Brother Asa to unlock the door. To the west, over a scrim of naked treetops, the sun was going down in a pink-gray soup of cloud. Once inside, she asked to be taken to see Mrs. Stokes. Brother Asa did not immediately comprehend.

"The, uh, prisoner," Jane Ann said, disliking the sound of the word.

Brother Asa then nodded and directed her to a room in a distant part of the building. She found her way there through eerily familiar hallways she had not been in since her only child, Evan, was a student there, before the school shut down for good. Elements of the original decor remained, for instance the sea-foam green tiles in the entrance lobby and the halls, but several classrooms were turned into workshops and she saw signs of reconstruction at every turn. She knew from talking with Robert Earle that the old gymnasium had been converted into a labyrinth of chambers for the mysterious woman they called the Queen Bee, who was never seen in public, and her attendants. Portraits of Jesus Christ hung conspicuously in the hallway while candles burned in wall fixtures, giving the place the air of a monastery. She thought of Rome and all the ancient buildings that had been used for different purposes over the centuries. It made her sad to think she would never see Italy again. The building was quite warm. She knew that the group had a way with practical things. They'd rigged the old hot water radiators to a wood-burning furnace in the basement. Several members had been engineers in the old times. They'd helped fix the town's decrepit water system only weeks after they arrived the previous spring. Now, they were partnering with her husband, Loren, and Robert Earle to build a community laundry in the old Union-Wayland paper mill on the Battenkill, the river that ran through town.

Jane Ann could hear choral singing distantly. This Christmas night, most of the brothers and sisters were at their devotions in the old school auditorium. As she made her way through the hallways, she passed classrooms converted into dormitories. They were extraordinarily neat and orderly. She wondered if it was fun to live that way. It reminded her of boarding school, which she had loved. When she reached her destination, she came upon one Brother Enos posted in a chair beside the door there. He stood up.

"Why, you're the first of her people to visit," he said.

"Is that so?" Jane Ann said. She did not know who Mandy Stokes's friends in town were, or if she had any at all. "My husband is the Congregational minister."

"I know, ma'am."

"How do you know that?" Jane Ann said. She was sincerely curious.

"We was there last night at your church, some of us, for the music."

"Oh? Did you enjoy it?"

"Very much. You got a different spirit than us, more like the old times. Are you here in an official capacity, then?"

"I make calls sometimes."

"Have you got something for the poor lady in there?"

"Yes, I do."

"I'll have to peek inside your basket, ma'a . . ."

"It's just some things to eat."

". . . case you might be trying to bust her out."

"Don't be ridiculous."

"Two lives have been taken, ma'am" he said, lowly.

Jane Ann regretted snapping at him. She held out the basket. Brother Enos inspected the contents, finding a jar of currant preserves along with little fruit and nut cakes and cornmeal cookies in the shape of crescent moons.

"I can't let this jar in there," he said.

"Why not?"

"It's glass. She could break it and hurt herself with a piece of it."

"I see."

"You can have it back when you leave."

"Okay."

He looked back up at her. His demeanor had changed. "Do you s'pose I can have one of them cookies?" he asked.

His plea was so much like that of a small boy's. It was Christmas night, after all.

"Take two," she said. He smiled and helped himself and made to unbar the door to the room. Jane Ann stepped past him.

It was dim inside. Twilight came in from the high clerestory window. There were no candles or lanterns. It appeared not so much a prisoner's cell as a kind of austere guest room. Mandy had been lying on her side in the dwindling light with her face turned to the outside wall. After Jane Ann entered the room, she stirred, rolled over, swept the hair out of her eyes, and propped herself up watching Jane Ann but saying nothing.

"May I sit down?" Jane Ann asked. Mandy offered no visible clue to her disposition. Jane Ann had been advised by Loren about Mandy's state of mind. She pulled a plain wooden school chair closer to the bed, sat down with the basket on her lap, shrugging off her cloak so that it fell over the chair back. She explained who she was and proffered the basket, but Mandy just stared back.

"Has anyone been to see you?" Mandy did not respond. "No? I'm sorry about that. I don't know who your friends are. Have any of them been here? Who are your friends? Do you understand what I'm saying?"

Mandy sighed and swung her legs around so she was now sitting primly on the edge of the bed. She gazed down at the floor and seemed to struggle with her thoughts. Over the previous two days, these thoughts had changed from an overwhelming barrage of fierce instructions and imprecations issued by invasive malign personages extrinsic to her essential self to a dull roar like tinnitus in a low register. A change was coming over her, the resolution of the symptomatic aftereffects of meningitis. The oncoming clarity frightened her as much as the mental confusion she was leaving behind.

Frustrated, Jane Ann went to the door and tried to open it but it was barred again.

"Open this up!" she cried and hit the door twice with the heel of her hand. Mandy looked up.

"Is that you, ma'am?" Brother Enos said.

"Of course it's me."

He opened it a crack.

"Can I have a candle, please."

"I can't leave my post."

"Why isn't there one in here?"

Brother Enos put his face right up against the slot between the open door and the wall. "Ma'am," he said, whispering.

"What?"

"We have to be careful," he said. "She might burn the building down."

"Oh . . ."

"For now, she has to make do with the natural daylight," he said.

"There's hardly any left."

"I'm sorry," Brother Enos said. "Mebbe you can come back another time when it's not so dark." He craned his neck around and peered inside, holding a candle aloft. Flickering light seeped into the room. He made eye contact with the prisoner. She held him in her gaze and it seemed to affect him. "Lookit," he said. "You take this here candle. It's my own personal one. Just don't be too long, now. I'll be out here in the dark, waiting."

"Thank you," Jane Ann said.

She returned to the chair, set the candleholder on the table, and rummaged in the basket for one of the little fruit and nut cakes, which she held out for Mandy.

"I have some sweet things for you to eat."

Mandy's eyes turned up into Jane Ann's. A fraught gleam came into them and Mandy seemed to try to form a word. She raised her hand tentatively, took the little square of cake, and began to eat it daintily without having said anything.

"There are more in here," Jane Ann said. Mandy chewed the cake slowly and deliberately, as if sampling something good for the first time ever. When she was finished, she reached for the basket and put it on her lap. She tried a cookie, then several more. The speed of her eating increased markedly the more she ate, until she couldn't cram the next one in fast enough. Jane Ann was a little unnerved. Then, Mandy suddenly stopped and passed the basket back to Jane Ann. When Mandy was finished, Jane Ann poured water from a white enameled metal pitcher into the metal cup on the table and gave it to Mandy. She took it and drank, looking at the floor. Then her lips moved as if she were forming words but no sound came out. She handed the cup back to Jane Ann and wiped her mouth on the sleeve of her sweater. Her gaze returned to Jane Ann again and she reached tentatively toward Jane Ann's face. Jane Ann made a conscious effort not to recoil from Mandy's reach. Mandy touched the long, thick braid in which Jane Ann wore her gold and silver hair. She touched the braid the same way she ate her first nut cake, daintily. Jane Ann took a chance, left her chair, and sat beside Mandy on the bed.

"Here, let me braid yours," Jane Ann said, and began working Mandy's lush dark brown hair into a single braid, like hers. She worked quickly, being well practiced. She could not help noticing the acrid odor of Mandy's body. In these new times people did not bathe often, and they had no manufactured cosmetics, colognes, or deodorants. The people in trouble or in sickness who Jane Ann made ministerial visits to often smelled ripe. Jane Ann recognized it over the years as the odor of human despair. Mandy submitted docilely to having her hair braided, just sitting still while Jane Ann worked. When she was finished, Jane Ann sat quietly next to Mandy for a while. It was now dark outside the clerestory window, and the candle on the floor shed a weird flickering uplight over the two women in the bare room, like the lighting in a horror movie of the previous century.

"I had a cat once," Mandy said clearly, out of nowhere, gazing into the floor. "Oh, how I miss him."

Jane Ann was startled to hear Mandy speak. Her voice was throaty, musical, not what she expected. She was not sure how to respond to her.

"What was his name?" Jane Ann said.

Mandy didn't answer. Jane Ann repeated her question more than once, and asked a few other questions about it, but Mandy continued to stare into the rug on the floor.

Jane Ann rose from beside Mandy on the bed. She gathered up her cloak from the chair and the basket and picked up the candle on the floor.

"His name was Sweetie-pie," Mandy said. Her head remained lowered.

Jane Ann waited a moment but Mandy said no more.

"I'll come back soon," Jane Ann said and moved to the door and knocked on it.

Brother Enos cracked it open.

"Everything okay in there?" he asked.

Jane Ann didn't know how to answer that. She felt tears coming on.

"I'll be going now."

Brother Enos opened the door wider and she squeezed through.

"Thank you for lending us your light."

"Thank you for the treats," he said.

TWENTY-SEVEN

"You know nothing," Daniel Earle said "Nothing!" The vehement utterance, apparently from a bad dream, startled his father, Robert, who sat half asleep, squinting at his book in a battered but comfortable wing chair beside Daniel's sickbed in the first-floor parlor. It was late Christmas night. The clock on the mantel read 11:35. Britney had gone to bed, but Robert wouldn't leave Daniel's bedside. Daniel had been sleeping for almost twenty-four hours. He still had an intravenous line in his arm. The doctor had left more bottles of prepared fluid and shown Robert how to change them. Now Robert watched Daniel claw ineffectually at the IV cannula just below his elbow. Robert put his book down and moved to sit on the bed beside Daniel. He held Daniel's arm to prevent him from ripping out the IV line and was surprised at the size of his son's hands, and how hairy they were, and the sinewy strength of his arms. Daniel was no longer a boy in any sense. As he struggled, Daniel opened his eyes and appeared to take in his surroundings for the first time. "Ohmigod . . ."

"It's all right," Robert said. "You're home."

"Oh . . ." Daniel let out a deep groan. "Father."

"Yes, it's me."

"When did I . . . get here?"

Robert told him and explained about the IV lines and the doctor's instructions.

"Aren't I a mess, though," Daniel said.

"You were a sight," Robert said. "Like a walking hairball."

"I'm sorry."

"What for?"

"Being disgusting."

"You're okay now. You're going to be all right."

"I walked so far."

"What happened to Evan?"

"He didn't make it."

"Oh God."

A shimmery veil of beaded sweat had formed on Daniel's face.

"I'm so hungry, Dad."

"What can I get you?"

"Anything."

"Okay," Robert said, standing up. "Leave that IV line in your arm alone. The doctor is coming back to see you in the morning."

"Is there something . . . down there?"

"It's a catheter, so you don't piss the bed. Leave it alone too."

Robert hurried out to the kitchen, found some cheese, cut a large chunk into bite-sized pieces, cut some large squares of corn bread and slathered them with butter that was soft from sitting out on the counter, and brought it all back to Daniel in the parlor. Daniel struggled to elevate himself but there was no headboard. Robert fetched a nearby sofa cushion and wedged it behind Daniel as his son hunched forward.

"There."

"Oh, that's better," Daniel said.

"See if you can get this down," Robert said, handing Daniel the plate of bread and cheese, which he rested on his lap. Daniel devoured the food rapidly and systematically, as though it were a job that urgently needed to be done.

"You're so much older," Robert remarked.

"Yeah, I've about caught up to you, feels like," Daniel said with his mouth full.

"Your sense of humor's still there."

"It's not so funny, what's out there in America. I need something to drink. Make me wobbly cow."

"Okay," Robert said. A wobbly cow was a glass of milk with honey and some whiskey or apple brandy in it. He gave it to the kids when they were sick. Its power as a medication was limited, but it eased the mind a little. Robert went back to the kitchen while

Daniel continued eating. The kitchen stove still had live embers in the firebox and the steel surface was warm enough to dissolve the honey in a mug of milk. He was generous with the whiskey. When he brought the beverage in, Daniel asked for more food. It was after midnight when he had finally finished eating. He had just handed the empty plate back to his father when Britney came down the stairs. Daniel followed her with his eyes, as though she were making an entrance on a stage. She wore a floral robe that had once belonged to Daniel's mother, Sandy. Britney had lost all her own clothes when her house burned down in June. She stopped at the end of the bed.

"Hello, Daniel," she said with her usual directness. "I'm glad to see you're okay."

"Do you live here?"

"Yes, I do."

"What about Shawn?" Daniel said.

"Shawn's dead."

"I'm sorry. I was friends with his little brother Cody. He's gone, too, of course. Evan's gone. So many people dead. What happened to Shawn?"

"He got shot at the General Supply. Your father was there when it happened."

"Did Wayne shoot him?" Daniel said. Wayne Karp was head man of the tribe of former bikers and motorheads who ran the old town landfill as a salvage operation.

"No," Robert said. "Bunny Willman pulled the trigger."

"He's dumb enough," Daniel said. "You didn't see it?"

"I was in the office buying nails and stuff from Wayne when it happened out by the gate. Wayne's dead now too."

"Is anyone I know still alive here?"

"A lot's happened since you left home. Last June, a bunch of Christian evangelicals arrived here, about eighty people. They came from Pennsylvania somewhere, but that was just a stopover from where they started in Virginia. They call themselves the New Faith Church. They bought the school . . ."

Daniel gagged slightly on his warm milk and whiskey.

"It was just sitting there, unoccupied," Robert said. "They've done a lot to it, turned it into a . . . a hive of activity. I've worked in there myself doing renovations. You'll see. The old ball fields are gardens and pastures now."

"Evangelicals," Daniel said, bitterly. "You have no idea."

Robert flinched. Daniel as a grown man seemed a stranger to him.

"This bunch are pretty good sorts," Robert said. "They've done a lot for the town."

Daniel lowered his mug and focused his gaze on Britney. The clock on the mantel ticked. Britney looked directly back at Daniel.

"Are you two hooked up?" he said.

"I guess you could say so," Britney said.

Robert quelled the urge to explain himself. Being intimidated by his own son was a startling mental adjustment.

"I remember you had a little girl," Daniel said.

"Sarah's eight years old now."

"Is she here?"

"Of course," Britney said and pointed upstairs.

"Oh," Daniel said. "Has she been healthy?"

"Yes."

Daniel turned back to his father.

"Well, I can find a place of my own, then."

"You don't have to think about that right now," Robert said.

"I'm not angry at you, in case you're wondering. Mom's been dead for years. I understand." Daniel's declaration hung awkwardly in the silence that followed it. "There must still be plenty of empty houses around town."

"You can stay here as long as you want."

"Sure, thanks," Daniel said, settling back against the sofa cushion, with a sigh.

"You feeling okay?"

"A lot better. The food and all."

"Maybe you should rest now."

"I'm tired of resting. Don't you want to know what happened . . . out there."

"You have all the time in the world—"

"I need to start telling you now."

Twenty-eight

Daniel's Story: To the Lakes

"It was fine spring weather when we left," Daniel said.

May. All the trees finally leafed out, fruit blossoming, people putting crops in here and there where they had the wherewithal to farm. Not everybody out on the land did. They didn't have tools, or draught animals, the knowledge to farm, or even the will to live after all they lost. The landscape was beautiful but you could smell death everywhere. The scent of lilacs and death. That stuck.

We didn't have to camp outside much. We found empty houses wherever we passed. You could take your pick. They were always full of people's stuff, even though they were gone. Nothing of value, usually, 'cause pickers had always been through. Everything a mess, usually. Things strewn all over, broken, trashed. Now and then we came across a body where a person died alone and nobody came to get them or bury them. Once a whole family of four, all in one room. The bodies were pretty far gone. We figured the father probably killed them all and then himself because the largest corpse had a gun in what remained of its hand. It had five live rounds in the magazine, a nine-millimeter semiautomatic. We kept it. It's a terrible thing to see a human being that has been unburied for some time. You could smell it down the road before you walked in the door. We never stayed over in a house where the dead lay, though obviously we went inside some of them to look.

The condition of the towns we passed through varied a lot from place to place. Based on what we saw our first weeks on the road, we rated Union Grove better than average. The towns at the center of a farming district were the best off because people could work for food, like here, and work at trades around the farming. All the population centers big and small had shrunk way down, of course. The suburban stretches were the most desolate. Wherever we went, people struggled to carry on. A lot of physically healthy people seemed to have mental problems. Maybe they were still dazed by how quickly things were changing. They had also come through another hard winter.

Here and there we came upon places like Mr. Bullock's where some honcho had set up a domain for himself and ran things, somebody with good organizing skills and a commanding personality. These were like strongholds in a wasteland. You could tell them because all of a sudden, after many miles of raggedy farms where half-starving scarecrow people grubbed around in the soil for subsistence, you'd come upon well-tended fields, well-fed people working in groups together in an organized way, with draft animals pulling mechanical tillers and drag rakes, usually a big house in good condition visible from the road, sometimes armed guards or signs telling you to keep out. We stopped at a couple along the way those early days. Once, we offered to work for a meal and they laughed at us because we were just two jokers who didn't know how things were done around there, but they gave us lunch anyway. Another place, they thought we were pickers and ran us off. I guess we could've been mistaken for pickers, but we were just travelers off to see the country.

The first town of size we came to on our quest to get to the Mohawk River was Amsterdam, New York, where the old Mohawk carpet mills stood on a bluff above the town like a giant Tibetan Buddhist monastery overlooking the valley. The buildings were so enormous. It was hard to believe that our society had produced these immense things, as if the people of the twentieth century were a race of giants who could do anything. We went inside. They were brick shells, gloomy and rank. The roofs were collapsing. The machinery was long gone. Some people had lived inside for a while, but the remnants of their campsites were old and we figured they didn't make it through the winter.

Evan was great company, always bright and chirpy, crack-
ing jokes, keeping it light when, if you had been all alone, after
a while you might want to find a hole in the ground to crawl
into just to hide from the reality of where things had gone to, or
throw up, or maybe hang yourself. Evan called the dead people
we came across "mummies." He spun out an ongoing story as we
hiked along about how the mummies had colonized the USA,
and taken over the government, and infiltrated every level of
society, and wrecked everything—and we were among the few
survivors battling our way across Mummy Nation. Evan had
quite an imagination.

We knew that boats were running on the Mohawk River,
which fed into the old Erie Canal system, and we were hoping
to catch a ride west. We didn't have any wish to go down to
New York City because it was supposed to be a pretty terrible
situation all around there, and farther south in Washington, DC,
where the bomb went off, forget it. The town of Amsterdam had
all concentrated down by the riverfront. Everything up the hill
around the old factories was abandoned. They'd destroyed the
center of town way back in the old times by bulldozing most of
Main Street so there would be more room for cars. The ruins of
an old downtown mall still stood there, in all its stupidity. The flat
roof was shot from so many winters of ice and snow. Front Street
down by the river was where people did business now. There were
a few new buildings, merchant houses, they called them, doing
trade on the river, a tavern, a general merchandise. They'd put in
docks and slips and a yard where they were building new boats
for the canal trade. That's where we met the boatman Randall
McCoy, master of a barge called *Glory*. The boat's name was an
exaggeration and he was in on the joke. I wish we were. He and
Evan struck up a jabber as we searched among the vessels on the
waterfront for a way to the west. McCoy gave off a lighthearted
impression and that snared Evan's sense of fun. McCoy was about
thirty years old, a full-hearty grown-up dude well over six feet,
brawny arms, thick neck, and kept his hair long, braided in the

back like an Indian of yore. He wore good linen hand-sewn, pattern-made clothes, not the old-times shiz like our people wear around here, T-shirts with pictures on them and all that. McCoy was going for respect, even if he was a jokester.

The *Glory* was seventy feet long by about eight feet wide with a draft of four and a half feet loaded. Cabin near the back end. McCoy had a team of mules in the bow, another in the stern. It was easy work for them once you got the boat going. They had a nice life. If reincarnation really exists, I wouldn't mind coming back as a canal mule. McCoy had just tied feed bags on the bow team when we came along. He seemed to find us comical at the get-go. Evan told him we were searching for a long lost land called the United States.

McCoy goes, "I think I saw it under a rock at the Marengo Marsh cut."

Evan goes, "What was it doing?"

McCoy's like, "It's just a feeble crawling little thing now. A shadow of its former self since they ran that General Fellowes out of office."

"We're out to see what's left," Evan goes. "We hear it's lovely out on the lakes."

"Trade's picked up there or we wouldn't be in business," McCoy goes. "I've got a load of halite and hops going west, leaving tomorrow."

I'm, suddenly, like, "Can we catch a ride on your boat?"

He goes, "If you pay for your own food and sleep on deck and work to offload the cargo at Lockport where they're rebuilding the flight of five locks."

"What's that?" we both go.

McCoy explains that the original Erie Canal ran pretty flat across western New York until it got to the Niagara Escarpment where they had to build a big set of five locks to get boats up to the level of Buffalo and Lake Erie.

Evan goes, "Why not just go up into Lake Ontario and float into Lake Erie?"

McCoy's like, "Ever hear of Niagara Falls, doinky-doink?"

"What about it?"

"It's between the two lakes, is what. Kind of hard to sail up and over it in a boat."

"And his mom's the schoolteacher, back home," I go, giving Evan my thumb.

"Is she really?" McCoy goes.

Evan goes, "Hey, I knew that about Niagara Falls."

"Like hell you did," I go.

Evan's like, "You're so smart, what's the capital of Kentucky?"

I'm like, "Now how the hell should I know that?"

He goes, "We had to memorize all the capitals in the fifth grade, remember?"

"Well, I haven't thought about it in ten years, and who gives a damn?"

"We might travel through Kentucky. You never know."

"I'd stay away from there," McCoy says. He's all grins. I think he likes to see us go at it.

"How come?"

"Kentucky, Tennessee, that part of the country isn't safe. I think we're at war with them."

"Since when?"

"More than a year."

"What for?"

"They broke away from America."

"How come?"

"They never did like us? It's civil war all over again," McCoy says. "Remember the Alamo?"

"The Alamo was the war with Mexico," Evan says, "not the Civil War."

"They don't like Mexicans either," McCoy says.

"Seems like the country has just fallen to pieces," I go.

"As long as things keep moving on the Er-i-o, I don't give a damn," McCoy goes.

"So what *is* the capital of Kentucky, smart ass?" I ask Evan.

He ignores me. He goes, "Well, what about those five locks, mister?"

McCoy says, "They changed the system in 19 and 13 and built new locks that were bigger than the original ones, and only two to the set. But the gates ran off the electric, and with the electric out they don't work anymore, so now they have to rebuild the old five-step, which they are doing and hope to finish up by midsummer. It'll be dandy when they're done. Meantime, we have to offload our cargoes at Lockport and put it in wagons up the slope and then the Buffalo boats take it the rest of the way. You could work on the locks when we get to it. They're paying silver, I hear. I'll introduce you to the boss there, if you like."

So we just looked at each other, Evan and me, and knew we'd go west with Randall McCoy for a ways and then take it from there.

Daniel slid down from the sofa cushion, saying only, "So tired, got to sleep now."

Robert removed the sofa cushion and placed a regular pillow back under his son's head, tenderly, as though Daniel were not the mysterious man he had become but still a small boy who needed his father to take care of him.

Twenty-nine

The next morning Robert Earle, Loren Holder, and Brother Jobe convened at the old former Union-Wayland mill down by the Battenkill River. Brother Jobe had brought a thermos bottle of real coffee and a little sack of raised donuts made of real wheat flour and dusted with real powdered sugar. The New Faith people had a knack for coming by scarce commodities in their trade dealings. Brother Jobe was attended by Brother Shiloh, chief engineer of the project ongoing in the old factory: a community laundry that was near completion. Brother Shiloh left the others in his office room equipped with a wood-burning stove and went off to inspect the new boiler fabricated in the New Faith's own metal shop.

Without electricity, the old way of everybody having washing machines at home was out of date, and laundry was a laborious task. A few people had set themselves up to take in other people's wash, but there were not enough laundry facilities for everyone, and some people could not pay to have it done, and on the whole the townspeople suffered from a lack of clean clothes and bedding. They had hoped to get the community laundry—which was originally Loren Holder's idea—up and running by Christmas as a present to the town, but a few kinks in the mechanicals remained to be worked out.

The office was in one corner of the large open factory floor. It had a wall of windows that looked onto the works. Seven thousand square feet of space remained of the twenty-four thousand square feet the complex comprised in its heyday. The building had started its life in 1854 as a linen mill, was converted to a toilet paper factory in the early twentieth century, and produced cardboard boxes after the Second World War. It ceased to produce anything in 1971 and had languished for decades. The weather had its way with the flat roof and the rubber-asphalt cladding that cracked and split under ultraviolet exposure. Things started to leak, rot, rust, flake off, spall, and molder inside.

All the debris and rottenness had been cleared away in the past six months. Beams, joists, and flooring had been replaced and gleamed brightly with varnish made right in Washington County out of turpentine and seed oil. Robert had put in many extra hours of labor on the project when he wasn't working elsewhere and the Reverend Holder had collected silver coin from the members of the Congregational Church toward paying for the fittings fabricated by local smiths, coopers, and craftspeople. At the center of the main workroom now stood two rows of four hundred-gallon oaken tubs four feet high, mangles made of the toughest and most rot resistant black locust wood with wrought-iron fittings for wringing out wet fabrics and several big tables for sorting clothes and sundries. An overshot water wheel on the river turned leather belts overhead connected to gearing that ran the paddles in the wash tubs.

"Shiloh thinks we can test-drive her in another week or so," Brother Jobe said, pouring coffee into the cup that screwed off the top of the thermos. "Help yourself to a durned donut, you two."

Robert and Loren did not hesitate. Robert closed his eyes as he savored the first bite and the sugar melted on his tongue.

"We've got four of our people and four of your people hired up to start," Brother Jobe continued, "and if we need more we can hire up more. I know quite a few of your farm labor folk are idle this time of year. By and by some might like working in here better than out in the fields. We can shake out the operation in the weeks ahead. If you boys want some of this here coffee, we all got to drink out of the same cup. I didn't bring no extra mugs."

"Can your bunch cover those wages we'll be paying until we get cash coming in?" Robert said.

"Sure. It'll come out of you-all's cut until we're square."

Robert and Loren glanced at each other. Both then nodded okay. Robert reached for the coffee. It had been many months since he'd tasted any. In the old times, when he was an executive at a computer software company in Boston, Robert's steel coffee mug was his constant companion. Colleagues joked that it was a prosthetic extension of his brain.

"Meantime," Brother Jobe said, "we got to assemble twenty-three upright individuals to sit on a grand jury to review criminal charges against poor Miz Stokes. Mr. Bullock has asked me as an officer of the court to direct you as constable"—he looked at Loren—"to notify these potential grand jurors." He dug into the inside pocket of his frock coat, withdrew a folded document, and handed it to Loren. At the top of the first page, in florid cursive script, the document said, *On Order of the Magistrate, Union Grove, New York, Hon. Stephen Bullock,*" followed by several paragraphs of dense legalese that fogged Loren's brain as he attempted to parse it. He flipped the page.

"There's only fifteen people on this list," Loren said. He knew them all. "You say we need twenty-three."

"Well, he told me to tell you to scare up the rest, plus a few alternates."

"Jesus Christ," Loren said.

"No need for cussing there, Rev."

Loren rubbed his temples as though he had a headache. "All this constable bullshit is taking over my life," he said.

"Well, whyn't you quit grousing and seek some upright and mature fellow amongst your regular townspeople to take your place as constable whilst you discharge this particular final obligation, which is your duty as long as there ain't nobody else to fill your boots."

Loren made a face, then sighed and reached for another donut. "Maybe I will."

"I know we all got a full plate these days," Brother Jobe said. "If it's any help, I can nominate a few grand jurors out of our outfit."

"You think our people would mind that?" Loren said to Robert.

"His people live here now too," Robert said. "They're citizens of Union Grove."

"My wife visited with Mrs. Stokes last night," Loren said, turning back to Brother Jobe. "It sounds like she's not fit for any trial."

"That was my impression, too, frankly, but the wheels of justice are in motion, my friend. We got to roll with them."

Brother Jobe poured some more coffee into the cup and handed it to Loren.

"Those wheels are attached to a runaway wagon," Loren said, "and the wagon is named Bullock."

THIRTY

Einhorn's General Merchandise at the center of Union Grove was the favorite gathering place, casual meeting spot, and business exchange in town. It was also the only place within an eleven-mile radius of Union Grove to buy household goods and groceries. It occupied a one-story cinder-block structure built in 1957 originally for a store called Carpetland, which had replaced the burned-down Beeman Block (completed 1899), a far more elegant and substantial exercise in the small-town Beaux Arts that had housed Beeman's Hardware on the first two floors for almost six decades. When the economy crashed and the government withered and everything about daily life changed, Terry Einhorn acquired the long-vacant Carpetland building, built a wide and comfortable porch on front, and an icehouse on the rear alley, and started his business, which for a number of years was the only going concern in town besides Allison's livery and the Fixit Shop.

In the old times Terry Einhorn had represented a kitchen and bath products company, selling high-quality fixtures to vendors in a sales territory that included all of eastern upstate New York, western Massachusetts, and Vermont, a region, back then, with a large number of wealthy people in fine houses who spent their money on gourmet cooking equipment and home spa furnishings. He made a good living. On a fluky, nervous hunch that things weren't going so well in the world, a few months before the outbreak of war in the Holy Land, Terry took $70,000 out of his investment account and bought gold coins in half and quarter ounce denominations. He bought as many again just before the Los Angeles bombing. When the economy cratered soon after that, and the banks with it, he was one of the few citizens of Union Grove left with fungible wealth. Being a deeply practical person, and one who cared about his town, and someone who could connect the dots and see where the collapse was leading, he used a fair portion of this wealth in setting up the store. The Kmart was already done for by then and the Hovington supermarket was on its last legs with intermittent deliveries, half-empty shelves, and irregular electric service that rendered the freezers inoperable. Of course, the corporate managers of the supermarket chain had no interest in finding local sources of food, while Terry arranged his new network masterfully, helping the local farmers to organize and cooperate with one another as a beneficial side effect.

His wife, Leslie, was a mainstay of Andrew Pendergast's music circle (cello) and of the Union Grove Theater Company—she played Cousin Nettie in the fall production of Rodgers and Hammerstein's *Carousel,* directed by Andrew Pendergast. Terry and Leslie lost one child in the Mexican flu epidemic, a girl, Kristan, fourteen. Their son Teddy, eighteen, who survived, made daily rounds in his wagon of the farms throughout the county, picking up produce, meats, cheeses, cider, and other merchandise instead of waiting for the farmers and craftspeople to bring it in. Einhorn's store was therefore always reliably supplied. Teddy had not been old enough when the world changed to have developed more elaborate career plans involving college, an office job in a faraway city, and all the other trappings of bygone modernity. He was a happy, busy, well-adjusted young man of his own new time. He loved plying the hills and vales of Washington County in the double-spring-mounted wagon with its snug driver's box behind the big steady Belgian gelding Lancelot. He had a girl over at Center Falls who he got to visit with at least once a week on his rounds, and he was developing the notion of opening a branch of the store there.

After the death of their daughter, the Einhorns had taken in the orphaned Buddy Haseltine, then sixteen. Buddy was born with Down syndrome and was classified as "higher functioning" by the medical establishment. As it happened, he'd attended a special-ed class until the schools closed and was able to read and write at the level of a normal seven-year-old, as well as to add up simple sums—though subtraction baffled him. Buddy worked in the store, too, and by the time he was twenty-one had begun to campaign to live away from the Einhorn house on his own, the answer to which was a comfortable room in the rear of the store, the store being the center of his universe. All day long the people came and went and Buddy Haseltine enjoyed the human traffic immensely and went about his simple duties of stocking, and sweeping, and sometimes waiting on customers, and delivering their orders around town in a handcart he pulled himself, as though he were a horse, and was well loved by everybody, and may have been the happiest soul in Union Grove despite the disadvantages life dealt him from the start. In a troubled period of history, Einhorn's store was a happy place.

Buddy was bringing potatoes out of cold storage that morning and filling bins at the front of the store when he overheard the conversation of Robbie Furnival, Bruce Wheedon, and Walter McWinnie, all gathered around the potbellied stove at the center of the store, and all enjoying mugs of an herbal "coffee" made from roasted dandelion and angelica roots, fennel seeds, and rhodiola, which Leslie Einhorn blended herself. Terry Einhorn stood behind his counter, helping Lucy Myles get her groceries.

"It's out that they're calling a grand jury," Walter said. "From all I heard it sounds like she was defending the child from him."

"I knew Rick Stokes," said Robbie, "and I just don't see him as the type of man that would kill his own son."

"Something terrible went down in that house that night," Bruce said, "and I suppose it's the purpose of the grand jury to find out what, exactly."

"I've been called to serve on it," Terry said from behind his counter. "The rev came by earlier with a writ from you know who."

"Terrible, what happened," Lucy said. "Did you get any of that Shushan cheddar in by any chance?"

"Yes I did, dear," Terry said.

"I hear the doc says the baby was shook to death," Walter said. "Spinal cord all squarshed."

Buddy's head perked up at the potato bin.

"Rick would never shake a baby like that," Robbie said. "He loved that kid."

"There was no knife wounds on the baby," Bruce said. "It must have happened that the baby was crying or carrying on and Rick did something. It doesn't take much, you know. Little snap of the head is all."

"She shake the baby," Buddy said from over at the potato bin. His speech being impaired by his deformed palate, it came out as a kind of mere vocal noise that did not get the attention of the men around the potbellied stove.

"So she sees him do this and goes berserk and stabs him with a kitchen knife," Walter said. "Must have happened like that."

"Shake the baby," Buddy repeated. It sounded like a kind of honking: *Hee hake da baby*. This time he caught the attention of Bruce and Robbie.

"It's the only way that makes sense," Walter added.

"Hee hake da baby!" Buddy said. In his pigeon-toed way he stepped closer to the center of the room where the men sat in rockers.

"What's he sayin'?" Walter said.

"Da baby!" Buddy said. "Hee hake da baby." Up at the counter, Lucy turned to look. Buddy then acted out what he remembered. He held his stubby arms out and as if holding a parcel in them he shook the imaginary bundle violently. "Hee hake da baby ike da."

"He's got a theory," Walter said. "Imagine that!"

"No, I saw ih! I saw ih," Buddy said.

Now Terry came around the counter.

Buddy pantomimed what he saw again.

"Hee hake da baby!"

Everybody was now looking at Buddy, who stopped the pantomime, suddenly nervous about the attention focused on himself.

"What's he saying, Terry?" Robbie asked.

"He's saying 'she shook the baby,' I think," Terry said.

Buddy wagged his head up and down. "Hee hake da baby."

"You see that?" Bruce said to Buddy, then to Terry, "Did he see that?"

Buddy continued nodding his head.

"Did you see that?" Terry asked and then he mimicked what Buddy had done, holding his arms out stiffly and shaking.

Buddy wagged his head again.

"How could he see that?" Bruce said.

"He lives here in the store now," Terry said. "He's here after we close up. Where'd you see this happen, Buddy?"

Buddy pointed toward the window.

"The street," Buddy said. *Da hreet*.

"The street?"

Buddy nodded.

"When was that?"

"Ni'time. Hefo Crimmis."

"Nighttime. Before Christmas?"

"Yah!"

"Christmas Eve?"

"Ya! Crimmis Eeh."

"That's when it happened, all right," Robbie said.

"Does he really know what he's talking about?" Bruce said.

"Yeah, he probably does," Terry said, and turned back to Buddy, who seemed abashed and uncomfortable and squirmed in place.

"Are you sure it was a woman you saw?" Terry asked him.

"She! She!" Buddy said, pointing outside. "*Hee, Hee!*"

"Is that a he or a her?" Walter said.

"Woman!" Buddy said. *Hooman!*

"A human?" Walter said.

"You mean a lady?" Terry said.

Buddy nodded again.

"I gah go," Buddy said, overcome by anxiety. "Mo 'tatoes."

"Wait a minute," Walter said.

"No, let him go," Terry said.

They all watched Buddy pigeon-step to the storeroom in the back, across the hall from his living quarters.

"Well, this puts a new light on things, don't it?" Walter said. "You're going to have to inform you know who."

It took Terry a longish moment to digest that.

"Buddy can't testify," Terry said eventually.

"Why not?" Walter said.

Robbie Furnival just shrugged his eyebrows and lit a splint in the stove to relight his pipe.

"Is it legal?" Bruce Wheedon said. "Being who he is and all."

"Well," said Lucy Myles from over at the counter, "we can't pretend we didn't hear it. Sounds like she killed them both."

Thirty-one

"We signed on with Randall McCoy to voyage west on the Erie Canal in exchange for helping them load and unload cargo along the way," Daniel said, sitting up in bed at four o'clock that afternoon as twilight gathered in the windows of his father's house. Loren and Jane Ann Holder sat beside the bed. Thirteen-year-old Mary Moyer was looking after their four young adopted children back at the rectory.

Robert Earle put a log on the fire. Britney worked on a splint basket in a seat at the end of the bed. Britney's child, Sarah, stood in the kitchen nearby in a nimbus of candlelight, making corn bread. Daniel clutched a mug of rose hip tea in both hands. The color was returning to his face.

Daniel's Story: Incident at the Five-Step Flight

The night before we left the town of Amsterdam, McCoy took us to the boatmen's tavern for a meal and what he called "sport." The place was rough but lively. In the big front room men played cards. It was good weather, though, and they had an open-air deck overlooking the river. Out there a geezer was playing fiddle with an old gal on the mandola. The boatmen put dimes in a hat for them. The food there was pretty good for that time of year: corned beef and potatoes, all kinds of pickles, bacon and beans, and fresh shad from the spring run over to the Hudson that boats brought up the Mohawk. I don't care for shad roe. It tastes like liver from another planet. But others were shoveling down great platters of it. The meat's bony as hell. They say that a porcupine chased by a mountain cat once took refuge by jumping in the river and God turned him inside out and that's how the shad got created.

McCoy was popular among the boatmen. Many stopped by our table to joke with him, being old friends, I thought, and the society of the canal being a close one because they saw each other coming and going all the time and in the canal taverns along the line. They asked who we were and McCoy told them we were bound west to the end of the line at the five-step locks of Lockport, and from there God knew. When they heard that, more than a few raised their eyebrows as if impressed or busted out laughing. I supposed they were all pretty drunk. The tavern was that kind of place, and it was that time of day—the purple hour of twilight—when workingmen were inspired to drink quick and hard. McCoy bought us ciders with our meal and whiskeys after we finished, and some ladies came around our table. They were in skirts, all clean and buffed up, and we understood what kind of girls they were. Anyway, McCoy left us there, the girl with him tugging at his arm, and said we could sleep on deck of the *Glory* that night and get under way in the morning. Two girls remained with us, Haven and Lily. They informed us that they were at our service. I'm like, "I never paid for it."

Lily goes, "Well, you don't have to because Mr. McCoy took care of it." She was most winsome, let me tell you.

"I'm not sure I want to hear this," Jane Ann said.

"I'll spare you the details," Daniel said. "Let's just say we went with them."

"Oh, my little Evan."

I never saw Evan so happy as that evening. He liked Haven because their names sort of rhymed. He thought that was, like, fate. Anyway, their establishment was up the street and we went with them. We weren't allowed to sleep there. So after that, we made our way back to the docks and lay out our bedrolls on the *Glory*'s deck between the mules on the bow and McCoy's cabin.

The air was chill, perfect for sleeping, and the sky full of stars. We're lying there, pretty buzzed on drink.

Evan goes, "I'm gon' come back and marry that girl."

I go, "No you're not. By the time we come back she woulda had a thousand other dudes and I'm sure at least half of them'll have the same idea. And she'll say yes to one of them, I'm sure."

"She was the most beautiful li'l thing I ever saw in my life."

"More beautiful than Abby Sweetland?"

"I never did it with Abby. Tonight was my first time."

"Oh God . . ." Jane Ann said, groaning.

"Well, it was our lives," Daniel said. "You've already had your lives and done things like that when you were young, and it was our turn."

"Let him tell it," Loren said.

Robert shared a glance with Jane Ann.

"Please go on," Loren said.

Okay, so we heave off in the morning, early. McCoy's in great spirits, singing on the cabin roof. Evan and I take turns walking the mules, two hours at a time walking the towpath. We changed mule teams every four hours. McCoy would rotate them from the so-called barn in front to the "barn" in the stern. It wasn't any kind of real barn, you understand, just a portion of the deck where they stood happily munching flakes of hay on the slow, gentle, steady boat that never rocked because the water was never rough. Our work was easy. We occasionally offloaded a few barrels of this and that and took on a few barrels of this and that.

Walking the towpath with the animals was loveliness itself, except when it rained, which was only a very few times, it being a dry spring, and quite warm too. Everything about canal boat work is slow and stately. You never hurry up. Everybody along the way knows each other. The only danger is being around mules, and McCoy's were exceptionally well behaved, Spark and Goose on one team and Shadow and Beans the other. I think they liked towing the *Glory*. You could hardly even call it work for them. Flowers were out. Yellow and blue iris in the marshy spots, May apples in the woods, wild mustard along the towpath, fruit trees blooming in old abandoned orchards.

The towns floated by: Fultonville, Canajoharie, Fort Plain, Herkimer, Ilion. The Mohawk River finally funneled down into the canal for good at the town of Frankfort, which was abandoned except for the lock keepers, who ran a rude tavern with lodgings there, of course, and charged a dime toll to pass through their lock. They couldn't charge more because the boatmen couldn't stand it and stay in business. We checked out the center of town. You could tell it was mostly ruined, before the old times ended, with parking lots. The three older brick buildings left were burnt out—by firebugs, the lock keeper said. They liked their situation there, with a cow and gardens and boats bringing them stuff to trade for all day long, and the dimes adding up.

We stayed in their lodgings for one night in crude bunks because it started to rain and McCoy wouldn't let us in his cabin on board, and Evan got lice there. McCoy had a razor so in the morning he shaved Evan's head. Evan was very discouraged by it and said no girl would ever look at him again. I told him that in the old times it was all the fashion for men to shave their heads. He said it was the ugliest look he could imagine and would grow his hair out as long as McCoy's and wear it braided up like he did. He and McCoy got on like big and little brothers, their sense of humor being very similar. I began to feel a little like odd man out.

Utica was spooky. It was set back half a mile from the canal past a wasteland where the old state thruway ran, now all busted up, with mulleins and sumacs poking through the pavements. Utica was once big enough to have some tall office buildings in the downtown and they were all vandalized, windows shattered up to about the fourth floor where, I guess, the vandals couldn't throw rocks any higher. A big old hotel, too, from over a hundred years ago, all forsaken. We went inside. The lobby was a mess of fallen plaster, broken furniture, and stinking carpets. Must have been sweet when it was new. Hard to believe people lived so grandly in this land then. Utica was one of those places that just couldn't get back on its feet. There was nothing left even to steal, if you were a picker. We didn't linger.

Despite what McCoy said about us having to get our own food, he shared his with us. It was a stupid waste of effort, he said, to cook two separate breakfasts. Anyway, he kept four hens on board and we usually had enough eggs, and you could find butter along the way, and honey or jam, and bacon, and beans, various kinds of bread and corn bread, hardly any fresh greens besides dandelion and ramps that time of year, no fruit except preserves. The farther into western New York you went, the more wheat flour turned up. Sometimes we'd make real pancakes. We didn't see coffee at all in the west. We caught carp and perch in the canal. Not great eating, but better than shad, and scorching it on McCoy's on-deck brazier made it edible. There were many other taverns in the towns along the way, mostly low-down filthy establishments full of rough boatmen. You could fill up a plastic gallon jug of rough cider for ten cents and a pint of whiskey for a silver quarter. Supper wasn't much in those gully dens.

We carried some hardwood lumber on deck from Brewerton just west of Oneida Lake to Onondaga Lake just north of Syracuse. The city was the chief trading town of the central Finger Lakes. Its population was down to five thousand souls but it was like a big city compared to Union Grove. They had a hotel with fifty rooms, all new wooden construction, with a fancy dining room, so McCoy said. He left us in charge of the *Glory* and rode Beans the mule five miles to the town and didn't come back until morning, still a little wobbly. They told him down there that the stretch of the canal from the Tsache Pool to Blue Cut was having Indian trouble—his very words. Imagine that. The Senecas were harassing farmers over three counties and law enforcement couldn't contain them. Of course, there was no law outside of Syracuse, McCoy said, and even there it was the personal law of a certain Boss Fouts, who ran the town. Anyway, they burned

some farmers out and two boats on the Erie had been attacked
and plundered that month.

McCoy talked to himself much of the morning working off
his headache, debating out loud if we should go on or lay back.
When we tried to comment he just told us to shut up, he was rea-
soning in his own mind, and around noon he came around to the
view that there was nothing else to do but go on and try our luck
getting through. He had but one firearm on board, an old single-
shot twenty-two, a child's gun, really. I didn't want to tell him that
I had a pistol and I warned Evan not to let on about it either. So
we just set off for Rochester, about a hundred miles, or five days
west since we didn't run at night. McCoy, cradling his popgun, sat
on the roof of the cabin with whichever of us wasn't walking the
towpath with the mules and we scoured the woods and swamps
and breaks of open country for signs of Indians. McCoy said he
doubted they would look different from us—like, not to expect
breechcloths, feathers, and whatnot—but we didn't see any groups
of men that looked like marauding Indians, or rogues, or pickers,
or anything of the sort. We passed several eastbound boats along
the way and they didn't report anything out of the ordinary either.

The canal crossed a quiet part of the Genesee River several
miles south of Rochester. It originally traversed the river in the
center of town on an aqueduct, but they took an easier route
in the rebuild of 1912. The city had been especially hard hit by
disease in recent years and was in the throes just then, we heard,
of a meningitis scare, so McCoy didn't dare visit, and we passed
on south of it. And then, once you're west of Rochester, there's
little but farm country and a few tiny hamlets the rest of the way
to the five-step locks. We heard no more talk of Indians after
that. We just fell back into the easy rhythm of the days and the
early June weather, all beauty and peacefulness walking with the
mules and watching the world go by. I tell you, I liked that life
on the canal except for what happened next.

We arrived at the end of the line, Lockport, where the Niagara Escarpment forms the last barrier to the lakes. It was the

center of a fruit-growing district, and had the canal traffic and the construction works, so it was not so run-down as these other places. And it was active with people. We offloaded the last of McCoy's cargo and he took us as promised to the offices of the superintendent of the locks. We could see men laboring down there on our way into the building, moving big stone blocks on wooden cranes with machinery driven by oxen yoked to rotaries, gangs of men digging and moving earth, scaffolds everywhere. It was impressive, the grandest work I ever remember seeing since I was a little child in the old times when everything was done by motor machines. The hall outside the super's office was busy, men coming and going, foremen, laborers, riggers, tradesmen, jobbers, boatmen. It had the aura of excitement, of men working on a thing with purpose, which gave me the thought for the first time that something might be coming up in this country instead of running down, and I was thrilled at the chance to be part of it. Evan, too. He expected all along that they would be paying good wages in hard cash because labor was scarce, especially among our age group that had suffered so much in the epidemics.

So there we are in the hall before the super's office, and McCoy confabs with a man seated at a desk, who's nodding, and I figure that means they need men. So he disappears for a bit and comes back out and by and by ushers the three of us in to see Mr. Farnum, the super. It was a nice big office, too, with a view of the works and wooden models of the locks on a big table. Two other men stood at another table fussing with some metal apparatus of chains and plates I assumed was machinery for the locks. Farnum came out from behind his desk all cheerful to see Randall McCoy, his old crony. He was even bigger and broader than McCoy, with a handsome drooping mustache and even better pattern-cut clothes than McCoy, and he gave off that glow of authority you sense about men used to telling others what to do. They did a man hug with backslapping and all.

Farnum's like, "Look what you brought me, you bobtailed sonofabitch of a gondolier!"

He looks Evan and me up and down and pinches our flesh a little, all smiley, and makes a kind chortling laugh with his teeth clenched, manfully, to show how great it is to have us on board, like we were new members of a select club. McCoy joined in admiring us and said we were good boys and strong, willing workers and all. And this goes on just long enough so that I get this . . . funny feeling, and I guess Evan picked it up too.

Then, Farnum goes to his desk and takes a steel box out of a drawer and unlocks it with a key on a chain he's wearing around his neck and takes a bunch of silver coin out of the box, stacks it up on his desk, sweeps it into his hand, and gives it to McCoy. We're watching all this.

Evan goes, "Mr. McCoy says you have employment for us."

Farnum's like, "Oh, I've got work for you, all right."

Evan goes, "Okay, what's the pay like?"

Farnum goes, "Fifty dollars in hard silver."

I go, "Fifty each?"

Farnum's like, "No, twenty-five apiece."

Evan goes, "For what? The week? The month?"

Farnum laughs. "No, that's what I pay Mr. McCoy here."

That bad feeling I had turns sickening.

Evan's like, "Well, what are you paying *him* for? That's supposed to be our money."

Farnum goes, "He just sold your indenture to me."

Evan's like, "What the hell's that?"

Meanwhile, those two dudes in the back grab that iron off the table and start toward us, and it's clear to me, like the air in the room had powers of magnification, what's going on.

I go to McCoy, "You sold us?"

He's just beaming like he pulled off the world's best practical joke.

"I guess I did," he goes, and busts out laughing.

Evan's carrying on, "What's this mean! What's he saying? What's this about?"

The two other men approach us with what I can see are leg irons and chains. Farnum steps closer to us.

I can feel that automatic pistol lodged right in the small of my back, under my shirt, and I fast yank it out and rack the frame. Farnum backs off at once, with his wrists snapped back and up, and the others stop in their tracks. We're all just standing there, eyeballs jumping around from one to the next for what seems like forever but probably no more than ten seconds.

"Aw, boys," McCoy finally says, like we disappointed him.

"It ain't loaded, I'm sure," Farnum says. "Give it here to me, we'll forget all this and you can go right to work, today."

I'm like, "Forget it, we're leaving. Go stand in that corner and turn around facing the wall."

Farnum's like, "Well, we're not going to do that, sonny. Are you going to shoot us, then?"

I'm like, "Maybe I will." I actually wasn't thinking that far ahead. And God knows I never had to think about shooting anyone before. But he did put the idea in my mind and I was quickly coming to the conclusion that I might have to pull the trigger.

Evan goes, "Don't shoot Mr. McCoy."

I'm like, "I won't shoot anybody if they just go stand in the corner and turn around and let us leave peacefully."

So it's a standoff. Apparently, none of them are armed. Who carries a gun around these days in places of common business?

Farnum goes, "Where'd you get the piece?"

"Does it matter?" I say. "Get in the goddamn corner and turn your face to the wall."

He's like, "I'm not going to do that, sonny." He's remarkably calm, at least on the surface, though I can sense the wheels turning in his brain and I'm pretty sure he's just trying to buy a little time. He goes, "You can't get store ammunition these days. That thing ain't loaded." He takes a step toward me, now with his hand out. "Give it over here to me." He extends one hand and makes little flicks with his fingertips.

I tell him, "Back off and go to your corner like I said."

McCoy stands his ground too, with that big disappointed look on his face and his hands on his hips.

"I won't ask you again," I say.

"Don't shoot 'em!" Evan is begging me. It distracts me for a moment. Farnum sees an opening and lunges at me and I pull the trigger and he drops like a sack of meal, groaning on the floor. We can still hear the sound of hammers banging and construction out the open window, a real din out there. The two other company men drop those shackles and hurry into the corner, saying, "Don't shoot," and like that. McCoy is just gaping at me.

"You shot him, you green-gilled gutter punk," McCoy says.

"I'll shoot you too," I say. "Hand over all that coin you sold us for and then go lay down in front of that desk."

McCoy goes, "Do what?"

"You heard me. Give that money to Evan."

He does, sneering, and goes, "You're just a pair of common thieves."

I kick him in the balls and swiftly down he goes, vomiting up whatever he ate for lunch. I tell Evan to take whatever coin remains in that metal box. One of the two dudes in the corner tries to peek around at McCoy squealing and Farnum groaning. It appears I shot Farnum in the gut. He's all curled up on the floor clutching his midsection with blood all over his hands and his vest. I go and tip the desk over onto McCoy so he's pinned to the floor. I smash one of the company men on the side of the head with the flat part of the pistol and the other fellow crumples too. I think he just fainted. All this happened faster than I'm even able to tell it.

Then I'm like, "Come on!" to Evan and he follows me rushing out of the place. We bust through into the hall with all its hangers-on still there. I suppose they heard the shot because they're all stock still, gawking at us, and all their heads turn as we dash out the door.

Once we're outside, Evan's going, "O shit, O shit, O shit, O shit" all the way to where we're headed, which is Randall McCoy's boat. It's barely a hundred yards away from the super's building. We're there in about ten seconds. Quickly as I can I take the hobbles off the piebald mule in the bow, that's Beans, and Evan does like I'm doing with Shadow, the black one. They're wearing their halters and I grab the lead lines and tie them crosswise 'round my shoulder and under my arm. I give Evan a boost to mount Shadow and then climb aboard Beans, using the gunwale to mount, and we bust across the gangway onto the towpath bareback on the mules.

By now, we could see that the super's office is in a state of alarm. Men are coming out the portico, pointing at us, shouting. I squeeze off another shot into the roof and they all dash back inside like bugs into a rotten log. Then we gallop off, ride up the slope, to the canal towpath on the plateau up there heading west toward Buffalo.

We rode like hell for a quarter of an hour, I guess, and found a quiet place to let the mules drink.

"This money is making my pants fall down it's so heavy," Evan says.

"Well give me some," I say.

"Sure," he goes, "but we'll count it out later and split it even, right?"

It kind of dismays me that he's talking like we were a couple of common thieves, but he had a point and I wanted to calm him down because he was obviously in a half-hysterical state. So I go, "Of course, we'll split it even."

"You shot that man," Evan said, with something like admiration.

I go, "Evan, listen to me. We're not going to talk about it anymore, never again. As far as you and me are concerned it never happened."

"Well sure it happened—"

I grab him by the front of his shirt and pull him right up to my face. He's slighter than me and the age difference matters, I guess, and he doesn't resist. "You just forget about it and act like it never happened. Especially if we're around other people."

"Okay," he says. "What are we going to do now?"

I let go of his shirt. This was the first time I'd actually thought about it in all the excitement. McCoy had told us about Buffalo. He'd been there. It had a lively waterfront district, he said, and received all kinds of trade goods from around the lakes. I told Evan we'd go there and figure something out.

He goes, "Won't they be looking for us?"

"I expect they will be. Now give over some of that coin to me and let's get moving."

Evan pulls it out of his pockets and dumps handfuls into mine. I notice there's some yellow coins mixed in with the silver.

"Goddammit," I go, "there's gold mixed in with this."

"Huh?" Evan goes and he's finally seeing it. "Goddammit, you're right!"

We counted the gold. Fifteen half-ounce and three tenth-of-an-ounce coins. Plus all that silver.

"Goddammit," Evan goes. "We're rich."

At that moment I knew exactly what we were going to do when we got to Buffalo.

"I'm awfully thirsty, and hungry, too," Daniel said.

Loren flinched as though he had awakened from a trance. He had been leaning forward hanging on Daniel's every word.

"The corn bread's done," Sara said. "And so's the pudding."

By pudding she meant what had, in the old times, been called scalloped potatoes au gratin with bacon. In the new times, just about everything baked in a casserole with cream and often cheese was called pudding.

Thirty-two

Brother Jobe, the prosecutor appointed by the magistrate Bullock in the murder case of Rick and Julian Stokes, agreed to meet the defense attorney Sam Hutto that evening and suggested his Union Tavern as the place. Since the tavern had opened, the novelty had begun to wear off, but half a dozen men lingered at the bar enjoying their whiskey, cider, and tobacco, all of them townsmen, none of the New Faith. Brother Jobe sat alone in a booth in the back room, where the other tables were otherwise unoccupied at that hour, about half past eight. While he waited, he scribbled in a book of foolscap paper by candlelight with a pencil stub in an attempt to compose his sermon for the coming Sunday, always a chore. The pony glass of Coot Hill applejack on the table made the chore a little easier, as it filled him with a sense of gratitude for being, and his appreciation for the forces greater than himself responsible for it. This week's message would be based on the use of the word "mystery" in the book of Ephesians, credited to Paul the Apostle. Faith is a mystery at its core, he mused, but mysteries are still for real.

Just as he wondered whether this was an original thought, he looked up upon hearing the front door open and close. Brother Micah, the tavern manager, had hung a set of sleigh bells on the door. Sam Hutto, lanky and long, a man people said was born sad-looking, dusted some snowflakes off his slouch hat, spotted Brother Jobe in the rear, and strode to the booth.

"Evening, counselor," Brother Jobe said and waved a hand at Brother Micah. "You got some discovery for me?"

"I do."

"Well, have a durned seat."

"You did a nice job in here," Sam said, looking all around the place. "I remember when it was a drugstore."

"How come you ain't been in till now."

"I don't drink," Sam said. "Anymore."

"Oh . . . ?" By now, Brother Micah had come over to the table. "What can I get you gentlemen?"

"You can give me another," Brother Jobe said. "Esteemed counsel here is teetotal. Think you can scare up a pot of tea for him?"

"Mint all right?" Brother Micah said. "It's alls we got."

"Sure."

"And if sister is still in the kitchen," Brother Jobe said, "ask her to send out a basket of tater tots." Then, to Sam, "We make 'em ourself. Taste just like the real ones used to. Our ketchup brand's coming along too. Before you know it, it'll be just like old-timey times around here."

Brother Micah scurried off back to the kitchen.

"What have you got for me?" Brother Jobe said, looking over his reading glasses, his voice returning to its lower business tone.

"It appears Mr. Einhorn's chore boy saw Mrs. Stokes shaking her baby out on the street the night of the murders."

"Yeah? What's that mean?"

"Possibly that she shook him to death. Shaken baby syndrome. It's well known. And consistent with Dr. Copeland's autopsy report."

Brother Jobe reflected while he sipped his jack.

"That ain't good for your client."

"Nope. But I'm bound by law to tell you in case you haven't heard it yourself yet."

"That boy's a half-wit, ain't he?"

"He's Down syndrome, actually."

"How'd this come to light?"

"A bunch was down at Einhorn's store talking about the murders. The boy, Buddy, was around and he weighed in, so to speak, on something he saw out on the street that night. He lives in a room back of the store and he often sits outside at night, even in winter. You're going to have to depose him."

"Is he credible, this boy? I ain't never deposed a half-wit."

"He's an adult. More or less functional. Reads and writes a little. Does some simple figures. I suppose the others would corroborate they heard what he said, though. It's your call."

"Well, I got some discovery for you too," Brother Jobe said. Brother Micah came by the table with a pot of mint tea, a mug, a honey jar, and the basket of tidbits composed of deep-fried cornmeal and potato with a little dish of sweet red sauce to go with it. Brother Jobe took the first one, and several more. "I can't get enough of these ding-danged things. This place was a pizza parlor for many a year, you know."

"Oh, I know," Sam said, pouring his tea.

"'Course you would. Well, we're working on a pizza recipe. You know how hard it is to get wheat flour. And Bullock's so durned stingy with that spelt he grows. Let's face it, corn bread just don't make much of a pizza."

"Yes, we all miss real pizza," Sam said. "You say you got some discovery for me?"

"The Stokes gal was in here the night of the murders."

"I think we know that already."

"Yeah, well, I got a boy was working in the kitchen that night, young Brother Enos, says he was taking a bucket of swill out back in the alley and caught Miz Stokes in a carnal congress with a town man in the box of the horse truck, baby all bundled up there beside it on the ground, crying all the while. It don't make her look too good."

Sam sipped his tea, ruminating.

Brother Jobe continued. "Enos can identify the fellow. Says he's in here most nights since we opened. Farmhand over to Larmon's. I'll find and depose the sumbitch."

Sam tried a tater tot. He was surprised how good it tasted, how forcefully the taste projected him into the past. The two men both foraged in the basket silently for several minutes.

"Ain't they tasty?" Brother Jobe said.

"They're quite good," Sam said. "I have every intention of pleading Mrs. Stokes insane."

"The burden of proof is on you-all," Brother Jobe said.

"She was very sick, you know. The brain fever."

"I do know."

"She's probably not competent to stand trial."

"I intend to have that conversation with our magistrate, for what it's worth," Brother Jobe said, then knocked back the rest of his applejack. "It seems to me that Mr. Bullock's in a hanging mood these days. Much as I think we need to see justice done around here—and just between the two of us, off the record—I don't think hanging this poor girl is the right way to go."

THIRTY-THREE

Daniel finished eating and put his plate aside. The others—Loren, Jane Ann, Britney, and Robert—remained in their seats in the parlor, the warm air in the room fraught with dreadful expectation. Sarah sat at a remove in the inglenook across the room, practicing her handwriting with one of the manufactured pencils that had become increasingly scarce and valuable.

"Yeah, this part is hard," Daniel said. "I apologize in advance."

Jane Ann and Loren knew what that meant and shared a nervous glance.

Daniel's Story: On Board the *Kerry McKinney*

We got to Buffalo by midafternoon. I figured they'd be looking for Randall McCoy's mules as much as for us, so we abandoned them in a plowed field in what I suppose was once a city park. There was a statue on a granite pedestal that the farmer had plowed around. Evan had to go over and see who it was of. Grover Cleveland, it turned out, a long ago president. The corn was about as high as your ankle. We walked on from there. We'd left our packs and all our stuff behind on McCoy's canal boat, of course, so we weren't burdened by anything.

Buffalo was the biggest city I'd ever been in, but there wasn't much of it left alive even once you got well into it. Most of the streets of houses appeared to be long abandoned, weeds and shrub trees growing in the old front yards, things hanging off everywhere, shutters, rain gutters, plastic siding, a lot of broken windows, hardly anyone around except some pickers going for the last scraps. The old business district with the tall buildings was vacant too. But closer to the lake you started to see some activity and some streets of close-together new wooden buildings, shoulder to shoulder, and finally a broad street on the waterfront with all kinds of businesses going.

There was a kind of man-made harbor there with a stone jetty that hooked around out about a quarter mile, and a lot of docks and slips with boats, the biggest sailboats I ever saw, and tall wooden structures along the shore where corn and grain that came in from far away across the other lakes were stored. There were lots of people, too, working around the docks, moving cargo on hand trucks and horse trucks, and an open-air market under a big wooden shed roof with farmers selling the first early crops, radishes and greens and mushrooms and cheeses and fishes, whatever they brought in. Evan and I had a stupid argument about whether the big water out there beyond the jetty was Lake Ontario or Lake Erie. It was Erie, of course. One thing amazed me: you couldn't see across it.

We'd talked along the way about what we might do when we got to Buffalo, being a couple of desperate characters on the run, and I came up with the idea to buy a boat and just get the hell out of that part of the country to somewhere they wouldn't even be looking for us. Evan went along with it. I admit, it seemed a little sketchy until we saw what was going on at the Buffalo lakefront and all of a sudden I was sure we really could do it.

There were two big new wooden hotels on Front Street, the Niagara and the Eagle. We agreed it would not be smart for us to go around being seen together since they'd be looking for a pair of desperados, so we decided to split up and each stay the night at a separate hotel. We agreed to meet up the next morning at the restaurant on the same street called O'Brian's Meals and then just sail away, nice and easy. It was my job to go search around the docks for a suitable boat to buy because I was a year and a half older than Evan and supposedly I knew more about such things, which I didn't, really. Anyway, there was only one sticky problem. I had to ask Evan to give me his share of the gold because I didn't know yet how much I'd have to pay for a boat, but I figured it could be a lot. I didn't even know what kind of a boat we would get, except it had to be something the two of us could handle.

In the meantime, Evan's all upset about handing over his gold. He goes, "What if while we're split up they capture you and take you in custody with all our money?"

I'm like, "I don't know. If that happens, you better run like hell and hide out and maybe try to get back home."

Evan's like, "I'm not ready to go back home. But if I still had my share of the gold, then I could buy a boat of my own and make a getaway."

I'm like, "Hey, lookit, before you did anything you have to try to bust me out of jail."

He goes, "I don't even know where the jail is."

"Well, I guess you could ask somebody, huh?"

"What! And risk getting captured busting you out? No way . . ."

I grab him by his shirt and drag him around the corner to a little alley between two buildings. I draw out the pistol and press it into his hand.

"Here, you take this," I say. "If I get captured, use it to bust me out. And if they come after you, use it to save yourself."

He just gawks at it in his hand like it's the most amazing object he ever saw.

"Put it away, goddammit," I tell him. "Tuck it in your pants and wear your shirt over it like I do."

He does. Then he's like, "It's still loaded, right?"

"Of course it is," I go. "So don't take it out or mess around with it unless you're in a serious jam, okay?"

He's like, "Okay."

"You trust me a little more with the money now?"

He's like, "I guess so."

I'm like, "You go get a room over there at the Niagara. You've got enough silver for that, I'm sure. Take a quiet dinner by yourself and don't talk to any strangers. No girls either. Not tonight. You meet me at nine o'clock in the morning at that meals place over there and I will have a boat ready for us to sail away on."

He goes, "What about food and stuff for the boat?"

"I'll take care of that."

"Don't forget maps," he says, and finally hands over all his share of the gold coins.

I was glad he mentioned maps because it hadn't occurred to me. But I didn't tell him that. I just go, "Of course."

So that's where we split up. I went down to the docks intent on finding a boat. There were about a dozen separate boatyards in that harbor aside from the public docks and slips. These were businesses that repaired boats, ones that built new ones, and others that outfitted them. I looked around at a lot of boats, trying to get an idea of what was on offer. The ones for sale all had signs on them saying, "Inquire at So-and-So's office," with no prices posted. I figured you had to go in and bargain over it. While poking around I kept my questions to a minimum so as not to show how little I knew about boats. I learned a lot just looking around.

There were many very pretty boats, some of them grand. Who doesn't like sailboats? I began to look for how they were rigged to get a clue whether two men could handle them. Many were old-times boats, built just for the pleasure of sailing around to nowhere in particular for no good reason. They had hulls made out of plastic that you'd have a hard time fixing if anything happened to them, and they had complicated riggings and they didn't have much room for cargoes. They were designed for a sleek look that didn't have much practical value in these times. The idea began to form in my mind that we should have a boat that you could carry a lot of stuff on, like McCoy's canal boat, but with sails, that we could go into business once we got somewhere far away enough to feel safe and where we could transport freight from one town to another. I went into several offices of the boatyard managers and inquired about boats and even started bargaining to get the feel. I'd make them pitch an opening price, even when they tried to goad me to make an offer first. We established that all prices were hard money and I did the arithmetic in my head.

It was getting to be evening when I found the boat for us. It was a broad-beamed, twenty-eight-foot long, nearly flat-bottomed cargo scow, all wood with leeboards instead of a keel or centerboard, what they called junk-type sails, light canvas with battens all through, easy for reefing in high winds, with a big sail forward and smaller in the rear, the stern, I learned to say, what Mr. Fourier, the boatyard owner, called a ketch rig. The hull was painted dark green with red trim. There was room below for four to sleep and a galley with an alcohol stove and a table bolted to the floor. The toilet was a little room with a steel basin that you had to take on deck and dump over the side. In the old times, Fourier said, they had machines that sucked all the nasty stuff out of a storage tank when you got into port, but nowadays it was just over the side with it. I was getting more and more interested in this boat. She was boxy and homely and looked pretty simple to run and I fell in love with her. Her name on the transom was *Pearl,* but I decided to rename her *Kerry McKinney* in honor of that girl I loved in Starkville who died of the cholera just before I left home.

Then Fourier and I got down to the haggle in his office, which was a nice room with maps and stuffed fish on the walls and big windows where you could see the evening sun hanging above the jetty. He seemed skeptical at first but eventually he understood that I meant business.

"What do you intend to do with her?" he asks.

I'm like, "Why, sail the great inland sea and carry some cargoes and have a life on the water."

"It's not such an easy life," he says.

"I can always sell her if I get sick of it," I say.

"I guess you can at that," he goes. "Well, a hunnert fifty-five will do it."

He meant ounces of silver. I jawed him down finally to a hundred forty.

"Will gold do?" I say.

His eyes bugged out. "If that's alls you got," he goes, twiddling his beard and chuckling.

Because of spending that time around Randall McCoy doing trade, I knew what the conversion was. We settled for six ounces. That left us with three half-ounce plus three tenth-of-an-ounce gold coins and a good bit of silver. We'd still be rich.

Fourier's like, "Mind if I ask how a young dude such as yourself come into such a treasure?"

"My dad was a gold bug in the old times," I say. "One of those ones that didn't trust paper money."

The others in the room all glanced at Robert Earle, who immediately said, "Well, that's bullshit, of course."

"It was just something I heard you talk about once long ago," Daniel said, "the year the banks shut down."

Anyway, Fourier says, "You're a rich boy, then?"

I'm like, "Well, since you asked."

He goes, "You look like a damn picker."

I try not to appear insulted. Or nervous. I'm like, "It's hard traveling these days."

He's like, "I assume you rode to Buffalo in comfort."

I'm like, "Indeed I did, sir. And I aim to sell my horse here. Are you interested, by any chance, in a fine seven-year-old mare?" I'm bluffing of course.

"Nope," he says and spits into a mug on the desk. "But you might try Arnold Fluke over to Genesee Street."

I'm like, "Would you write that down along with a bill of sale for the *Pearl*?"

"Yessir," Fourier says. "And for a change of clothes I recommend Salter's Dry Goods right up there on Front Street."

"Why, thank you," I go. "I'll stop there on my way to the hotel."

He's like, "Which one are you at?"

"The Eagle," I tell him, foolishly, and immediately regret it. Suddenly this conversation is making me nauseous, despite the fact that I haven't eaten anything since early morn, east of Lockport. I'm trying my damndest to sound breezy and cheerful after a long day of tribulations. "Is she ready to go, as is, the *Pearl*?" I ask. "I'd like to set sail tomorrow, late morning, let's say."

"She's shipshape," he says. "Turnkey, so to speak."

He's got a big framed map of the lake on the wall. I drift over to look at it and ask him where I can get some maps like it. He corrects me, "Charts, you mean?"

"Of course," I go. "Charts."

"I sell charts," he says. "The Great Lakes series will run you two ounces of silver."

I don't aim to bargain over it. I just want to get the hell out of there. I'm like, "I'll take the set. I'd like to study them in my room tonight." So he pulls a bunch of these charts from a big flat file and ties them up in a roll with twine, then hands me the bill of sale for the boat and everything. We settle up. I give him a bunch of our gold. I've got plenty of coins left on me. I notice him hearing it all jingle in my pocket. I turn to leave, finally.

Fourier goes, "You plan to set sail by your lonely?"

"My cousin is meeting me here tomorrow morning."

"Oh, where's he from?"

I glance up at the map on the wall again. I can see the towns near the shore of Lake Erie. I go, "Down in Hamburg." It's a few miles south of Buffalo.

"You don't say? I'm from Hamburg," Fourier goes. "What's his name, your cousin?"

"Uh, Perry Talisker," I say. It just popped into my head, the name of that river rat we call the Hermit. I just figured nobody would know him, hundreds of miles from Union Grove.

"Don't know any Taliskers," he says. "You sure he's from Hamburg, New York? It's not much of a town anymore."

I'm still fixed on the map. I go, "Perry, he just manages some family property there. He's learning to farm."

"What sort of farm?"

"Fruit," I go. It was a wild guess based on what we saw in the vicinity coming west. Fourier takes it in, though. I can't wait to get out of there. "The family's actually from . . . East Aurora." That's another town I spot on the map.

"It used to be a rich town in the old times," he says. "Doctors and lawyers. Is he a rich boy, too, your cousin?"

I turn around and look him straight in the eye and say, "I was taught it's not polite to brag about such things. Especially now when times are so difficult for so many."

"It ain't bragging if it's true," he says, tugging his whiskers again.

I'm like, "We've got enough to buy a boat and go into business, sir, and that's what we aim to do. It was a pleasure trading with you. She's a fine boat. I'm going to rename her after a sweetheart of mine back home that died of the cholera just three months ago. Now, if you don't mind, I need to go purchase some provisions for tomorrow before the shops close on Front Street."

"They're open till nine in the evening," he says. "People come here from miles around to trade on Friday night. You'll be all right."

"Sweet," I say. "And thank you. I'll be back here around nine, ten o'clock tomorrow morning."

"With your cousin?"

"Yessir, with my cousin."

"What about that farm, then?"

"The farm?" I say, caught off guard.

"Yeah. Who's going to manage that farm?"

"Oh, his brother Jerry is taking over that position," I say.

Fourier stares at me for a moment. "Perry and Jerry," he goes. "That's downright tuneful."

"You know how folks are. See you tomorrow morning," I say, pleasantly, on my way out.

"See you then," he goes.

I thought I might puke from nerves, on an empty stomach no less, but finally I can leave. It's a mild evening out, though, and when I get up there Front Street is busy, but I couldn't relax and enjoy it. It was weighing on my mind that I'd told Fourier I was staying at the Eagle Hotel because there was a pretty good chance that people would be coming after us. I felt foolish for not minding the urgency of our situation until then, but I was intent on getting that boat. So I decided right there, on the front porch of Salter's store, with its lamps just lit on each side of the big front door, that we would not spend the night in Buffalo after all, that we would shove off in the *Kerry McKinney* that night, and that I would hurry up and get what provisions I could to last us just a few days on the water before we had enough distance out of Buffalo to land and resupply.

Salter's was a cut above Einhorn's store, I can tell you—nothing against Mr. Einhorn—but they had all the goods you could ever want, even a wall of books from the old times. I bought a big slab of bacon, hunk of cheese, hard sausage, five-pound sacks of onions and potatoes, honey, jam, butter, applejack, licorice candy, salt, hot pepper sauce, fish hooks and line, blankets, candles, matches, alcohol for the stove, a bucket and some rope, and two books—because they were famous and very long and would last us a long time, reading them out loud in the evenings for entertainment when we anchored somewhere: *Moby-Dick* and *War and Peace*. Altogether I'd spent nearly seven ounces of silver. I had to buy sailcloth totes to carry the provisions in as well and made two trips from the store to the boatyard to stow it all aboard. Night was falling. No light burned in Fourier's office. I didn't want to see any more of him.

Then I went back to find Evan at the Niagara. I inquired at the desk and the woman there sent me to a third-floor room, but he wasn't there. He wasn't in the hotel dining room either, or at O'Brian's Meals down the street, so I went back to the Niagara. He still wasn't in his room. It was going on nine o'clock. I got so angry I thought of setting sail without him, but I just couldn't do it, leave him there, him being younger and sort of my responsibility. Then I happened to glance in the Niagara barroom and, what do you know, there he was sitting at a card table with four other men, his back to the front window. He also had on new clothes, including a linen sack coat and a fine cotton shirt, which is how come I didn't know him when I'd peeked in from the street. He had little stacks of silver coins on the green cloth tabletop. I went over just as he was winning a hand of poker and bent down and whispered in his ear: "What the hell did I tell you about going out and about?" The other players shot me dirty looks. I smiled back pleasantly. I notice there's a glass next to Evan's elbow with whiskey in it, just like the others. Me and him, we're trying to argue in whispers.

Evan goes, "I was bored out of my mind in the room, and it was hot up there."

I go, "You're goddamn immature. Come on. We're going."

"But I'm on a hot streak," he says.

"I don't care," I say.

One of the other players, a workman from his burly looks and clothes, complains about me disturbing the game. I have to yank Evan out of his chair.

"He's going," I explain.

"Who the hell are you, anyway," says another player, who has a narrow, toothy face like a human crocodile.

"I'm his big brother come to take him home," I say.

"He's got our money," Crocodile says.

"I won it," Evan says.

"He's got to give us a chance to win it back," says a third man.

"I won it fair and square," Evan says.

I'm like, "I'm sorry, but we've got to go."

"You can't do that," says Crocodile.

"It's a free country," Evan says. He's drunk, I'm sure.

"It ain't a country anymore, kid. It's Buffalo and Buffalo rules."

Just then, I notice through the window six men on fine horses canter up to the front of the Eagle Hotel, across and up the street a little ways from us. Two of them hurry up the front steps of the Eagle. The others wait in the saddle cradling rifles. They're looking all around as if they're searching Front Street. Just seeing them I'm sure it's us they're looking for. The memory of Farnum curled up on the floor of his office oozing blood all over his hands flashes through my mind and I'm afraid I must have killed him after all.

Evan scoops his money off the table and gets most of it into his pocket, but I'm man-handling him and a few coins fall down and ring on the floor. He scrambles around down there to get them. I practically drag him out of the room. When we're out of earshot of the poker players, I'm like, "I just saw a bunch of men ride up in front of the Eagle. I bought us a boat and we're getting out of here right now. You hear me?" I give him a shake and, being smaller, he stops resisting me. He smells like a distillery. He has to keep hiking up his new pants, the coins are weighing him down so. I tell him to follow me.

We steal out the barroom, across the front room where the hotel desk is, and into the restaurant on the other side. I figure there's a back door through the kitchen and indeed there is. Evan follows me. The cooks and bottle washers are all occupied and barely notice us passing through. We slip out into the side alley. I can see two of the mounted men are still out there on the street, minding the horses, which tells me maybe two more of them have gone into the Niagara where we just came from. I tell Evan to watch where I go and to follow twenty yards behind me, like we're not together. I creep out of the alley onto Front Street and hurry down toward the boat basin. The sun has set and there are no streetlights. As far as I can tell nobody has noticed me. Once I'm down by the docks, I jog toward Fourier's slips. I turn around and see Evan coming. I'm on the dock waiting.

I go, "I ought to thrash you for that, you goddamn fool." I drag him over to where the *Kerry McKinney* is tied up. Of course, it still says *Pearl* on the transom.

He's like, "Is this the boat you bought?"

"Yes it is," I say. "Get aboard. We're shoving off."

He's like, "We can't see anything out there on the water. Maybe we should wait until day."

"Didn't you hear me?" I go. "There's men back there in town looking for us."

He goes, "This boat is ugly as a pig."

Finally I just lose my patience and shove him into the cockpit where he lands with a thud and a loud jingle of silver and a cry of pain when he splits his lip. I free up the mooring lines, shove us off, and leap aboard. There's no wind but there's a long sculling oar lashed to the cabin wall and it fits into a cleat on the transom. You push it back and forth and the boat moves clear of its slip. It's a bit clumsy working our way out. We bump into other boats, but before long we're clear of the slips. Evan is sobbing. I tell him to shut up. I can dimly see the rise of the jetty that encloses the basin and I follow along it, sculling in the darkness. It looks like someone has lighted a lamp in a building back at the slips just as we get to the tip of the jetty. I scull around it heading down the back side of it into the open water of Lake Erie. The jetty is a hump of rock and fill standing maybe ten feet above the waterline. Where we are, behind it, it blocks out Front Street and the boatyards and the lamps of town are no longer visible, just a million stars above, but I can hear some shouting from back on shore. I know from having studied the map on Fourier's wall which way is which. Running down the back side of the jetty, I'm sure we're headed south following the lakeshore, toward Pennsylvania and Ohio. I didn't want to go north and get anywhere near the Niagara River and its current, which would take us over the famous falls and surely to our death.

Evan had stopped blubbering and was now apologizing drunkenly over and over. Once we were out into Lake Erie proper, a breeze came up and a quarter moon was rising over the darkened land so you could see things again. I told Evan how to raise the small stern sail at the rear of the cockpit. He stumbled around in the dark, but finally he figured it out and raised the sail. We didn't bother with the larger forward sail. Moments later, you could hear the water purling against the hull as the breeze pushed the boat forward at a very modest pace. I stowed the sculling oar and took the wheel, which was on the right side of the companionway into the cabin. The *Kerry McKinney* felt very safe and trustworthy and I was now a sailor on the Great Lakes. I was sure we had just barely escaped getting captured there in Buffalo, and very likely hanged. I was sorry I killed Mr. Farnum, if that's what happened, but I would not be sold into an indentured slavery. And if that was the normal way of things now in the country, I was opposed to it, even if that made me an outlaw.

I kept the dark shore in view at all times. The moon rose higher in the sky and I could see the outline of the treetops and even hear the little waves breaking on the shore. We coasted along it, a few hundred yards off land, until the last vestige of the city of Buffalo was far behind us. Evan had crawled off into the cabin. I was starving, but there was nothing I could do about it. Some time later—I don't know how long—I lowered the sail and let the little waves push us closer to the shore. The moon was high and bright now and there was nothing but woods there. I went up to the bow and gently lowered the anchor over. It went down maybe ten feet to the bottom and grabbed. When I was sure we were anchored fast, I crept downstairs. I could hear Evan breathing on one of the bunks. Moonlight came through the portholes and the transom windows of the cupola above. I rummaged through our totes for the cheese and hard sausage and devoured a fair portion of our store. It was growing chill out on the water. I found the blankets and put one over Evan. Then I curled up on the other front bunk and went to sleep.

THIRTY-FOUR

Jack Harron lay awake in the darkness in his room behind the kitchen in Andrew Pendergast's house, his mind roiling with perturbations about the order of the universe and his place in it. He felt grateful and aggrieved at the same time and he could not sort out his feelings, nor understand why a mysterious fate had chosen to place him in the company of his new . . . the word "master" resonated in his head. He saw himself as something like a dog. Andrew, as Jack was instructed to call him, trained him relentlessly all day long, one task after another, things that he had seen other people do, things that he had never troubled himself to learn, things he had no prior conception of doing: how to clean a kitchen with vinegar; how to polish silver with salt and alkali made from burnt wood ashes; how to make corn bread (properly); how to dress a turkey; how to beat a rug (he'd never heard of it before); how to grind the pigments that Andrew used in his artistic endeavors; how to take apart a mechanical clock (though not yet how to put it together); how to use the scores of tools Andrew had carefully collected before the old times suddenly became the new times, and countless other things that Jack had also never considered before.

He was confused but not sure he still felt broken, in the way he had during those desperate days before Christmas—in need of being fixed. He was confused about feeling tied down to a place and to another person and about what otherwise might be his lot if he wasn't tied down but cast back into a world that seemed utterly without kindness, fairness, or meaning. He wondered what sort of world this was where people could have masters, just like dogs used to have masters, when people owned dogs. Maybe this was what people did now, in the new times, lacking dogs. He was confused about liking the attention and care that Andrew showed him in teaching him how to do things, but he dreaded the moment he was sure lay ahead, maybe days, perhaps weeks, when Andrew would venture to touch him in a personal way that would offend his manhood, for everybody knew the sort of person Andrew Pendergast was.

He also began to suspect that his fears about the world—which before had seemed set, as though he were constantly surrounded by a circle of scary totem poles planted in the ground, designed to remind him at all times that the world was a frightful place—might be subject to revision. He was no longer so certain, for instance, that the world was unkind, unfair, and devoid of meaning. He took the example of Andrew, who so casually assumed the task of Jack's redemption and was going about it in a way that appeared to be kind, fair, even generous. And Jack had glimpsed inklings of meaning and purpose in the tasks that Andrew had put him on to. He saw how a job of work defined a chunk of time and, when it was completed satisfactorily, made that time spent seem worthwhile, and when it worked out so he felt an ease in his mind to which he was unaccustomed. There were duties he looked forward to and enjoyed, especially tasks in the kitchen, where it was warm, and there was always something to eat, or a cup of tea with honey, and Andrew gave Jack the impression that he was welcome to eat what he wanted from the larder, if it was not prepared for guests. He even discovered pleasure and satisfaction in routine chores such as splitting stove billets, visiting the chickens morning and evening with their rations of cracked corn, and setting out new candles. Andrew Pendergast was the richest person Jack had ever known in mysterious ways that went beyond his possessions and whatever treasure he had.

Jack was lonely, of course, in the sense of longing for the comforting touch of a woman. But though he dreamed of it, he considered himself still hopelessly unworthy. He had not been with a female since his year at the community college, when his entanglement with a girl named Debbi DiCiccio propelled him into the disgusting circus of her troubled relatives, with their addictions, hatreds, jealousies, morbid interests, evil motives, and illnesses. It ended one night when Debbi, high on weed and painkillers, smacked him with the butt end of a pool cue for casually saying her uncle Matt was a child molester, which was just a statement of fact, because he had been in Comstock prison for four years. She was the first real girlfriend he ever had and the liberty of her body was like being let into the Garden of Eden to him, but he was afraid she might kill him next time. Since then, with the college shut down, and all the other touchstones of normality now things of the past, his day-to-day life had been too desperate and miserable for even the thought of romance. There was something fundamentally unromantic about the world falling apart all around him, and himself with it. Now, things were changing inside of him and around him.

Several women around town began to excite his interest. There was the dark-eyed beauty who ran the New Faith haberdash on Main Street, the place Andrew had taken Jack just after Christmas to show him how a man was measured and fitted for new trousers and shirts. Sister Annabelle had a magnetic glow that amazed and baffled him. He wondered which of the New Faith men he saw about town was fortunate to keep company with her. He had heard tales about the living arrangements at the New Faith compound— that a certain freedom of liaison prevailed among them—and he sometimes wondered what it might be like to go over to them, surrender to their manners, their ways, and their religion, and get swept up in the musky raptures of free love. But Jack had bad memories of a church his mother had taken him to in the old times, in a building that looked like a muffler shop on a highway of strip malls with wig shops and manicure parlors. In that threadbare church people had fits in the aisles and the preacher seemed like a crazy person even to a five-year-old child. Besides, he reckoned his position in Andrew Pendergast's house was altogether a better deal than a perpetual orgy with people high on Jesus.

About town with Andrew, he saw women of various ages with good figures, laughing eyes, ringing voices, wise faces, and he imagined them filled with feminine bounteousness, like the way the landscape was in October, giving forth all its fruits and nutriments, a natural abundance of what life required. He was beginning to wonder whether what Andrew told him about the generosity of the universe might be true, and if he might be as much a party to it as anyone else. He was growing sleepy again, having worked out in his mind what he needed to work out at the end of a long busy day, and as he fell down the slippery hill of dreams his last conscious thought was of gratitude that another long and busy day would surely follow.

Thirty-five

"Maybe you should rest now," Britney said as Daniel finished the mug of warm milk and whiskey he'd asked for.

"No," he said. "I have to tell them what happened to Evan."

Loren and Jane Ann remained nervously alert in their comfortable seats. Robert put another log in the woodstove. Britney told Sarah it was time to go to bed. She refused.

"No, I want to listen," Sarah said. Britney did not want to start a quarrel. She replaced two candles that were burning down to stubs and invited Sarah to snuggle close to her on the sofa. Loren poured himself another whiskey.

"Please go on," Jane Ann said.

Daniel's Story: Adrift on the Inland Sea

It was a beautiful peaceful morning and the next week and a half was the most beautiful time . . . ever. We woke up on the boat. Evan didn't feel very good. He had a nasty-looking scab on his lip where he split it the night before falling into the boat. We were both awfully hungry. One of the things I'd forgotten to buy in my haste to gather up supplies before leaving Buffalo was cooking utensils. I had alcohol for the little galley stove but nothing to cook any of our food in, and I wasn't too keen for raw bacon and potatoes. The bucket I'd bought was a plastic one from the old times. Couldn't cook in that. The only thing that might serve for cookery was the steel toilet pan. So I scooped some sand and gravel off the lake bottom and scrubbed that toilet pan and ended up frying our bacon and potatoes and onions in it, and it was the best meal we ever ate. After that,

Evan felt better. I showed him around the boat and explained how things worked and he began to see what a good boat she was and how we would have a career carrying cargoes about the lake for the summer, or until we got sick of it, or found a better situation somewhere. But the big thing was that we were free and out of danger and on our own, and when we hoisted the anchor and raised the sails our spirits flew.

Evan took the wheel and I studied the charts Fourier sold me. We had a compass built into the pilot station and it was easy to understand where we were as long as we weren't out of sight of land. There were no natural harbors along the lakeshore for many miles and few signs of life. We coasted off it all morning in a fair breeze coming in from the southwest. Evan knew some things that I didn't about sailing a boat—how you could move forward even sailing partly into the wind because of the way the air flowed over the sail and the air pressure on each side. It was physics, he said. I wasn't any good at math and physics but Evan was a whiz. He mastered the operation of the boat that first day and taught me things I didn't know.

The weather was perfect. It was even getting hot, being June. We stopped wherever we liked that first day. The *Kerry McKinney* had a very shallow draft. We could raise the leeboards and bring her in close to shore, drop the anchor, and wade onto the land carrying our boots. We could swim or lie about, or read our books, or sleep. When we felt like it, we moved on. We passed little towns that seemed uninhabited, an old state park with pavilions overgrown with Virginia creeper, crumbling factories, abandoned rail yards. There were occasional orchards and farms along the shore, some raggedy, some better-looking. We stopped at one late that first afternoon. It was a big, handsome old house in the Greek temple style of the long ago times of early America, like the machine age never happened. There were people working about the place, well clothed and healthy-looking, good fenced pastures with horses and oxen, fields planted far to the horizon, workshops and out-buildings, a smith banging away in one of them.

We went to the kitchen door of the big house and asked to trade for a fry pan and a pot and some spoons and forks and a flipper and like that. The cook must have been making supper. It was quite hot in there. She had pots simmering on a big stove. She was a good-looking old girl, forty or so, substantial in the right places, with a gypsy-looking head rag on, and she was a little flirty with us. She had two helpers, both younger, both homely, one with a pushed-together face and kinky red hair and the other quite fat. She said she doubted we had anything worthwhile to trade. I said we had silver and could pay in hard money. That perked her up. We bargained and got what we needed, plus a loaf of real wheat bread, a sack of cornmeal, two dozen eggs, more onions, and some oat cookies. She asked who we were and how we came into a pocket full of silver. Evan said that we were pirates. It was one of his jokes, but I could see it didn't sit so well with the girls. The cook said that was a dangerous career and perhaps we might not want to keep at it. She said that her farmer boss was looking for strong young men and was a good provider. Evan said, no thank you, we liked being pirates out on the Great Lakes. She said we would probably get ourself hanged inside a year. I asked if the people out on the property worked on the indenture and she said no, she didn't even know what it meant, and all were free to come and go, but there was no better situation in western New York than Miller's farm, which was famous in the region. I took it that Miller was a grandee like our Mr. Bullock. She had never had a better life, she said. In the old times, she worked for a company that had a thousand restaurants all over the country, all the same, and all they did was heat up food that was made far far away and came frozen in trucks. She said the new times was the best thing that ever happened to her and Miller's farm the best place, and if we got tired of being pirates we should come back there and sign on for honest work. She was a jolly spirit. I suspect she had a free hand with the cider in that kitchen too. She said we could both kiss her before we left because she had never been kissed by pirates before.

When we got back to the boat I had to lecture Evan about shooting his mouth off like that and he said I had no sense of humor. I said no, he just had no sense, period, as in common sense, telling people we were pirates. For all I knew there were pirates out in the lakes just like there were pickers all over the land, and I hoped we didn't encounter any because they would have no reason not to leave us for dead after stealing our money. But apart from that little upset, the period that followed was a dreamtime. We had fine weather, day after day of bright sun and cool, still nights. We turned brown basking through the long days as we followed the shore and stopped and swam and ate. Evan suggested that we try crossing Lake Erie to the Canadian side, to see how things had gone in that country, but I wasn't ready to sail out of sight of land yet. Those lakes are like little oceans. It was a good forty miles across to Canada where we were and you couldn't see across. A few times, a wind came up and the water got rough, quickly, and forced you to be respectful of it. I didn't want to be caught out there at night, unable to get to dry land if necessary.

We broke out the fishing lines and easily found bait ashore under rotten logs and down in the leaf litter and brought it back and fished off the boat at evening time when the lake grew still. At first we hooked the common bass and perch that we knew from the ponds back home. But for really great eating we discovered another fish I was not acquainted with. It wasn't any kind of a trout or a salmon but looked like a stretched-out bass, yellowish brown colored, with a dorsal fin like a sail. I later learned it was a walleye. We called it the golden snapper. It was superior to the others, which we threw back. We weren't out deep enough to get lake trout, if they were in there at all. We'd roll the fillets in cornmeal and fry them in bacon fat. Often, we made supper on shore over a wood fire if there was a pretty little beach. We had pancakes and jam for dessert and took turns reading out loud from *Moby-Dick* until it was too dark to see the page, and then we'd wade back to our bunks aboard the *Kerry McKinney* and sleep to the gentle rocking of the little waves. It was a glorious time. Nobody bothered us. After a while we stopped worrying about being followed over what happened way back in Lockport. We also developed a plan to sail clear up through the lakes, past Detroit, up into Huron and around the Mackinac Straits. From the charts, it looked like you had to go through a set of locks to get into Lake Superior. But I didn't think we'd go that far in one summer, or know what we would do when winter came on, or whether we'd keep on sailing the lakes more than one season. Evan had some idea about sailing as far as Chicago and going west from there to the Pacific Ocean, where Lewis and Clark went—he knew all about them, and I didn't, except that they were famous Americans of long ago—only now if you went all the way to the Pacific Ocean, Evan said, there would be Americans there, whereas Lewis and Clark met up only with Indians. Well, I wasn't confident that things were going so great out on the West Coast since the bombing of Los Angeles, but it gave us a lot to talk about, making plans and all by the campfire.

After five days, we were running low on supplies again and we came upon a town with an excellent harbor. It turned out to be Erie, Pennsylvania—we'd made it out of New York State! It had a great big hook of a sand spit with woods on it that sheltered a bay a good mile across. We sailed in and found the public dock. A harbor master was on duty to keep order there, which was reassuring. Like other cities we visited, Erie was well reduced from its former glory of the machine age, with many blocks of abandoned buildings and houses and old factories and a population pared down by sickness and hardship. But down around the harbor they had built new buildings for warehouses and dealers in goods and they had a lively trade going on. We bought new clothes there, and straw hats, and more bacon and a nice ham and some Ashtabula whiskey, a deck of cards, a pound of taffy, and two fishing rods made in the old times, with good line, and they had a bathhouse on Short Street where we got cleaned and shaved, and then we went out for supper at the Star Hotel overlooking the harbor and had beefsteaks with spring greens and good crusty wheat bread and learned the news of the day, which was the first we heard of the Foxfire Republic.

Some enterprising person had put out a newspaper there, of the style from the far-back old times where all the stories and advertising were crammed on two sides of what was called a broadsheet. I guess paper was in short supply, like so many other things. But I was most taken by it and thought wherever fate led me I might someday like to run a broadsheet newspaper like that if I got sick of sailing around on a boat.

The Foxfire Republic was a new nation broken away from the USA composed of Tennessee, Kentucky, Virginia and West Virginia, North and South Carolina, Arkansas and Missouri and the southern part of Illinois. It was led by a woman president who was a famous roustabout for Jesus on TV and, before that, a star of country music recordings before she turned politician. This Foxfire Republic was engaged in hostilities with another new nation of former states that called itself New Africa, or *Uhuru-wardi*, which was Swahili for land of freedom, the paper said. That country was made of Georgia, Florida, Alabama, Mississippi, and Louisiana and the two new nations had sorted themselves out just like it sounds, between the white and black races, which is how come we encountered so few people of color anywhere we'd been since leaving home. Texas had apparently gone its own way for a while, with Oklahoma for a sidekick, but was now fighting off a takeover by Mexico. Then there was the country still called the United States, which I concluded was made up of whatever else might be left over, with the government most recently located in St. Paul, Minnesota, because of what happened in Washington, and rumors of yet another move of the capital elsewhere. We talked to various men in the barroom before supper about these new developments and they didn't know much else about the fate of the nations besides what was in the paper, or what was going on in the Pacific coast states, or the Rocky Mountains, for that matter. People were not journeying far between the regions unconnected by rivers or the Great Lakes because there were no cars, railroads, or airplanes anymore.

The story in the newspaper was titled "Rumors of Atrocities Down South." A battle had taken place around Marietta, Georgia, in a failed attempt by the Foxfire army to take back the city of Atlanta. Both sides were executing prisoners in horrific ways and the roads were festooned with soldiers hanging from trees, or crucified, or decapitated, with the heads displayed on poles, very brutal stuff. The paper said there were unconfirmed incidents of cannibalism on both sides. The USA was trying to stay out of it but there were rumors, too, of an imminent Foxfire incursion to take over Cincinnati and to therefore control the traffic along the Ohio River. An advertisement across the bottom of the sheet called for volunteers for the U.S. Army, mustering in Cleveland on the Fourth of July, with the promise to pay in hard money. The men in the barroom laughed at the idea of joining up, saying they would be damned to fight in a new civil war, and that they couldn't depend on the government of Erie County, let alone the state of Pennsylvania, which was bankrupt and useless, and that the U.S. government was just a ghost of a government, haunting the land—and thank God for it because that was the end of the taxes that almost crushed everybody in the "last days of the empire," they called it. I told them we hadn't heard anything from the U.S. government back home for quite a while, which at once I regretted bringing up, in case anybody came around inquiring about two young men from New York State. Anyway, Evan and I had no desire or intention to travel south of the Mason–Dixon line, or go off fighting when we were free as a couple of birds on the lakes.

I tried to talk Evan out of seeking some romantic adventure that evening in one of the parlor shops, as the men in the barroom called places where love could be bought, and he was all grumpy when we returned to the public dock, especially when I said we would shove off that night, and we argued about that because I think he intended to sneak back into town once I was asleep and find a girl, and I said I would feel like a sitting duck sleeping tied up to the town dock if anyone came looking for us, and he says, "We must be fifty miles away from Buffalo now."

I go, "That's not far away enough for my comfort."

"We're not even in New York State anymore," he says.

"I doubt that any pack of regulators would care about state lines."

He's like, "Who appointed you captain, anyway?"

I go, "I'm the senior member of the crew."

He's like, "And half of what you know about sailing this tub I had to teach you."

"Well, I bought the boat," I say.

"Partly with my money," he goes.

"Shut up and get on the goddamn boat," I say.

"Can't make me," he says.

I just stop for a long minute, drilling my eyes into him, and finally I'm like, "All right, you want to go your own way, then go. But I'm not sleeping here in the slips tonight, so I guess this is farewell. I won't be here when you come back and neither will the *Kerry McKinney.*"

He's like, "You can't do that!"

"I can and I will," I say. "We're not out of danger in my judgment."

"And when will that be?" he goes.

"It'll be when I say so and not before," I say. "You don't have the sense of a box of rocks."

Evan walks around in little circles on the dock, kicking at the planks there in frustration, like he would like to kick me, but he can't. I'm bigger.

"Come on," I say, "Get on the boat."

Finally, he goes, "You're no fun at all," and climbs aboard.

We sailed in a light evening breeze until the sun went down and the moon came up, and we moored offshore, as usual, where there was no town and no people, just woods. We had bought candles back in town among the other things and we ate taffy as

I read to him that night about Ishmael and Queequeg in their room at the Spouter tavern before they sailed off on Captain Ahab's *Pequod*.

Evan came around to himself the next morning and apologized for being pigheaded and made me read the charts and say when exactly we could start enjoying ourselves and I said maybe Sandusky, Ohio, because by then we would be well away from any pursuers, and it looked to be much the finest natural harbor on Lake Erie, and I said we might even begin asking around there about taking cargoes for hire and beginning our business and that satisfied him.

It took us the better part of the rest of the week to beat a course west toward Sandusky. We decided to skip Cleveland altogether so as not to get dragooned or indentured into any military venture that might be marshaling there to fight at Cincinnati. We continued to live very easily and comfortably. Time seemed to stand still. It rained one day and we were glad to just laze around our bunks at anchor reading and napping, and then it was sunny again the next morning, which was our last on the *Kerry McKinney*.

We were coasting off Ohio now. We picked up some cheese and sausage in a hard-up little town called Vermilion, maybe twenty miles from the mouth of Sandusky harbor. It was early afternoon when we got back on board and under sail again. The sky had darkened and the wind was picking up but the boat handled nicely. We zigzagged in a close reach always following the shore, perhaps a quarter mile from land at most. I had a rough idea where we were from the charts and thought we could make it to our destination easily by late afternoon, and it was around the solstice, too, the longest day of the year, so we would have plenty of daylight in any case. We didn't know what was coming our way, of course, which was a fierce and deadly blow. The rain started and pretty soon it was hitting us horizontally. It came down so hard that the shoreline disappeared. I tried to navigate by following the compass directly to the west, but that put us in the teeth of the wind and, from what I determined later, we blew off course, side-slipping toward a shoaly area around a set of islands and reefs to the north of Sandusky. I was beginning to despair of making it to the safe harbor there, and we were getting farther out into the vastness of the lake, exactly where I didn't want to be in this kind of situation. Evan took down our forward sail and reefed the small one in the stern as the waves got higher. Soon, it was like being out in the ocean, the troughs were so big. They were huge rollers with whitecaps on top, probably thirty feet high. It happened so suddenly. The boat was like a toy on them. We'd get pitched up on the crest of a wave and then the bow would drop with a great crash on the other side so hard I thought the hull would shatter. The sky just grew darker and angrier, even though it was far from evening. Then, we came down off one particular wave and hit something that felt more like solid ground than water and the pilot wheel went slack. I realized that the steering cable had snapped. We were at the mercy of the wind. The boat spun around and we started taking the waves broadside and water was sweeping over the deck. It was a struggle not to get washed overboard. I cut the halyard of the stern sail into two pieces of about ten feet each and told Evan to tie himself to something on board. The storm and the crashing waves made a terrible din. Evan couldn't hear what I was saying. I demonstrated by tying one end of the rope around my ankle and the other to a cleat on the starboard gunwale. Evan yelled that if the boat capsized, and we were tied to it, we'd drown. I yelled back that he'd drown if he got swept overboard and I think he was about to do as I had done when another wave caught us and swept over the cabin, and when I came through the wash Evan was gone, swept overboard.

There was nothing I could do. We didn't have any life buoy on board and I could not maneuver the boat at all. I could only scream out his name, and that didn't do any good. I stayed with the boat. What else could I do? Evan was gone. The storm just blew and blew. I couldn't tell how much time was passing except that night still hadn't fallen. Finally another giant wave smacked the boat down on something hard again—a sand bank, a rock, I don't know what. The forward mast cracked as though it had been hit by lightning and crashed down on the deck, crushing the cabin roof. Whatever the boat hit, she didn't stay stuck on. We blew back off into the waves. Shortly after that another wave capsized the boat. I went over with her into the lake and thought I would drown. I was underwater for what seemed the longest time, and it was so strangely silent down there like the peace of death itself. But I managed to bust back up for air, and I was lucky to be tied to the boat by my leg because I was able to catch hold of the starboard leeboard and clung on to it for life. Eventually, the storm died down and I hoisted myself onto the flat-bottomed hull of the capsized boat.

"You probably don't want to hear about how I was rescued, but obviously I'm here, so I was," Daniel said.

Loren leaned forward in his seat with his head in his hands and Jane Ann held her hand over her mouth as though to prevent something from escaping.

"I never saw Evan again," Daniel said. "I've been informed that he didn't come back home. At least not yet."

Jane Ann shook her head. Tears began coursing over her fine cheekbones.

"Maybe he's still alive," Daniel said. "He might have made it to shore. It's possible. I don't know. Just because I couldn't see anything out there in the rain doesn't mean we weren't close to land, maybe one of those shoal islands on the chart, and we kept on smashing onto things so wherever we were was shallow water. Anyway, we were separated for good by that storm. I'm awfully sorry. I tried to look out for him. He had a fine spirit. It wasn't easy for me to get back here, and maybe he's struggling to get home right now."

Daniel subsided against his pillows. Loren squeezed his leg and mouthed the words "thank you." Jane Ann kissed Daniel on his forehead. And then they both left the house.

THIRTY-SIX

Stephen Bullock was up late in the library of the house built by his ancestors near the confluence of the Battenkill and Hudson rivers, watching a video recording of a favorite movie from his younger years: *Goodfellas,* a picture about mafia lowlife in New York City directed by the immortal Martin Scorsese. His wife, Sophie, who did not appreciate movie violence of that amplitude, had read herself to sleep upstairs (a novel about court intrigue swirling around Henry VIII and Anne Boleyn). Bullock was able to enjoy the movie because he possessed the only functioning hydroelectric generator in Union Grove and, as far as he knew, all of Washington County. It produced enough electricity to run his household and a few of his workshops and was frequently down with annoying mechanical problems of one kind or another. Bullock had originally laid in three Pelton runner wheels—the guts of the system—among many replacement parts some years back when he sensed that the economy was going south. But they were disappointingly fragile and impossible to repair once broken. He was on the last one now and he knew that he lacked the critical metallurgical resources to fabricate any more of them. So he lived in a perpetual mood of resigned precipitous nostalgia, thinking that any day would be his last with electricity. He drew some consolation from observing the townspeople of Union Grove make do, and even remain generally civilized, without electricity. But he feared the eventual discontinuity of being cut off from all the recorded culture of the times now bygone, as though he would be cut off from hundreds of old dear friends. These premature regrets were dogging him as he munched a bowl of buttered popcorn (prepared by Lilah the cook) and watched Joe Pesci's character Tommy DeVito stomping Billy Batts (Frank Vincent) to a bloody pulp in the bar owned by Henry Hill (Ray

Liotta). Moments after the body was wrapped in a tablecloth and dragged out of the bar, someone knocked on the library door. It was highly irregular for Bullock to be interrupted so late in the evening. He stopped chewing in mid-munch and said, "Come in."

It was Dick Lee, his most trusted subaltern, wrapped in a greatcoat with a hat made of muskrat fur and a gray wool muffler hanging down over his shoulders.

"Got some bad news, sir," Lee said.

Bullock had to get up from his comfortable chair to manually press PAUSE on the DVD player because batteries were no longer available to run remote control devices. His hamstrings ached from riding around the property all day and he was annoyed to have to stop the movie.

"Well . . . ?"

"Perses," Lee said. "He's not doing so well."

"How bad?"

"He's dead."

Bullock absorbed the blow.

"Yes," he said, "that's about as unwell as it gets."

"I'm sorry to tell you."

"Okay," Bullock said. "Give me a minute then."

Bullock stopped the video and shut down the electronics. In the mudroom he pulled on his boots and bundled up in a raccoon coat made on the premises by a talented seamstress among his people out of varmints trapped on his own property. It featured a hood, which made him look immense, like a Sasquatch. Outside, it was sleeting. He stopped in the tool shop among the outbuildings and barns near the house and picked up a stout unfinished hickory ax handle. Then he and Dick Lee trudged a mile uphill to the site of the village where his people lived. Dick Lee carried a candle lantern that shed minimal light along the gravel road. But it was easy footing. The roads on Bullock's property were much better cared for than the long-neglected county roads and state highways with their potholes and fissured pavements.

"Don't kill him," was all Dick Lee said on the way up.

"All I have is an ax handle," Bullock said. "You're the one with the pistol."

The cottages of Bullock's village were situated along a little main street with the larger community building at the end of it, set into a formal village square. At this hour, no lights were burning inside it, and only here and there did windows of the cottages glow. Several narrow lanes ran perpendicularly off the main street, the cottages built close together on narrow lots with dooryard gardens, the fall stubble in them now glazed with ice. Dick Lee directed his boss to the home of Travis Berkey. It was dark within. Bullock rapped stoutly on the door. After waiting a minute he rapped again, this time with the ax handle. Shortly, the door opened a crack and a frightened woman in a muslin nightdress peered through the slot.

"Let us in, Molly," Dick Lee said. She opened the door and backed away. Dick Lee raised his lantern. The interior of the cottage was tidy but smelled of fermentation. "Sorry to come by so late," he continued gently, while Molly Berkey's gaze was fixed on Bullock, in the immensity of his fur coat. "Would you ask Travis to come down."

"He's . . . not here," she said.

"Who's that?" said a man's voice from up the staircase.

Molly looked away from Bullock and wrapped her arms around herself. He noticed that she looked old, though she was half his age.

"Get down here, Travis," Bullock bellowed. The three of them waited. The first floor of the cottage was effectively one room: a kitchen with a long table, some rustic chairs, and a wooden bench with a crude back. Much of one end wall was taken up by a fieldstone fireplace with an iron crane for hanging cook pots and trivets and other iron furnishings disposed around the hearth. Bullock was a little shocked to discover how primitive the arrangement was, like life in the Thirteen Colonies. His mind was still sojourning in the formerly modern world of the movie he had been watching. Most of his people at least had proper cast-iron woodstoves, which Bullock had taken pains to collect in the initial crash years of the economy. It was cold enough in the room so that their breath came in visible huffs of steam. Finally, they heard a commotion on the stairs and Travis Berkey appeared, slender and crooked like an old hand tool, in patched wool pants, shirtless and barefoot.

"Get in here," Bullock said. There was more noise on the staircase. A small boy's face appeared near the top of the stairs in the meager lantern light. Berkey came closer, moving sideways, as though expecting a blow.

"What's up," he said.

"Perses is dead."

Berkey did not reply but his eyes slammed shut and he hung his head.

"Get into your warmest clothes and your best boots," Bullock said.

"What about them?" Berkey muttered, cocking his head at his wife.

"They stay."

"What's he mean?" Molly said.

Berkey turned his head sharply and said, "I'm being run off."

She rushed across the room, not to her husband but to Bullock, and threw herself at his boots. "Don't make him go," she said and repeated it several times until her voice turned to blubbering.

The boy on the stairwell, who was six, began keening.

"You can't come between a man and his family," Berkey said.

"Go finish getting dressed," Bullock said, pointing upstairs with the ax handle.

Berkey glared, then turned, climbed the stairs, tenderly scooped up his son, and disappeared.

"What'll I do?" Molly blubbered.

"You'll stay here. Our people will care for you. You'll work. You'll have food and a place to live," Bullock said. The child could be heard weeping above.

"What about him?" she said tremulously.

"He'll be fine."

"Maybe we should go too," Molly said. Bullock detected the lack of conviction in her voice.

"You can't," Bullock said. "He might survive out there on his own this time of year, but with the two of you weighing him down you'll all perish. I can't allow that."

"But he's my husband," she said.

"He's an ill-tempered rogue. He beat my horse to death and I'm aware that he beats you too. You can find a better man. When the time comes, as magistrate, I'll annul your marriage, if that's what you want."

Molly grasped at Bullock's leather boot tops and her sobs turned racking in a manner that seemed theatrical. Bullock didn't fail to notice that she did not dispute the idea of finding a better man. He also noticed that she did not so much as attempt to prepare a parcel of food for Travis to take on what was bound to be a difficult journey. Berkey soon came downstairs followed by his son, who then clamped his arms around Berkey's leg as he keened. Dick Lee separated them with some difficulty and the boy then threw himself, shrieking, on his sobbing mother. Berkey stuffed his feet into a pair of ancient manufactured hiking boots, grabbed a wool coat and knitted toque from pegs on the wall, and pulled on two thick, crudely assembled shearling mittens.

"Do you want to say good-bye to them?" Bullock asked, meaning the wife and child.

"I'll send for you," Berkey muttered.

The child lifted his head but Molly did not.

"Do you aim to thrash me with that thing when we get outside?" Berkey said, pointing his scruffy chin at the ax handle.

"Not if you leave peaceably," Bullock said.

"Let's do it, then," Berkey said, twin billows of steam issuing from his nostrils as he struggled to contain his emotion. He glanced back at his wailing son and then left the house followed by Bullock and Dick Lee.

Thirty-seven

Brother Jobe, snug in his personal quarters, the former office suite of the high school principal back in the day, was notified late at night that the prisoner had been weeping strenuously and carrying on for several hours in her cell. Her guard for that shift, Brother Levi, was distressed and didn't know whether something ought to be done about it, so he sent for guidance. Brother Jobe asked his companion for the evening, Sister Susannah, to excuse him, wearily pulled on his clothing, and wended his way through the large building to the prisoner's place of confinement. He could hear her plainly enough himself through the barred door.

"Let me in," he said to Levi.

He brought a candle with him and set it on the table. Mandy lay heaped on her bed in something like what the yoga instructors of yore used to call the *child position,* her knees drawn up to her belly, face buried in the blankets. Her body shuddered with her sobs.

Brother Jobe took a seat and sat with her patiently, leafing through a Bible he had brought in with him. At first, Mandy seemed unaware of his presence. By and by her sobs subsided, she unfolded herself from her compact position on the bed, and slowly, with a feline economy of movement that impressed him, came to sit erect on the edge of it with her feet on the floor and her head down, as if waiting for some pronouncement, which was not long in coming from Brother Jobe.

"It says here," he read, "*And the prayer of faith will save the one who is sick, and the Lord will raise him up. And if he has committed sins, he will be forgiven.* The him in here," he said, "that could be a her, of course. Could be you."

Mandy lifted her head and looked up at him. Her eyes were directly level with his. She had stopped weeping and she wiped the residual moisture away from her eyes.

"I've done terrible things," she said. "It's all become clear."

"I'm afraid that's so. You know who I am, don't you?"

"Yes. You're the minister up from Virginia."

"And you know where you are?"

"Somewhere in the old high school?"

"That's right. In confinement, of course."

"In confinement," she repeated. The words fell off her lips as though they had weight and seemed to crash on the floor.

"I've been amongst your mind a few times recently."

"What does that mean?"

"Let's just say I have, uh, special abilities that would puzzle your average folks. It don't matter. The thing is, you come back to yourself now. You been a sick girl. Your mind was affected. I know it. Now, apparently, you know it."

Mandy's shoulders humped as a spasm of despair ran through her and she choked on a fresh sob. She wiped her eyes again and came out of it.

"I'm in a nightmare," she said.

"Well, you've woke up, at least, and that's a start. I can tell you that the sickness itself, it's gone out of you. Now the law don't easily separate acts done in sickness from the person that done them. It also happens that I'm an officer of the court that is going to try you for your acts. I'm concerned that justice is done. And to do that we got to get down to some serious bidness. Lookit here at my pointing finger."

Brother Jobe held his index finger up to his right eye. It was his key to unlocking the door to someone's interior. She slipped into his thrall easily. Her jaw fell slightly and her own eyes went glassy.

"One thing I got to know," he said. "Do you want to live?"

"I don't know," she said. "I killed my husband and my son. How could I deserve to live?"

"You can let God be the judge of that question. The answer to death does not have to be more death. Tell me how you were in this sickness and who was in it with you, and what they did with you."

Mandy complied, recounting her journey through the meningitis, and the demon-like entities who held her captive, and all the particulars of the fateful night when the baby Julian died and she slew her husband upon his discovery that the baby was dead.

It was well after midnight when Brother Jobe concluded the session.

"You going to come out of this after I count backwards from ten," he said. "When you do, you gonna suspend judgment on yourself while the law works its way with this. It is important for you to know that grace means getting mercy that you may not deserve or think you deserve. God is abundant in grace and mercy. It is what God means, what He is all about. His greatest grace is salvation, and He loves us with a love everlasting. It says here in Hebrews: *Let us then with confidence draw near to the throne of grace, that we may receive mercy and find grace to help in time of need.*"

"What do you want me to do?" Mandy said.

"You don't have to do nothing for now but be open to God's grace," Brother Jobe said, then began counting backwards from ten.

Thirty-eight

Daniel Earle was up on his feet early in the morning, well before dawn, restless with returning energy. He kindled a fire in the cookstove, made himself a pot of mint tea, found a ration of leftover corn bread and the butter tub, warmed up the bread on top of the cast-iron stove, sat down, and enjoyed the leisure of a breakfast indoors, unharried by trouble and hardship. He was making a second pot when Britney appeared in the doorway, wearing a flannel robe that once had belonged to Daniel's mother. The sight of her in it startled him.

"It's only me," she said.

They exchanged a fraught glance that seemed to suggest many possibilities of thought, emotion, action, and judgment.

"I hope you don't mind that I rustled up some breakfast for myself," he said.

"Mind? It's your house."

"It's my father's house. I'm in the way here."

"Don't be silly," she said, and swept her hair out of her eyes.

"I ate the last piece of corn bread too."

"It's okay. I came down to make more." She moved around the table where he sat, getting the cornmeal out of a large tin, a steel pan from a cabinet, a jug of milk. "I'm glad to see you up and about," she said over her shoulder.

"I feel just about human again."

"Would you like some eggs?"

"I couldn't find any. Would have made them myself."

"Allow me. Scrambled?"

"Okay, sure."

He watched her move in the predawn candlelight, in the robe, things shifting liquidly around inside. He saw a lot that he understood his father would like. She took three eggs out of a stoneware bowl high atop a cupboard.

"Sometimes it gets so cold in here the eggs will freeze," she said, so we keep them high up where the last bit of heat from the stove lingers."

"You're a good cook, I've noticed," Daniel said.

"Thank you. You have to be these days," Britney said. "Remember when you could buy lots of things already made? You know what I miss? All that crunchy stuff that came in bags: potato chips. Taco triangles. Cheez Waffies?"

"Cheez Waffies. Never heard of them."

"They were these bright orange round waffley crackers, really salty, with even brighter orange cheesy, salty sludge in the middle, probably incredibly bad for you. God were they good. Washed down with a Diet Coke . . . Ha!"

Daniel saw the girl in her, the person who was closer to his age than his father's and the cargo of experience that it represented.

"I don't remember as much about that stuff," he said.

She peeked inside the firebox of the cookstove. The top was heating up nicely and she put a finely tempered cast-iron pan on it. "Things have changed around here since you left."

"Well, yes, they have," he said. "You're here."

"I don't mean this house," she said. "I mean the town."

While he ate his eggs, and she prepared another corn bread batter of the never-ending corn bread, Britney told Daniel about the coming of the New Faith people and the odd, dominating figure of their leader, the preacher who called himself Brother Jobe, and changes in town politics that propelled Robert into the mayor's job, and the rescue of Mr. Bullock's boatmen from being hostages of the gangster boss of the Albany riverfront by Daniel's father and the New Faith rangers, and the hanging of the nine pickers on River Road by Bullock after they had invaded his house late one night in October, and the death of Wayne Karp, the headman at Karptown and controller of the salvage operation that the old landfill had become, and the many other doings about town since Daniel left.

She also ventured to explain how she had burned down her own house by accident in the dark weeks after Shawn was killed.

"I'm sorry about Shawn," Daniel said of her murdered husband. "I was a friend of his little brother Cody." Cody had died in the same flu epidemic that swept away Daniel's little sister Genna.

"I want to tell you something very personal," Britney said. She put down the corn bread pan that she had been buttering and looked directly at him.

He lifted his face from the plate and met her gaze. His demeanor told Britney that she had his permission to speak freely.

"Shawn and I weren't very happy for quite a while before he got killed. Your father had nothing to do with that or with Shawn's death, though he was with him at the General Supply when it happened. Shawn was very bitter about what the world had come to, and about what happened to his plans for the future, and all. He was working on the Schmidt farm as a common laborer and he was angry about it. He was messing around with one of the girls in the dairy there."

"Why are you telling me this?"

"So you understand how I came to be with your father so soon after Shawn died. There's a lot of gossip around town. You'll hear it sooner or later."

"I think I already understand. It's good that he found someone to be with."

"He's a good man, your father."

"You're a good woman."

Their gazes locked again for a moment longer than what felt completely comfortable. Britney adjusted the top of her robe and turned her attention back to the corn bread she was making.

Thirty-nine

Donald Acker woke up freezing in his house off Huddle Road thinking that everything in his life had gone to shit. He lay on a bare mattress bundled in half a dozen blankets and quilts, which the cold still penetrated. The bedclothes stank and Acker could feel tiny things crawling on his skin under the layers of shirts and pants he was wearing in bed. Gray daylight in the window was filtered by a glaze of ice on the inside of the glass that formed through the night from Acker's exhalations. Ordinarily, he would have gotten up, gone to the front parlor, and stoked the woodstove, but he had the nagging feeling that he had run out of matches, which led to the realization that he would have to walk the nearly two miles into town to get some matches at Einhorn's store—except, he also realized, he was completely out of cash money. He'd made a little silver in the fall working as a "super" on the Schmidt farm, which is to say a nonregular seasonal employee doing stoop labor in the squash rows—hubbard, butternut, acorn, kabocha, pumpkin. He detested squashes of every kind. The several acres he cultivated behind his house produced onions and potatoes, a little corn, which lasted perhaps a month in season, but not much else. He didn't like to eat most vegetables and he had neither the skills nor the equipment to put up food in jars. He hadn't eaten meat in months. His gums were so inflamed that several of his teeth were loose. Lately, he was afraid to eat anything except mashed potatoes and onions. Now that the prick of a constable or priest or whatever he was had taken his horse away, he would not be able to get a crop in next spring even if he survived the winter.

Donald Acker watched his prospects of surviving another year grow so narrow that he couldn't really see through the aperture of his destiny to any plausible future. It was like looking through a knothole in a fence at twilight only to see a dingy brick wall on the other side. He was sick and shaky, but he was afraid to visit the doctor, who he wouldn't be able to pay in any case, not even in barter. He didn't have a drop of whiskey left. He had some potatoes and onions but no lard or butter to fry them in or salt to make them palatable. He had absolutely no idea what he might do. There wasn't any government left to turn to for help. Becoming a beggar wasn't even feasible—on any normal winter day there weren't enough people on Main Street in Union Grove. Most of the people who lived in town worked on the farms outside town, the big farms owned by rich pricks like his neighbor Ben Deaver, and Bill Schmidt, and Carl Weibel, and Ned Larmon. He'd heard that the other big prick of the locality Stephen Bullock took in people to live and work on his so-called plantation, on a basis that sounded like some kind of serfdom to Acker. Bullock was their lord and master. Anyway, he doubted that Bullock would accept him if he presented himself, sick and messed up as he was.

As his choices dwindled and the anger rose in his gorge like a wad of matter he could neither swallow nor spit out but just remained there choking him, Acker began to entertain thoughts about ending it all. There was nothing else to think about, no more old magazines left to take his mind elsewhere that he hadn't read three times, no plans to make, no resources to call on, nothing but the constant reminders of all the body parts that ached, throbbed, stung, shook, and itched because he was simply decrepitating, journeying hour by hour to a place that was all darkness and silence. So why endure the misery of the journey? Without stating it clearly in his own mind, Donald Acker reached a decision. Only two questions remained. One was how to accomplish it. The other was what to do about that wad of anger pulsing in his throat. It occurred to him that he could fix that by taking down one or more of the rich prick farmers who treated him like something other than a man who had lived a perfectly normal, honest life in New Jersey, playing by all the rules, before the world went to shit and infected him with all its shittiness.

FORTY

A little later in the morning, Daniel told Robert that he wanted to venture out of the house to get some fresh air and see the town in daylight. Robert's instinct, which he suppressed, was to try to argue that Daniel should wait for the doctor to sign off on that. Then he realized, again, that Daniel was now a grown man, not a child to be managed.

"Sure, let's walk downtown," Robert said. "There's something I'd like to show you."

He gave Daniel his puffy old goose down expeditionary jacket made by the EMS outfitters back in the days when American men liked to think of themselves as high-tech adventurers. It was stained and the rip-stop nylon had several rips in it. Robert wore it to cut wood with Robbie Furnival's crew when his other work was slow, which had not been the case since the New Faithers showed up and employed him steadily much of the past year. As the year had wheeled around, and he had acquired some silver, he had developed some other ideas about how to get on with his trade as a journeyman carpenter.

Robert and Daniel stepped out into the gray morning. There was a glaze of ice on the sidewalks. They walked out in the middle of the street where years of horses passing by had overlaid the old asphalt with a layer of grit and horse manure and the footing was better. Daniel said little along the way. His eyes darted restlessly from one house to the next, off scenes and places he remembered from childhood. When they got to Main Street he was startled to see Brother Jobe's new Union Tavern on the corner of Van Buren with its gold-on-black sign and its Christmas decorations still up.

"What happened to Luddies Pizza?"

"Gone," Robert said.

"Jeez, I thought somebody might reopen it someday."

"The great age of pizza is over."

"That was my all-time favorite food."

"The new place is pretty nice. They serve food in there."

"Who opened it?"

"The Jesus people from Virginia. Brother Jobe's bunch."

"They allow drinking?"

"They seem to be quite in favor of it."

"Isn't that odd?"

"Yes, they're pretty odd."

"Do the people in town actually patronize the place?"

Robert laughed. "Yeah, they do. Maybe we'll have lunch in there."

"Well, I've got to say, the building looks a whole lot better now. This town is coming back from the dead."

"Yeah, in some ways I think that's true," Robert said.

They rounded the corner onto Main. Robert steered Daniel up an alley between two empty shop-front buildings. It led back to a large gray barn. It had been a stable and a harness shop before the advent of the automobile. Robert unlocked a padlock and let them in. The inside was a cathedral-like space flooded with light from the tall mismatched windows, many of which Robert had collected and installed the past year. Robert had also assembled sets of workbenches and racks for his tools and jigs. There was a substantial old top-loader sheet metal woodstove against the far wall and a collection of mismatched sofas and chairs around it.

"Is this your place?" Daniel said.

"More or less," Robert said. "One of the perks of being mayor is I've learned a lot about which properties are in title limbo, where the owners are known to be dead or can't be found."

"What if some relative does show up from . . . out there . . . and claims rightful ownership of the property?"

"So far that hasn't happened. If it does, I'll go find another barn. There's plenty of vacant property around town and not enough people left to inhabit it. The trouble is that none of it is being cared for. It'll all fall apart if people don't use it. That's how buildings are. How do you like the layout?"

"It's sweet," Daniel said. "You always wanted a big workshop."

"Let's get a fire going and sit a while before lunch."

"All right."

There was plenty of split cordwood in a rack beside the stove. Robert started some kindling with ancient newspaper, which he had found bales of in one of the old horse stalls when he first cleaned the place out. It amused him to read these news stories from the 1990s, before anyone had a clue how fragile the economy really was. He got the stove fired up in short order. A fan stood on the top powered by an ingenious Stirling engine that ran off the heat of the stove itself. Soon it was wafting warm air across the room.

Daniel kicked off his boots and reclined on an old sofa with sprung, sagging springs.

"I suppose you want to hear what happened after I capsized on Lake Erie."

"Yes, I do," Robert said. "I'll make some tea for us." He had a five-gallon plastic jug with some water in it and he put it near the stove to melt the ice inside.

Daniel's Story: *The Great Northern*

Of course, Evan was gone. The boat was upside down in the water. There was no way to right it. The mainmast had snapped off. I hung on to the leeboard going up and down those big storm swells. It was like riding a bucking horse. The lake was horribly cold, even though it was late June. The storm did end. The water calmed down. I was able to climb all the way onto the hull and get out of the water. The sun eventually came out, pretty low on the horizon. It was evening. The air cleared. I could see a shoreline a couple of miles away, a slim little gray band on the horizon, and some darker islands between it and me, but still too far to try and swim to. If I stayed with the boat, I had no way of propelling it in any direction. I thought, if I could just hang on maybe the wind would push me close enough to something I could swim to. Then again, there was as much chance that the wind would shove me farther out in the lake. I decided to just stay with the boat. Then the sun finally started to sink down into the lake. My clothes were nearly dry by then and the lake was calm again, but I knew if we got the usual night breezes that the waves would slap against the hull and I'd get wet again and I worried about hypothermia and getting disoriented, losing my grip, slipping into the cold water . . . I don't know. I kept on calling Evan's name in bursts every half hour or so, but there was no response from out in the darkness. I figured I'd be dead, too, before long unless somebody came along.

As it happened, I was on that hull all night long and nearly froze to death. It wasn't even that cold, maybe sixty degrees, but I got splashed and soaked, and my clothes kept the wet against my skin and even the mild breeze chilled me to the bone. I was shivering so hard I found it difficult to keep hanging on to the leeboard. I fell into a strange state of despair where you're convinced that it's all over for you, but you're still there hanging on because the instinct to stay alive is so strong. The immensity of the sky and all the stars overwhelmed me with a feeling of my utter insignificance and the indifference of the universe. I didn't sleep for a moment though at times I felt I was in a dream. I heard your voice, Mom's voice, Genna, the voices of the dead. I've never felt so far removed from life, from humanity, even in all the breakdown of our country that I had already witnessed, as I did alone that night riding the hull of my wrecked boat, with Evan lost on top of all that. Then, the sky turned a luminous blue green and as a clear morning broke I saw two things: one, that I was completely out of sight of land at all compass points and, two, a white sail on the horizon a mile or so away.

I couldn't stand upright on the hull, it was too unsteady, but I got up on my knees and waved my arms and screamed and hollered and the boat seemed to get bigger and come closer. As it did, I could see it was a large boat with more than one sail. It turned out to be, in fact, the most magnificent sailing boat I ever saw, what they call a topsail schooner. She was well over a hundred feet with the hull painted forest green to just above the waterline and red from there below. She had both a cabin and a pilothouse, three masts, mostly gaff-rigged sails, and three square topsails on the forward mast. I kept waving and hollering, even as she closed on me, and I could hear men hollering on deck. They reefed the three mainsails and turned into the wind maybe a hundred yards from me. I untied the rope from my ankle that had kept me tethered to the *Kerry McKinney* in the storm. I said a quiet good-bye to the boat that now seemed so tiny compared to the behemoth before me and dove into the lake and swam to the ship. The name on her bow was *The Great Northern*. Crewmen threw lifelines with buoys toward me, but I didn't even see them until I reached the hull, where they dropped a boarding stairway down along the side. The water was so cold that my head throbbed as I struggled up the stairs. Crewmen in blue uniforms met me on deck, wrapped me in a wool blanket, and trundled me down a companionway to a stateroom.

They gave me towels and blue coveralls and fresh underwear and left me alone. I dried off and got dressed in their clothes. There was a built-in bunk in the corner and I was just about to go collapse on it when someone knocked on the door. Before I could answer, a crewman in a white tunic came in with a tray that he puts down on the table. He takes these silver half-globe covers off the plates, like I imagine the royalty of old used to be served. The crewman leaves. I shuffle over and sit down. The shivering is coming only in spurts now. There's a plate with three over-easy eggs, bacon, ham, some really fancy wheat rolls, butter, cherry jam, a bowl of oatmeal, a little pitcher of cream, a little sugar bowl, a big glass of milk. I dig in. I wolf down the oatmeal in about eleven seconds. It's warm and delicious, and when it's gone I swish the rest of the cream from the pitcher in the bowl and dump more sugar in it. I demolish the eggs and meat after that, and then I crawl off into the bed. I haven't slept under sheets in almost two months. The luxury is beyond belief.

The next thing I know someone is knocking on the door again. I say, "Come in," and it's the crewman, the same steward. He says to come with him. I'm confused, like who are these people? Have they been looking for me and Evan for what happened back in New York State? I get out of bed and peek out the porthole. The sun is low on the horizon, about the same as when they pulled me out of the water, but I don't know what direction it is—east, west?

"What time of day is it?" I ask.

"Evening. You're called to dinner."

"Did you find my friend out there?"

"Your friend?"

"There were two of us on that boat," I say. "He got washed overboard in the storm."

"You're the only one we pulled out of the water," he says.

"He could still be out there somewhere. Can they look for him?"

"We've been under sail all day long. We're far away from where we came across you in the morning. Twenty leagues or more."

My heart fell into my stomach. I just stood there staring into the floor.

"Come with me. I'll show you to dinner," he says.

I'm so stupefied I just do what he tells me to do. He leads me down a long passageway to another part of the ship, to a dining room, or cabin I guess you'd say, very fancy, with dark wood wainscoting and nautical paintings, luxurious furniture for a boat. The table is a lot bigger than the one in the room I slept in. It's set for two. There are chunky candles in little glass vessels and some oil lamps in gimbals on the wall, a sideboard with squashed-down nautical decanters on it so they won't topple over in rough water. The steward pulls out a chair for me. Before I can ask him who else is coming, he leaves the cabin. I sit down. I'm there alone for quite a while. There's a tablecloth, ironed napkins, a bread basket and butter. I start eating these wonderful chewy rolls and I can't stop. Plus, I'm nervous wondering who I'm waiting for. I end up eating all of them. Finally, there's a knock and without me saying come in a woman enters.

That was the first time I laid eyes on Ms. Valerie Estridge of the U.S. government, or what was left of it. She was tall and slim, around forty years old, I thought—at least that was my first impression. Her face had a sculptural quality, clear planes and angles, that was austere at first. Her hair was a silvery-gold helmet with bangs that framed her face as if it were a portrait of a face. She wore a plain tan skirt, a white blouse with a frilly front that buttoned to the throat, and a dark blue jacket, all factory-made stuff, like what a person might wear to work in a company office of the old times. She stood at the door examining me, I thought, with a kind of mysterious smile that you were never sure signified actual amusement or just her mouth in its natural relaxed state. It was what she showed people in the political world that was her realm of action, like the grin of a shark who prowls the coral reefs among fishes of all sizes and colors.

I'm like, "Sorry, I ate all the rolls."

She closes the door behind her. I can hear the latch click, like I'm stuck in a trap with her.

"Don't worry, we'll get more," she says, and steps up to her seat at the table.

I notice she's wearing some flowery scent. It wafts my way.

"Whose boat are we on?" I ask.

"I like to think of it as mine," she says, "but it's the U.S. Navy's."

I'm like, "There's still a navy?"

She just smiles. The steward comes in with a cart. More goodies. Ms. Estridge sits down. The steward uncovers our plates. There's a hunk of fish, creamed potatoes, and fresh asparagus on the plate, quite big portions.

"Do you like fish?"

"Pretty well."

"We get a lot of it right from the lake," she says. "They're coming back nicely."

"That's a plus," I say.

"Would you bring us some more rolls, Terry?"

"Yes, ma'am," the steward says and leaves us alone.

"Dig in, Daniel," she says.

I'm bamboozled. Since I came aboard, nobody has asked my name. I watch her pour herself some red stuff from a pitcher.

"Want some?" she asks.

"What is it?"

"Michigan red," she says. "It's not bad."

I'm like, "You know my name."

She pours me some of the wine, though I didn't ask for any.

"I do," she says. "We stopped in Buffalo to provision."

I'm like, "This is making me kind of nervous, ma'am."

"Don't be," she goes. But I'm still on edge. I can picture Mr. Farnum lying on the floor of his office in Lockport with blood all over the place. I watch her eat for a while. She has a good appetite. She eats deliberately and gracefully, like somebody brought up well. She's an imposing presence, actually quite pretty for a forty-year-old.

"What did you find out in Buffalo?" I ask.

"Your name," she says. "And that you shot a man on the Erie Canal."

"And you're serving me a fine dinner and all? How come I'm not in the whaddayacallit."

"The brig."

"Yeah."

"We don't have one on board. We'd have to lock you in a storeroom. I don't think we'll do that. The truth is, you saved us a lot of trouble."

I try to absorb that.

"If I may explain, ma'am, we were about to be sold into slavery by an unscrupulous boatman. What they called an indenture, for twenty-five dollars each."

"Exactly," she says. "Go ahead, eat."

I'm quite hungry, actually, so I do. It's walleye, with a perfect crispy crust on it in a puddle of butter sauce. Delicious.

"I assume your companion was on that little boat with you."

"You know about him too?"

"Of course."

"He got washed overboard. I couldn't save him."

"I'm sorry," she says.

"What else do you know about us?"

"That you left Buffalo together on that scow just ahead of the regulators."

"I knew they were coming after us."

"Yes, they were."

We ate silently for a while. The tension was driving me crazy.

"Well, am I under arrest or what?"

She put down her knife and fork. "We're against these practices," she says, "selling people into indentures. It's barbaric and un-American. Criminal, really. We intend to stop it. But we have limited enforcement capabilities these days. You were within your rights to resist."

"Does that mean I'm free to get off this boat when it lands somewhere?" I ask.

"Where would you go?" she asks.

"Where are you landing next?"

She just grins her shark grin.

"Are you toying with me, ma'am?" I say.

"No," she says. "You're a kind of gift from the sea, so to speak. I think you might be useful to us, Daniel."

"In what way?"

"In the Service," she says.

"What service is that?"

"You'll see."

I can tell she won't elaborate.

"Who are you exactly?" I finally ask straight up. "And where are we going?"

She tells me she works for the government, but she's not a military officer. She's returning from an inspection of the Great Lakes ports to the new capital that the government is setting up in a place called Huron City, Michigan. They're going to change the name to New Columbia. They have moved their people, she says, from St. Paul, Minnesota, which was unsuitable. The future of the nation lies with the Great Lakes, she says, America's freshwater Mediterranean Sea at the center of the continent. I'm burning to know more about what is going on, but she grills me about our part of the country. She says the government has a very "poor presence" back east.

"It has no presence, ma'am," I tell her. "Same for the state and county governments. We're totally on our own."

She asks about the town, about my family. I tell her how Mom and Genna met with the epidemics, and how you used to work for the computer industry and switched to being a carpenter, and all, and how things are kind of slowly grinding downhill for us back home.

"But it's a very beautiful corner of the country, Washington County, New York," I tell her, "and from what I've seen traveling west it's not much worse off than any place we passed along the way."

"Why did you leave home?" she asks.

"To see the country for myself," I tell her. "I'm of the age where I remember quite a bit about the old times when I was a young child, but most of what I've lived is the new times. I know what we lost. I wanted to see what happened to it all."

"Fair enough," she says.

The steward returns with dessert: cheesecake with raspberry sauce.

"You're really not going to arrest me?" I ask.

"Correct," she says. She goes and gets one of those decanters off the sideboard and brings it back to the table. She pours two drinks into heavy-bottomed glasses. "Michigan cherry brandy," she says. "Not half bad. What do you know about the recent history of our country and what's happened around the world?" she asks.

"Next to nothing," I say.

"Would you like to know? I think it will provide some perspective for you in the Service."

"Am I already signed up for this service?"

"Why did you leave home?"

"To see what was going on out here."

"What's going on is stranger than you ever imagined. Did you not expect to have some adventures when you left home?"

"I suppose I did."

"Well, my gift from the sea, you're going to have the adventure of your lifetime, and we're going to train you for it, and here is a condensed version of what has been going on in the world."

She tells it. President Ted Sharpe made the decision to send troops into the Holy Land. Israel was surrounded by failed states and it was being pounded and harassed by jihadists of every sort. Classic fourth-generation asymmetrical warfare, she called it. Even the Israelis, who were so astute about self-defense, couldn't contain these adversaries. They certainly couldn't use their nukes. Against what? Egypt? Egypt was a basket case. It didn't even have a national government anymore. All the other nation-states of the old Levant were in collapse: Jordan, Lebanon, Syria. Iran never did produce a usable nuclear weapon, though it pretended for a while. Then the Iranians made the mistake of electing the maniac Mousa Forood president and he started a civil war, which bled over to Iraq and wrecked most of the remaining oil industry in both places. Desertification was becoming extreme in the region with the annual average temperature rising. It was all about too many people in places that couldn't support them all, Ms. Estridge said, but it expressed itself in widespread religious war, all against all and everybody against Israel. For Israel it was like being stung to death by fire ants. So we went in to help and it was Vietnam, Iraq, Somalia, and Afghanistan all rolled into one. We might have lasted longer on the ground, perhaps, but the bombing of

Los Angeles kick-started the collapse of the economy. It had been running on fumes for decades anyway. Ms. Estridge said she was personally surprised that the American public did not rise up against the government even before the LA bomb, given the disastrous inflation and the gasoline lines.

Elsewhere, Europe had broken down economically. England and Scotland separated. England went fascist, she said, and tried to deport large numbers of nonwhites on ships. That only started an insurrection and then a dirty bomb went off in Birmingham, she said, which poisoned much of the country downwind, as well as the Netherlands. The Germans decided by consensus to go medieval, meaning a planned, orderly retreat to historically lower economic conditions and political arrangements, all managed by a parliamentary process. The government performed an official search for a new king, like he would be the head of a company, and divided its states into semiautonomous principalities. Russia went in a similar direction minus the orderly planning and, of course, more people died there as a result. All over the continent, old borders dissolved and new, smaller places emerged from the wreckage, run by every type of party, gang, popular savior, and despot. A lot of people froze to death. Many starved. Disease came later.

Asia was hit by everything at once and at full force: broken supply lines to the oil supply, economic collapse, ecological collapse, epidemic disease, famine, natural disaster, and war. Ms. Estridge said her people—meaning the government, I suppose— believe that China attempted to reduce its population by an engineered epidemic. The estimate was over a billion dead in the first wave. An elite received vaccinations beforehand. The population problem was solved in a few months, but the country was left with a ruined, poisoned landscape, a depleted water table, and not enough able-bodied people alive to bury all the bodies. So that brought on a second and then a third round of epidemics, the old standby killer diseases such as cholera and typhoid fever, which swept through China and killed off many of the elite.

While that was still happening, an earthquake struck the port city of Tianjin and destroyed the infrastructure of the entire region, including Beijing, Cangzhou, and Baoding. She said that the stories about China putting a man on the moon are nonsense. The Chinese are heading back into the twelfth century mocked by the standing remnants of the ghost cities and highways they built in a stupendous orgy of construction that lasted only a few decades. A lot less is known about Japan, she said. When the airplanes and the trading ships stopped moving, the country went into lockdown. There are rumors of widespread starvation and radiation sickness. Nothing goes in and out of there now.

India had run out of water and attempted to seize the Indus River valley and its watershed from Pakistan. Ms. Estridge said that Indians hacked and disabled Pakistan's nuclear launch capabilities—I'm not sure what she meant by that—and a grinding war on the ground ended in the political collapse of both nations. The test-tube epidemic in China spread across the ancient trade routes, the Great Silk Road, where stuff was still moving in the absence of global shipping and aviation. India was especially savaged by the secondary diseases because of its tropical climate. Africa was a zombie continent of ghost nations returning to the wild kingdom. The region where Argentina, Uruguay, and Paraguay meet retained a veneer of old-time modern life because of the vast hydroelectric capacity that was still operating, but these countries shunned contact with the distressed, deindustrialized former big countries in the north. Similarly went Norway, which still had some oil out in the North Sea as well as hydropower and incorporated the rest of Scandinavia under its administration. Its attempt to organize a Greater Federation of Northern Europe, with itself as boss, failed. Very little information was coming out of Australia and New Zealand, she said. It was thought the two countries were doing okay because of their small populations and relative isolation and just wanted to be left alone.

Then there was us. Ms. Estridge shook her head and stared into her brandy glass for a long moment before continuing.

General Walter Fellowes was the army chief of staff when things went south for us, she said. He was vehemently against the War in the Holy Land, as it came to be called, and organized an opposition to it in the Pentagon. He used the bombing in Los Angeles as a pretext to shove President Sharpe out of office, along with his own boss, the chairman of the Joint Chiefs, Admiral Royster, and many other of Ted Sharpe's people, and he took over the management of the nation's affairs—a classic coup d'état, she said, like in a banana republic. It's true that the government was paralyzed in a state of chaos. It could do nothing about the fuel shortages and the bank failures. General Fellowes invoked the continuity of government policy and he got Congress to go along because the politicians violently opposed the war, too, including many in the president's own party, and they didn't see any other way out. Fellowes began to pull troops out of Israel and Lebanon right away. They put Ted Sharpe in Fort Detrick, Maryland. He turned up dead in his quarters two weeks after he arrived. Detrick was the center for the country's biological weapons program, so they could have just dialed up room service to give him a lethal dose of something, she said. He was sixty-three years old and it was called natural causes. It didn't really matter because a few weeks after that the bomb went off in Washington, DC, and killed off most of the rest of the government, including General Fellowes and all his people in the Pentagon, plus all the parasitical contractors and lobbyists, plus the news bureaus that covered the affairs of the nation, everything, all gone.

"Who was behind the bombs in Los Angeles and Washington?" I ask.

"Los Angeles, we think the Sinaloa Cartel."

"What's that?"

"Organized crime on the giant scale, initially organized around drug trafficking but by then a shadow government. It was a crude device. But effective enough."

"And Washington?"

"Several Sunni extremist groups and Hezbollah all claimed

credit. We never got to the bottom of it because the federal government was effectively disabled when it happened. We may never know. It was a more powerful bomb than the one in LA."

I asked Ms. Estridge, "Where were you when all this happened?"

"I was in St. Petersburg, Russia, in the American embassy which we'd moved out of Moscow," she said. "They didn't know what to do. They decided to just stay in place and wait. They thought sooner or later a government would reorganize and issue instructions. As it happened, Speaker of the House Clayton Rhodes was back in his district, which was Nashville and its environs, when the bomb went off. He was second in the line of succession to Ted Sharpe. Vice President Corcoran was out of the picture, presumed vaporized in DC. They treated the Fellowes coup as if it hadn't happened and invoked the continuity clause again. Rhodes organized a kind of rump federal government in Nashville. He called himself 'acting president' to be polite. He asked the state governors to appoint and send new congressional delegations there. It took a while. Communications were bad and the governors had terrible problems to manage in their own regions, food shortages, bank closings, failures of water, sewer, electric. Many states didn't respond at all. The people of Tennessee were very anti–federal government and they weren't alone. Their aspirations lay elsewhere, and all the disorder gave them a chance to act on it, as you'll see presently," she said.

"Meanwhile, that new Congress convened in the old state-house there, and because the sentiment in Nashville was so poisonous the first thing they did was vote to move the capital to Chicago. By this time the economy was in freefall. Not only had we stopped receiving oil imports, but shale oil production had plummeted years earlier and the Canadians wouldn't send us any of their tar sand oil because they wanted it for themselves. There was agitation in this new Congress to try and seize the Alberta tar sand region, but the military was in a state of disintegration. There wasn't enough fuel for its ships to get all the troops out of the Holy Land or to mobilize a force here in North America. Troops weren't getting paid, or even fed, and they just walked away from their posts. Most of the command structure from the Pentagon was dead, and there was no appetite among the surviving generals for another invasion of a sovereign country. Some of them even thought Canada might kick our ass.

"The move to Chicago was a debacle. Violence had broken out there. Too many poor people were not getting food. The banks were shut. Nobody was getting paid. The gas stations were down. The place was ungovernable. Many of the invited congressional delegations didn't even show up, mostly the ones from southern states, plus California, which was in near anarchy. The only thing that Rhodes was able to do was organize a new constitutional convention, which took place that summer, ironically right around the Fourth of July. The delegates to the convention called a special election for president to be held among the governors of the remaining states. Things were too disorderly to organize a popular vote. The governors elected Harvey Albright, governor of Minnesota, to head the new federal government. He moved the capital to St. Paul, which was one of the few cities in the country that had put a transition plan into action for a future without oil. The city had substantial hydroelectric power from the Falls of St. Anthony, the only waterfall on the upper Mississippi. Clayton Rhodes himself eventually went back to Nashville, to be part of its own special thing."

Ms. Estridge said she got back from Russia on a chartered oil tanker ship with twenty-eight thousand tons of crude aboard that the U.S. government bought with gold held in the embassy for just such an emergency. They landed at a place called the MTX Terminal in Bayonne, New Jersey. Ambassador Peletier was a former navy pilot. They swapped the oil cargo for a Gulfstream III jet, fueled up, and flew out of Newark to Minnesota. That was the last time she was ever up in an airplane, Ms. Estridge said. What had happened those months she was marooned in St. Petersburg was the breakup of the United States. I told her I read about this thing called the Foxfire Republic in a news sheet back when we were coasting Lake Erie before the storm and the wreck. She affirmed all that. It was a southern white supremacist breakaway nation, she said, dedicated to the unfinished business of the old Confederacy. It was ruled by a woman named Loving Morrow who had been in show business before she turned to religion and politics. They were running all the black people out of the Foxfire states, committing wholesale atrocities in the process: theft of property, detention, deportation, murder, just like the Germans a hundred years ago. The blacks fled deeper into the south, Georgia, Alabama, Florida, Mississippi, Louisiana. Some of the whites down there fled north in turn to Tennessee, the Carolinas, Kentucky, and Virginia. But many of them wouldn't leave their property behind and, when they tried to defend it, there were violent clashes with atrocities on all sides. Eventually, the black republic formed out of those Deep South states. It was led by a man who called himself simply Sage, real name: Milton Steptoe. He had run a check-cashing and payday loan empire all over the Deep South. I didn't understand what that was so Ms. Estridge explained it. She had to explain a number of things to me that evening. Sage had organized an African-American militia to counter the Foxfire attempts to control northern Georgia, including Atlanta. The Foxfire government was very pugnacious, Ms. Estridge said. Loving Morrow was a fanatic, a religious maniac, claiming to follow injunctions directly from Jesus Christ to expand her territory, in effect to refight the Civil War and win it this time. Ms. Estridge called her a cornpone Nazi. "Think of Hitler with a Bible, big boobs, and a guitar," she said. They were now threatening Cincinnati in order to control shipping on the Ohio River. We wouldn't allow that, she said, meaning the federals.

She went on. California was a basket case. A million people died in and around Los Angeles as a result of the bombing, and millions more were displaced. Agitators north of San Francisco started an aggressive movement to dissociate politically from the southern half of the state. Refugees overwhelmed the San

Francisco Bay Area and beyond. It was not like the Dust Bowl days of a hundred years before when refugees from one part of the country could get work picking fruit. Many survived only as robbers and bandits and their careers were generally short as word got out and they met armed resistance. The Chinese-engineered bird flu got over to the West Coast in one of the few cargo ships still delivering goods. The epidemic ripped through the population, and the refugees who stayed on the move carried it up the coast to Oregon and Washington. Along the way, people started calling it the Mexican flu but it was Chinese. Mexico had plenty of problems of its own, largely growing out of its attempts to control Texas and what remained of Southern California, plus Arizona, which was also a gigantic mess because there was no gasoline to run Phoenix, a place where you could get around only by car. Mexico's land grab was at odds with the fact that it was crumbling internally, just like the United States. Did you know that Mexico's full name is the United States of Mexico? Many of its states were breaking away from the center too.

While all this was going on out west, Asian freebooters fanned out over the Pacific, especially Indonesians in their own naval vessels—they still had some oil as well as a fleet of secondhand, 1970s-vintage Russian destroyers—and began raiding operations along the long coast of North and South America. Among other escapades, they docked in San Francisco, marched up to the Federal Reserve Bank building on Market Street in broad daylight, and carted off fourteen tons of gold in pushcarts that they'd brought with them for the job. They knew exactly where to go. Sacramento was negotiating with Oregon, Washington, British Columbia, and Alaska to form a Pacific Northwest political union, but the last Ms. Estridge heard they hadn't accomplished it. Colorado, and the plains states north of Missouri, stayed with the federals, but Idaho, Wyoming, and Montana did not fill their congressional seats. They were economically stranded and too distant from the seat of government. The Northeast suffered terribly, too, from epidemic disease and the wholesale dysfunction of the massive smear of human settlement that ran from Portland, Maine, clear through Virginia. What people called the Mexican flu in the east was neither the Chinese strain nor anything from Mexico but a natural bird flu that had evolved in the Canada goose population. In the big eastern cities, the social services collapsed and the people lost the ability to maintain their infrastructure. New York was especially afflicted because it had so many office skyscrapers and high-rise apartment towers that just didn't work without reliable electricity. A breakdown in sanitation led to cholera. Diseases of the subtropics had become well established in the Northeast, including West Nile virus, several kinds of encephalitis, and meningitis. Yellow fever made a comeback in Philadelphia. In New York and Boston a lot of people just starved. The food trucks stopped coming. Others realized this was not a temporary situation and fled the cities. But most didn't get very far. They got wet and got sick and, in the places they came to, the locals met them with firearms.

"This country has changed so much that my own parents wouldn't recognize it," Ms. Estridge says. "That is what happened. That is the way of the world. Sometimes things change drastically. We endeavor to carry on in what everybody seems to call these new times. Harvey Albright is a good man. I report to him directly. Our government is nothing like the leviathan that existed in Washington, but we remain Americans, with our history, our language, and our commitment to the common good. Is there anything you would like to ask me?"

"Yes," I say. "Where is this ship going?"

"Channel Island."

"What's at Channel Island?"

"Your nation's future."

That was the end of one part of my life, right there. Ms. Estridge left the table in a little cloud of her flowery perfume.

FORTY-ONE

In the middle of the day, which had turned colder with full-bellied dark clouds crowding the blue out of the sky, Andrew Pendergast and his servant Jack Harron hiked east on the old county Route 29 to the Deaver farm a mile and a half out of town. Jack carried a wooden box fitted with shoulder straps on his back containing Andrew's painting equipment. He also toted the 24 by 36–inch plywood panel Andrew had prepared with a gesso of rabbit-skin glue and marble dust. The panel was fitted with an old suitcase handle screwed to the side so Jack could carry it like a piece of luggage. Andrew carried a portable cherrywood easel under his arm. They were going to Ben Deaver's house, where Andrew would begin the project of painting the distinguished man's portrait.

A few stray snowflakes drifted in the still air as they marched along. Jack enjoyed walking in the boots that Andrew had given him. They were greased with beeswax and tallow to keep the wet out and very comfortable with an extra pair of socks, since Andrew's shoe size was one greater than Jack's. He was bundled in a warm blanket coat that draped to his shins and a conical rabbit-fur helmet that looked like something a spear carrier in the army of Genghis Khan might have worn. As they hiked, Andrew offered a running commentary on the lives and techniques of the portrait painters he admired: Velázquez, Rembrandt, Édouard Manet, and John Singer Sargent. Sargent, the American who hardly lived in America during his lifetime, was the very best, Andrew said, but then he lived in the very best moment in the history of the late, lamented recent old modern times: the turn of the nineteenth to the twentieth century, the Beaux Arts era. Jack tried to process the word "bozart." He could only imagine it referred to a time when clowns reigned. Though self-conscious and ashamed of his ignorance, he ventured to tell Andrew that he didn't know what a bozart was. Andrew proceeded to explain it to him. He even paused to spell out the words "Beaux Art" in the snow at the side of the road and explain the pronunciation. Jack had taken the compulsory two semesters of foreign language in high school, but it was Spanish, and he just squeaked through with C's. At the time, it seemed that knowing a little Spanish would be handier, the way things were going in America. Now he regretted not having opted for French.

They continued up the road and Andrew resumed his disquisition on Sargent. His painting materials were first rate. The finest colors from the new chemical industries of Europe. Beautiful linen canvases, the best handmade brushes. Now, in the new times, there were no places to purchase art supplies. There was progress for you. Andrew was running out of the vivid colors he had managed to stockpile in the collapse, and before long his palette would be limited to simple earth colors plus black and white, he said. He'd have to plumb the science stacks of the library and read up on chemistry, he said, to make his own colors. Jack was not sure what it all meant, but he was surprised to find himself listening with keen interest, struck by the notion that he was actually learning something, and that it would lead him in the direction of a life worth living.

They turned off old Route 29 onto the Huddle Road, passing the delaminating house of Donald Acker along the way. Andrew remarked that there was no smoke coming out of the chimney. That was one way, he said, of telling whether buildings were inhabited, for who could live in such a place this time of year without fire? They continued up Huddle Road, a steep grade, around the back of Pumpkin Hill, until they came to the drive that led up to Ben Deaver's house. It was a new house, built in a style and using methods that had been long forgotten in the United States of America. Deaver built it after giving up on the so-called *contemporary custom* house he had originally bought when he retired from United Airlines, a few years before the collapse. That first house was a grandiose thing of soaring angles and gigantic triangular plate glass windows designed to erase the boundary between being inside and being outside. It proved impossible to heat without propane gas and electricity, and as the economy dissolved the house's conceits annoyed him to an extreme, so Deaver decided to build a new house in the traditional style and manner. At the center of it was a substantial stack of masonry chimneys that acted as a heat reservoir for the house's multiple fireplaces. The system incorporated several ovens and a cook surface made of sheet steel in the big kitchen. The house was sited over a water well drilled with great effort without power machinery. The plumbing was copper and steel pipe salvaged from the old house, run in a stack proximate to the masonry heating stack at the center of the house to a tank in the attic. Water had to be hand-pumped up there by a servant assigned to the routine daily maintenance of the household systems. In the new times, human servants replaced many of the functions formerly performed by machines and automatic switches. These arrangements allowed for fewer bathrooms than was the case in the old days of so-called McMansions, with their profligate amenities. But Deaver had a very grand bathroom on the second floor that was practically a spa. A wood-fired boiler provided hot water for bathing and for the kitchen on the floor below. It was fired up twice a day so hot water was available when needed, morning and evening.

On the outside, Deaver's house looked like it was built in the times of James Madison, with a pedimented portico, a wood fan ornament in each gable end, and shutters that actually closed. Along the hundred-foot-long entrance drive he had planted a formal allée of shagbark hickories. They were still young and he knew that he would not live long enough to see them in their glory, but was it not the case, Ben Deaver thought, that everyone in history who planted a big tree did it for succeeding generations? As an investment in the future? To express confidence in the continuity of the human project?

Andrew and Jack approached the house between the ranks of the young hickory trees in silent reverence induced by the beauty of the large building and its setting. Smoke curled out of the chimney top with its castellated cowl. The pair were greeted at the door by a servant who took their coats and hats. The servant was named Harry, a cheerful former loan officer at the Glens Falls National Bank in the old times, and his new job title was "houseman" because it had been so long since servants were an ordinary fixture in American life that people did not know what to call them, and Deaver disliked the term "butler." Harry showed Andrew and Jack into the sitting room, as he called it, where Ben Deaver sat by the fire with his nose in a novel from the previous century about international hugger-mugger involving a Russian submarine. The room was delightfully warm and painted a genial yellow, a color that was especially pleasant at a time of year when the world outside presented only various tones of gray and sepia.

"Gosh, you're punctual," Deaver said. The clock on the mantelpiece, a rather fancy 1881 Ingraham, had been refurbished by none other than Andrew Pendergast. Andrew checked it now against his own pocketwatch.

"It's seven minutes slow," he said.

"How do you know yours is accurate?" Deaver said.

"I check it against the old almanac tables for sunrise and sunset."

"Hmm. Imagine that."

Andrew said they were ready to set up and proceed with the task at hand. Deaver asked Harry to bring tea and something to eat. Andrew took a drop cloth that was lashed to the paint box Jack carried on his back and laid it on the rug. He examined the room and asked Deaver to try standing in various places around it. He decided to make the portrait with Deaver posing by a window that faced east. It offered a nice view off of Pumpkin Hill down Deaver's own fields to the valley where the Battenkill River ran and to the gentle hills behind it. The hills in their snowy mantle had a voluptuous quality. Mount Equinox, just across the Vermont border, was visible on the far horizon. Deaver had dressed for his portrtait in a fine herringbone tweed jacket with a scarlet sweater vest, a green plaid necktie, and gray moleskin trousers, all factory-made back in the old times. With his shock of silver hair he looked every inch the former airline executive that he had been and the wealthy farmer he was now.

"Do I look all right?" he asked Andrew.

"You look like a gentleman," Andrew said. He directed Jack to move the drop cloth closer to the window and to set up the easel. He had trained Jack how to do the setup and prepare his palette. Some of the colors he made himself did not come in metal tubes, of course, which were no longer available, but in small glass jars manufactured in the old times, still plentiful and reusable. By the time everything was ready Harry had arrived with a pot of peppermint tea and a plate of cookies made of cornmeal, walnuts, honey, and plenty of butter. Deaver's wife, Nancy, fluttered into the room briefly to say hello, before going down to the workshop beside one of the barns where the wool from her Merino sheep was being cleaned, degreased, and prepared for dyeing to fulfill a contract for the New Faith blanket-making operation.

Ben Deaver took up his pose beside the window and Andrew began the portrait by establishing reference points and lines of the composition in thin brown paint on the gessoed panel, humming a slip jig called "The Snowy Path" as he worked. He had just begun to establish the masses of Deaver's figure when a commotion erupted in the hall outside the sitting room, accompanied by the raised voices of Harry and another man. Then there was a sharp cry, the door to the hallway crashed open, and the baleful figure of Donald Acker flew into the room with an eight-inch hollow-ground cook's knife aloft in his hand. They smelled him the same moment they saw him. Behind Acker, Harry staggered two steps and collapsed with blood running down his arm. Both Ben Deaver at the window and Andrew Pendergast, brush in hand, stood frozen like jacked deer, but Jack Harron sprang from his place near Andrew, left his feet, and flung his shoulder into Acker's knees, as he had learned to do years ago on the football field. The two of them crashed down on a coffee table in a heap of flailing limbs, one of which was Acker's right arm with the knife plunging twice into the conjoined mass of clothing that was the two of them. Then, in a movement that was simply a continuation of all that kinetic motion, Jack rolled onto his feet toward the fireplace and, while Acker struggled with the great bulk of himself to rise from the floor, seized a fireplace poker that rested casually against the marble hearth and swung it with such force against the side of Acker's head that his skull split open like a muskmelon, with large bits of bone and gobbets of brain flying against the furnishings and draperies of the beautiful room as his body crumpled back onto the splintered coffee table like a puppet with its strings cut.

Forty-two

Robert and Daniel Earle slid into a booth in the back room of the new Union Tavern. Brother Micah was polishing glasses behind the bar where some idle farmhands passed the winter midday nursing glasses of cider. The only other patrons that lunch hour were two young men from Bennington, Vermont, twenty-three miles to the east, who occupied another booth in the back, having just that morning delivered to Brother Jobe's chief engineer, Brother Shiloh, a belt and roller assembly manufactured in one of the first small factories started anywhere post-collapse in the struggling region. Their factory turned out equipment for water-powered machinery and was destined to run the washers and mangles in the Union Grove Community Laundry.

A New Faith sister took Robert and Daniel's order: soup (bean and cabbage with ham) and two variety plates with corn bread. Robert did not generally like to drink alcohol during the day. He ordered rose hip tea; Daniel asked for cider, Holyrood's Frosty Jack.

"So you were on that schooner . . ." Robert said, filling his mug from the steaming teapot.

Daniel's Story: Summer, Channel Island

We sailed up to the place where the federals had set up their new capital on Lake Huron, stopping only in Detroit, which had endured repeated typhoid fever epidemics that left it little more than a trading post on the river between the lakes—so odd to behold, with the skeletons of the huge old factories standing mute at Wyandotte and River Rouge and then, farther up, the decrepitating glass skyscrapers of the old city center, where ospreys now roosted. There were hardly any signs of life along the riverfront. I didn't have any duties and spent much of the next two days on deck watching the shoreline or, once we got out into it, Lake Huron in all its moods. We passed some other sailing vessels, apparently transporting cargoes of goods. It made me sad for what I'd lost: Evan, the *Kerry McKinney*, and the freedom of being on our own. I had several sessions with a navy doctor who put me through a battery of tests and interviews to determine my mental disposition, I believe. I had supper twice in the officers' mess along with Ms. Estridge, her two civilian subalterns in the Service, the captain of *The Great Northern* and his officers. The chatter was all of our strained relations with Canada.

The town of New Columbia was alive with construction when we docked there, rising out of the detritus of an old-times town, a place of no significance. What startled me upon landing there was the sound of electric tools, the whine of circular saws. The first thing that the government did was set up two electric wind turbines on Channel Island, a half mile out in the lake, and run cables to the mainland. The electric power was intermittent; it didn't work when the wind wasn't blowing. There weren't sufficient batteries to store the power, so sometimes workers could use power tools and other times you heard the slower rhythmic sound of hand saws. Same with electric lights. Sometimes they just didn't work but it sure was nice when they did.

They weren't trying to reconstruct Washington, DC, in this new place. They were aware of things being lost for good and of the country being something other than what it used to be. The scale of the new stuff was very modest. To me it was like a frontier village. Harvey Albright had a philosophy that the new government should relinquish any pretense of imitating what had been destroyed. He had disdain for the overblown conceited beliefs of the old system, especially the idea of American exceptionalism that got the nation in so much trouble. The new capitol building under construction was a modest redbrick structure, smaller than a high school, with no dome and two very austere chambers for the House and the Senate. Few representatives or senators even showed up when I was there. What little there was of government ran out of the president's office and the headquarters of the Service. There were no cabinet secretaries and no agencies, just a few dozen men and women around Harvey Albright.

All of them actually lived and worked on Channel Island. They had begun constructing stone revetments around the shore to defend it, perhaps from the Canadians, if they couldn't come to terms. The president lived and worked in a former coast guard station on the side of the island that faced out into Lake Huron toward Canada, protected by a battery of artillery. They did call it the White House, though. The building was painted white. Many of Albright's inner circle of advisors and assistants lived in the station too. Other government people of lesser status occupied a four-story wooden hotel built hastily on the side of the island facing the town on the mainland. Ms. Estridge and the Service had their own precinct in woods behind the president's house. It had been a summer colony for rich people from Detroit back in the heyday of the old times. She had a house in a piney glade near the shore, very private and secluded from the other things in the compound. It had been built a hundred years ago by a lubricant tycoon, I learned.

The Service was the residue of the State Department and the intelligence agencies. It was never clear to me exactly what assets it still controlled. At least twice a week all the personnel on Channel Island were asked to attend gatherings in a building called the Commons, which was a pavilion with a ballroom and quarters for visiting dignitaries next to the White House. This was done to keep up morale, as far as I could tell. The government was very insecure. It had little real control over anything. Most of the visitors who came in the weeks when I was there were from Canada. President Albright was negotiating with the province of Ontario to unite with his government. That was the reason behind Ms. Estridge's journey on the schooner *The Great*

Northern when I was plucked out of Lake Erie, not any "port inspections," as she told me.

I spent the first night and day on Channel Island in a kind of navy lab where I was run through more tests. They wanted to know just about everything I ever did or thought or felt since I was a baby. They badgered me, trying to find my limits. I think on at least one occasion I was given drugs. I was not told what for. It was "classified." The next afternoon, an ensign brought me to Ms. Estridge's house, where I was assigned quarters. It was a very grand place. He left me on a stone terrace. You could see the lake through the pines, flickering evening light playing through. She stepped out on the terrace, looking different than when we were on the ship. Her hair was down. She was dressed in a blue velvet gown. She took my breath away.

"You're working for me now," she says, clipping on an earring, very businesslike in contrast to her costume.

"What are my duties?"

"We have a mission for you."

"Does that mean I have to go somewhere?"

"Yes, you'll see more of the country, just like you wanted to."

"What is the purpose of this mission?"

"It's . . . a special assignment. You'll understand what it entails when you go through the training."

The Service was very big on testing and training. Of course, they couldn't train you for everything.

So it started. She went to the Commons that night in her gown. Harvey Albright hated slovenliness. It was a big part of our country's decline, he said. So things were quite formal there. I began my training the next day. It was extremely rigorous, both physically and mentally. They had people who knew how to do things you would never learn in a normal life in normal times. Ways to hurt people. Ways to deceive people. Ways to get through an unfriendly country. Ways to survive. The mission was revealed to me in slow stages, like the petals of a flower blossoming over a period of days, a black rose. My destination was Tennessee. I knew that was the heart of the Foxfire Republic.

Looking back, I think the purpose of quartering me in Ms. Estridge's house was to excite me, to light a particular flame of desire in me, to make me a little crazy in preparation for what would happen in Tennessee. There were moments when I wondered if she was toying with me. The house was full of her perfume. Once, she came back from a diplomatic dinner with the Canadians and stood in the doorway of my room in a distant wing of the house asking about my girlfriends back home. I think she'd had quite a bit to drink. She told me to call her Valerie. She made a V with her fingers to emphasize it and then peered at me through the notch between her fingers as if she were aiming a rifle. She told me her husband was killed in a food riot in St. Paul the year before. He was a major in what was called the Home Guard. Someone pitched a television out a fourth-story window onto the street he was standing on and it broke his head open. She missed him terribly, she said. It was nice to have a man in the house, she said, meaning me. She said I was a very handsome young man and that it would surely help me on my mission.

I thought something might happen between us that night, but she went only so far with her suggestive behavior and no further and I didn't dare make a move. She waxed philosophical, standing there in the doorway, in the candlelight, beautifully dressed in one of her gowns. These were completely abnormal times, she said, but they would stay that way, things would never be normal again. She said she was worried about what they were sending me off to do and she started to cry a little. Not sobbing or carrying on. Just some tears and a sniffle. I almost reached out to her. But she turned and left abruptly. I listened to her pad down the stairs and then the door shut, and I lay awake for hours thinking, wishing she might come back.

I was there, on Channel Island, for about a month. The trainers toughened me up. I think they got pretty deep inside my mind. They worked hard on me. Things changed inside of me. Subtle things. The way I saw the world. My feelings. The mission I was being prepared for took on more of a reality than where I was, except for the reality of Valerie Estridge, which continued to torment me with irresolvable tension.

The government kept a launch at the island dock with four oarsmen, which was rowed back and forth to town every hour, and I went over on a few occasions to look at the construction and walk the few streets, just to get out of the suffocating conditions on the island for a while. I was encouraged to come to gatherings in the Commons, where I got to see just about all that was left of the U.S. government in one big room—smart, ambitious people in midlife who were thrilled at having survived a wrenching transition and clearly enjoyed their roles in the strange new order of things. I was given a lieutenant's uniform to wear, though I wan't commissioned. It was very formal, pretty grand there, like a ball in a fairy tale, with Harvey Albright as Prince Charming. The pavilion itself was very beautiful, with a vaulted ceiling, fireplaces big enough to walk into, and a view west toward New Columbia. The late summer sun would be setting over the new construction just as the ball picked up momentum and people loosened up. They did a lot of drinking on Channel Island. They were a very high-strung bunch, those government people. The food was outstanding. Groaning buffet tables of beef and Great Lakes salmon and cheeses, plenty of wheat bread. Everything was coming into season and Michigan was overflowing with produce like a cornucopia. There was music and formal dancing in lines with complicated figures. Valerie Estridge was not the only attractive female there. On one occasion I met a girl who worked in the Office of Correspondence, as it was called. She was a lovely dancer. Her name was Sienna, dark-haired, delicate, with a low throaty voice, obviously smart, a Chicago girl. All I did was sit at her table chatting for half an hour after dancing and the next day a navy special ops guy met me on the path from the training building to the commissary and said if I ever talked to her again he would rip me a new asshole. I don't think he realized that I had been taught some of the same tricks he knew, and for a moment I was tempted to try some of my training on him, but I just let it pass.

The day came in August when I was told to prepare to leave Channel Island for my mission. They meant prepare mentally because I had gotten pretty comfortable there and now things were about to change again. To my surprise, Ms. Estridge came in around eight that evening with President Albright himself. It was twilight, beautiful reflections off the lake playing on the ceiling. I was in her library, lying on the sofa reading a big book about the First World War full of pictures of the slaughter of the trenches. I had been in the Commons many times when the president was there but had never spoken to him. He was a solid, rather blocky man of fifty-two, built like a wrestler, clean-shaven, which was the federal style, with brown hair that he wore to his shoulder. He was a very avid rider and wore tall boots with buff trousers and a black double-breasted tunic with a flap collar partly opened. He even smelled a little like horse sweat. He had an obvious air of authority, like some other people I'd met since setting out from home. I could see Albright's security detail through the window, down by the rhododendron plantings, three soldiers dismounted, holding the reins of their horses.

Ms. Estridge poured two glasses of brandy. I was standing now and the president gestured for me to resume sitting. He took a seat directly across the low coffee table from me in a plush chair and leaned in with his forearms on his knees. She stayed in the background standing by the fireplace.

"You'll be traveling as far as Cincinnati with Major John Thomason and his company," he says. "From there you'll assume the identity we've supplied you with and some printed identification. When you cross the Ohio River you'll be in enemy territory. You'll continue to go by your own name, of course, since it would only confuse you to change it, and nobody in Tennessee will know who you are, anyway, but you will have a new biography. When you get to the town of Franklin you'll report to Hector Tillman, better known as Barefoot Tillman—"

I'm like, "Barefoot?" I couldn't help laughing. "Excuse me, sir. Is that really someone's name?"

Albright flashes a momentary smile. Then it's gone. He's like, "These are hard-core Appalachian crackers, young man, if I may be blunt. Barefoot Tillman, he's our man on the inside, all the way and deep. He is a patriot. We trust him absolutely. And so do they. He has been among these extreme Christian reconstructionists since before the real trouble started. He will be your handler on the inside. You will receive your instructions from him. The Foxfire leadership are dangerous people and we knew what they were up to before the"—he made a gesture with his hands as of disposing of something unpleasant—"the trouble our country has been through. They were bent on systematically destroying the government and our institutions. The Foxfire gang effectively had political control of the whole mid-southern region before the war and the oil shocks and they took the opportunity in our moment of weakness to set up exactly the kind of theocratic despotism they have advocated for decades. They are unapologetic white supremacist fanatics who would banish people unlike them and, in fact, have, and, in further fact, will destroy them should they not submit to banishment and have done exactly that. Their leaders claim to speak for God and rule with the authority of God and are not subject to any checks and balances. They have the power of life and death over people with no due process of law. They believe in liquidating homosexuals, Jews, anyone they perceive as foreign, adulterers, blasphemers, and, of course, anyone who opposes their methods and beliefs. They have run most of the African Americans out of the region they control, and killed many, and stolen their property, and have not stopped trying to get rid of those who remain and resist. They are very aggressive and have formed a military. They endeavor to take over southern Ohio and northern Georgia. We oppose them in southern Ohio and are preparing to defend Cincinnati with our military against a siege of that city. They initiated hostilities against the city of Atlanta, or what remains of it, months ago, but so far that place has been successfully defended by the forces under Milton Steptoe, aka Sage, head of state of so-called New Africa. We believe the Foxfire Republic leadership intends to try to control as much of the old lower forty-eight states as they can conquer. They're refighting the Civil War. They are very determined to win this time and they are quite crazy, in my opinion, the way the Nazis were crazy. The thing is, we're determined too. We're determined to not let history run over us and jump feetfirst into a dark age. We intend to keep this government running up here in the Lakes and get the American project going again. I would like to put these dangerous fanatics out of business in a way that the German Nazis should have been put out of business, by striking at the head of this mad beast and decapitating it. Are you following all this, young man?"

"Yessir."

"Mr. Tillman—and that's what you will call him—is as close as anyone can be to the leader of the Foxfire Republic, the woman known as Loving Morrow, formerly Caroline Woodfin of Luck, North Carolina, a self-created personality and a danger to the human race. Do you remember television, son?"

"A little."

"Loving Morrow preached over the airwaves," he went on. "She had a cable TV station in Nashville and raised enormous sums of money on it from her Foxfire Church of the True Holy Light pulpit. She used that to finance a news operation, which was just nonstop hateful propaganda inveighing against the Wall Street Jews and the Won't Work Nigger monkeys, as they called them, and the fags, ditto, and also against the federal government, of course. We know a great deal about Loving Morrow. One thing we know is that she has a weakness for young men. And that is why we are sending you down there to kill her."

President Harvey Albright looked right at me as he said this and I didn't flinch or make a peep because I knew clear into the center of myself that this was exactly what I was going to do. I also knew that it was at the heart of the training I had received. Odd, isn't it? To know that your mind has been meddled with and still feel like you have free will?

A New Faith sister brought their food order to the booth. As she leaned forward to slide the plates onto the table, Daniel noticed her shapely figure, her breasts straining against the cotton fabric of her blouse. The emotion it aroused seemed to exhaust him momentarily. When she was gone, he turned his attention to his bowl of steaming soup. He closed his eyes and savored the journey of the warm, smoky-spicy bean mush down his gullet into his belly.

"You were programmed," Robert said. "We used to do that with computers. You enter a set of coded instructions and the machine just executes them. They used to do that with people too. They called it brainwashing."

"Brainwashing," Daniel said. "Yes. They certainly scrubbed it good there on Channel Island."

Daniel's Story: In Enemy Territory

Much later that night, after Albright left the house, I had trouble sleeping. The wind banged around outside. Moonlight skittered all over the walls and ceiling as it played among the windblown tree branches through the window. The door to my room opened and Ms. Estridge, Valerie, appeared in a robe, like a vision or a dream. She let the robe slide down her shoulders and fall at her feet. The moonlight flashed over her naked body for a time before she came onto the bed as though she was purposely putting herself on display. I just yielded to her like she was a force of nature. I felt that this was something I must let happen with the greatest urgency, something beyond my own desires and intentions—as you said, programmed into my brain. No words were spoken. She overwhelmed me. It went on a long time, I think, and when it was over I fell asleep immediately. I never got to say good-bye to her, at least in words, and in the morning when the sergeant came to get me she wasn't anywhere in the house.

We started to Cincinnati that morning, an infantry company of 120 men, officers mounted. I was permitted to ride, too, but I received many a resentful glance from the men marching. I was in civilian clothing, good clothing. Over the days to come we passed through Flint, a ghost town, Ann Arbor, where the big university was all closed up, Toledo and Columbus, everything smaller, reduced, struggling. Cincinnati's riverfront was alive, at least. The vast parking lots between the ball parks had been turned into a stockyard and several new concerns had been built for salting pork and making sausage. They were brewing beer too. Many were employed at these operations and lived close by in the blocks behind the vacant district of skyscraper buildings in the old row-house district. But the city was very much compressed, as were all the places I had been to over the months, into the habitable precincts of its old center, with everything beyond a half mile walk from the riverfront empty and deserted. Many had died in the epidemics there and malaria was now also a seasonal visitor.

From down in the stockyards, across the Ohio, you could see some fortifications over on the Kentucky side and soldiers slouching on the parapets with rifles. Nobody was shooting at anybody yet, but Kentucky was a Foxfire Republic state and there was a sharp feeling of animosity in the air, like something could bust out at any moment. Cincinnati had its garrison, too, between a swathe of disintegrating elevated highway and the river, east of the stockyards. The prevailing winds prevented the place from being overwhelmed by the odor of hundreds of confined pigs. Fort Schenck was very much a makeshift establishment, still under construction. Some two thousand soldiers were billeted there in tents, shacks, and half-finished barracks. After a month living with at least some electricity it was back to candlelight for me.

But I wasn't there long. They took me across the river the second night about ten miles downstream from Fort Schenck where a little creek called Rapid Run spills into the Ohio. The Kentucky side was just some farms with the old Cincinnati airport behind them. It hadn't been used for over a decade. Nobody was around. The bank across the river down there was known by the federals to be unguarded. I was rowed across in a pilot gig with a Lieutenant Ainsley. There was just a sliver of moon above the horizon. A horse was waiting for me on the other side. Kentucky had its share of federal sympathizers, people who objected to the Foxfire methods and religious persecution and didn't like being pushed around. My horse was furnished by two men, not young, dressed in town clothes. No one told me, but I got the feeling they were lawyers. Lieutenant Ainsley gave them a pouch that contained hard money. The horse was a chestnut gelding named Ike. He was tacked up with an unmarked military saddle on him. I was also given a money pouch. Not a large amount, because the Foxfire region was said to be infested with bandits and pickers, but enough to cover my meals and lodging, if I could find any, in the two weeks it would take me to get to my destination, Franklin, Tennessee, a town south of Nashville, now the Foxfire capital. These transactions on the Kentucky side were completed very quickly and all these men were strangers to me so, having no further business, I just thanked them, mounted, and rode off.

I had memorized the route during my training. I was not carrying any maps, which might suggest I was a spy. I had a compass and a few documents: false identification that indicated I was a merchant of Covington, along with bills of lading and promissory notes pertaining to fictitious business I had in Franklin, in case I met up with any Foxfire military along the way.

I soon made my way beyond the abandoned housing tracts south of the airport and followed a set of back roads through deeply forested, crinkled hills to Big Bone Lick, where I caught up again with the south-turning Ohio River. I slept out that first night in a cemetery, in warm weather, and had plenty of rations for my breakfast and some oats for Ike, who I'd hobbled inside the cemetery fence with me. The next two days I made excellent progress to Frankfort, Kentucky. It rained hard there and I stayed inside the Meeting House Tavern where I put up for an extra night. That was the first place on my journey I encountered a painted image of Loving Morrow, set up like a little shrine on a table in the common room, with Foxfire flags, some old plastic flowers, and a statuette of Jesus Christ. The painting was done by an obvious amateur who depicted the Leading Light of the Foxfire Republic, as she called herself, with a sort of golden halo, as if she were a saint. The artist had put a slightly mad look in her eyes. Her figure was pictured as very generously filling her robes, such as to be an object of desire. Her physical presence was not a small part of her appeal, I was given to understand. Anyway, the food was very good there. I got a plate of fried chicken and three ears of sweet corn. It was that time of year.

Aside from a little rain the first week of my journey was easy. The route I passed along was sparsely inhabited between the towns, almost like a wilderness, and many of those towns were reduced to very meager terms. At one crude tavern at Campbellsville, I overheard talk of "confiscations, tithings, and oppression," and I believe they were referring to their own Foxfire government; the Brunswick stew I was served there fetched up on me afterward. Two days farther down the road I met bandits coming through a rocky defile outside of Horse Cave, Kentucky, about a day's ride from the Tennessee border. I was walking Ike to take in the rugged scenery when I heard hoofbeats. They rode up behind me and I reined Ike around to face them. I believe they were all younger than me. The youngest reminded me of Evan, which sent a pang of remorse through me because I would have to defend myself if it came to it. They were a scruffy-looking bunch in country clothes and mean little hats, and one rode a mule. The youngest rode up closer to me on his squatty swayback nag with just a blanket for a saddle and a rope bridle.

I'm like, "You're following a little close, aren't you?"

He was apparently their spokesman. He might not have been older than sixteen, with peach-fuzz whiskers. "That's a nice horse you got, mister," he goes. The other two looked blank, slack-jawed, like they might be drunk. Their heads appeared a little lopsided too. We all just swapped eyeballs for a long moment, one to the next.

"If you're in hurry, pass on by," I say.

"How much you take for him?" the young leader says.

"He's not for sale."

He goes, "We got something in trade I expect you can't resist."

"What would that be?"

"A five-minute head start," he says. "On foot." And then he busts up laughing.

I'm like, "I don't think so."

He's like, "We'll see about that." He goes directly for the butt of a pistol that's jammed in the side of his trousers and he can't withdraw it. It's stuck. His cohorts guffaw. When they do, I see they have no front teeth. Finally, he frees up his firearm and draws it out. It's some kind of homemade piece of junk, like out of a piece of steel pipe, with a crude wood grip and an awkward assembly of levers and springs at the breech end. Meanwhile, I've drawn my own pistol, which is an old-times factory-made .38 caliber military revolver, and my heart is sinking as I am about to use it on this pathetic boy. As my gun comes out, his two cohorts rein around and ride off up the road, apparently unequipped with any firearms of their own. The boy doesn't even look up or see me brandish my weapon, he's so intent with that piece of junk. He has to pull the hammer contraption back with both hands to set it, like it was a crossbow. I fire into the air just to get his attention. A split second after I do that his gun misfires. The discharge vaporizes one ear of his poor old horse in a little cloud of red mist, and the recoil blows him off his mount in the process. His nag bolts away, screaming and bleeding from the stump of her ear, up the road where the others skulked off. The boy is squirming in pain on the road. He must have landed hard on something. The road is fissured old blacktop that hasn't been repaired in his lifetime.

Now I dismount to attend to him. As I do that, out comes a dark steel blade that he would have stuck in my liver had I not been lucky to kick it clean out of his hand, and then I was on top of him with my knee in his chest and my hand on his throat. He is fulminating at me, blowing snot on my jacket. I strike him in the head repeatedly until he stops it.

"Keep it up and you'll get yourself killed for certain," I say.

"Why don't you then?" he says, and his voice is all strangled with my hand on his throat.

"Because I don't want to," I tell him.

"Why not? It's your right. Look who's on top."

"Is that how it's done around here?"

"Sure it is," he says. "Anyway, I don't care if I live or die."

"Well you ought to," I say and cuff him on the head one more time. "What's the matter with you?"

"Nothin'. If it was me on top I'd kill you."

"You come at me with one more weapon, I might change my mind."

He quits struggling and I get off of him. He's got a pretty bad powder burn on one side of his face. He sits up and spits some blood out of his mouth. Up close, he smells like those pigs back in the Cincinnati stockyards.

I'm like, "You're a poor excuse for a bandit. Why don't you take up some other line of work?"

"Like what?"

"Farm. It's safer."

He spits. "Person like me can't get land. It's all owned by the masters. They run your ass off if they don't kill you outright. That's why I'm up to robbing folks."

I go, "Looks to me like this country is ninety percent empty, woods coming back where the fields used to be, nobody around. I'm telling you, just grab yourself some acres and settle in, raise some chickens and corn."

"You can't just set down on a place," he says. "Them Foxfires'll get you and put you in their damn army and send you off to fight the niggers."

"Maybe the army wouldn't be such a bad place for someone like you."

He squints up at me like I'm out of my mind. "You're not from around here, are you?" he says.

"I'm from up in Covington, Kentucky, on the Ohio."

"You sound like a damn socialist." He spits again.

"Well, I'm not."

He's like, "Just kill me and get it over with." He squeezes his eyes shut, with blood dribbling down his chin, and waits for the bullet.

"You're a dandy, you are."

"I'm sick of it all is what I am."

"Don't you have any interest being in this world? It's a gift, you know."

"It's just affliction and a torment," he says, eyes still shut. "Go ahead. Do me like I would have done you."

I'm like, "I'll just be on my way now, if you don't mind."

"You a preacher?"

"What if I was?"

"Then I would hate you double," he says. "They just serve the masters is all. I don't know what you are, mister, but I'm real sorry I failed to kill you. You want to know a secret? I like that even better than robbing folks. I've killed seven men since I took up this career. What do you think of that?"

"Life must be cheap in this part of the country," I say.

"It ain't worth nothin'," he goes. "Guess I'll be on my way now too."

When he stands up fully, I doubt he's over five and a half feet tall. He dusts himself off and picks up his mean little chewed-up-looking hat, which is like a cloth bowl on his head. While he's doing that, I go get his firearm, which is lying in the road.

"You gawn keep that?" he asks.

"I'm going to throw it in a creek at the first opportunity," I tell him.

"Why not give it back to me then?" he says. "I'll just have to make another one."

"You do that," I say. "Maybe you'll get better at it, if someone doesn't kill you first, and you'll grow up to be a gunsmith, with an honest trade."

He just snorts at the idea and begins humping back up the road where his cohorts and his nag ran away. When there's a hundred yards of space between us I mount up and go on my way. I did throw that pitiful gun away at the first chance I came by. The land there was full of limestone sinkholes, like perfectly round little ponds, from all the caves that ran underground in that part of the country.

Judging by what I saw on my journey from the federal states, the Foxfire Republic was even more deeply impoverished and run-down than the north. Some towns had nobody whatsoever in them. One evening by the fireside of a crossroads tavern in Owen's Chapel, I heard talk for the first time of a smallpox visitation that passed over the region a few years back. They had new diseases that had never been seen there before. Snail fever, dengue, whipworm, black jaundice, sand fly rot, chagas, yellow fever, and malaria, on top of all the other sorts of epidemic flu plus the encephalitis and meningitis that was everywhere.

I finally came into Nashville on a hot morning late in August. The very center of the town around the north side of the old state-house had mostly been parking lots when the collapse happened. Men were at work erecting buildings of two and three stories in red brick that they salvaged from elsewhere in the deserted quarters of the city. Many strangely shaped skyscrapers loomed balefully over the blocks between the old capitol and the Cumberland River. They were empty now. The glass had been removed, starting from the lower floors. The sort of office work they were built for no longer existed and they contained a lot of material that nobody manufactured anymore. You could imagine the work of careful disassembly going on for decades, centuries. I know from my history classes people were still pulling marble off the ancient Roman monuments a thousand years after the empire fell. The smallpox outbreak had devastated Nashville. The survivors fled, and the Foxfire government had moved to Franklin, some twenty miles south. Nashville was the headquarters of the Foxfire military these days. In the distance on a grassy mall down the statehouse hill, a company of foot soldiers drilled. Their drumbeats and shouts carried in the still air. Their formations were slapdash. They didn't seem like a match for the federals back at Fort Schenck. Officers on horseback came and went. Their uniform jackets looked homemade, as if they were trying out all different styles, which is to say they were hardly uniforms. I got a meal of fried potatoes and ham at the makeshift outdoor market that operated next to the statehouse, patronized almost entirely by workmen and soldiers. I saw very few women in the city passing through that day. I didn't want to linger where so many soldiers casually gathered.

I got to Franklin in the early evening. I came in straight from the north on old State Highway 31. The asphalt pavements were stripped off the surface starting some five miles out from town, and a gravel road was laid the rest of the way, which was well maintained, excellent for horses and wagons. Closer to the old center, the highway eventually became Main Street and I had to wait my turn to pass through a gate manned by soldiers, who were checking cargoes and persons wanting to enter. There was considerable traffic with wagons backed up from that point, most of them commercial but some military. They were especially on the lookout for people who showed signs of ill health. The gatehouse was a substantial, handsome structure of red brick that made a graceful arch over the street with offices on each side for the soldiers to do their business and congregate and a room in the arch itself, where a soldier sat in a window with binoculars surveying the procession down the road. It was clearly built to impress, to send the message that Franklin was a special place, exclusive, orderly and well protected. The soldiers manning the gate wore gray tunics that all did look the same and hats with the brim tacked up on one side, giving them a dashing air. I dismounted and felt nervous waiting. My sidearm was stashed in my blanket roll but, when my turn came, they barely searched my person or asked more than my name and my business in town, which they recorded in a ledger and then said I could go in.

Friday evenings in Franklin was the time of the week when people of the Foxfire capital did their shopping and put themselves on display, a time of socializing in public. Now, the most amazing thing happened. Around eight o'clock, as the sun sank below the little hills to the west, electric streetlights flickered on as well as the lights in buildings around town. The storefront windows and rooms in the second and third stories came alive. Many people were out on the sidewalks, a good number of them in fancy town clothes. A lot of these were government employees. They paused to clap their hands, applauding the amazing display of electric power, like a little ceremony, and then went back to their business promenading or visiting the shops along the street. One of the larger emporiums in the center of the business district was called Walmart. I dimly remember the name from the commercial folklore of the old times. It occupied a building that had once been a movie theater. As far as I could tell it was just a glorified dry goods operation. Pairs of soldiers mounted on fine horses surveyed the scene on street corners. Now and then, a fine open carriage came along the street with a prosperous couple or a family, as children were a sign of high status in these days of frequent epidemics. I admit that I was thrilled to find myself in this busy, bright place, though I would learn a lot about its dark side.

The original old heart of town, where activity now concentrated, was a set of ten blocks disposed around a broad traffic circle with a square rose garden set within it and an obelisk in the middle. A lot of new construction was evident. Since the Foxfire government relocated from Nashville and extended its administrative tentacles far and wide, the wealth from its territories flowed into Franklin. Much of the town had been relegated to parking lots in the old times. The lots were being filled in now and the work was impressive. The new buildings were made in the traditional style of the region, using red bricks and wood trim painted white, sometimes with black shutters, which gave you the odd impression of being somewhere that was neither exactly the past nor the present. The buildings that most stood out were the awkward and ugly things left over from the twentieth century, buildings that looked like machines, or packing crates, or spaceships, and were built with materials that aged badly. These were being torn down, to great public approval. Of all the strange sights my first night in Franklin, the most startling was the glimpse of a big black automobile rolling past a cross street two blocks off the town center. It was there for a moment, and then it was gone, like a phantom. I had not seen a car in motion since I was a young child.

I found a stable for Ike on South Margin Street and proceeded according to my instructions to the Yancey Hotel on Church Street, a new establishment named after the Confederate "fire-eater" politician. The big, four-story place was busy and bright, and when I signed the register the clerk, a slight fellow my age with a concave chest, asked how things were up in Covington.

"They're just fine," I go, not really thinking.

He's like, "Is that so? Well, things will hotten up there soon, you bet."

"You think so?" I say.

He lowers his head and whispers, "It's all the talk we're gonna lay siege to Cincinnati, right across the river there. Didn't you see our soldiers coming in?"

"I've been away from home on business for weeks."

"Well, that's the news, friend. The barroom here is the center of the Foxfire universe. Government bigwigs come and go all day and all night. You'll hear it all first at the Yancey. Just wait and see. We'll take the Ohio and from there it's on to the lakes.

Gonna push the federals clean up to Canada—and maybe we'll have that, too, by and by."

"Perhaps you should join the army and enter the fray," I go. He shoots me a look.

"I'm needed here," he says indignantly.

I realize I'd better check my banter and study up on my *legend*, as they call your cover story in the Service, so I can be quicker on my feet.

Meanwhile he's turned all business with me. "The electric goes off at ten-thirty p.m., midnight on weekends," he says. "After that you have to use candles so please take the usual precautions. Welcome to the Yancey, and praise her."

He was referring to the Foxfire leader. I'd learn that most formal transactions in Franklin finished with that praise salute to Loving Morrow. I would employ it myself in the days ahead. Apart from that, I was happy to find that they were serving real old-times pizza in the barroom when I finally got down there. There was plenty of wheat in Franklin. These people had plenty of everything.

In the morning, I found an envelope slipped under the door with instructions to report to the paddock at Stokely's mule barn out on Acton Street at ten o'clock. When I got downstairs to the restaurant it was already 9:15, so I had to bolt some eggs and biscuits and hurry over. There were half a dozen men there at Stokely's, some country people, some in good linen suits. I was just standing at the fence, like I was a buyer, looking at the stock. It was already very hot and the mule paddocks were dusty. Soon, a slight man about fifty sidled up to me. He was delicate in his figure, dressed in good clothes and high boots, with a broad-brimmed hat and steel-rimmed eyeglasses.

"I'm Hector Tillman," he says.

"Then I am the one you are looking for," I say.

He tells me to go out the checkpoint on the Murfreesboro Road at the edge of town and cross the bridge and go up by the path along the creek and wait for him in a cottonwood grove. I do just like he says, directly. It's a quarter mile, just a five-minute

walk past some half-demolished highway strip buildings, fields
of asphalt, old-times desolation. The checkpoint on that side of
town is much less grand than the one coming in on the Nashville
Pike—just a shack and a fence with a gate in it. It happens that
the solitary soldier there is tilted back in his chair napping in
the sunshine. He smells like a distillery. I duck under the gate
and continue on my way. I take the well-trodden path beside the
lazy stream, find the grove, and shortly Mr. Tillman appears. He
takes my hand in both of his.

"I'm very glad you're here, son, and none too soon," he goes.
"How is our Mr. Albright?"

"I think he's got his hands full, sir."

"I hear they got a new headquarters up in Michigan. Lakefront property."

"It's not as grand as this place," I say, which seems to annoy
him.

"This place . . ." he goes. "Hmph. Well, you're a fine speci-
men," he says. "Our Leading Light is going to like you, I believe.
You give ole Harvey my fond regards, you get out of here alive."

That threw a chill in me for a moment. Mr. Tillman plucked
a grass stem with a seed head and sucked the stalk, searching the
riverside for an awkward interval. A faraway look came over him,
as though for a moment he clearly saw a lurid fate beckoning him.

"Is it true that you're called Barefoot?" I say.

"I was a fast runner as a child," he says. "I'm still pretty quick.
Might come in handy yet. Well, here you are at last," he says
coming back to himself and sizing me up more. "They promised
to send me someone who is prepared and capable. You feeling
up to your task, son?"

"I guess I do, sir."

"Looks like you arrived in good order."

"I met up with robbers just the other day."

"I gather you prevailed."

"They were sickly, inept, and depraved," I say. "And they don't
have a lot of love for their rulers, you might be interested to hear."

"I know all about it," he says. "Sounds like a very general run of the Foxfire populace. Beginning to catch on to the hoodwink nature of their deal, which is they get to stay poor while their rulers wallow in luxury."

"That's how they put it in so many words," I tell him.

"It breeds resentment and grievance, of course."

I'm like, "It's hard not to be impressed by things here. The electric, the goods flowing in, the activity."

"Well, you'll be more astounded before long."

"I saw an automobile last night on a back street."

"Yes, the Leading Light goes about in one, like a goddess in a machine," he says. "I reckon that's what you saw. She likes to patrol the streets, inspecting her domain. She's met not a few young men that way, I hear, but she has a tendency to dispose of them when she's had her fill, so to speak. You stay alert once you're on the inside, and make your move wisely. Before long, this will all seem like a strange dream you had."

"I'm twenty years old and lived through the change from the old to the new," I say, "and I've never seen anything like this place."

"This is the new Rome, boy. Only we not doing it exactly the Roman way. More like the Disneyland way."

I'm like, "What's Disneyland, sir?"

"Long ago and far away," he says. "You take a left at Never-Never Land and keep going."

"I think I see."

"This thing here ain't going to be no thousand-year endeavor. It'll be a miracle if it goes five more, with or without Miz Praise Her. We stripping all the value out of these poor-ass states as fast as we can so the fantasy of wealth and power might linger on here for a little while longer. It's a scavenging operation. The people behind all this look like adults, but they have the minds of children. What was your impression up in Kentucky?"

"It was some sorry country I rode through coming here, sir. With few and sorry people."

"I had a trip over to Arkansas a year ago, visiting with the home folks," he says. "Looked like scenes out of the fourteenth century over there. They just about picked clean. What I'm saying, something you'll come to understand about the Foxfire Republic, these people here in Franklin were determined to not change with the world when the world changed. They still living like it was the old times, as much as they can, but because there's so little left out there, this town and a fraction of its inhabitants are the only ones that get to live this way. In the meantime, they strangling and starving and bleeding down the rest, like a demon tick on a sick dog. That is, the ones that don't get killed or run off outright. They already killed fifty thousand at least, and they're hot for more. Seems the more they kill, the more they like it. They call their policy the Unspeakable, which is funny, 'cause if you spend enough time around them on the inside you'll realize it's nearly all they talk about: eliminating the nigger and the Jew and the Spanish and anyone else they regard as less than one hundred percent Foxfire. They a goddamn menace to life and decency in North America."

Mr. Tillman took off his hat and wiped his brow with his sleeve. His eyes were rheumy, like he didn't sleep well.

I'm like, "Pardon me for asking, where do you fit in, sir?"

"That's just it, I don't," he says. "I was old time federal, going way back to Bubba himself. When the Service was called CIA. Being deep in and deep down is my element. You want to know how come? I got an acute aversion to despotism. I never met with the devil and his associates, but I know political evil when I see it and this here's the real deal. We saw where these folks were going a long time ago, and I been in so long and deep amongst them that it's like living underwater. Tell you the truth, I'd like to breathe again."

"What happens now?" I ask.

"You'll be assigned to work in the Logistics Commission," he says. "It's the civilian side of quartermaster. That's mostly seeing to the flow of goods into the city, keeping track of cargoes, grain shipments, inventories, distribution of provisions, accounting for excise taxes, and such. Soon, you'll be brought into the inner circle. You will not be connected to me in any manner people know about. I'll see to that. She's a piece of work, our Leading Light, Loving Morrow. She's well protected, though. You got to be inside on the inside to get to her, otherwise I might have tried to do the job myself. It never ceases to amaze me how this nation managed to raise up its own little Hitler, and how it turned out to be a down-home gal who likes fried food and Jimmie Rodgers songs. You know, history is nothing if not a prankster. Well, this is the last and only one on one you and me going to have. I've played a dangerous game here and I dare not make a misstep at this point. You'll receive instructions at your place of business and I wish you Godspeed with your mission."

We shook hands, both of us pretty damp with heat and nerves. He left me down there by the river and told me to wait awhile before returning to town. The guard was awake when I passed his checkpoint, but he just waved me through, like his head hurt too much to even ask my name. I moved later that day from the Yancey to a rooming house on Fair Street, where I was to live modestly until called to my duty. The town was full of people from elsewhere all over the Foxfire states who worked on government business, true believers but strangers to one another. I was as anonymous as anyone. I reported to the Logistics Commission offices across town on Monday and I began to learn a few things about how the Foxfire Republic actually functioned.

The electric was kept going in Franklin by means of "the eighth wonder of the world," as they called it: an oil well in Overton County, a hundred miles to the east, that was capable of producing thirty-seven barrels of oil a day. Unfortunately, the largest oil distillery able to be built was capable of refining only twenty barrels a day, and the output could not be moved by old-time motor truck because the pavement on the roads was in such poor condition and there weren't the resources to fix a hundred miles of roadway. So what they managed to distill at Miller Mountain came all that distance to Franklin in horse-drawn vehicles. There was a daily train of these wagons coming and going to power electric generators that ran a few hours in the evening in the central district of town. The journey for each wagon took the better part of a week, and each one required a team of six mules, so you can imagine the expense. Generators ran in the wealthy villa neighborhoods of Loving Morrow's higher-ups and another portion of diesel fuel was allotted to the Leading Light's personal compound west of town. There were some ideas about using armored motor vehicles in military operations to shock and awe the Foxfire enemies, but the battlegrounds were so far flung—Atlanta, in the first instance, and presently Cincinnati—that there wasn't the fuel to get the vehicles there, let alone run them once they got there. So they gave up on that idea and went back to cavalry.

I worked that first week at the Logistics Commission, which had me in and out of an office, going to warehouses about town to physically inspect stores of commodities, entering the figures in ledgers, and compiling reports for a Mr. Bodrew, who I never met, at the head of the commission. I got the impression in just that first week that an awful lot of stuff was being spirited away by anyone who could manage to fob off with it, and therefore that I could make up numbers in my reports and it wouldn't especially matter. But my duties allowed me to get out and about and see things and not have to consort with the others at headquarters. It was lonesome, nervous work in an enemy land, and I awaited my call.

I found a packet on my desk Friday morning. It contained a printed ticket for an event the next afternoon called the Carter's Creek 312 at a place called the Carter's Creek Speedway and also my first week's pay in silver, which amused me because it was made in old-times pre-1965 federal U.S. silver coin. The Foxfires hadn't got their own mint going, apparently. There was another item in the packet, a card with the letters VIP printed on it and the words "Speedway Sanctum" under them, bearing the signature at the bottom of one Hunter P. Call, Chief of Security. It said "Enter Via Gate E." A ribbon was attached to it for wearing around your neck.

This speedway was a ten-minute walk southwest of town, beyond the limestone quarries that figured so large in the old-times economy there. I went out at midafternoon along with hundreds of others from town and many hundreds more streaming in at all compass points from the countryside, a few in wagons or horseback but most on foot. It looked like the old county fairgrounds back home, except everything was new. A wooden grandstand rose out of the surrounding cornfields, all recently built and freshly painted. Harking back to Mr. Tillman, it did seem like how the Romans had built their arenas with the wealth of far-flung provinces. The track itself was a great oval a mile and a half around with a surface of what looked like tar sprayed onto crushed stone. There were Foxfire flags and standards and bunting all over the place. The Foxfire flag consisted of the old Confederate Stars and Bars in the upper corner, like the blue canton of white stars in the U.S. flag, and then a Christian cross with flames coming off the top on a snow white field in place of the old stars and stripes.

I migrated out to the grassy area inside the oval called the infield to mingle with the crowd for a while. Many of the country people were out there with their wagons and animals. They passed around plastic jugs of homemade liquor and not a few hawked food they'd brought with them, crying, "Pies! Boiled peanuts! Corn dodger! Sausage! Pickles! Punch! Muscadine! Divinity!" The grandstand across the way had two levels. I was so much in the habit of counting things after a week at the Logistics Commission that I toted up the rows of seats to estimate it held fifteen hundred people and it was getting filled up now. There were easily another thousand on the apron in front of it and two thousand more in the infield. In the center of the upper level of the grandstand was a distinctly separate large box, a substantial room, really, with a balcony at center. Even at a distance you could see they were the elite milling up there, in fancy clothes and hats. A diesel generator started up and soon a haze of oily smoke drifted over the speedway, then a loud crackling noise provoked the crowd to cheering and a man's voice came over loudspeakers praising Jesus and thanking him for the blessed oil to power the race cars in Jesus' name, and the whole while he spoke the crowd got louder and rowdier and more excited and expectant. I left the infield and strolled back across the track to the apron below the grandstand so as to get a closer look. Another roar erupted and I looked up to see the figure of a petite woman in a white robe, with a big mane of blonde hair, step onto the balcony above. She extended her arms as if embracing everyone in the crowd. The cheering and roaring died down quickly.

"My dear sweet precious angels," Loving Morrow began, her amplified voice reverberating over the loudspeakers. "Thanks so much for coming out here on my fifty-first birthday. We gawn have some fun!"

Another roar from the crowd.

"You want to know how I feel at this, *ahem,* advanced age?"

People in the crowd shouted both "yes" and "no," which provoked laughter and more roaring.

"I feel great," Loving Morrow said. "Fact, I feel like I could take over the world. But what do I want with all those niggers and Jews and Islams and gooks and whatnot out there? Let the winged horsemen ride among them, I say, and winnow down their numbers naturally, and give this ole earth a little breathing room. I got my sights set on what's here, in this precious corner of the globe. We are on the verge of taking back the country, and by that I mean the federal territories, like should have happened last time we come to differences on things."

Another cheer, and whoops, plus respectful applause from the crowd.

She resumed. "First of all, I want to thank him, you know who, the Big Guy, for scheduling me to be born at the right time

and all, and taking me on this wonderful ride I been on, and all
the good fortune of becoming your Leading Light, my dear sweet
precious angels. Praise him! Praise Jesus!"

The crowd does, so strenuously—some of them fainting in
the heat from the intensity of their exertions—and for so long
that Loving Morrow has to extend her arms again to get them to
leave off of all their praising. She's just getting warmed up, though.

"There was a time," she says, "when someone of true Foxfire spirit could find comfort only in the past, while the present
was something to be ashamed of, the years of welfare socialism,
bridge-to-nowhere-ism, decline of faith, decay, corruption, race
mixing, Jew usury, same-sex consort, moocherism, me-tooism,
abortion, and every other evil whatnot that Godless vandal mutts
could contrive to rot our character and turn us into slaves of
Mammon. They dragged us into that Holy Land War to save
the bacon of wicked hypocrite, lawless, mongrel Zionists and
stood by as those monsters stabbed our boys in the back and
left them to die out in the Wilderness of Zin. And that is why
we dissociated these blessed Foxfire states from the depraved
federals, just as our great-great-great-grandfathers stood on the
righteous ground of self-determination at Charleston and Ball's
Bluff, Chancellorsville, Pittsburg Landing, Antietam, and all the
rest, including the unfortunate event of November 1864, just up
the road a ways . . ." She's referring to the Battle of Franklin, a
disaster for the Confederates.

The crowd whoops, cheers, and emits lots of other interesting
noises to demonstrate their range of emotion. Loving Morrow
gazes out over her people with supreme confidence that they
were in thrall to her, nodding her head slightly as if to affirm
herself, a demi-smile on her full lips, and her eyes slitty with
determination. You could tell she knows they were enjoying every
minute of her antics. She lets them run themselves down naturally
before resuming.

"There was only a handful of us back in the day who sub-
scribed to the Foxfire vision, back when it was just a political

party. But it grew and grew. Fifty core members, then five hundred members, five thousand members, fifty thousand, five hundred thousand, five million. The time will come when those who condemn and oppose us will join us. What started as just a teeny-tiny movement is now a nation, the Foxfire Republic, one nation truly under God, and the right God, too, praise him, Jesus Christ!"

The crowd eats it up. Grown men stagger in the direction of Loving Morrow's pulpit and fall to their knees. Some break into babbling nonsense speech, what the Foxfire true believers call *the tongues*. People of all ages, both men and women, are shedding tears, even bawling.

"It was our recognition," Loving Morrow goes on, "that a vicious gang of criminals tried to destroy our Foxfire founding heritage in the halls of Washington and the law courts, which provoked the need to separate, and we will not rest now until we overcome their vile and illegitimate so-called government and restore that founding vision among all the states, from Maine to Minnesota, praise him, praise Jesus. And likewise to that rapist, murderer, cannibal, self-proclaimed N-word prophet, Sage, also known as the usurer Milton Steptoe, in lawless occupation of our legacy cotton states, we proclaim a warrant of eviction! Let those monkeys move south to a monkey land in the South American tropics were they can laze under the banana tree all the live-long day and make monkey babies and do nothing worthy of the true human being."

The crowd commences, as if on cue, to making monkey noises and gestures—going *hoo hoo hoo* and pretending to scrape their knuckles on the ground and scratch their flanks. The Leading Light beams at them and nods her big gold-maned head with approbation. This goes on for some time. They are all excellently rehearsed and orchestrated in their roles, the leader and the led.

"Do you know the true origin of the Jew?" she continues. "In sixth-century before-Jesus Babylon, where all the bad apples of Judah's barrel got mongrelized. And, then, you see, they return to Canaan and mingle with the mongrel descendants of Esau, and this bunch become the self-righteous, blaspheming Pharisees of our New Testament times. Didn't the apostle John say of them: *Ye are of your father the Devil, and the lust of your father ye will do?* With the rise of these Pharisee Jews and the Christmas Nativity comes the battle between the racially pure holy Christian ones of the world and the unholy mixed mongrel Jew. The dearest belief of the Pharisee Jew is that they are the highest life-form on earth. They are special—chosen people!—while the white Christian is on a par with the beasts of the field. Can you beat that?"

"No-o-o-o-o ..." the crowd replies as one. They're going wild, brows knitted in righteous rage and eyes all scrunched together, turned-down mouths, and fists pumping in the air.

Loving Morrow's voice has begun to get a little shrill as she winds up to a carefully calibrated higher pitch of demagoguery. "These are the same ones that teach that Jesus was the bastard offspring conceived of a menstruating prostitute, and that Jesus dead on the cross was consigned to hell to forever boil in hot semen."

Shouts and catcalls.

"The Pharisee Jew theology goes by the names secular humanism and dialectical materialism, but it all just boils down to atheism, hatred of God, denial of God, worship of God's enemy Satan. Didn't these same Pharisee Jews of Wall Street bring down the dollar money system with their thievings, their necromancies, their black arts, and their sharp practice? What we saw in those dark days at the endgame of the old times was nothing other than the ritual murder of our economy. Yessir! They drained the value out of it as surely as they drank the blood of our forefathers and it was the same ritual murder that tried to destroy our way of life, which we strive to preserve here in your Foxfire capital city. Who tried to cut off the oil?"

"The Pharisee Jews!" the crowd bellows.

"Who tried to cut off the electric?" Loving Morrow yells.

"Pharisee Jews!"

"Who set the nigger up in arms against us?"

"Pharisee Jews!"

"Who took the cars away?"

"Pharisee Jews!"

"That is the God's truth, my dear, sweet, blessed precious angels. But we still got 'em and here they come, Foxfire angels, here they are!"

It's like a signal. Heavy rumbling starts up at the far end of the speedway. The crowd is going wild. A section of the fence at the far end rolls away, opening up like a gate, and automobiles start pouring through the gate onto the oval track. These cars are painted in wild, hot colors: flaming yellow, orange, red with big numbers on them and the names of people or places or things painted wherever there isn't a number: "Lowes," and "Wix," and "Kobalt," and "Moog." Perhaps those were the names of pilots or the owners. I don't know. There were eight of them altogether. I haven't seen so many cars running since I was a small child. These cars jockey into a double-line formation and begin to circle the track on parade. The crowd is delirious at the sight of them. Loving Morrow is not quite finished, though. She puts out her arms again and galvanizes the crowd's attention back from the purring, smoking cars.

"My precious angels! The future belongs to you, not to the mutts and rascals! You are the highest embodiment of Foxfire faith and principle! Time and time again, the appeal must be made to renew the struggle. And so I say, Foxfire today, Foxfire tomorrow, Foxfire forever! Y'all have a nice day!"

The crowd takes up the chant, "Foxfire, Foxfire, Foxfire," as their Leading Light throws her arms around herself, as if in an embrace of them all, and soaks in the rabid love of her followers.

She remained out there on her pulpit a very long time, until you sensed that the people were running out of energy to keep up the display of affection and worship. Anyway, by this time the racing cars had all assembled at a starting point below the grandstand, their engines winding, ringing, and sputtering. A fat man handed Loving Morrow a green flag on a stick. She waved it left and right and the race cars jumped off their marks with their engines screaming. Out in the infield horses reared. One got loose among the crowd with a wagon behind it, knocking several people down before being brought under control. The cars reached their racing speed in the first lap around the oval and so began an event that was punishing on my nerves with its violence of noise and stink of burnt oil. I struggled through the crowd to the inside of the grandstand to get away from it. Foxfire soldiers were posted at frequent intervals around the interior, with its fried-food stands and beverage stations and vague stink of urine. I showed my VIP card to a lieutenant and he directed me to a stairway that led to the so-called salon where the dignitaries were all gathered. Two more soldiers at the door examined my card and patted down my body before admitting me.

It was a large and luxurious room, like a hotel lobby, with carpets and wicker chairs, and potted palms, and a bar at the back end, and at least a hundred people in finery with drinks in hand. The noise was not quite so intense up there, though the roar of the engines was now competing with a voice on the loudspeaker making commentary on the action of the race. The Leading Light was making her way around the big room, stopping to chat with these favored subjects of her realm, leaning in close to listen to their remarks and tributes, mindful of giving them her touch, laying her hand on a shoulder or another hand to establish intimacy, sometimes on a cheek, nodding and smiling at what they had to say. She conducted herself like someone keenly aware of her own physical magnetism. Her white gown was cinched at the waist emphasizing the abundance of her flesh. Her bosom shifted visibly within as though she were filled with gelatin. I watched her closely with the most extreme fascination, trying to imagine how my assignment might develop. You couldn't fail to see how hard she worked at her role, the dedication she brought to it. She gave some attention to everybody. Hector Tillman was in the room. He ignored me completely and likewise me him. He had his own somewhat smaller orbit of persons around him, like a smaller sun with its own planets.

I obtained a sweet whiskey drink called a julep, suggested by the bar man who had a pitcher of them at hand, and watched Ms. Morrow work the assembled admirers. Waiters wove through the crowd with trays of tidbits: fried things, ham biscuits, cheese nuggets, sugary nut squares—I tried them all. They left me queasy. I began to notice some things about the salon and the people in it. It was a little shabbier than my first impression registered. The potted palms were plastic and soiled with a film of greasy dust. The wicker chairs were all flimsy plastic, too, made in the old times, I'm sure. The carpets were threadbare and stained. The VIP men and women elite of the Foxfire government tended uniformly to plumpness, as though they ate too much and moved about too little, with sallow skin, dull-looking eyes, and careworn creases on their faces. Close up, their clothing was not so well made, and not always very clean. It reminded me of the costumes we wore back in the Union Grove theatricals. Some of them gave off a bad odor of people not used to bathing, or in a state of never-ending terror that produced a stink of anxiety. Not a few of them were visibly drunk. Of the women present, none of them was a match for Loving Morrow in appearance, or even close, nor did I spot one close to my own age. I was feeling the effects of that julep myself when Loving Morrow finally came around to my side of the big room and stepped up to me. She had an undeniable power of presence.

"Have I seen you 'round here before, young man?" she says, with an interesting lopsided smile. She wore a great deal of cosmetic decoration about her eyes, to make them look bigger and more dramatic, I suppose, but there was no denying she had a naturally beautiful face.

I'm like, "No, ma'am. I'm new here in town."

She's like, "Where from then?"

I tell her Covington up in Kentucky and a little of my legend and when I'm done she puts her hand on my upper arm and squeezes it.

She goes, "That's across the O-hio from Cincinnati, iddn' it?"

I'm like, "Yes, ma'am." Her eyes are working me up and down, like I was a perfectly fried chicken thigh and she hasn't had her lunch yet. She asks my name and I tell her.

"How come you're not in the army, Daniel," she says. "You know we have a big initiative about to get going up thataway."

"I don't know about that, ma'am," I tell her. "I'm here to serve."

She goes, "I think you'll serve just fine. Where you working at, darling?"

"Logistics Commission."

"Is that so?" She leans in to whisper to one of her army attendants, a dark-haired sergeant with a single eyebrow that makes him look like a cookie jar. He takes out a pad of foolscap and writes something down. Then she turns her attention back to me. "You one of Mr. Bodrew's boys, then?"

"Yes, I guess I am, ma'am."

"Oh, well, that's important work, all right, moving materials and commodities and whatnot. You know I'm a very hands-on executive. I like to check up on the commission work from time to time. Maybe you could consult with me on it sometime. She slides her hand down my arm to my hand, gives it a squeeze. Her hand is smooth, dry, and warm. She stands so close I can feel heat pulsating off her. Then she steps back as though to take me in more fully before moving on in her clockwise transit of the room.

When she completed the circuit, she headed for the stairway and left the salon with her retinue. After she was gone, few in the room paid attention to the race. They continued drinking heavily and then long tables groaning with grilled meats and other treats were set out for them. I didn't want to become familiar with any of them. The roaring engines outside perfectly matched the gale of emotion inside of me as all the theoreticals of my mission resolved into real flesh and blood. Even as I left the salon, I could still feel the heat between us. My call was not long in coming after that fateful encounter.

Daniel rubbed his eyes with the heels of his palms and then stared emptily across the table at his father as though utterly depleted. A pallid gloom had settled over him. He looked like someone not just grown out of boyhood but disfigured inside by experience since then. It made Robert uncomfortable to see him that way, all the innocence drained out of him, the dreadful untold conclusion of his tale oppressing him like a judgment.

"I expect I'll learn what happened?" Robert said.

"Yes," Daniel said, "by and by you will."

Robert craned his head around and glanced at the front of the Union Tavern barroom. Winter darkness filled the big window. Night had fallen here in Union Grove. The barroom had filled up with workmen and laborers. Someone began plinking a mandolin, a jaunty tune in a minor key with a sad edge called "The Wren." It was still a novelty for such a place of warm conviviality as the tavern to exist in the village, Robert thought, and such a contrast to the chilling tribulations of a nation consuming itself in hatred, poverty, violence, and death.

FORTY-THREE

It was dark when the doctor finished cleaning and stitching up the outer layers of the three knife wounds in Jack Harron's thoracic cavity. Donald Acker's blade had missed Jack's heart but neatly sectioned part of the lower right lobe of his lung. The eighth right rib was broken by another thrust and the doctor had to repair a nick in the inferior mesenteric vein. The doctor placed a drain tube in the pleural space of the right lung. Jack was resting comfortably in the doctor's surgical suite in the clinic building, formerly a carriage barn behind the doctor's house. Donald Acker's remains occupied a wooden table in the cold, damp, and dark of Dr. Copeland's nearby springhouse, sometimes recruited for use as a morgue. Jeanette, the doctor's wife, swabbed Jack's sutures and the drain tube exit with alcohol.

Harry Melzer, Ben Deaver's houseman, had been taken home to Pumpkin Hill with superficial wounds and a sprained shoulder.

Andrew Pendergast and Ben Deaver waited in the doctor's office next door to the surgical suite. The office was a large room filled with interesting artifacts of medicine and natural history as well as some comfortable furniture and a wood-burning stove. On the cabinet behind Deaver's head, a rampant stuffed porcupine surveyed the scene with dead eyes. The two men had taken up the doctor's offer to enjoy some of his pear brandy while he worked on Jack Harron and they waited. They had already covered the questions pertaining to Acker, his feckless attempt at farming, his misfortune, the horse he had kept starved in the barn, and his grievance over being turned in for it.

"Disagreeable as he was," Ben Deaver said, "I felt sorry for him."

"Why didn't you just ask him to work for you?" Andrew said.

"Oh, I did, more than once. He wouldn't. Said he wasn't cut out to be a peasant. When he put it that way, it got me thinking.

To be honest, I'm still not used to how this is all working out in these times," Deaver said. The brandy had made him garrulous. "In the old times, at the airline, I had a lot of employees. But they got good wages, benefits. The corporate structure took care of it all. Now, it's gotten all personal. There's no human resources office doing payroll. I'm basically cash poor. I've got the house and the furnishings and the operations, and my animals, but that's all sunk costs, a lot of it paid for when there was still paper money circulating. Now, we don't have enough hard silver revenue coming in to pay these people properly in the old sense of money wages. They know it, I know it, but it is what it is. They get some coin and most of their food and some goods. Also on the plus side for them, there's no taxes these days and no mortgage payments, no car payments, no gasoline to pay for day in and day out. I like to think that the benefits balance out for us and them. But it's a different social structure now, real different, and I imagine over time the lines between us will just grow sharper, and that's troubling. We couldn't run our household without help now, with the electric down, no machines, no vacuum cleaner, no washer and dryer. Now everything has to be done by hand. In the old times, we had a housekeeper who came every other day. It was enough. Everything seemed to run itself. Now it seems we need all these . . . servants. I'm uneasy with it."

"When things ran on automatic, a lot of people had no jobs and no purpose." Andrew said. "People need a place and a purpose. We have an obligation to provide that now. It's probably the best we can do."

"The way things are going, this won't be a democracy anymore."

Andrew had to laugh. "Democracy?" he said. "We don't even have a government, as far as I know."

"Pretty soon, those of us with property that's been maintained and improved and kept productive will have to go the way Bullock does—straight-up feudal. This thing of ours is going Middle Ages. Who knows, maybe knighthood will come back into flower. Where did you find this boy Jack?"

"Right on Van Buren Street on a winter night," Andrew said. "He was drunk and in a bad state of mind, failing in every way. He turned up in my parlor later that night. Just snuck in while I was out rehearsing the Christmas program over at the church. Scared the shit out of me."

"Did he try to hurt you?"

"Well, no, he asked for help. He asked me to fix him."

"Like he was a piece of broken equipment?"

"In so many words, yes."

"And how did you accomplish that?"

"I gave him a lot of chores to do in a structured life. I provided him with some basic comforts. I trusted him. I introduced him to the idea of improving himself. I think he began to see the advantage in all that."

"He can improve himself all he likes," Deaver said. "But he's not likely to change his social or economic status. He's a servant now."

"Maybe people can find contentment just being where they are, as long as they're treated fairly. What's wrong with being a good and faithful servant?"

"Not everyone will go along with the program," Deaver said. "Just saying. Frankly, Christmas night when we first saw him, we thought he was your new boyfriend."

"Well, that's just not the case, Ben," Andrew said.

"Excuse me for going there. It's been a strange day and I've got a buzz on. I owe that young man for saving my life. I don't know how I can repay him for that."

"Throw a levee in his honor. I'll bring my musicians over."

"Well," Ben Deaver said. "That's an idea."

In the adjoining room, Jack lay sedated with morphine that the doctor had extracted laboriously by reflux, filtration, and distillation from opium grown under contract by farmer Bill Schmidt. The doctor, by urgent necessity and limited means, was developing new skills as a chemist. Jack was not exactly asleep but floating in a plane of existence where all the sensory discomforts of the physical body were gloriously absent and he enjoyed a crystalline mental clarity that simplified everything. He was aware of having engaged in a deadly battle and prevailing. The entity he had vanquished somehow seemed related to a previous iteration of himself, something violent, empty, and foul. Out of this battle he, Jack Harron, was being re-born into something new and entirely different, something clean, filled with purpose, untroubled. Under the influence of the drug, his thoughts came in images and sensory impressions. All of these were of places of comfort and things of satisfaction: the kitchen at his new home with its copper pots, baskets of apples and squashes, things simmering on the stove, roasted birds, hanging bouquets of herbs; the joy of splitting kindling with a sharp ax in the cold knowing you would shortly be back in the warm; the movement of his limbs walking in good boots while word clouds of history and art floated around the perimeter of his attention; a warm parlor with yellow walls full of light on a winter's day; the smell of paint and turpentine. What changed for him was just this: his energies no longer went into opposing the world. Something had allowed him to go where the world was tending to go, allowing him to ride with it. All he had to do was remain in service to that flow of things the way a person of religious faith put himself in service to God. He watched the doctor roll down his sleeves and put on a cardigan sweater. He didn't comprehend what the doctor said to him, but he was content to let it be. He felt safe and protected and filled with gratitude. The woman drew another wool blanket over him and moved a candle stand to a marble-topped chest beside the bed. Jack's eyes followed the flickering shadows on the wall as the doctor and his wife left the room.

FORTY-FOUR

On the morning of New Year's Eve, Brother Jobe received a letter from Stephen Bullock summoning him to a conference in the matter of convening the grand jury for the Mandy Stokes murder case. Brother Jobe would have preferred to be on hand at his own headquarters to receive the two mulefoot boars he had ordered from the breeder over in Shaftsbury, Vermont, and was annoyed at the imperious tone of Bullock's summons, which stated, "You will appear . . ." as though the prosecutor himself, Brother Jobe, that is, were some kind of common vagrant to be ordered about.

He stopped in on Mrs. Stokes before leaving. Someone had brought a rocking chair into her room where she was sitting in a beam of winter light coming through the clerestory window. She was leafing through a large book about the life and work of Claude Monet, the French painter. A stack of art books that had been brought to her from the old school library in the building lay on the table near her bed.

She looked up as Brother Jobe entered the chamber and took off his broad-brimmed hat. Her demeanor struck him as resolute.

"How you getting on, ma'am?"

"I'm prepared," she said.

"What are you prepared for, ma'am?"

"Anything."

"Have you spoken with your attorney, Mr. Hutto?"

"I have."

"I believe he aims to plead you insane and I intend to not oppose it."

"I told him I want to plead guilty."

Brother Jobe felt his innards slide like the wall of a glacier into the cold sea. He had once seen it on television.

"If you do that, Mr. Bullock will hang you," he said.

"I don't deserve to live."

"Miz Stokes, I seen a lot of death these years, just and unjust. Our Lord said, *I desire mercy and not sacrifice*. The book says, *God is faithful, and he will not let you be tempted beyond your ability, but with the temptation he will also provide the way of escape, that you may be able to endure it.*

"As far as I can see, death is the only way I can endure it."

Brother Jobe peered over Mandy's shoulder at the open book on her lap. It was turned to a page that depicted the artist's little studio boat on a quiet backwater of the Seine at a late hour of a summer day with reflections in lavender light playing on the water and the artist's wife, Camille, a shadowy figure within the boat's little cabin.

"You see yourself on the boat in that pitchur?" Brother Jobe said. He knew that she did.

"She died," Mandy said.

"Well, we all do, and that was what? Back in the nineteen hunnerds?"

"She died young, a few years after he made this painting of her. See how dark and alone she looks inside there, and the world outside remains . . . so beautiful!"

"I'm going to see Bullock in a little while about the proceedings," Brother Jobe said. "You give some more thought to that pleading."

Mandy turned the page. Brother Jobe lingered a moment, then knelt down beside the rocking chair and spoke softly into her ear. "I'm sure you feel sick unto death about what has happened," he said, "but I don't see that throwing another life away is the right thing."

Boaz had Atlas the mule saddled and waiting for Brother Jobe when he emerged from the front entrance of the old high school building, and he had also readied the sorrel horse named Brownie for himself. The temperature had dropped into the mid-20s and clouds coming from the west over the Hudson Valley were so dark that the tree branches on the hilltops stood out in bright relief as if they were lit from the inside, like lamps. The two men, cloaked and swaddled in scarves, rode out toward Bullock's plantation four miles away. The animals were frisky and didn't have to be cajoled to canter. All along the way, Brother Jobe's thoughts belabored his conscience and he barely noticed the grandeur of the winter landscape with its many grays, sepias, and the occasional startling splash of the crimson staghorn sumac bobs.

When they got to Bullock's establishment and were relieved of their horses, the magistrate kept them waiting in his library office for thirty minutes. Boaz rather enjoyed the idle time there. The fireplace was lit and they were served lemon balm tea with little walnut cakes by Jenny the housekeeper. Bullock had many interesting antique artifacts on display there, a brass British naval telescope, an armillary sphere made in Geneva, 1749. The mantelpiece held a display of Japanese ivory and jade carvings: comic figurines, netsuke in the shapes of animals and birds, a Buddha, and a boat shaped like a dragon. Where there was not a run of bookshelves on the wall, an oil painting hung in a gilt frame. The hand-lettered title on a gilt scroll at the bottom of the frame read: *Arrival of the First Delaware & Hudson Train in Shushan NY, 1878*. Boaz stood before it in thrall. Brother Jobe sat by the fire with his tea and tried not to stew. A clock ticked loudly. At length, Bullock came through the door followed by his versatile factotum Dick Lee.

"Nice of you to drop by," Brother Jobe said. He did not get up from his seat.

Bullock ignored the remark, saying, "I've summoned the grand jury for ten a.m. Monday. You'll have your witnesses ready, and I'll assume your people will get what's-her-name down—"

"Miz Stokes."

"—to the conference chamber in the old town hall, and we'll get right on with the festivities."

Brother Jobe put his teacup and saucer on the side table at his elbow.

"Festivities?" he said. "This is a grave and solemn matter, sir, not some dang fish fry. A person's life hangs in the balance."

"And in the balance of things, she might hang," Bullock said.

"In fact, that outcome is looking more and more likely, based on what's come to my attention."

"You refer to the testimony of a half-wit."

Bullock affected to be shocked. "For the sake of decorum we call them developmentally disabled. Yes, that and other information."

"You used to call 'em 'retarded' for the sake of decorum. A spade is a spade, sir, and a half-wit is what it is that you propose to be the principal material witness on the life of somebody."

"Whose side are you on?" Bullock said, sincerely perplexed.

"I'm on the side of justice and righteousness," Brother Jobe said.

"The circumstances surrounding the case have developed sufficiently to necessitate that the developmentally disabled witness testify at the trial," Bullock said. "Consider that my ruling."

"You mean grand jury, don't you? Putting the cart before the horse there."

"Whatever," Bullock said with annoyance.

Boaz must have been eyeballing the repartee too strenuously, because he caught Bullock's attention.

"What is your man doing here in my chambers listening to all this?" he said.

"Brother Boaz is my scribe, my aide-de-camp, and my all-around right hand. He's attends all my business."

"Not the business of this court," Bullock said. "You"—he glared at Boaz—"wait outside."

"Is that so," Brother Jobe said. "What about *your* man?"

"He's an officer of the court."

"Like fun he is."

"He's my bailiff."

"You're just saying that. You keep this up, sir, and I'll move for dismissal myself."

"I'll get another prosecutor."

"No you won't. Beside Mr. Hutto, who is occupied for the defense, there ain't another living attorney left in this town except for Mr. Murray, and he's crawled so deep into the bottle that you could slice him lengthwise and serve him on the side of a hamburger with coleslaw."

Bullock circled his desk like a confounded predatory animal stalking a resourceful prey. After rotating around it, he slid into the padded leather chair and slumped with an air of resignation.

"All right," he said of Boaz and Dick Lee with a peevish flapping of his hand. "They can both stay."

Now it was Brother Jobe's turn to rise out of his seat. He enjoyed the new perspective of looking slightly down on the magistrate.

"I'm not altogether right with this prosecution," Brother Jobe said. "Your eagerness to dispense a certain harsh justice is . . . unsettling."

"It's going forward now," Bullock said. "The machinery of justice has been put in motion, just as you exhorted me to do when first we met way back in the springtime of this year. I'd have thought you'd be delighted."

"I'm concerned that you're moving too fast."

"Doesn't this woman deserve a speedy trial? Didn't you want me to set a tone for the rule of law in this jurisdiction?" Bullock said with his voice rising. "Didn't you push and prod and hector me to get this court up and running? Why, we would have chaos around here if people thought they could get away with murder—"

"Are you remonstrating with me, sir?" Brother Jobe said.

"You kill me," Bullock said.

"Kill you?" Brother Jobe said. "If that's a suggestion, it's gol-durned interesting, considering—"

"It's a figure of speech," Bullock said, overspeaking him, and rather loudly. "I mean by it that you are funny. You crack me up sometimes. The things that come out of your mouth."

Brother Jobe absorbed the remarks.

"Well, sir, this ain't no laughing matter," he said.

"You can address me as 'your honor' in these circumstances," Bullock said.

"All right, then, your honor, I hereby resign as your prosecutor. Do you want it in writing?" He placed his index finger at the outside corner of his right eye.

Bullock met Brother Jobe's burning gaze and recoiled. Not for the first time since he had made his acquaintance did he see in the fiery pools of Brother Jobe's eyes a disquieting something that made him twitch and shrink. Then something else came over him, a fugue of sensations and emotions that, when processed in his mind's temporal lobe, sent a message of generalized alarm to the more primitive regions of his brain. He had to grip the edge of his desk to resist an impulse to flee the room.

"No," Bullock said almost inaudibly, glancing down at the documents on his desk and then shuffling them without purpose. "I'll accept the verbal."

Brother Jobe glanced at Boaz to signal he was ready to depart.

"Oh," Bullock said without looking up as they crossed the room. "I'll be sending for the prisoner. The court will have to take responsibility for her custody now."

"You got a decent place to keep her?"

"Adequate enough."

"I'm sure."

Dick Lee followed them out and saw them off silently.

Brother Jobe's spirits had improved by the time he left Bullock's property, despite the fact that he didn't have so much as a notion for his next move, except that he would be damned to let the girl hang. Riding his mule Atlas toward home, Brother Jobe enjoyed the passing landscape in its severe grandeur. Though it was midday, the clouds had grown only thicker and darker. A few rogue snowflakes drifted on the air. Atlas was eager for a fast trot. Boaz, who had been riding behind on Brownie in his own globe of equanimity, came up abreast of Brother Jobe.

"Ain't that ole boy a piece of work," Boaz said.

"I'll say this, the sumbitch ain't never left me bored. But never wanting more neither."

"For what it's worth, you by far the better man," Boaz said.

"You been measuring?"

"Just observing."

"Well, thank you, son. You are a sure enough good and faithful servant."

FORTY-FIVE

Stephen Bullock remained at his desk many minutes after Brothers Jobe and Boaz departed, waiting for his vascular system to return to its normal parameters from the state of alarm that this latest encounter with the New Faith leader had provoked. Something had to be done about that man, Bullock brooded. For the moment, no remedy came to mind. But he had a more immediate problem: the lack of a prosecutor in the capital murder case that was going to the grand jury Monday morning. It was just then that Dick Lee returned from seeing the visitors off on their mounts.

"Shall we go castrate those calves now, sir?" Dick Lee said, referring to the next chore on that day's long agenda. Oxen were in short supply around the county.

"Dick, I'm going to have to ask you to step into the breech here."

"Beg your pardon, sir."

"I lack a prosecutor at the moment and I'm going to appoint you."

"Uh, sir, I didn't go to law school."

"I know that. However, there are no more law schools in operation these days, so far as I'm aware, at least not around here. Under the circumstances we have to revert to prior arrangements for manufacturing attorneys at law."

"I'm, uh, not following you, sir."

"Say you're Abe Lincoln, Dick, a young fellow who reads Shakespeare by firelight. You take a notion to become a lawyer. You're in a semiwild country. The law is trying to become a presence there so that people can manage their affairs in a civilized way. But there are no schools of law on the frontier. So you intern with a practicing lawyer, learn at his feet, so to speak, and by and by, when you have

absorbed enough knowledge, you apply to the courts for admission
to the bar. You follow me?"

"Yes. The apprenticeship model."

"Precisely!" Bullock said, slapping the desk so hard that his
fountain pen jumped. "Obviously we have to return to that method,
right?"

"Well—"

"Otherwise there would be no new lawyers and after a while—a
rather short while—there will be no law. In fact, that's more or less
our situation here today, wouldn't you say?"

"Uh—"

"We're back in the frontier all over again. Where are the courts?
What have we got for law enforcement? Where are deeds and titles
being filed? Where would one even find a notary? We're adrift in
history, Dick. As magistrate, I'm the only force standing between
chaos and the orderly regulation of daily life around here. Now
we've got a capital murder case that begs to be tried expeditiously
in the name of due process and justice, lest the people get the idea
that we exist in a state of savagery. Am I being clear?"

"But you didn't even want to serve after they elected you, sir."

"I was hoping that somebody else would step up to the plate,
Dick," Bullock said with his voice and his pulse rising again. "I don't
even live in the goddamned town of Union Grove! Don't I have
enough to look after right here?" This time, when he pounded the
desk, his fountain pen bounced onto the floor. It was a Montblanc,
a gift from his father on the occasion of his graduation from Duke
University Law School. It cost nearly a thousand dollars at the time.

"Of course," Dick Lee said. "But—"

"So back to my point. We're going to accelerate your apprenticeship a little bit. I happen to be an attorney and you have been in
my employ for, what, going on eleven years? You must have picked
up a thing or two. Now, since it also happens that I am the only
officer of the court in this district, I'm going to admit you to the
bar right here and now."

Bullock lifted a riding crop off his desk and waved it before Dick Lee as if it were a magic wand.

"There," Bullock said. "You are hereby admitted to the bar to practice law in Washington County and the State of New York. Do you feel any different?"

"Uh, sir, I have no idea how to conduct a criminal prosecution."

"Yes, I suspected as much," Bullock said. "So I'm going to help you out. I will tell you exactly what to do, step by step, every inch along the way. I will make out all the paperwork for your signature. All you have to do is show up and follow the script. This is all just ritual anyway, you know. The evidence I've seen is overwhelming that this woman murdered her husband and child."

"Okay, but what about this idea that she was out of her mind with the brain fever, sir?"

"Whoa. Wait a minute," Bullock said. "Is there some confusion about what side you represent? I think I said you will prosecute. Leave the defense to Mr. Hutto."

"Sir, why is it necessary to hang this poor girl?"

"Because there's nothing else we can do with her. There's no prison for the criminally insane. There's no locked hospital ward. There's no madhouse. We don't even have a goddamn snake pit to put her in. The facts are going to show that she committed these acts. I'm quite sure of it. I've seen all the depositions. And, when it comes down to it, there really isn't anything else we can do."

"I'm not comfortable with it, sir."

"What?" Bullock said. "You hanged that whole damn gang of nine pickers who busted into my house in October."

"They were professional, hardened criminals, sir, caught in the act of armed robbery, brandishing weapons and all."

"Dick, the people over in town just buried a young man and his baby boy, put into their cold graves before their time by this woman's hand. The trial will confirm that, I assure you. I think it's fair to say categorically that all murderers are insane in the commission of their crimes to some degree. It may be pitiable in her case, but these times don't leave us much latitude. The institutional support just isn't there like it used to be."

"What if you just cast her out?" Dick Lee said. "Like we did with Berkey."

"You mean ride her off somewhere and dump her on a snow-covered rural byway, like a dog that has bit somebody? I don't think so. She'd almost certainly die and maybe by slow degrees after an awful struggle. Then there's the question of precedent. We're trying to reestablish a coherent legal system here with consistent procedures. What happens the next time? Plus, she's potentially a great danger to others. How can you be so sure she won't kill again?"

Dick Lee appeared to struggle internally. The lines of his forehead knitted together and he ground his teeth.

"Do I have to be prosecutor and executioner both, sir?" he said.

"Oh, gosh no. That wouldn't be proper. I'm confident we can find a hangman. However, it might be necessary for you to instruct him."

Dick Lee stared into the rug.

"I don't relish what has to be done in this case," Bullock said. "But I'm burdened to have to do it. It's my duty. If I can't depend on you, who else is there?"

Dick Lee sighed. "You can depend on me, sir," he said.

Bullock nodded gravely. "Thank you, Dick," he said. "Now what do you say we go castrate us some calves?"

When he stood up and came around his desk, his boot heel crushed the Montblanc pen on the floor.

FORTY-SIX

At midday, Daniel ventured out by himself to the center of town for the first time since his arrival on Christmas Eve. His father had gone over to Tom Allison's livery earlier that morning to discuss the possibility of starting a regular mail and passenger carriage service between Union Grove and the other towns in the county, perhaps as far as Glens Falls, twenty miles to the north, where the Hudson River spills out of the Adirondack Mountains. Tom had purchased an antique Concord Coach from Esther Callie's barn in Battenville. It was in poor condition. Tom wanted Robert's opinion as to whether it might be fixed up or, if not, used as a model for Robert building a new one from scratch. To Robert, constructing a coach seemed an immense challenge. There was no surviving knowledge base in the county for constructing such a vehicle.

Daniel felt a little nervous on his own at first. The sheer cadence of walking by himself reminded him of those lonely months trudging back home from the west. But his feet had healed nicely since Christmas and his new boots were comfortable. They were a belated Christmas gift from his father, who had them made by Walter McWhinnie, the town saddler and bootmaker.

Like many people raised in the north country, Daniel could tell instinctively from the look of the sky that snow was coming. A New Year's Eve levee was organized for that evening at Carl Weibel's farm around the back of Schoolhouse Hill, and Daniel looked forward to being out in general society for the first time since his return, including among people he had grown up with and hadn't seen in two years. He had decided to get the stubble on his face shaved and his hair properly trimmed at the barbershop run by the New Faith people on Main Street.

With the return of his physical strength and energy also came a return of his sense of having a future. But a gnawing anxiety that something inside of him might be damaged, that he had lost the capacity for any kind of love, was with him constantly. He paused in his footsteps at the corner of Linden and Salem Streets and watched Teddy Einhorn pass by in his delivery wagon. He waved, but Teddy appeared not to recognize him. If he found a girl, a wife, Daniel thought, there would always be a part of his history he could never explain to her. Had he been able to explain it to himself yet? he wondered. He leaned against the metal pole of the battered street sign and filled his lungs with cold air, bringing him back to refuge in the present. In a little while, he continued on his way.

His route meandered so he could take in some familiar, comforting sights. Farther along, Salem Street opened up to a steep prospect above a bend in the Battenkill that afforded a good view of the river and the two old bridges, road and railroad, that crossed it. Here the river had a natural fall of eight feet, one of several in its winding course through town. A cambric factory was established here in 1861 that produced a linen fabric renowned for its weight and luster, used to make officers' dress uniforms for the Union army. Nothing remained of the mill except a revetment of gigantic granite blocks that stood up to every spring flood for almost two hundred years. He recalled the works at the five-step flight of locks, the cranes and ox-powered rotaries, and the marshaled manpower, and how the people of Union Grove might accomplish similar feats of reconstruction. Perhaps building a water-powered factory was something he could do in the future, he mused. Below the falls was a big pool, good for swimming, where the monster trout of his boyhood lurked.

Once he got to the barbershop on Main, he did not have to wait long to be attended by Brother Judah. Despite his gloomy demeanor, Judah initiated a conversation as he brushed the warm soapy lather on Daniel's face. He was eager for snow, he said, because where he was born and raised it hardly ever snowed and didn't stick long when it did.

"Where was that?" Daniel said.

"Memphis, Tennessee," Brother Judah said at the very moment he brandished his straight razor at Daniel's neck. "Ever been down to that part of the country?"

FORTY-SEVEN

When he returned to the old high school compound, Brother Jobe went straight to the winter quarters of Mary Beth Ivanhoe, the Queen Bee of the New Faith Brotherhood Covenant Church of Jesus. She lay, as usual, propped up in bed in her warm windowless chamber with its mingled odors of sweetness and rot and its luxurious furnishings. Daylight filtered dimly in from a cupola high above and beeswax candles scented with lavender burned on several tables and cabinets. Sister Zuruiah, chief of her attendants, had been folding clean linens. She didn't have to be told to excuse herself. Brother Jobe drew a chair to the bedside.

"How you getting on, Precious Mother?"

"I'd get on better with a dish of banana pudding, truth be told."

"Ain't no bananas to be had these days."

"Mebbe that's why they don't bring me none."

"I expect that's so, dear."

"Ain't anybody around here remembers how to make a red velvet cake, I wonder?"

"I'll set someone to task on that directly."

"Come closer, I can't hardly see you."

Brother Jobe moved the chair so close up against the bed frame so his legs hung over each side. He could hear her wheeze. She seemed, if anything, physically larger than ever. Her neck had disappeared completely into the folds and wattles of her many chins and Brother Jobe worried if, before long, her head might be subsumed in all that blubber, too, turban and all.

"Maybe you should ease up on them desserts," he said.

"What else I got left in this earthly life?"

"Yes, well, okay," Brother Jobe said. "The thing is, I just come from a confab with the magistrate—"

"I know all about it. I done tuned in. That sumbitch don't like you."

"I wish I knew why. I been as nice as pie."

"I could stand some pie. You tell them that down below."

"Keep your eye on the ball here, Mary Beth—"

"They can make a chess pie, I'm sure. It don't take but mebbe three ingredients, and one of 'em is eggs. They still got chickens around. I made it myself years ago, before I come to be the sancti-fied monster you see before you. Can you believe that once upon a time I fit into a two-piece swimsuit, with two fair enough titties and all, and had more'n one man waiting on me? That was Pine Knoll Shores, North Carolina, 2005. Look what I come to."

"I'm sorry, Mary Beth. Some things can't be undone."

"You more right than you know. Food is my only comfort now."

"I'll order you up a chess pie."

"Good," she said, eyelids fluttering, as in prelude to one of her recurring seizures. "Now, I was you, I wouldn't waste another minute with that Mr. Bullock."

"I can't get deep in enough amongst his mind to bend his will."

"And you won't, neither. He's what you call a nemesis. You got to get that gal out of here, is all. She ain't sick no more and all the wickedness that brung on her dire acts went out with it. Hanging her don't make no sense, and I guarantee he aims to get it done."

"I see it that way too. It'll be dark in a matter of hours. And it's fixing to snow. Where do I take her that'll do for more than a temporary hideout? I'm stumped."

"You listen up. I got a idear."

Forty-eight

Travis Berkey had spent two nights in an unoccupied house on the Windy Hill Road. He had to burn half the furniture in the place to keep from freezing, and most of the heat went up the fireplace flue. He had killed a ewe and stolen the meat from the Zucker farm but had nothing to go with it, not a potato or a turnip, and the kitchen implements in the house had all been pilfered previously so he had to spit ragged chunks of mutton on a green stick and roast it on the open fire like a caveman. By the second day, he was sick to death of plain roasted mutton. The worst part, though, was that he had no duties, no activities to attend to, nothing to do all day long except stew about his bad luck and the injustice of the world. Much as he held Bullock and everything about the plantation in contempt, he saw clearly now how important a structured existence had been to his peace of mind. As the hours went by, he pondered the necessity of presenting himself to another farmer for labor. With all the sickness raging year on year, and the population drawn down, able workers with skills were valued, and he was sure to find a position, he reasoned. But he held back on trying because the other farmers all knew Bullock and did business with him, especially business involving livestock, and Travis figured that sooner or later his true story might be found out.

Then, late morning after that second night on Windy Hill Road, with his meat all gone, Travis had an inspiration: he would go sign on with that New Faith bunch over at the high school. He'd heard over the months that they were actively recruiting. He'd heard that they had nice quarters for the members, and that there were a number of good-looking women among them, and he'd even heard rumors that they engaged in something called free love, which put him in mind of orgies, something he'd been rather fond of in the old times back when the porn websites were running. The New Faith people had done quite a job, apparently, renovating and outfitting the old high school as their settlement. They had lots of workshops on the premises like Bullock had, making useful things. The members all got regular hot meals, clean clothes, and even showers, since the old athletic facilities were still there and the town had a working, gravity-fed water system that didn't require any electric to run.

One time back in October when Bullock sent him to town with a wagonload of sorghum horse feed for Einhorn's store, Travis saw for himself that the New Faith had laid out impressive gardens and fenced-in paddocks and pastures on the old athletic fields. He took particular note of their horses and mules, as that was his area of know-how, and how sleek and clean they looked. Thus ruminating, Travis concluded that he should clean himself up and go over there forthwith to sign on. It was what used to be called a "no-brainer" in the old times. The only reservation he had was the religion part. He'd never been a churchgoer and didn't have a whole lot of interest in pious matters, but he figured he could pretend easily enough and, after all, sitting on your butt in a pew and singing a few hymns wasn't exactly hard work. You could probably even catch a few winks while the others had at it.

And so it was that when Brother Jobe returned to his personal office and quarters that afternoon, after consulting with Mary Beth Ivanhoe, he found Travis Berkey waiting on the bench in the hallway. Brother Jobe was in a hurry to layer on yet more apparel for a trip of about fifteen miles on horseback, with snow looking ever more likely. He ignored Berkey, who rose from the bench with his hat in hand, and simply swept past him. But Travis persisted and knocked on the door to the suite—once the school principal's headquarters—as it practically closed in his face. Boaz finally answered, heard his request, sized him up, and reported to Brother Jobe, who was pulling on an extra pair of wool socks.

"There's a feller out there wants to come over to us. Male, mid to late thirties, wiry but strong-looking, says he's good with horses and stock."

"All right, send him on in, but tell him I ain't got time to waste."

Boaz showed Travis into the private sanctum. Brother Jobe was putting on heavy, insulated construction boots factory-made in the old times. He listened to Travis's story, which was some nonsense about his farmhouse burning down up to Argyle, and the wife and children gone up with it, and now he was bereft and without a family or a place to live and he'd had a dream where Jesus told him to join the New Faith.

"You say you're good with animals?"

"Yessir," Travis said.

"You got yourself some?"

"I've got a few cows, pigs, chickens."

"Horses?"

"Uh, sure, two, uh, Clydesdales."

"Uh-huh. I guess your barn didn't burn down then."

"No, sir, just the house."

"Family all gone?"

"Like I said."

"Any hands?"

"No, sir, I farmed it on my own. I'm not rich."

"You say you come down here day before yesterday?"

"Uh-huh."

"And you're ready to move right in here, this afternoon?"

"Yessir."

Brother Jobe pulled a wool tunic over his double layer of shirts.

"Mister, that just don't add up," he said.

"How's that?"

"Well, who's taking care of your stock while you been here? You just stash 'em in the barn without no feed or fresh water? Or you leave 'em out when a snowstorm's coming?"

"I, uh . . ."

"Lookit here, son." Brother Jobe held his index finger to the corner of his right eye. "Look right at my fingertip."

"This a vision test?"

"In a manner of speaking."

Brother Jobe was able to enter Travis Berkey's mind as easily as walking into a toolshed. What he saw in there was a poor candidate for the brotherhood.

"We going to have to respectfully pass on your application."

"Huh? I can't join up? Why, I'm crazy for Jesus."

"That's good. He'll guide and keep you. We don't have no openings at present. Sorry. Now, if you'll excuse me, I got some rather urgent business to see about. Boaz here'll show you out."

He left Travis Berkey there and hurried down the long maze of corridors to Mandy Stokes's cell. Brothers Seth and Elam were waiting there along with Sisters Judith and Esther, who clutched bundles of clothing. The former were both veteran soldiers of the Holy Land War. Brother Amos, the duty guard, admitted Brother Jobe to the cell.

Mandy sat on the edge of the bed, alert, bright, apprehensive. He could see tension in the muscles of her slender neck, like wires under her pale skin. And in noticing, he imagined a length of heavy rope looped around it. He approached warily.

"Ma'am, something come up rather sudden and we'd like to move you to a safer location."

"Here? In the school?" she said.

"No, elsewheres. Can you ride a horse?"

"Not really."

"Well, I expect your education on that is about to begin."

She shrank back.

"I'm afraid," she said.

"I know you are. You going to have to trust me."

"Where would you take me?"

"Away from here. A ways away."

"I've prepared myself to answer for my crimes."

"Mercy triumphs over judgment, girl. Self-judgment too."

To Brother Jobe's dismay, Mandy fairly exploded in sobs. He took a seat beside her on the bed and put his arm around her and she turned to clutch the awkward mass of him bundled in many garments. She gave off competing scents of clean laundry, summer fruit, and fear.

"Listen here, Miz Stokes," he said quietly and his hand moved to tenderly cup the back of her head. "I can't imagine what it's been like for you, what you gone through with all this, but I done made up my mind to intervene, and we going away from here now. So I ask you to suspend all them mental preparations and get ready to ride. I got two of my best rangers coming with to guide the way and look out for our safety, and in another day, or two, or ten, or twenty days, this world is going to look different to you, I promise."

She didn't answer directly but her body stopped heaving.

"The sisters are standing by to outfit you for your journey," Brother Jobe continued. "We putting you in men's clothing for both comfort and disguise. We got a fine, calm mount for you and the country is very beautiful out there while there's daylight. Will you come along now?"

She pulled herself off him, wiped the tears from her eyes, and nodded her head.

Forty-nine

Robert Earle and his family rode to the levee at Weibel's farm in Tom Allison's open chore wagon along with the Allison family. Robert and Tom sat up front on the spring seat while the others occupied cushions in the wagon box all under lap robes and with bottles of hot water. The wagon was drawn by two dainty Haflingers the color of caramel and marshmallow. Candle lanterns hung above the mudguard up front. The trip was but a ten-minute trot out of town on mostly level road and around the other side of Schoolhouse Hill in the last glimmers of twilight with snow falling sparsely and gently over the landscape. When they came upon Weibel's big red farmhouse the windows were alive with light and two of his hired men waited at the top of the drive to take charge of wagons and horses. Many others were parked in the paddock beside a nearby barn.

Inside the old house, built in the boxy Italianate style in 1858, with its spacious rooms and high ceilings, seventy people in their best clothes, the prospering ones of the county, circulated around tables filled with roasts, ham, a turkey, smoked trout, chicken livers, puddings, gratins of potatoes and turnips, the ubiquitous corn bread, fritters and apple butter, cakes and pies made of scarce wheat hoarded over the year past, preserved fruits, walnuts, filberts, nougats and fondants, cider, beer, whiskey, and punch for the little ones.

Daniel Earle, a nervous weariness overcoming him, took a seat on a sofa in back of the big parlor and was content to observe the festivities with a glass of Weibel's own Schoolhouse Hill cider. He marveled that the farmers had emerged from the disorders of recent times to become the wealthiest citizens of the region. When he was a little boy, the farmers all seemed old, beaten down, and poor while the men of affairs in town were car dealers and holders of the hamburger franchises. Daniel recognized that farming was not in his blood. All the talk at the levee was about the heinous, bloody invasion by one Donald Acker in Ben Deaver's sitting room and the heroic defense by one Jack Harron, a little-known young man lately taken on as a servant by the polymath Andrew Pendergast. In fact, there was some dismay that Andrew was not present this evening to lead the musicians, Daniel's father, Robert, now among them on fiddle across the room. They were, at that moment, playing the rousing English country dance tune "Portsmouth," and a few couples were executing swings and figures to it. One of them was Britney, on the arm of Robbie Furnival, who loved to dance. Daniel studied her liquid movements with a gathering sense of ominous disturbance.

By and by, a barrel-chested towhead with a red beard the same age as Daniel took a seat on the sofa. It was Corey Widgeon, a classmate of Daniel's all the way up into the final years of the high school before it shut down. Daniel wrenched his gaze away from his father's girl.

"Hey, Danny," Corey said and playfully performed a kind of hand jive around Daniel's face that they used to do to torment each other as twelve-year-olds. Daniel pretended to be charmed by it. "I hear you've been all over out there in the country."

"I guess I was," Daniel said, and took a long draught of his cider.

"Where'd you go? What'd you see? Is it true the Chinese landed on the moon?"

Daniel struggled to formulate an answer. All he could do was crack a pained, artificial smile and pull in his chin as if he wished he could make his head disappear. His inability to answer his old chum frightened him a little, as though he were sitting on the lid of a box filled with demons.

"I don't know, Corey. I saw a lot but . . . I don't know . . ."

"We heard about Evan."

"Yeah, Evan." Daniel drained his glass and shook his head.

"He'll be missed," Corey said and all Daniel could do was nod. "I see Reverend Holder and his wife aren't here tonight."

"Yeah," Daniel said. "They're taking the news hard, I guess."

They were not children anymore and Corey sensed Daniel's unease, though not the intensity of it. "I've been working over at Schroeder's creamery," he said. "It's pleasant work indoors in the wintertime. They could use another hand. They pay silver."

"Thanks, Corey. Maybe I'll come over and see about that."

"And there's a new tavern in town. The Jesus bunch opened it. Go figure."

"I've been in there."

"Let's meet for a tipple some time."

"Sure, Corey. That'd be great."

Daniel had to get up before his head exploded.

FIFTY

Brother Jobe and his rangers Seth and Elam, along with Mandy Stokes, made good time on their journey north into the highlands of Washington County, by turns walking and trotting up the old county roads. They encountered no other travelers this dwindling day of the old year. Snow started to fall in earnest after they passed through the moribund village of Argyle where, months before, store owner Miles English was discovered to be trafficking in boys for labor and sport and where he had hanged himself in a root cellar. Dead leaves clumped in the vestibule to the store's doorway, suggesting it had not reopened since. There was no wind and the lilting snowfall mesmerized them as they pushed on in the winter stillness. Mandy rode a black mare named Jinx between Seth in the lead, followed by Elam, with Brother Jobe taking up the rear on Atlas the mule. They rode solemnly. Now and then Brother Jobe hummed a favorite hymn to himself swaddled in the cozy insulation of his cloak, scarves, woolens, and fur-lined hat.

They had departed around one-thirty in the afternoon. By a quarter after four they had crossed into the rural township of Hebron. The farther they penetrated the uplands, the more forested the landscape became and the wilder the forests. The bare treetops were hardly legible against the gray westering twilight when the travelers came upon a homestead in a dell on the lee side of Lloyd's Hill that afforded a comforting sense of enclosure to the scene, as though nothing bad could find one who sheltered there. The homestead consisted of a yellow and white cottage in the Gothic style, with porches and pointed windows and bargeboards figured with trefoils in the gable end. A barn also painted yellow stood twenty yards to the left of it. Candlelight within the cottage was visible from up on the road. Brother Jobe rode Atlas up to Seth in the lead.

"Reckonize the place?" he said.

"I sure do."

This was the house where Brother Jobe had been carried in the fall, delirious with illness, where an emergency surgery was performed on him by the doctor's boy, who had run away from town after poisoning Brother Jobe's horse and then fallen into the company of the bandit Billy Bones. This was the home of Barbara Maglie, who some in the county referred to as the Witch of Hebron.

Brother Jobe reined Atlas down into the drive, past the fenced garden. The others followed.

"You'all wait out here a minute," he said. He dismounted and walked up the porch to the door. It took the lady of the house a moment to register the identity of the visitor, swaddled in winter traveling garb as he was, but then a look of delight brightened her face, which was the face of an enchantress inside a cascade of silver hair. Two people who could not have been less alike, Brother Jobe and Barbara Maglie had struck mutual chords in each other and gotten on like the oldest friends back when he was recuperating from his aforesaid ordeal. She was a refugee from New York City who had left in advance of the trouble that brought down the economy and the nation and established herself in this sheltered little corner upstate. In the old times, she'd appeared as a model in advertisements, and had a husband who ran a major ad agency, and had a summer house on the South Fork of Long Island, and consorted with the notables of what were once called the media, Wall Street, and show business. Now she was a recluse, a healer, a seer, a signal beauty of a certain age, who more than a few men of the county, and even beyond the county, mostly married men, visited regularly for stimulation, pleasure, counsel, and renewal. Otherwise, she lived happily alone.

"Why, it's you!" she cried with silver ringing in her voice, "and on such a night, and New Year's Eve!"

"It's nice to see you again, ma'am."

"Oh, come in, please come in."

She was so delighted that she did not notice the others sitting their horses in the shadows up the drive.

As Brother Jobe stepped into the house a figure emerged from the rooms deeper within.

"Oh," Brother Jobe said, stopping short, "sorry to bother you."

"It's no bother," she said.

The stranger was a tall man, about forty, balding but handsome with a groomed full beard, well dressed as if for a levee in a fine cream-colored linen shirt with blousy sleeves and a wool vest embroidered with satin birds and flowers in gay colors. His name was Blake Harmon, a "scientific farmer," as he described himself, from the nearby Camden Valley, where his thousand acres of orchard, pastures, fields, and excellent hardwoods straddled the New York–Vermont border. He held a stemmed glass filled with amber liquid, his own Tug Hollow whiskey. Barbara Maglie was also dressed for festivity in one of her characteristic long skirts of many colors, a clingy black sweater that emphasized all the pendant appeals of her flesh, and dangly earrings that sparkled in the candlelight. She introduced Brother Jobe to Mr. Harmon, who shook hands, with a hint of amusement visible in the set of his mouth. The house was infused with buttery aromas of things caramelizing in the oven and the perfume of herbs hanging to dry off an exposed beam: rosemary, bergamot, sage, yarrow, lavender, tansy.

"What are you doing so far from town on such a night?" Barbara said, helping dust the snowflakes off his shoulders, though Brother Jobe had begun to sweat under all his layers of clothing.

"Ma'am, we have a situation where I believe you can help a fair great deal."

She asked the gentleman from Camden Valley to excuse them and she led Brother Jobe into a small room off the kitchen that had been set up as a cozy retreat for reading. There he briefly explained the predicament of Mandy Stokes. It was not necessary for him to go into extravagant detail because Barbara Maglie easily was able to infer more than he could convey in mere words.

"I believe you can help her get right in her mind," Brother Jobe said, summing it up. "She's come far but she's got a ways to go."

"Please, ask the others to come in," she said. "There are stalls in the barn, and hay, water, and grain for your animals."

"Thank you very much, ma'am."

Brother Jobe went back outside and waved to the others to come down the drive. The accumulating snow muffled the horses' hooves as they walked and swayed toward the house. He told Seth to stable their mounts. Broad-shouldered Elam took Mandy in his arms, helping her down from Jinx. She slid against his firm solidity to the snowy ground as if returning to the earth after a long absence.

FIFTY-ONE

Daniel had moved his bed from the parlor downstairs to his childhood room on the second floor. After the family's return from the New Year's Eve levee at Weibel's farm, Daniel lay awake in an enervated cocoon of anxiety as he dimly apprehended sounds of amorous exertion from the room where his father had retired with Britney. Long after the house fell silent again, trapped in the haunted room of his childhood, Daniel remained wide awake as his mind waded beyond the confounding tumult of the present moment to his final deadly days in Franklin, Tennessee, capital of Loving Morrow's Foxfire Republic.

The Monday following the automobile races at the Carter's Creek Speedway, and the reception that followed, he found an envelope with instructions waiting on his desk when he returned to the Logistics Commission after making the rounds of the warehouses and grain storage depots. The instructions told him to meet an automobile that would be sent to convey him on official business to "executive headquarters" and to bring the summons with him as a pass. So, at the designated hour, late in the afternoon on a late summer day, he waited at the curb on a quiet block of 4th Avenue North, where a large blocky black car manufactured years ago under the brand name Lincoln Navigator pulled to a stop right in front of him. Daniel marveled at the near soundlessness of the engine—so unlike the roaring race cars at the speedway. The big machine had the presence of a large animal. Fluids pulsed audibly through its churning guts. It even had a kind of face in front, a grinning grille and two eyelike lights. A tinted side window dropped, revealing the operator of the car, a middle-aged sergeant in a dress tunic.

"Got your letter, boy?" he said.

Daniel presented it.

"Okay. Git in."

Daniel heard a thunk as of a switch being thrown. The rear door opened.

Several civilians at the far end of the block had gathered to gawk at the car.

"What you dallying for, boy?" the sergeant said.

The seats were butter-colored leather and the surfaces within appeared to be made of fine polished wood, though they were plastic. Daniel discovered that he could see out of the windows more easily than he could see in from outside.

"You're a dandy," the sergant said. "She gawn like you."

"Where are we going exactly?"

"You'll see," the sergeant said and he did not speak again for the duration of the journey.

They drove past a military checkpoint at the western edge of town without stopping, and then three miles out into the countryside. The road was in excellent repair the whole way. Daniel was not used to moving through the landscape at such speed. It made him dizzy. He had only the dimmest memory of riding in cars as a small child, except for the vivid discomfort of the plastic safety seat in which he was encased and immobilized like an astronaut. The car climbed a steady, looping grade into some low hills where there were no visible habitations. Then it turned through a gatehouse manned by more soldiers onto a gravel driveway lined with stately tulip trees. An enormous house appeared at a distance. As the car drew closer the house resolved into a chaotic pastiche of historical gestures, architectural conceits, and mixed modular building components made of materials not found in nature. The various parts seemed to be at war with one another: Corinthian columns battling with mansard roofs, corbeled turrets, Victorian chimney pots, Palladian windows, stained-glass windows, leaded oriel windows, and soaring triangular bay windows, vinyl clapboard-clad facades joined to half-timbered facades next to redbrick plastic veneer facades—the whole fantastic heap piled onto a wedding cake of landscaped terraces with statue-like topiaries, including a cavalryman on a rearing horse, a race car of the type Daniel had seen at Carter's Creek, a fanciful baby elephant, a Tyrannosaurus, and a pair of gigantic praying hands.

The car bypassed the broad porte cochere in front of the mansion, where two other black cars sat parked among soldiers mounted on horseback, soldiers on foot, and a bustle of people coming, going, and confabbing. The car turned around the rear of the building to an inconspicuous gray service door on a far wing, where a lone soldier sat with a complex firearm Daniel had never seen before, a machine pistol. The guard checked Daniel's pass, opened the gray door, and said, "Gawn up."

At the top of a short stairway another door opened to a spacious hallway with a vaulted ceiling painted clumsily in the manner of Michelangelo's Sistine Chapel fresco. Instead of God and Adam, the vignette portrayed an airborne Jesus reaching to touch the extended hand of an enrobed female figure recognizable as Loving Morrow, recumbent on a pink cloud. Rather than angels and cherubim, Jesus was surrounded by deceased luminaries of country music: Elvis, Dolly, Garth, Waylon, Willie, Tammy, Patsy, Mother Maybelle, June and Johnny. Daniel had no idea who they were. Two more soldiers were posted by a door there. They were in size relation to ordinary soldiers as prize oxen are to common steers. They asked Daniel to produce his "letter of conveyance" and, satisfied, admitted him within.

It was a very grand suite of rooms, each one larger than the entire downstairs of his family's house back home in Union Grove. The furniture, too, was oversized and overstuffed. Nobody else seemed to be there. The pictures on the wall caught Daniel's attention. They depicted cottages in idealized twilit landscapes with blazing windows, as though complex thermochemical reactions were happening inside. He was studying one intensely when a door opened deeper within the suite. Footsteps. Moments later, Loving Morrow stood before him. She was shorter than he remembered because she was barefoot. Her hair was held up in a pile atop her head with a big tortoiseshell plastic clasp. She was dressed not in her customary robes of office but in cutoff blue jean short pants with fuzzy frayed hems and a stretchy pink camisole with string straps, with apparently nothing beneath it.

"Hi," she said. "'Member me?"

"Yes, ma'am."

"You like that pitchur?"

"The house. It's so bright. Like it's about to burst into flames."

"I'll tell you, I'm 'bout to burst into flames," she said. "Mr. Tillman won't let me run the a.c. as cool as I like it. He knows best, of course, and anyway we got to pinch pennies, so to speak, if we're going to take the Ohio River from the federals. You got any idea how much it takes in hard cash money to move and supply a battalion of twelve hundred foot soldiers with mounted officers?"

"No, ma'am."

"You don't want to know. I got all this junk on my mind twenty-three hours of the day." She stepped closer so he could feel the heat radiating off her. "Then there's the blessed hour when I like to forget all that. That's where you come in."

"Yes, ma'am."

"You are an obliging young man," she said, and ran an index finger down his breastbone, then executed a dancelike step around him. "This here pitchur is an original Thomas Kinkade," she said. "He was an old-times *artiste* of California. It's worth a fortune. Those others, they're just reproductions. He was known in his time as the painter of light."

"That's a bright house for sure," Daniel said.

"Do you like my home?"

"I've never seen a house like it. It's . . . roomy."

"Yeah, and this is just my personal hideaway. You should see the gubment part. Lemme show you around."

She took his hand and led him through a series of rooms. Her hand was small, soft, and warm. One room was an exercise parlor filled with machines that required electricity to make a human being operate her muscles. Flat screen televisions hung on three walls. The screens were dark. Another room had a billiard table at center and video game consoles around the edges.

"This one here is for the boys," she said. "You like to play pool?"

"I never played, ma'am."

Loving Morrow shot him a sideways frowny look.

"You a space alien, honey?"

"Not as far as I know, ma'am."

"Naw," she said. "You look human enough."

They came to a kitchen with vast granite countertops, pot racks festooned with copper cookware still bright with their original protective varnish.

"You hungry?"

"No, ma'am."

"'Course you are. Why, I bet you're still growin'. I got just the thing for you. We can share."

Loving Morrow produced two jars from a cabinet. One had brown paste in it and the other white. Then she pulled a bulbous loaf of wheat bread out of a drawer and sawed two slices off it. Of these materials she composed a sandwich and held one end up to Daniel's mouth.

"Where do you get peanut butter?" he asked.

"They make it for me, special."

"Been a long time since I tasted that."

"Poor thing."

"What's the white stuff?"

"Didn't you ever have a Fluffernutter?"

"No, ma'am."

"You weren't raised right."

He watched her address the sandwich as though she were demonstrating how all the various complex parts of her mouth worked: lips, teeth, tongue.

"You know, I was quite the tomboy as a girl," she said, coming closer to him again. "I'd like to climb you like a tree." She put the sandwich on the counter and reached up, joined her fingers around the back of his neck, pressed herself against him, and made a pouty face. "I'm still hungry," she said.

Daniel was experiencing such a bioelectrical surge that he saw little spots of light before his eyes. Theta brain waves battled his hormones and enzymes in a fugue of acute sensation, fear, lust, rage. Behind it all loomed the governor of his emotions: the training. Loving Morrow turned her head up. Daniel noticed that her pupils were dilated, as he had been taught to observe.

"You wanna play with me?" she said.

"Yes, ma'am," he said.

"That is exactly the right answer. You're good. I can tell already." She slid her hands down and took one of his in both of hers and guided him out of the kitchen, down a hallway, and into a bedroom. It was heavily curtained and dimly lit. He had never known that there were so many shades and tones of pink as were evinced by the decor in this room. The bed was proportionately as large as the room. It could easily sleep more than two, and at various times had. She backed him up to it and tipped him onto it with a push of her finger. A fierce look of determination came over her face. "You gawn see something very special now, young man."

She seized the plastic clamp from the back of her head and tossed it aside. Her ghostly silver-blonde hair fell around her shoulders and she swept a knot of it out of her face with an aggressive gesture. She wiggled out of her shorts and let them fall on the floor. Then she crossed her arms and briskly pulled off the camisole. Daniel watched the spectacle in a state of inflamed paralysis as she leaned over him, all soft roundness, and started undoing his things: shirt buttons, belt buckle.

"Skootch up out of that, now," she said and she pulled it all off. "My goodness, will you look at that."

Then she was upon him, lightly and softly at first, businesslike, as though trying out the saddlery on a new horse. He was startled to discover that the body of a woman fifty-one years of age was not, in her case, materially much different from the body of a younger woman, and that all their components worked exactly the same way. He obliged her even with the tumult churning inside of him, allowing her to choreograph changes of positions, activities, and themes until he was wedged up between her legs like a plowman and her wet mouth formed a gaping O emitting yelps of animal extremity, and she threw her head back culminating with a choked sob and a tender shriek that subsided into a giggle. In that train of events Daniel, too, spasmed, subsided, and rolled off to her side on the gigantic bed.

"Oh, thank you, Jesus," Loving Morrow murmured with a conclusive sigh and no irony. She pushed herself up against the padded headboard. "You are good," she said. "You'll come back, won't you?"

"Yes, ma'am."

"Of course you will. I'll order you to," she said playing at being stern before her mouth turned up again in its high-wattage smile and she bumped his thigh with the heel of her palm, and laughed musically. "Just kidding," she added.

"I'll be happy to see you again," Daniel said.

"My heart," she said, making a little fluttering gesture with her hand over her bare breast with its broad, pink tip. "I will send for you again. Meantime, don't work so hard. "You take a little more time to yourself, hear? Save some of that youthful energy for me."

"Yes, ma'am."

"I don't get up until 'bout one o'clock in the afternoon, so our time will be around now, most days. Most nights I'm in the studio recording with the gang until three, four a.m. Once in a while we see the sun come up."

"What are you recording, ma'am?"

"Why, my music, of course, silly. You wanna watch us sometime. It's just like seeing a live show."

"I'd like that, ma'am."

"I like how you call me that. So polite. I bet you were well raised after all, Fluffernutters or not. Well," she said, fairly bouncing off the bed, "I'ma shower off my little wet bottom, and put the robes of statecraft back on, and get back on my own job," she said, and by this time she was closing the door to an enormous adjoining bathroom with only her head still peeking out. "Can you believe I run this whole shebang?"

"Yes, I do, ma'am."

"I mean, I got help and all. But still. Sheesh . . . Oh, the car's outside down below whenever you wanna go. Bye now."

In the days that followed, Daniel made regular visits to the place that everybody in the capital of the Foxfire Republic called the White House, with all its multiple layers of meaning. Loving Morrow's temperament was steady and generally buoyant, her appetites reliably avid. Daniel always received his written instructions by ten o'clock in the morning and was able to plan his day with the object of meeting the sergeant and the car late in the afternoon in a different place near the center of town each time, "for security," he was told. Every morning, after checking in and out of the Logistics Commission office, he rode his horse Ike on a twelve-mile loop across the patchwork of farms and plantations outside of town, down crop lanes and through woodlots, pastures, cornfields, and meadows, even jumping the hedgerows here and there. In the process, he became a better rider. And it was only on these lone sorties away from the bustle of Franklin that he forced himself to think about his mission and tried to plan exactly how he might carry out the primary deed itself, and what he would do in its aftermath to get away successfully. The Service people back on Channel Island had taught him many skills, given him many ideas, and run through many scenarios for the carrying out of his mission, but it was left to Daniel to determine the final details of execution, depending on what he discovered about *conditions in place*, as the jargon had it during training.

He fretted over these matters while riding Ike and he hoped somehow to formulate a final plan that would allow him to escape from Franklin on horseback. He looked for places outside the town checkpoints where he might be able to stash Ike and his tack for a few hours while he carried out the mission and got away from the scene. Being adjacent to the Foxfire capital, the farms and plantations surrounding the town were well-run operations. There were no run-down barns or abandoned sheds as he'd seen just about everywhere else in the country, though he noted several fenced pastures that were occupied by numbers of horses where he might hide Ike in plain sight among them for a little while.

And whether he brooded directly on one plan after another, or just let the matter percolate at the margins of his consciousness while losing himself in the exertion of riding through a landscape that had turned the russet colors of autumn, he could not arrive at a course of action that might accomplish its main objective as well as save his skin.

He continued to receive his pay in silver, and he saved a lot of it to finance his escape, but he allowed himself a leisurely lunch every day in one of several restaurants in town, his favorite being the dining room of the Yancey Hotel, which served a fried chicken special with onion rings, collard greens stewed with bacon, wheat biscuits and fresh butter, and, at this time of year, an excellent squash pie for dessert. Before leaving home, he had never eaten in a restaurant. When he was not diverted by riding or eating he was increasingly conscious of a generalized bad feeling inside himself, a vivid corrosion of the spirit in which he seemed to be marinating. He soon identified it, with a certain strange relief in doing so, as self-hatred. And having done that, he just as readily recognized the source of it as the dissonance between the pleasure he was taking in the company of Loving Morrow and his very deliberate intention to murder her. Even as he ruminated darkly on these things, he also consciously took pleasure in the leisurely routines that allowed him these ruminations, his mornings on horseback, the fine napery of his table at the Yancey, his meals, his pie, his chicory root and barley "coffee," his fine clothes and boots, and the illusion of his independence.

Then, one late afternoon, as instructed, he met the big black car behind the Methodist Church off Cummins Street and was surprised to find Loving Morrow in the rear compartment with a splint basket and a guitar. The sergeant was behind the wheel as usual.

"How you doing, sugar?" she said as he climbed in beside her.

"I'm just fine, ma'am," he said, sensing she was not.

They drove off through the checkpoint, out east on the Lewisburg Pike a mile or so out of town. Loving Morrow remained quiet, pensive. She chewed on the pad of her thumb, looking out the window at the passing landscape.

"Where are we going, ma'am?" Daniel said.

"You'll see," she said with a pained smile. "My special place."

Daniel felt himself slip into a state of heightened alarm.

They passed tobacco barns, orchards, work gangs stooping in the fields digging yams and picking squashes and okra, people gawking in their dooryards at the queer sight of the automobile rolling along the bumpy road.

"How I'm gonna feed all these moochers, I'll never know," Loving Morrow muttered to herself.

"Something wrong, ma'am?"

"That goddamn Milton Steptoe is laying siege to Chattanooga now," she said. "Just what I needed."

The car turned onto an inconspicuous dirt lane in a patch of woods. A quarter mile up the road stood a little log cabin of impeccably accurate historic design, complete with dovetailed corners, moss chinking, a mud-and-daub chimney, and a broad porch. It stood on a bank yards from the lazy Harpeth River. The car stopped and Loving Morrow got out with the guitar.

"Grab the basket, would you, sugar?"

Daniel climbed out behind her. She was wearing a cotton print dress with a button-front pink sweater and beaded moccasin slippers on her small feet. She looked like a schoolgirl, Daniel thought.

"Why don't you take off, Rusty," she told the sergeant.

"I'm supposed to stick by you, ma'am."

"Would you please just do what I say. Come back in two hours."

"That's not regular procedure, ma'am."

"Well goddammit, dontcha think I know that?"

"Just sayin', ma'am."

"Can't I just have a few moments on my own like a regular human being?"

"You're special, ma'am. It can't be helped."

"You get out of here right now, Rusty, or I'ma send your ass to fight that goddamn Milton Steptoe over to Chattanooga, goddammit. I got this strong, upright young man to protect me. Go to the Yancey, for Gawd's sake, and get some ribs or something and come back in two hours."

"You know I can't do that, ma'am. I got orders from General McBride."

"Hell, I give McBride his orders!"

"Well, the general's orders are to stick by you no matter what you order me to do, including like now tellin' me to get lost. If that means I have to go to Chattanooga, so be it, ma'am."

Loving Morrow uttered a grunt of exasperation, stamped her foot in the grass, and shook her fist at the sergeant through the open passenger-seat window.

"What's it come to when a woman that runs a damn country can't give a simple order to a noncommissioned officer."

"Security procedure, ma'am. That's what."

"Would you just git your ass two hundred yards up the road, then?"

"I can do one hundred, ma'am. That's all."

"Aw hell . . . Well, git, then!"

"Send that young man up when you're ready to go home," the sergeant said.

The big car rolled back up the lane.

"See what I have to deal with?" Loving Morrow said. "Come on inside."

The cabin was furnished with a reproduction rustic bed and some other simple antique furniture. As soon as Daniel put the picnic basket down on the table, Loving Morrow was pulling off his jacket and unbuttoning his shirt.

"Do you know what that goddamn Milton Steptoe did?" she said, opening his belt buckle. She didn't wait for him to answer. "He invaded our camp at Ooltewah and let loose over two thousand niggers. What do you think of that?"

"What were they doing there?"

"They were hard cases. Ones that wouldn't leave the state or took up arms against us."

"I see."

"I'm telling you I aim to stop this sonofabitch for once and for all. I got to send an army over to Chattanooga to whip his ass, and those are troops that were all ready to go up to Cincinnati. Now we're gonna have to postpone that operation and winter's coming on and all. Oh goddammit . . ."

Loving Morrow left off undressing Daniel, stepped back to the bed, sat on the edge, and cried.

"Look at me," she said between sobs, "cryin' like a little girl."

Daniel felt helpless.

"Sometimes all this just, I dunno, gets to me."

"I understand."

"Armies and niggers and responsibility and all."

"Sure, ma'am."

"Do me a favor, sugar. There's a bottle of whiskey in that hamper there. Pour me three fingers in a glass and fix yourself one too. Then take the rest of your damn clothes off and git over here and comfort me."

Daniel did what she asked. It occurred to him as he swallowed his whiskey that this was an opportunity to complete his mission. But he had none of his silver nor his compass, nor had he been able to prepare his horse in advance, and he was unsure just how close the sergeant really was, so he decided to wait for a better opportunity, wondering darkly if he was making a fateful decision. He knocked back his whiskey and drank another, and two more, and Loving Morrow kept pace with him, and after an hour they were quite drunk. By now, they were both out of their clothes and in the throes of desperate sloppy copulation, which brought Loving Morrow to her usual dependable conclusion and left Daniel tumid and frustrated.

"Poor little thing," she said. "Is it something I said?"

"No, ma'am," Daniel said. "Just the whiskey, I think."

"You men. You're so damn sensitive."

She kissed him on the belly, got the hamper from the table, and they sat up in bed eating egg salad sandwiches and pecan bars with more whiskey.

"We gotta go soon," she said when they were done eating, puffing out her cheeks. "Back to all the madness."

"I know."

"I wanted you to hear me sing, though. Let's go outside and watch the sun go down and I'll sing for you."

"Okay."

They put their clothes back on and went outside. In fact, the sun had already gone down over the hills to the west, where the White House was, but the sky was incandescent with lingering reds, pinks, and violets. They sat out on the porch with the whiskey bottle and their glasses on the table. Loving Morrow picked up her guitar and began noodling on it, finger-picking complicated versions of "Little Maggie" and "Three Forks of Cheat."

"Okay, I'm limber," she said. "This one's a traditional tune about a man who's love won't have him cuz he's too poor, so he leaves his home country and lights out for the other side of the Smokies, but he will never forget her. It's called 'Pretty Saro.'"

It was a melancholy modal tune. She had a way of making every note she played on guitar count, Daniel thought, not like pikers who just bang away. Her voice was crystalline and transcendent. He understood how she had been a professional recording star in the old times.

> Oh I wish I was a little sparrow, had wings and could fly
> Straight to my love's bosom this night I'd draw nigh
> And in her little small arms all night I would lay
> And think of pretty Saro till the dawning of day

"Did you like that?"

"I did, ma'am. Very much. Your voice is lovely. And you're a hell of a guitar player."

"I been playing twice as long as you been on this planet, my friend," she said and giggled, then finished another whiskey. "Here's another. Traditional Appalachian murder ballad. It's called 'Banks of the O-hi-o.' It's about a young man who takes his love down to

the river on a little walk to pop the question and things go awry."
She sang the opening verses. The next two seized Daniel's mind
like a glimpse of perdition.

I took her by her lily white hand
And dragged her down that bank of sand
There I throwed her in to drown
I watched her as she floated down

Was walking home 'tween twelve and one
Thinkin' my God what I had done
I killed a girl, my love you see
Because she would not marry me

She finished the song with a graceful walk down on the neck
of her instrument, landing gently back on the E chord.

"You wouldn't do that to me, would you?" she said, pretending
to be serious.

"I couldn't ask you to marry me," Daniel said. His statement
terrified him.

Loving Morrow gave him a long hard look, then softened and
smiled.

"Of course, you're right. Anyway, I'm already married to all my
Foxfire angels," she said. "Whoa, I'm a bit tipsy. We'd better go."

The next two days, his instructions arrived promptly at the usual
time, but they said his attendance was not required and to await
further orders. Daniel's anxiety level reached an intolerable pitch. He
worried that he had insulted Loving Morrow by dismissing the idea
of marriage. He wondered if it was something else he said or did,
perhaps something as trivial as his failure to come to orgasm when
he was drunk. He worried that he didn't have the nerve to carry out
his mission after all, if he had the chance to. He worried about all
that would ensue if it turned out he could. Or if he tried and botched
it. He resolved that if he was not ordered back to the White House
before the week was out he would leave Franklin with his horse, his

silver, and his pistol and make his way back north. He spent those two days of nervous uncertainty riding Ike hard and drinking more heavily than he was accustomed to. On the third day, his instructions said to meet the car again on a particular back street in town.

He was both relieved and in a heightened state of agitation when the car pulled over to get him. The sergeant, as usual, was behind the wheel up front.

"Everything all right up at headquarters?" Daniel asked.

"There's some bit of hubbub going on," the sergeant said. "It appears the niggers are trying to take Chattanooga. We're holding on so far. It's got everybody's knickers in a twist up there."

"She all right?" Daniel asked.

"Far as I know. I haven't seen much of her lately," he said. "You've had good long run with the lady."

"What do you mean by that?"

"Well, her boys don't generally stay around more'n a few days. It's been about two weeks for you. You must be a dandy."

"What happens to them?" Daniel said.

He saw the sergeant glance at him in the rearview mirror.

"She don't kill 'em," he said and cackled.

"Where do they go?"

"They get reassigned. Most are army boys. They go where the battle is. Most of 'em want to be heroes, you know, to shine for the Leading Light. You got some hero in you, son?"

"I don't know."

When he got up to Loving Morrow's private quarters in the White House she was not there and he waited two hours for her, reading the old copies of *Southern Living* magazine that she kept in the bedroom, and drinking some of her whiskey as he did that, and marveling with ever more incredulity flipping through the pages at the massive losses the broken nation had endured in his lifetime. She came in around seven-thirty in the evening. She appeared even more anxious and distressed than he was.

"Hi, sugar. I'm sorry I'm late." She began undressing right away. "Come on, let's take a shower together."

He peeled off his clothes and followed her into the big bathroom with its luxurious appointments. In the shower, she held him tightly, letting the stream of hot water play over her neck while she groaned and pressed her ear against his breastbone. For the first time in their acquaintance he could see the weight of the years on her.

"Is everything all right?" he said after they'd been in there a while.

"Things are kind of screwed up right now," she said. "I got to release some of this tension. I just knew it would help if I came to you."

With that, she turned desperately amorous, kissed him, pressed her body into him, then turned around and asked to be taken, with her hands gripping the faucets on the wall. When the act was complete, she just slumped onto the floor, bawling. After a little while he hoisted her to her feet, finished washing her, and then toweled her off.

"You are an angel for sure," she said, coming back to herself.

Back in the bedroom, he poured both of them whiskeys. They moved to the bed.

"Here's what-all else is going on," she said as the whiskey began to calm her down. "Promise you won't tell anybody?"

"I won't tell anybody."

"One of my very closest advisors has gone traitor on me."

"What did he do?"

"It was him plotted with that goddamn Milton Steptoe to get up into Chattanooga. He sold us out. I can't believe it. I've known Hector Tillman from the beginning of all this when we went our own way from the federals."

Daniel felt an electric pulse of fear rise up his spine and go off like a blue spark in his brain.

"Who would've ever thought. Mr. Tillman," she went on, chattering nervously. "I always called him mister because he had this air about him of unshakable integrity. He was my rock. Did you ever meet Mr. Tillman?"

"No, never."

"Well, why would you. He's just another one of all those people over there." She made a dismissive gesture at the government's part of the gigantic house. "Of course you wouldn't know him. I could use another one of these, sugar," she said, presenting her empty glass. He got them both another.

"What'll happen to him?"

"Oh, Lord. I dunno. We'll take him out to the speedway at Carter's Creek, I expect. Drag him behind a race car or something. Skin him alive. Crucify him. Something like that."

"You mean, literally."

"Oh, yeah. We're gonna have to make an example of him, in case there's any more like him in the government. We got to make a damn statement. This is the part of being in charge that I really hate, believe me, but we can't have traitors among us. There's too much at stake. This is history at work here."

Daniel's brain was churning so violently he thought it would overheat and melt.

"I'm a mess," Loving Morrow said. "Please git me going again. Go down there, sugar, and do what you do with your mouth that's so lovely and calm me down."

Daniel did what she asked, his mind burning as he did, wondering if Hector Tillman had revealed anything about him. In time he understood that she was satisfied and he came back up to her.

"You're sweet," she said. "This is nuts, but I believe I'm falling for you a little."

"You'll get tired of me, I'm sure."

"No I won't!" she said. "Hey, lookit, I got an idea. Let's go out to my special place tonight."

"The cabin out on the river?"

"Yeah. Right now. Let's just get on out of this wretched place of treachery and strife for a little while before I lose my mind."

Daniel hesitated. "Okay," he said. "But I got an idea too."

"What's that, sugar."

"Let's go out there alone. Just you and me in the car."

"Yes, let's. Won't that be fun!"

"I want to drive that car myself one time," he said. "I never drove a car in my whole life. I might never have the chance."

"Well, all right. Sure. You made me happy so I'm obliged to do something'll make you happy. Maybe even more than what you ask. You never know."

"What?"

"You'll see when we get there," she said. "A special something. I bet you could guess if you put your mind to it."

Daniel grabbed the whiskey bottle on his way out and hid it under his jacket. They took an exit door off the home theater room, which brought them into a stairway to the basement. That part of the White House basement was an underground garage that contained seven cars, all identical Lincoln Navigators. It was dim in there. A young soldier sat in a little lighted booth. He had been tilted back in his chair reading a novelization of a TV show about the zombie takeover of the United States. He awkwardly got up and stood at attention.

"Ma'am," he said.

"Which car you want?" Loving Morrow asked Daniel.

"I dunno," he said. "They're all the same."

"How 'bout one that runs good, Corporal," she said.

"They all run pretty good, ma'am."

"Aw hell," she said. "Give me the keys to this one here."

The corporal fetched the keys from a pegboard in the booth. Loving Morrow tossed them to Daniel and told him to get in behind the wheel. She gave him five minutes of instructions for how to operate such a car.

"It's easy as pie," she said. "By the time they stopped making these things, they practically drove themselves." She reached over and turned the key in the ignition. The engine came alive and purred.

Daniel's hands sweated so much that the steering wheel felt slippery. The corporal threw a switch that opened an electric overhead door up a ramp. Daniel put the gear shift in DRIVE and steered up the ramp. They came out on the back side of the White House. Night had fallen. A sliver of moon hung in the treetops up a wooded hill.

"Turn here," Loving Morrow said.

She directed him down a long, curved, paved road and then onto a gravel lane.

"This here's the service road," she said. "We can git clear of this place without any fuss." The gate at the end of the service road was a plain wooden shed manned by two privates. The soldier who leaned in the window was shocked to see the Leading Light of the Foxfire Republic next to Daniel.

"That, you, ma'am?" he said.

"'Course it is, Private," she said. "You think I got imposters on the payroll?"

"No, ma'am."

"This here's one of my intelligence officers, Lieutenant Jones. We got a meeting down in town. It's classified business, need to know, and all like that. You follow me, soldier?"

"Yes, ma'am."

"We'll be back in a couple hours. You never saw us. Got that?"

"Yes, ma'am," he said and went to swing the gate open.

When they were out of the compound, Loving Morrow directed their way on back roads around the south side of town so they wouldn't have to go through any checkpoints. The roads were rough there. When they got onto the Lewisburg Pike, he reached for the whiskey bottle. Loving Morrow threw back her head and laughed heartily.

"What's so funny, ma'am?" Daniel said.

"I'se just thinking you shouldn't drink when you drive, but then I realized hey, there iddn't another damn car running in the whole state of Tennessee tonight, least as far as I know, so it iddn't like you're gonna crash into anybody out here."

"I'm doing all right, aren't I?"

"You doing just fine, baby," she said, and put her hand on his thigh and squeezed it.

As she did that, and the whiskey made a warm spot in his belly, he remembered what he was about to do and he shuddered.

"You cold, sugar?"

"A little."

"We can just turn up the heat."

Shortly, she told him to slow down and then directed him to turn down the gravel road that led to her cabin. When they got there, she lit some candles while Daniel made a little tepee of kindling in the fireplace and leaned some split logs against it. Loving Morrow came to him and sat down on a plush polyester bearskin rug in front of the hearth. When the fire was going and Daniel stood up, she got on her knees, seized his trousers at the hip, and rotated him around.

"Didn't I tell you I had a nice special surprise for you?"

"Yes, ma'am."

"Well, here she comes. Git that monster out now."

Daniel hesitated so she went for his belt herself.

"Wait," he said, and put a hand on hers.

"Is something wrong, sugar?"

"Yes," he said, and he fell down on his knees so they were face-to-face.

"Tell me, baby."

"I'm sorry," he said.

"What for?" she said, putting a palm to his cheek.

He shook his head and began to weep. But before Loving Morrow could utter another word, he reached out and seized her by the shoulders, flipped her around violently, and got her in a choke hold, as he was trained to do, with one forearm against the front of her neck and the other pressing against the back of her head. She bucked and kicked and one of her faux leopardskin flats flew off her foot and bounced off a near wall. Her strength surprised him. But in less than half a minute she slumped in his arms as her forebrain went dark, and he continued to hold her in that position for several minutes more, rocking as he wept into her fragrant hair, until he was confident that the life had gone out of her. Finally, he released her and let her body drop on the rug beside him. Her head made a dull thunk against the hardwood floor under the rug. He remained there on his knees, tears streaming down his face while watching her for any sign of life. When he saw a few fugitive twitches in her arms and legs, he pulled up her V-neck sweater and pressed his ear against her sternum between the breasts he had lately been kissing. He listened there for a long time and heard no sound of a heartbeat. When he raised his head, he noticed that her eyes remained open and glassy. Her mouth, too, was open in a manner he had seen before in different circumstances, with some gobbets of yellow-white foam at the sides.

Unable to look back one last time, he left her on the rug and briskly left the cabin. The cool night air slammed his senses as he went back to the car and turned the key as he'd seen her do. The sound of the engine echoed the feeling of the life pulsing through his own body. It took him more than a minute to figure out how to turn the headlights on. Being unacquainted with the reverse gear, he executed a tight circle on the grass between the cabin and the river, wiping the tears from his face with his sleeves as he did. Once he was poised to leave the little gravel lane that led to the road, he struggled to engage the higher functions of his brain to decide exactly what to do. He concluded right away that he shouldn't try to escape in the car because that would be the first thing they would be looking for, not to mention the condition of the roads beyond Franklin and the lack of any more fuel out there. But he knew it would be equally foolish to try to escape on foot, as he had considered in previous mental rehearsals of this moment. Instead, he decided to risk going back into town to get the things he needed and escape on horseback.

He drove back to the checkpoint on the Lewisburg Pike. To his surprise, the soldier on duty simply waved him through. He remembered that the car's windows did not permit people outside from seeing who was within, and it occurred to him that anyone traveling in an automobile would have to be an important government figure. Once inside town, he traversed the quietest streets, making his way toward the rooming house on Fair Street. On Acton, he turned down the alley of one of the grain warehouses he had visited on inspections, killed the engine, and left the car there. He walked the few blocks to his lodging house on Fair Street, collected what he needed, put on two extra shirts, and went to the livery on South Margin Street where he boarded Ike.

A boy of fourteen working the night hours there, a simpleton named Hootie Ray Blount, who would be hanged a week later, let Daniel saddle up Ike and sold him a five-pound sack of whole oats for his journey.

"Where are you goin' at this hour, mister?" he asked.

"Chattanooga," Daniel said, just because it had been on his mind.

"What's there?"

"Nothing."

"Then why you going there?"

"Just business."

"Watch out for robbers on your way."

"I will," Daniel said, and tipped the boy a silver dime on his way out.

With adrenaline making the blood pound in his temples, he carefully walked Ike across town, through the very center where the shops on Main were closed and things were quiet except for the Yancey Hotel, where a string band was playing a jolly tune called "Duck River" that was one of his father's favorites back home and it only prompted him to realize how far from home he was. He made for one of the lesser town gates on the Del Rio Pike at the west end of town, hoping to confound his pursuers as to the direction he was headed in.

At the gate, manned by three enlisted men who had been play-ing cards in their shed, the electric lights flickered out for the night just as he walked up on Ike. There were groans of consternation as the soldiers flung down their cards and two of them went to light candles while the third came out to talk to Daniel.

"Late to be setting out, ain't it," he said.

"I got word my ma up and died over to Dickson," Daniel said. "They're putting her in the ground tomorrow."

"Oh? For true? Well, sorry to hear that. Go on, then. And praise her."

"Praise her," Daniel said.

At that, he rode out of the capital of the Foxfire Republic, never to return.

He rode all night and the next morning in a rapture of grief and adrenaline and finally slept in the woods the second night. He shared the raw oats with Ike and found some apples along the way. It wasn't until he got halfway across Kentucky that he dared to stop at a little store for provisions in the Appalachian foothills village of Irvine. The store carried a newspaper out of Lexington and the latest copy was dated two days before he completed his mission, nor did he hear any chatter thereabouts about the murder of Loving Morrow, so he concluded that he still rode ahead of the news.

Luck continued to be with Daniel when, ten days after his deed, and seeking to avoid any bridges over the Ohio River, he managed to find a tractably ignorant ferryman in the village of Greenup who conveyed him and his horse over to the federal side for a little silver. Once in the state of Ohio he was able to put up at proper inns and buy meals in public taverns, and by that time the news of the assassination of Loving Morrow in the Foxfire capital was headlined in the occasional broadsheet he encountered. Though he was mentioned by name as the assassin, and described physically in words, no drawing of him circulated with the news. Nor did Daniel reveal his identity once he was safely back on federal terrain. Whatever anyone else thought of the deed—and there was considerable rejoicing over it—it was not something Daniel was proud of, and he didn't want to be known as the author of it. Rather, he traveled north, in increasingly cold weather, with the trees bare and the farm fields laid up for winter, raveled in shame, remorse, and confusion, wondering what sort of monster he was. His imagination was tortured as well by thoughts about the fate of Hector "Barefoot" Tillman. Without really weighing the matter directly, he reached the decision not to return to the seat of the federal government at New Columbia, Michigan.

What he wanted to do was hide from the world, indeed, hide from himself, and that was how he applied to join the community led by the Zen millenarian Usher Redfield in northeastern Ohio, a kind of secular monastery of men—no women—dedicated to the contemplative life, gardening, the preservation of literature, and the repurposing of useful items from the old times. He remained there through the winter, sleeping in an unheated cell, working in the shops and barns, and sitting in silent meditation for hours each day. He never spoke of his true identity or his mission to Tennessee or of the affairs of the nations of North America. By April of the following year he had sorted out his experience sufficiently to begin longing for home. And in May, when it was finally warm enough to endure the uncertainties of a long journey, he left the community on Ike with the belongings he had arrived with, including a purse of silver and the military pistol he had carried all the way down to Franklin, Tennessee, and back. These things were all taken from him by a band of thieves in Warren, Pennsylvania, who beat him senseless and left him for dead, the first of many vicissitudes and privations he endured on his eventually successful long trek home.

These memories of his months out in the American heartland occupied Daniel Earle in his bedroom as the first sunlight of the new year brightened the frosted window, and then he finally slept.

FIFTY-TWO

Brother Jobe and his rangers were given a fine New Year's Day breakfast of eggs, fried salt ham (brought by Blake Harmon), sautéed apples, corn pudding, and rose hip tea at the table of Barbara Maglie in the dell below Lloyds Hill in the rural township of Hebron, New York. As his men prepared their animals for departure, Brother Jobe met privately in the little library room with Mandy Stokes. She was still in her traveling clothes: men's trousers and linen shirt but with a turquoise silk kerchief around her neck that her hostess gave her the night before to wear at the table.

"Did you sleep okay, ma'am?"

She nodded her head.

"Something has changed," she said softly.

Sunlight streamed into the room through lace curtains behind her. Her face was bright, the dark circles under her eyes were gone.

"This lady here has an uncommon heart and a way with troubled spirits," Brother Jobe said. "You going to stay with her for a while, maybe a long while, and then, when you're ready, you will be rebirthed out into the world. You don't never have to go back to Union Grove."

Her eyes searched the room, the walls, the ceiling as though to capture the fugitive essence of the matter.

"Do you think I can ever forgive myself?" she finally said.

"The day will come when all your memories of that place and what happened there will feel like somebody else's story, and you can leave it all behind. That will be the greater truth of it, anyway, for you will be a different person then."

"Am I safe here?"

"I believe you are in good hands."

Mandy's eyes narrowed, her mouth trembled, and she stammered a moment.

"W-w-why did you do it?" she asked.

"Justice and mercy, ma'am. What's the world without it? I may be back around from time to time to say hello. The lady of the house is a special friend. You mind what she has to teach you."

Mandy threw her arms around Brother Jobe's casklike body and said, "Thank you."

Minutes later, having made all his farewells, Brother Jobe mounted Atlas and reined the big mule up the drive past the barn and the frozen garden to the road. Seth and Elam followed on their horses. Six inches of pristine white powder covered it and sleeves of snow clung to the tree branches overhead in the breezeless air. Clouds were beginning to move in again and Elam's aching right shoulder, which had caught a piece of shrapnel in the Holy Land years back and never lied about the weather, told him they were going to get more snow. They had determined to take a different, more roundabout route home, around Cossayuna Lake, than the one they came up on and they expected their tracks to be covered both coming and going.

"I had the craziest dreams last night," Seth said as they walked south. "That fine lady was all amongst them. And stranger yet, it seems I was all amongst her."

"What! I had the same dang dream," Elam said.

"Oh yeah?" Seth said. "I didn't see you around."

"You wasn't there," Elam said. "Not in my dream. I wouldn't have you in it."

"Well, don't you be coming around mine, neither, hear."

"If you see me there, blame your own dang self."

"I could say the same of you—"

"Boys," Brother Jobe said. "You ought to know by now: that there is a house of dreams and powers of a certain kind. Nobody goes in there ever comes out quite the same."

FIFTY-THREE

At midday, Stephen Bullock, once reluctant and now avid magistrate of Union Grove, with three of his men, rode over from his plantation to the headquarters of the New Faith Brotherhood Covenant Church of Jesus on the north edge of town looking for Brother Jobe, who was not there. Instead, he was directed to wait for Brother Joseph, second in command, a six-foot-four veteran U.S. Army ranger of the War in the Holy Land, who was called in from the barns to attend to the visitors. The wait itself annoyed Bullock hugely.

"I sent for the prisoner first thing today and now I'm informed that she has somehow escaped," Bullock said.

"That does appear to be the case," Joseph said.

"How the hell did that happen?"

"Her room was empty this morning, sir."

"That doesn't exactly explain how it came to be."

"It's all we know, sir."

Bullock rolled his eyes.

"Was she under lock and key?" he asked.

"The door was barred with a two-by-six."

"What about the windows?"

"Just little rectangular slots clear up by the ceiling. A child couldn't squeeze through 'em. Anyway, they don't open or close and they weren't broken. No, sir, I don't think she got out thataway."

"So she just disappeared like a little bunny rabbit."

"Beg your pardon, sir?"

"Like in a magic act? Presto! *Pffffft!* Gone."

"Frankly, we're stumped, too, sir."

"You're stumped . . ."

"It might have been the Lord took some kind of decisive action on her behalf."

"What? You mean as in some sort of miracle?"

"Every now and then unusual things do happen, sir. Our knowledge of this world is imperfect."

"Oh, please. I was born at night but not last night," Bullock said. He didn't like the look that was radiating off Brother Joseph's face. It made him feel like a fly about to be swatted. "Does it disturb you a little that you have let loose a killer upon this jurisdiction?"

"I'm told that she acted under the influence of a brain sickness," Joseph said.

"Yes, well, my court was going to determine that," Bullock said. He glared at Joseph, who paid it back in intensity, and then some.

"Well, are you going to do something about this?" Bullock said.

"I expect we will, sir."

"In the way of what."

"In the way of establishing her whereabouts."

"And when do you expect to commence that? She could be halfway to Lake George by now."

"When the boss returns from where he's at."

"And where's that?"

"He went to look at a jackass for sale over to White Creek. We're going all out for mules this year, you know. Do you have mules over at your place, squire?"

Bullock didn't relish that appellation but he didn't move to register his objection either.

"We prefer horses and oxen out our way," he said.

"You ought to give mules a chance, sir," Brother Joseph said. "Some folks look down on them as a lesser animal, but they can't be forced to do something stupid that would only harm them. They can take the heat better than most horses. And—I don't know if you're aware of all this—they actually ride much smoother than even your fancier saddlebreds. I'd say, a few years from now, this county is going to be crazy for mules."

"You tell your boss I want to see him posthaste as soon as he gets back."

"Sure, sir. You want to make an appointment now? When would it be convenient for you to come back here?"

FIFTY-FOUR

Daniel slept until the early afternoon and got up feeling as if some tremendous cargo had been lifted off him. He was the only one in the house at that hour. Britney had left a big crock of bean and ham soup warming on a trivet on the woodstove and Daniel found corn bread and cheese in the usual places in the kitchen. When he was fortified, he bundled up and sallied forth from the house into a town that was finally settling down to its regular business after the holidays. He had a particular destination in mind.

The last publisher of the *Union News Leader*, Paul Easterling, froze to death in his car years earlier trying to make it back from a Christmas visit to his daughter's home in Medford, Massachusetts, during one of the serial gasoline crises that paralyzed the nation before the Washington, DC, bombing put an end to the old times for good. By then the publication had devolved to the level of a "pennysaver"—a vehicle for paid legal notices, bake sale listings, and puff pieces about the activities of senior citizens, used mostly for lining cat litter boxes. Nobody had been in the building since the disappearance of Paul Easterling—for his fate was never learned back in town, so chaotic were those months. The little newspaper's headquarters was originally a temperance hall built in 1883 on Elbow Street off Main near Mill Hollow. Daniel entered through a broken window in the rear of the building. Easterling had not been a particularly tidy fellow, and every sort of animal from wasps to raccoons had brought organic debris into the place since he went away and never returned, but the equipment was all there and at least the roof had not failed, so no water had gotten in. Daniel spent hours poking around in it with a sense of rising excitement. There were several generations of letterpress machines, all requiring electricity to operate. But off in a corner, covered with dust, cobwebs, soda pop bottles, and wooden crates of metal odds and ends, stood a handsome 1891 Albion hand-operated flatbed proof press, and Daniel very quickly saw its potential value as he removed the junk on and around it. In his rising excitement, he also discovered cabinets of metal type, composing stones, paper cutters, and all the other equipment he might need to begin figuring out how to produce a simple broadsheet newspaper of the type he had encountered on his journeys out into the country.

Seized by this transport of ambition and inspiration, he hurried over to his father's workshop in the purple twilight. There he found his father with Tom Allison seated beside the woodstove enjoying whiskeys to celebrate their decision to form a partnership to build a coach and begin a service for passengers, freight, and mail around Washington County. Tom stood up at the sight of Daniel, whom he had watched grow up during all these years of change, hardship, and loss, and was stunned to see him suddenly as a full-grown man.

"Is that really you?" Tom asked.

The question quite stunned Daniel as he apprehended for the first time in more than a year that he had managed to come home not just to his town and his people but to himself.

"Yes, Tom," he said. "It's me."

FIFTY-FIVE

Some time after darkness fell, Travis Berkey ventured into the new Union Tavern in the center of town. He had spent the whole day freezing on his way to one farm after another, seeking a position, and nobody would have him. He began to wonder if Mr. Bullock had put out some kind of bad word on him, and when he got to the Schmidt farm late in the day and was told there were no positions, he asked straight out whether Mr. Bullock had sent any notice around to put a curse on him.

"You didn't tell me you worked for Bullock," Mr. Schmidt's crew chief Orrie Carrol said.

"Well, I did," Berkey said.

"When was that?"

"Uh, some time ago."

"There's no word on you from Bullock that I know of. But why didn't you say you worked for him?"

"We didn't get along so well, the squire and me."

Carrol regarded Berkey just slightly askance for a moment, taking in all the crookedness of his wiry body.

"I'm not sure you're an honest fellow," Carrol said, "and that's why we have nothing for you here."

Berkey trudged back to town in the gathering gloom and saw the lights of the tavern aglow through the falling snow. He had three silver dimes in his pocket, all the money that he had left. He thought about his predicament in the world, toted up the pluses and minuses, and decided to go inside and take whatever little last pleasures he could find in this life before throwing himself in the river.

There were a dozen men at the bar, some with wives and girls, all of them farm laborers on light winter duty. The place was still cheerfully decorated with leftover balsam sprigs and holiday swags.

Most of all, it was warm inside. Berkey had to stand for ten minutes by the woodstove in the front of the establishment before his lips could move freely enough to order a drink at the bar.

"What's the strongest beer or cider you got?"

"We've got a Buskirk Crosseye porter that kicks like a horse," said Brother Micah.

"I'll take it," Berkey said. He sat at the bar and took in all the fine furnishings of the place, the carved wood back bar with its arrayed bottles of distilled spirits and cider barrels, the glowing candles in their stands and the six-light chandelier overhead, the thrum of conversation and laughter. At first he regarded it all with the suspicion and disdain of the perennial outsider, but before long the active ingredient of the smoky-sweet porter made it into his bloodstream and he began to take a more charitable view of his surroundings. He recognized some of the people at the bar from around town over the years, but he was not acquainted enough with any of them to call them friends. So he sat at the corner of the bar drinking quietly and slowly, at two pints to the silver dime, for some time. By and by he asked Brother Micah if he could run a tab and the bartender, with a slight hesitation, said okay. He ordered a plate of meatballs with gravy sauce, cheese toast, and the special dessert, which was apple fritters with whipped cream, and ceased to feel painfully hungry for the first time in days.

After seven o'clock more people came into the tavern, townsmen and tradesmen. Eric Laudermilk, Dan Mullinex, and Charles Pettie came by with their instruments (guitar, clarinet, bass fiddle) and set up to play some old-times-style jazz music. Berkey was working on his ninth pint when he overheard a conversation down the bar between Doug Sweetland and Robbie Furnival in which the latter happened to remark favorably on Stephen Bullock's methods for organizing agricultural production in the new times, and Travis Berkey took exception to any complimentary talk about his old boss and his methods and started arguing loudly, and rather incoherently, back at the other two, who regarded the obviously drunken Berkey with increasing amazement, until Berkey started actually shrieking, cursing, and throwing swings at them. Robbie, who worked hard in the woods at lumbering and was very strong, was about to disassemble Berkey when the front door to the tavern opened and in walked Brother Jobe and his rangers.

They had made a wrong turn on the east side of Cossayuna Lake, where the snow was falling especially hard and deep, which had delayed their return to town. They barely shook the snow off their hats when the altercation at the bar broke out. Seth and Elam rushed over to restrain Berkey before Robbie could take him apart. Brother Jobe limped over on his half-frostbitten feet. Brother Micah put a glass of Tiplady rye whiskey in his hand as he swung around to see who the rangers were grappling with.

"You again!" Brother Jobe said.

"Well, goddamn you too," Travis Berkey sputtered, before throwing up a gutfull of meatballs, cheese toast, apple fritters, and Buskirk Crosseye porter all over the front of Brother Jobe's blanket coat.

"Get him out of here," Brother Jobe told the other brothers as he looked up from the stinking mess that dripped off his chest.

Seth and Elam trundled Berkey to the door and heaved him out of it in an impressive arcing flight that ended with a sickening thud as his body met the concrete underlying the accumulated snow. He lay on the sidewalk for a while before the cold got to him and then he got up, staggered back to the tavern entrance, and banged on the front door hollering for his coat. It was shortly tossed out the door at his feet. Berkey walked the streets of Union Grove for hours after that, sobering up and trying to work up the nerve to go throw himself into the Battenkill. But as the effects of alcohol wore off, his feelings shifted more and more from the loathing of himself and his hopeless lot in life to an aggressive fury at Brother Jobe and the New Faith brotherhood.

He returned to the Union Tavern via the alley off Main Street that led to the rear of the establishment and snuck into the kitchen after it had closed down at nine o'clock and the sisters who worked in it were all gone. He hid there, munching on sausages, ham, pickles, corn bread, and other items he found in the cabinets and the meat safe. When the last customers left the front room around eleven, and Brother Micah closed up for the night, and he heard the key turn in the front door lock with a clunk, Berkey ventured out of the kitchen to the delightful situation of having the whole place to himself. He found some matches and lit a candle and commenced sampling all the various whiskeys arrayed on the back bar—the Battenville blend, the Eagle Bridge corn, the Shushan what-have-you, the Tiplady rye, the Rupert Road tawny double malt, the Mount Tom silver lightning, the Duell Hollow fare-thee-well sour mash, the Ashgrove three-grain blend—until he was quite drunk again. Under the influence of all that, he arrived at the splendid idea of burning the place down. He fetched a generous scoop of embers from the woodstove in the little tending shovel and heaped them onto the shelf of the back bar. Then he tossed some kindling splints and stove billets on that until, by and by, the beautiful carved cabinetry of the back bar was well engaged and fingers of flame reached higher and higher up the shelves and bottles started exploding, which only intensified the fire. He kept pounding down the whiskey, wielding a bottle in each hand, while he admired the progress of his work, and then his brain chemistry crossed a boundary, the room started spinning, and Travis Berkey went down onto the hard floor. The last thing he saw before he lost consciousness forever was the beautiful filigree of smoke twisting and curling beneath the pressed tin ceiling in the hot barroom air.

Fifty-six

Earlier that same evening, the doctor had helped transport Jack Harron from his bed in the doctor's infirmary back home to his room at Andrew Pendergast's fine house on Cottage Street. Jack was recovering nicely from the wounds he had sustained in the attack by Donald Acker. He slept through the early evening and Andrew came in later to check on him before turning in himself. He brought in a painting he'd done in May of the Hudson Valley observed from Stark's Knob, an ancient volcanic plug of rock that afforded a view north up the river clear up to Buck Mountain above Glens Falls and to the blue Adirondacks beyond.

"I thought I might hang this on the wall for you," Andrew said, setting his candle holder down on the chest of drawers. "It'll give you something to look at while you're still in bed."

"Yes, thank you," Jack said. "It's . . . beautiful. Is it around here?"

"Yes, just up past Mr. Bullock's place on the river. We'll go there in the spring. I like to paint it in all its moods."

"I'd like that," Jack said. "How long until I'm allowed to get up and around?"

"A few more days, I think. The doctor said he'll be coming over to check on you."

"I'd like to get back to work," Jack said.

"That's a good sign," Andrew said and smiled. "Is there something else you need before I go upstairs? Are you hungry?"

"No," Jack said. "But . . . oh, I dunno."

"What?"

"You think you might read something to me?"

Andrew was a little surprised to hear that.

"Really?"

"Yes. Just a little while."

"Well, sure," he said. "Anything in particular?"

"You pick it," Jack said. "You'll know."

"Okay."

Andrew went to the big front parlor where he had encountered Jack Harron on Christmas Eve and thought he was about to be murdered. The memory stopped him for a few moments, but then he searched the bookshelves until he found what he wanted, one of the favorite books of his boyhood: Kenneth Grahame's *The Wind in the Willows*. He went back through the kitchen with the book and a ladderback chair, which he set down beside the table where the candle burned.

"What's it about?" Jack said when Andrew held up the cover.

"A rat and a mole and a badger and a toad who mess around in boats down by a little stream in the English countryside."

"They all get along, all those different animals?" Jack said.

"They're all friends," Andrew said. "It's a book about friendship."

He cleared his throat. "The River Bank," he began, reading the title of chapter one. "The Mole had been working very hard all morning, spring-cleaning his little home . . ."

FIFTY-SEVEN

Brother Jobe and dozens of brothers and sisters from the New Faith compound, along with more than a hundred townspeople, stood mutely before the smoldering ruins of the Union Tavern on the corner of Van Buren and Main Streets. All that remained was the three-story brick shell with its marble lintels and decorations. The volunteers had tried to save it, but it was not the kind of thing that a bucket brigade could avail to stop, especially at this time of year with the temperature below freezing. The generous alley had prevented the fire from spreading catastrophically down the other buildings along Main Street. The heavy snow, which amounted to ten inches by morning, had helped to dampen the blaze once the wooden joists and floors had been consumed and the interior finally collapsed. The ruin gave off a powerful stink. The charred skeleton of Travis Berkey inside would not be discovered for a week, when work commenced to clear away the ashes and debris.

As people began to peel away from the crowd in the deep morning cold to return to their homes, Stephen Bullock and three of his men rode up Main Street and tied their horses to the hitching posts along the block north of Van Buren where the barbershop and the New Faith haberdash still stood unburnt. Bullock, swaddled in fur, eventually made his way to Brother Jobe's side.

"We could smell it all the way over to the Hudson," Bullock said. "I'm not responsible, in case you're wondering."

Brother Jobe cut him a venomous glance and said nothing in reply. They stood quietly a while longer until a last lingering second-floor beam dropped into the rubble with an impressive crash.

"I don't suppose you have insurance," Bullock said.

"I got forty-six highly motivated skilled men with good tools," Brother Jobe eventually said, without looking at Bullock. "That's my insurance. And by the way, if you thought that was funny, it ain't."

"What's really not funny is you let your prisoner escape."

"You're right, squire. That wasn't no joke neither."

"She was in your charge."

"Thanks for reminding me."

"Are you going to search for her?"

"I don't think so."

"I could press charges against you for this."

"Try it." This time Brother Jobe turned and looked over at Bullock with the full force of his withering gaze. In a matter of seconds Bullock developed a breathtaking headache. Robert Earle, mayor of Union Grove, had just come over to offer some words of commiseration to Brother Jobe and have a few words with Stephen Bullock when Bullock turned away, looking greenish, and elbowed his way back through the remaining crowd to rejoin his men and the horses.

"What's wrong with him?" Robert said.

"Oh, he's just broke up cuz he never got to set foot inside the place," Brother Jobe said. "To enjoy all its comforts and marvels. Poor man just works too hard."

"Well, this is sure an awful loss," Robert said. "It was just starting to bring some life back into this town. I'm real sorry."

"Don't be sorry, old son," Brother Jobe said. "We gonna rebuild the sumbitch and I'm going to put up a proper hotel on the lot next to it where people can stay when they come here to buy my ding-dang mules." The idea arrived full-blown in his awareness with a dispatch that impressed even Brother Jobe himself at the hidden synchronous powers of Providence. "Always think positive, my friend. And if it don't come right away, just wait a little while."

And that is how the holiday season ended in Union Grove, Washington County, New York, in the year that concerns us, which is yet to come in the history of the future.